When the Stars
Go Dark

BY PAULA McLAIN

When the Stars Go Dark

Love and Ruin

Circling the Sun

The Paris Wife

A Ticket to Ride

Like Family: Growing Up in Other People's Houses

When the Stars Go Dark

*

PAULA McLAIN

A Point Blank Book

First published in Great Britain, Ireland & Australia by Point Blank,
an imprint of Oneworld Publications, 2021
This mass market paperback edition published 2022

ISBN 978-0-86154-197-3
ISBN 978-0-86154-081-5 (ebook)

Printed and bound in Great Britain by Clays Ltd, Elcograf S.p.A.

Maps copyright © David Lindroth Inc., 2022

Grateful acknowledgment is made to HarperCollins Publishers for
permission to use an excerpt from "I Am Too Alone in the World" from
*Selected Poems of Rainer Maria Rilke: A Translation from the German and
Commentary by Robert Bly*, copyright © 1981 by Robert Bly. Used by
permission of HarperCollins Publishers.

Oneworld Publications
10 Bloomsbury Street
London WC1B 3SR
England

Stay up to date with the latest books,
special offers, and exclusive content from
Oneworld with our newsletter

Sign up on our website
oneworld-publications.com

*For Lori Keene, there from the beginning
as I dreamed this dream*

Here is the world.
Beautiful and terrible things will happen.
Don't be afraid.

—*Frederick Buechner*

NORTHERN CALIFORNIA COAST

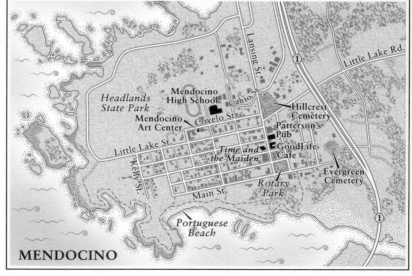

MENDOCINO

When the Stars
Go Dark

Prologue

The mother who tore off her dress when the police came to her house with the news and then ran down the street in only her shoes, while her neighbors, even the ones who knew her well, hid behind their doors and windows, afraid of her grief.

The mother who clutched her daughter's purse as the ambulance sped away. The purse pink and white, shaped like a poodle and smeared with blood.

The mother who began to cook for the detectives and her neighborhood priest while they were still trying to explain to her what had happened, her hands raw as she chopped a mountain of onions, washed dishes in scalding water. No one could get her to sit down. Sitting down meant she had to know it. Accept it.

The mother who left the mortuary after ID'ing her child's body and walked in front of a live Muni, the jolt throwing her twenty feet straight backward, her fingertips smoking where the current blew through, her lips black. But she had lived.

The mother who used to be a famous actress, but now waited for news the way glaciers wait at the far tip of the globe, frozen and quiet, half alive.

———

The mother I was that day in July, on my knees as the EMT tried to get through to me with words, sentences, my name. I wouldn't let go of my child's body. "Detective Hart," he said over and over as my mind gasped, plummeting. As if that person could still possibly exist.

1

Signs and Vapors

One

The night feels shredded as I leave the city, through perforated mist, a crumbling September sky. Behind me, Potrero Hill is a stretch of dead beach, all of San Francisco unconscious or oblivious. Above the cloud line, an eerie yellow sphere is rising. It's the moon, gigantic and overstuffed, the color of lemonade. I can't stop watching it roll higher and higher, saturated with brightness, like a wound. Or like a door lit entirely by pain.

No one is coming to save me. No one can save anyone, though once I believed differently. I believed all sorts of things, but now I see the only way forward is to begin with nothing, or whatever is less than nothing. I have myself and no one else. I have the road and the snaking mist. I have this tortured moon.

I drive until I stop seeing familiar landmarks, stop looking in my rearview to see if someone is following me. In Santa Rosa, the Travelodge is tucked behind a superstore parking lot, the whole swath of it empty and overlit, like a swimming pool at night with no one in it. When I ring the bell, the night manager makes a noise from a back room and then comes out cheerfully, wiping her hands on her bright cotton dress.

"How are you?" she asks. The world's most innocuous question, impossible to answer.

"Fine."

She holds out the registration card and a purple pen, the dimpled flesh under her arm unfurling like a wing. I feel her looking at my face, my hair. She watches my hands, reading upside down. "Anna Louise Hart. That's sure a pretty name."

"What?"

"Don't you think so, baby?" Her voice has the Caribbean in it, a rich, warm slant that makes me think she calls everyone "baby," even me.

It's hard work not to flinch at her kindness, to stand in the greenish cast of the fluorescent bulb and write down the number of my license plate. To talk to her as if we're just any two people anywhere, carrying on without a single sorrow.

She finally gives me my key, and I go to my room, shutting the door behind me with relief. Inside there's a bed and a lamp and one of those oddly placed chairs no one ever sits in. Bad lighting flattens everything into dull rectangles, the tasteless carpet and plastic-looking bedspread, the curtains missing their hooks.

I set down my duffel in the center of the bed, take out my Glock 19 and tuck it under the stiff pillow, feeling reassured to have it nearby, as if it's an old friend of mine. I suppose it is. Then I grab a change of clothes, and start the shower, taking care to avoid the mirror as I undress, except to look at my breasts, which have hardened into stones. The right is hot to the touch, with a blistered red mound surrounding the nipple. I run the water in the shower as hot as it will go and stand there, being burned alive, with no relief at all.

When I climb out, dripping, I hold a washcloth under the faucet before microwaving it, sodden, until it smokes. The heat feels volcanic as I press it hard against myself, singeing my hands as I bend double over the toilet bowl, still naked. The loose flesh around my waist feels as rubbery and soft against my arms as a deflated life raft.

With wet hair, I walk to the all-night drugstore, buying ACE bandages and a breast pump, ziplock bags, and a forty-ounce bottle of Mexican beer. They only have a hand pump in stock, awkward and time-consuming. Back in my room, the heavy outmoded television throws splayed shadows on the bare wall. I pump with the sound off on a Spanish soap opera, trying to distract myself from the ache of the suction. The actors make exaggerated movements and faces, confessing things to one another while I labor on one breast and then the other, filling the reservoir twice and then emptying the milk into the baggies I label 9/21/93.

I know I should flush it all, but I can't make myself do it. Instead, I hold the bags for a long minute, registering their meaning before tucking them into the freezer of the small convenience unit and closing the door, and thinking only briefly about the housekeeper who will find them, or some road-strung trucker looking for ice and feeling repulsed. The milk tells a whole sordid story, though I can't imagine any stranger correctly guessing at the plot. I'm having a hard time understanding it myself, and I'm the main character; I'm writing it.

Just before dawn I wake feverish and take too many Advil, feeling my throat catch and burn around the capsules. A breaking-news banner is running across the bottom of the TV. forty-seven confirmed dead in big bayou, alabama. deadliest crash in amtrak history. Sometime in the middle of the night, a towboat on the Mobile River has gotten off course in heavy fog and driven a barge into the Big Bayou Canot Bridge, displacing the track by three feet. Eight minutes later, running right on schedule, the Amtrak *Sunset Limited* traveling from Los Angeles to Miami has slammed into the kink at seventy miles per hour, shearing off the first three cars, collapsing the bridge, and rupturing the fuel tank. Amtrak is citing negligence of the tugboat driver. Several crew members are missing, and recovery efforts are still underway. President Clinton is supposed to visit the site later today.

I click off the set, wishing that the rubbery red button on the remote could work to shut off everything, inside and out. Chaos and despair and senseless death. Trains hurtling toward kinks and gaps, everyone aboard sleeping and clueless. Tugboat captains on the wrong river at exactly the wrong moment.

Eight minutes, I want to scream. But who would hear me?

Two

Once I worked a missing persons case, a boy we later found in pieces under his grandmother's porch in Noe Valley, the grandmother on a creaking, peeling porch swing directly over his body when we pulled up. For months after, I couldn't get her face out of my mind, the powdery folds of skin around her mouth, frosted pink lipstick painted just beyond her upper lip. The serenity in her watery blue eyes.

Her grandson, Jeremiah Price, was four. She had poisoned him first, so he wouldn't remember the pain. "Remember" being her word, the first word in the story she was telling herself about what she'd felt she'd had to do. But the story had no center, not to anyone but her. When we took her confession, we asked her the same question over and over. *Why did you kill him?* She could never tell us why.

In my dim room at the Travelodge, a rotary phone sits on the cheap, scarred bedside table with instructions for dialing out and the rate of long-distance charges. Brendan picks up on the second ring, his voice slow and thick, as if it's coming through concrete. I've woken him up. "Where are you?"

"Santa Rosa. I didn't get far."

"You should get some sleep. You sound awful."

"Yeah." I look down at my bare legs on the bedspread, feeling the Brillo pad scratchiness of the cheap fabric against my thighs. My T-shirt is damp and wadded, stuck with sweat to the back of my neck. I've wrapped my breasts in a tourniquet of bandages, and the pain, in spite of all the Advil, sends a pinging ache through me with each heartbeat, a ragged sort of echolocation. "I don't know what to do. This is awful. Why are you punishing me?"

"I'm not, it's just—" There's a long, freighted pause as he weighs his words. "You have to figure some things out for yourself."

"How am I supposed to do that?"

"I can't help you." He sounds defeated, stretched to the breaking point. I can picture him on the side of our bed in dawn light, his body hunched over the phone, one hand in his thick dark hair. "I've been trying, and I'm *tired*, you know?"

"Just let me come home. We can fix this."

"How?" he asks breathily. "Some things aren't fixable, Anna. Let's just both take some time. This doesn't have to be forever."

Something in his tone makes me wonder, though. As if he's cut the cord but is afraid to acknowledge it. Because he doesn't know what I'll do. "How much time are we talking? A week or a month? A year?"

"I don't know." His sigh is frayed. "I have a lot of thinking to do."

On the bed next to me, my own hand looks waxy and stiff, like something that belongs on a mannequin in a shopping mall. I look away, fixing on a point on the wall. "Do you remember when we first got married? That trip we took?"

He's quiet for a minute, and then says, "I remember."

"We slept in the desert under that huge cactus with all the birds living inside. You said it was a condominium."

Another pause. "Yeah." He isn't sure where this is going, isn't sure I haven't lost it completely.

I'm not so sure myself. "That was one of our best days. I was really happy."

"Yeah." Through the phone his breathing quickens. "The thing is, I haven't seen that woman in a long time, Anna. You haven't been here for us and you know it."

"I can do better. Let me try."

Silence spreads through the receiver, pools around me on the bed as I wait for his answer. Finally he says, "I don't trust you. I can't." The clarity in his voice is devastating. The resolution. For weeks he's been so angry, but this is worse. He's made a decision I can't fight, because I've given him every reason to feel precisely this way. "Take care of yourself, okay?"

I feel myself teetering on a dark edge. In other moments of our marriage, he would have thrown me a rope. "Brendan, please. I can't lose everything."

"I'm sorry," he says, and disconnects before I can say another word.

Nearly two hundred people came to the memorial service, many of them in uniform. Colleagues and friends and well-meaning strangers who'd read the story in the *Chronicle* and thought, *There but for the grace of God go I.*

I zipped myself into a dress I couldn't feel, so high on Ativan it could have been made of knives. I read lips through huge black sunglasses while Brendan said thank you over and over. Back at the house, I positioned myself in a corner of the kitchen, turned away from the aggressively placed flowers and condolence notes, the stricken faces around the table full of casseroles and cheese platters. My supervising officer, Frank Leary, found me there, a plate of food in his hands that he didn't even pretend to want.

"What can I say, Anna? What can anyone say about something so awful?"

His voice was usually gruff, not soft like this. I wished I could freeze him where he stood, him and everyone else in a child's game of statue, and walk away. Instead I only nodded. "Thanks."

"You should take as much bereavement time as you need for yourself. Don't worry about a thing, okay?"

The wall seemed to inch nearer as he spoke. "Actually I was thinking I'd come back next week. I need something else to focus on."

"C'mon, Anna. You don't mean that. It's too soon. You should only be thinking about your family right now, and taking care of yourself."

"You don't understand, Frank." I could hear my voice tightening around the words and tried to slow down, to sound less desperate. "I'll go crazy here with nothing to do. Please."

He raised his eyebrows and seemed just about to correct me as my husband walked up. Frank stood a little straighter and reached out his hand. "Brendan. Tough day. I'm so sorry, man. Let me know if there's any way I can help."

"Thanks, Frank." Brendan's gray knit tie hung loosely at the open collar of his shirt, but nothing in his body seemed remotely relaxed as he stood between Frank and me, glancing back and forth as if he was attempting to read a feeling in the air. "So what's going on here?"

"Nothing," I lied quickly. "We can talk about it later."

"I heard you." He blinked rapidly, his face growing pink. "You can't seriously mean to go back to work right now."

"Listen," Frank said, stepping forward. "I just said the same thing. I'm on your side."

"Who's on *my* side?" Behind me the wall felt smooth and cool against my palm, and yet I felt caged suddenly. Trapped. "I'm just trying to get through this, okay? If I can't distract myself—" I couldn't finish the sentence.

"I can't believe you!" Brendan clamped his lips together, his nostrils flaring. "How about us? How about focusing on your family? Don't we deserve that from you? Especially after what happened?"

It was as if he'd slapped me. I froze in my body. "That's not what I mean." I could hear how stiff my answer sounded, how defensive.

"Yes, it is."

Frank and I both watched him turn on his heel, then push his way through the room full of bodies with his head down.

"You should go after him. He's just grieving. People say all kinds of things when they're in pain."

"*People,* Frank? What about *my* pain?" Inside my chest, everything felt airless, sealed in a vacuum. "You blame me too, don't you? Just say it."

Three

The air temperature feels like bathwater as I leave Santa Rosa, and the sun glitters obscenely. Even the unkempt motel parking lot is a garden, half a dozen silk trees with feathery fuchsia drag-queen blooms. There are birds everywhere—in the branches, in the smudgeless sky, in the broken neon Jack in the Box drive-through kiosk, where three fuzzy chicks stare at me from a nest threaded with drinking-straw wrappers, their throats so pink and open it hurts to look at them.

I order a large coffee and an egg sandwich I can't eat before cutting over to Route 116, which will thread me through the Russian River Valley to the coast. Jenner is the town there, a postcard more than an actual village. Far below, Goat Rock looks like a giant's crude toy ball against the dizzying blue of the Pacific, the sort of magic trick Northern California seems to do in its sleep.

In thirty-five years, I've never left the state or lived anywhere south of Oakland, and yet the beauty still guts me. Stupid, effortless, ridiculous beauty that goes on and on and on—the roller coaster of the Pacific Coast Highway, the sea like a slap of wild color.

I pull over and park on a hard little oval of dirt just off the side of the highway, crossing both lanes to stand on a bald place above snarled brush and black saw-toothed rocks and bursts of spiky foam. The plunge is dramatic. Dizzying. The wind comes at me, clawing under every layer of clothing so that I have to hug myself, shaking. Then my face is wet, suddenly, tears coming for the first time in weeks. Not about what I've done or not done. Not about what I've lost and can never get back, but because there's only one place I can go from here, I realize, one road on the map that means anything to me now. The way back home.

For seventeen years, I've stayed away from Mendocino, locking up the place inside myself like something too precious to even look at. Right now, though, on the edge of this cliff, it feels like the only thing keeping me alive, the only thing that's ever been mine.

If you think about it, most of us have very little choice about what we're going to become or who we're going to love, or what place on earth chooses us, becoming home.

All we can do is go when we're called, and pray we'll still be taken in.

By the time I reach Albion a few hours later, coastal fog has blotted out the sun. It swirls ahead of my low beams, making everything vanish and reappear, the twisting coast road and clustered fir trees, and then the village, finally, like something out of a dark fable—Victorian houses floating white and anchorless over the headlands, the mist all around shuddering and releasing, seeming to breathe.

I feel a clamping sensation as each winding turn brings me closer to the past. The shapes of the trees seem to echo. The road signs too, and the long damp bridge. I'm almost on top of the stoplight by the time I register it and have to gun my way through, racing the yellow onto Little Lake Road. Then I'm out on the bluff, going on pure muscle memory.

Turning left on Lansing Street, I feel as if I've squeezed sideways through time. Above the roofline of the Masonic Hall and against a gauzy sky, the figures of *Time and the Maiden* stand sharp and white, the most iconic thing in the village. A bearded, elderly figure with wings and a scythe, braiding the hair of a girl standing before him. Her head bowed over a book resting on a broken column, an acacia branch in one of her hands, an urn in the other, and an hourglass near her feet—each object an enigmatic symbol in a larger puzzle. The whole carving like a mystery in plain sight.

Once, when I was ten, soon after I came to live in Mendocino, I asked Hap what the statue was supposed to mean. He smiled and told me the history instead. How a young millworker and carpenter named Erick Albertson had carved it from a single piece of redwood in the mid-1800s, working at night in his cottage on the beach. During that time he'd become the first master of Mendocino's Masonic Order, but never stopped laboring on his masterpiece. It took him seven years in all and then, sometime after the carving was erected in 1866, he had died in a strange accident the history books couldn't properly explain.

Hap had been a member of the Masonic Order for decades, longer even than he'd been a forest ranger. I assumed he knew everything, all there was to know. But when I asked him how Albertson's passing was connected to the figures and what they meant, he gave me a sideways look.

"Albertson's death doesn't have anything to do with you. And anyway, it happened so long ago. The symbols wouldn't make sense even if I explained them. They tell a story known only to Masons, never written down, only passed on by mouth as they take their Third Degree."

I was even more intrigued. "What's the Third Degree?"

"What you're giving me now," he said, and walked away before I even got the joke.

I park and pull on a baseball cap and sunglasses before stepping out into the chilly, fog-wet street. It's hard to imagine any locals recognizing me as a grown woman, but the San Francisco papers are widely read up here, and occasionally my cases had landed me in the *Chronicle*. So had the accident, for that matter.

In Mendosa's Market, I keep my gaze down, trying to grab only essentials, canned vegetables and dry goods, things easy to prepare. But part of me feels caught up in the spinning reel of an old movie. I was just here, it seems, right here by the lit icebox full of milk while Hap reached out for a cold gallon and opened it, drinking from the jug and winking at me before passing it my way. Then he was pushing the cart again, steering with his elbows, leaning over the basket. Idling as if we had all the time in the world.

But no one has that.

When I finish my shopping, I pay in cash, loading the bags into the back of my Bronco before heading down the street to the Good-Life Cafe. It was called something else when I lived here, but I can't remember what, and it doesn't matter. The sound and shape and smell of the place fit my memory exactly. I order coffee and a bowl of soup, and then sit in the window facing the street, comforted by the noises around me, dishes clattering in the bus tub, fresh beans in the grinder, friendly talk. Then, from over my shoulder, I hear two men arguing.

"You don't really believe all that bullshit, do you?" one barks at the other. "Psychics and whatnot? You know how much money that family has. She just wants a piece of it. Hell, I don't blame her."

"What if she really does know something, and no one follows up on it?" the other man spits back. "The girl could be bleeding out somewhere or worse."

"She's probably already dead."

"What's wrong with you? She's a *person*. A kid."

"A famous person's kid."

"That doesn't mean anything. What if the psychic is telling the truth? Haven't you ever seen or heard something you can't explain?"

"Nope. Can't say that I have."

"Then you're not paying attention."

Listening to them gives me a weightless, unmoored feeling. I pay for my coffee and soup, careful not to look their way, and cross to the message board on the far wall. It was always part of our morning ritual, Hap's and mine. He had a way of leaning back instead of forward as he scanned the board, a solid white mug in his hand, his eyes roving for something that hadn't jumped out just yet.

"How much do you think you can know about a town this size?" he asked me once, early on.

I'd lived in larger, dingier towns all through Mendocino County. By comparison, the village was spick-and-span, with only fifteen streets that even had names. In my mind, it seemed like a doll's house you could open like a suitcase and see into, room by room. "Everything."

"People you see every day? Houses you pass a thousand times without thinking?"

"I guess so."

"Think, Anna. What makes a blind spot?"

He meant like when we were driving. "Someone being right on your shoulder, too close to see."

"That works for people, too. Anyone under your nose just disappears. That's the danger zone, right next to you. Whoever it is you trust the most."

I was listening to him, listening hard. For as long as I could remember, people had been telling me that I *should* trust them, social workers and teachers and total strangers, all of them saying a version of the same thing, that I should let my guard down and open up. But the world had been showing me the opposite, and now Hap was, too. "What's the secret then?"

"There's no secret, just keep your eyes open. Open all the time, but especially when you think you can't be surprised. That's when you learn to pay attention, to listen to your own voice."

"What about other people?"

"They'll either earn your trust or they won't."

He meant himself and his wife, Eden, too. Some other type of ten-year-old girl with a different set of experiences might have felt nervous hearing this, but I was relieved. He didn't trust me yet, and I didn't trust him. Finally someone wasn't trying to pretend any of this was easy. Finally someone had decided to tell the truth.

The café's name may have changed, but the message board hasn't. I comb through the postings slowly, bright snatches of colored paper hawking guitar lessons and palm readings and garden soil. Someone is looking for an artist's model. Someone else wants free firewood. I take my time reading the messages one by one until I come to the missing girl, her lost lovely face under the words have you seen me?

Cameron Curtis
Age: 15
Last seen: 9/21
Red flannel shirt, black jeans
5'4" 105 lbs
Long black hair, dark brown eyes
Tips: 724-555-9641
Substantial reward offered

September 21 was yesterday, the day Brendan had finally had enough and asked me to go. The timing makes me feel shaky as I look at the girl again, her dark serious gaze, the spill of hair to her waist, all of her too beautiful to be safe anywhere for long. Something in the curve of her mouth tells me that very wrong things have happened to her, even before she disappeared. I've seen too many like her to believe otherwise. But this isn't San Francisco, where missing teen flyers are plastered on every Muni kiosk, a sight so familiar they become transparent. In a small place like Mendocino, I know all too well, any act of violence is personal. Everyone will be feeling this. Everyone will be affected.

I stare at the girl for one moment more and then reach for the number of a cottage for rent, just beneath her missing poster. The place is seven miles out of town and four hundred dollars a month. When I call the owner, Kirk, he explains that there's no TV service, phone line, or central heat.

"It's what you'd call bare bones," he says. "A nice getaway, though, if you like things quiet."

"I do."

Four

The first time I saw Mendocino, it hardly seemed like a real place. The tidy streets were lined with gingerbread houses, most of them white with lavish trim and picket fences. The whole village stretched out on the shaggy, rounded bluff against the Pacific, small enough to take in all at once, with one grocery store, a handful of cute shops, two cemeteries, and an elementary school.

"What are those?" I asked Hap, pointing at a wooden square-sided turret attached to a neighboring house. Mrs. Stephens, my social worker, had just left and we were standing in Hap and Eden's front yard on Covelo Street.

"Tank houses," Eden explained. "Water towers." Her body was soft and round and smelled of powder, while Hap was tall and tautly built, with wide shoulders and a handlebar mustache. If he looked like a cowboy, she looked like a grandmother, but wasn't one, I'd just learned. They'd fostered a lot, but never had children of their own.

Their house was beautiful, a large Victorian that looked to me like a ship. The second story was set wider than the first, with rounded front windows aimed at the headlands, a wild expanse of gold grass and wind-twisted cypresses. As we stood together, just getting the feel of one another and this new arrangement, the sun was setting in their front yard.

I'd just come from Fort Bragg, from a small, sad box of a house near the part of Glass Beach locals called "the dumps," where for years and years people had abandoned furniture, appliances, even old cars. From there, you could see the ocean too, but not like this. Nothing I'd ever seen was like this. The sun slid into the Pacific as if it was slowly melting, a ball of widening orange-pink taffy that seemed to pulse from the center, like a beating heart. I couldn't take my eyes off of it.

Then, just as the sun vanished completely, there was a sudden green flash.

"That's good luck," Eden said.

I'd stopped believing in luck, but *something* was happening. Mendocino had already begun to pull on me, like gravity.

Following directions from Kirk, I head out of the village on Little Lake Road. Five miles later, the road turns from asphalt to packed dirt and gravel. Firs and pines and Sitka spruce thicken around me, pushing in from all directions, black-tipped fairy-tale trees that knit shadows out of nothing, night out of day—as if they've stolen all the light and hidden it somewhere. God, but I've missed them.

After another two miles, I take a sharp left marked with a red flag and a battered wooden sign: no access. The earthen lane shrinks as it winds down a steep hill for three-tenths of a mile. Then I see the driveway and the silhouette of the cedar cottage winking through a stand of dense, towering pines. It looks like somewhere a hermit might live, like an island in the trees, a cave to disappear in. It's perfect.

Kirk stands waiting for me on the porch. He appears to be in his midsixties, with stiff shoulders and short-bristled gray hair in a military cut. His face is angular and his eyes flinty looking even as he smiles and gives me a small wave, keys in hand. "Trouble finding the place?"

"Not too bad." I notice the porch is neat, with cordwood stacked nearly to the window ledge on one side. "Was this a trapping cabin?"

"Once, I guess. Belonged to my wife's family. Now I rent it when I can." I feel him studying me, wondering about my story. "Most folks want a whole lot more, a romantic getaway. That sort of thing."

I only nod and stamp in after him. The main room is murky, full of dark paneling and smelling of mice, a slightly sweet and rotten odor, almost feral. A round-bellied woodstove sits angled in one corner, blackened from use. Rose-colored chintz curtains frame the windows in the tiny kitchen, where there's a dollhouse-sized sink and washboard counter, and a refrigerator better suited for a dorm room. A single threadbare dish towel hangs from a metal hook.

"You can see you have everything you need here," Kirk said.

If he only knew how little I do need. How much.

Off the living room, the dim bathroom has a closet-sized shower with a cheap frosted-glass door. The single bedroom seems to be an addition. When I step inside, the threshold gives like a sponge, but the room itself feels solid enough, with a metal-framed double bed and a simple bureau with a lamp. A picture window on the south-facing wall looks out onto thick forest etched against the fading light. *The gloaming,* Eden always called this time of day, a strange term that meant "to glow," even as it referred to the dark.

"It can get pretty cold at night," Kirk says. "I'd keep a fire going when you're here. You can use as much wood as you like as long as you chop more. That heater hogs propane." He shrugs at the standing unit against the wall. "Anything you use, you refill from town."

"That's fine," I assure him, only wanting to be alone now.

But there's more. The shower has tricky taps, with the hot and cold knobs reversed. The flue on the woodstove needs coaxing now and again. He shows me how to use the generator if the power cuts out, which it will sometimes, he warns.

"The loggers cut the lines. I think they're drunk more than not. The way they drive these roads you'll want to watch for them. And keep everything locked up too, at night. A woman on her own, I mean. . . ." His voice trails and dips as if he's just heard himself cross an invisible line into the realm of the personal.

"I'll be all right." Annoyance has crept into my voice.

Kirk coughs awkwardly. "Course you will."

When he finally leaves, the cabin ticks with quiet. I unpack my few things and then step out onto the porch, into cool dusk, purple light. The spaces between the trees have contracted. I breathe in the stillness and for one precarious moment let myself think of the life I've just swung away from, not by choice, of Brendan and our messy kitchen, toys everywhere, baby tub upended in the sink. Our names side by side on the mailbox, like a talisman that had failed in its purpose. We had seven years together—not nearly enough—but he was right to say I haven't been there for him. I haven't.

Above me, I look for the moon in the ragged gaps in the canopy, but can't find it. A screech owl sends up a trembling rhythm of hoots in the distance. From farther off a dog begins to yip, sounding plaintive. Or is it a coyote? The temperature has plunged. I shiver in my flannel shirt and jacket, wondering how cold it might get before morning, and whether the girl has a blanket or a fire wherever she is.

The girl.

I have no idea where the thought has come from, but immediately try to push it away. My whole world is still smoking behind me because of girls like Cameron Curtis. The missing and the damaged, their stories pulling at me like jagged little siren songs. For the last few years, I've been working for an initiative in the Bay

Area called Project Searchlight, focusing on sex crimes and crimes against children, those abducted and murdered by strangers, or stolen and rendered powerless by their own family members, or targeted by pimps and monsters, sold and resold invisibly.

It's the hardest work I've ever done, and also the most important, even if Brendan can't ever forgive me. I'm good at it, too. Over time, I've developed a kind of radar for victims, and Cameron Curtis is deeply familiar, almost as if a neon sign flashes over her head, telegraphing her story, her vulnerability. And not just to me. However the sign has gotten there, I know predators can see it too, luridly bright and unmistakable.

I think of the girl's family, losing their minds with worry and dread. I think of how lonely and lost Cameron might have felt for years, desperate even—disconnected. How sadness and shame are more than feelings; they're an illness, a terrible cancer that spins through the world taking lives in a hidden cyclical way that might never end.

When the yipping comes again, I flinch. It's definitely a coyote. More than any other animal in these woods, they sound almost human—cold and lonely and hungry. Scared, even. Crying on and on.

Five

That night I float bodiless above a white crescent of beach as someone stumbles, running through tangled kelp and shadows. But there's nowhere to go. It's a girl, of course. She trips and falls to her knees, stands and falls again, scrambling backward on her hands, screaming and shaking. And then she quiets suddenly. Quiets the way an animal finally does, when it knows the chase is over.

I wake with a start, my heart thudding, and my skin slick with sweat. My fever must be back, I think, throwing off the scratchy blankets. Under my thick sweater my breasts are still bound in their tourniquet, but the swelling hasn't gone down at all. My pain is dull but constant, a throbbing anchor point.

All around me, the dark is ice cold and seems to pool. I've forgotten how it feels to sleep in the woods, utterly isolated without street noise or neighbors, or light. Shoving my feet into a second pair of socks, I step out into the main room, where the blinking microwave tells me it's not quite 4:00 a.m. I've slept for five hours, maybe. Passed out is more like it.

I find some ibuprofen and another sleeping pill, and swallow them down with whiskey, hoping to clear my head of the nightmare. I can only assume the girl was Cameron Curtis, my subconscious fabricating a version of her disappearance, caught up in the drama that's always preoccupied me, long before I became a detective, even. As if cries for help that are forever ringing through the atmosphere get amplified as they cross my path, and sticky. As though they belong to me somehow, and I have no say in the matter, no choice at all but to try and answer them.

The first thing I see when I wake several hours later is the half-empty liquor bottle on the floor beside the sofa, my socks balled up on the coffee table. Behind my eyes, my hangover pulses, spangled. If Hap were here, he'd be concerned to see me drinking so much. He'd also be dressed already, face washed, coffee on the boil. He loved mornings and late nights, too. Sometimes I wondered if he slept at all, but it was comforting to think he was always there if I needed him, awake and at the ready. I wish that were still true.

I dress in layers, feeling the top button of my jeans sinking into the soft flesh at my waist, my fingertips grazing the puckered skin, like fresh scar tissue. I pull my hair back without checking my reflection and then fill my thermos with coffee before bolting the cabin door behind me and heading back toward the village.

When I reach the coast road, I turn the car north toward Caspar and Jug Handle Creek, a favorite place of Hap's for day hikes. When I was eleven, Hap and many of the rangers he worked with joined up with local activists to protect the bluffs from logging and real estate development—and they won. A legacy the entire area was proud of. Hap was only twenty when he first started working for the U.S. Forest Service, rising through the ranks until he became lead warden not long after I came to live with them, with oversight over dozens of rangers and fifty thousand acres of federally owned land.

His was a big job and sometimes a dangerous one. The stories he told were full of hunting accidents and hikers in dire straits, of teenagers pulled blue and lifeless from hidden quarries. He knew what an aggressive black bear could do to a man, and what men could do to one another out in that boundlessness.

Over the eight years I lived in Mendocino with the Straters, I became Hap's student and sidekick, his shadow. At first I didn't understand why he would want to spend so much time with me, or why he and Eden had taken me on to begin with. I'd already bounced through half a dozen homes without sticking. Why would this be different? It took time and numerous false starts for me to believe that Hap and Eden were what they appeared to be on the surface, just decent people who meant to be kind because they could. I tested and pushed, trying to goad them into sending me away like everyone else had. Once I ran off and slept in the woods, waiting to see if Hap would come and look for me. When he did, I thought he'd be angry or fed up with my nonsense, but he wasn't. He only looked at me, damp and bedraggled, shivering from my night on the ground.

Walking me back to his truck, he said, "If you're going to be out here on your own, let's get you smart about it, so you can take care of yourself."

"I can take care of myself already," I said, putting up my guard automatically.

"Things have been hard on you. I know that. You've had to be tough to get through it, but toughness isn't the same as strength, Anna."

It was as if he had shined a light directly into my eyes, into the crevice in my heart I thought I'd hidden better. "What do you mean?"

We'd reached the truck and climbed in. He settled himself behind the wheel, seeming in no hurry to answer my question. Finally he turned to me and said, "Linda told us what happened to your mom, honey."

Linda was Mrs. Stephens, my social worker. All I could do now was pretend I didn't care what he knew or didn't, what he thought of me or didn't. "So?"

"I can't even imagine what that must have been like for a kid your age. Honestly. It breaks my heart."

Whatever thoughts were in my head vanished with a forced pop. On autopilot, I inched nearer to the door handle.

Hap noticed and grew very still. Only his eyes seemed to move and they saw everything. "I won't stop you if you want to run away, but if you could take a chance on us and stay, I can teach you things that might help you later. Things that have helped me. About being in the woods."

Keeping my eyes on the front windshield, the scrim of dust above the wiper blades, I shrugged to let him know he didn't have my full attention.

"Nature demands our respect, Anna. It has a brutal side for sure, but if you can learn its language, there's peace to be found, and comfort too. The best kind of medicine I know."

"I'm fine the way I am." I faced him, daring him to say otherwise.

"Of course you are. How about one lesson before we head home, though? I can teach you how to find true north. An easy one."

I wanted to say yes, but the word had gotten stuck a long time ago, caught and fixed like a marble in the middle of my throat. Instead, I pulled my hand away from the door and into my lap.

"Or later is fine," he said. "It can keep. Let's go home."

That night before bed, he gave me a clothbound book called *Basic Wilderness Survival*. I pushed it into a drawer in my nightstand, but took it out again as soon as he left the room, scanning the chapter titles. "Signaling." "Sustenance." "Shelter." "Knots and Lashes." I stayed up past midnight devouring it. There were step-by-step instructions for testing the edibility of plants and bugs, setting traplines, building hobo shelters, catching fish with your hands. There was map and compass nomenclature to learn, field bearings and terrain considerations, fire building, personal protection, wound care, adaptability, overcoming stress and hypothermia and fear.

I didn't understand why I was drawn to these scenarios, at least not then, but they spoke to me on the deepest level. Hap was a wise man. He must have guessed from the beginning that this would be the way to talk to me, survivor to survivor.

Pulling into the small lot at the head of the trail, I double tie my heavy boots, zip up my anorak to my chin, and head off, skirting the main trailhead to follow a lesser-known route out to the headlands loop. Half a mile in, I come to a dense cypress grove and duck through a narrow break in the trees, holding one hand in front of my face to catch the cobwebs I know are there, though I can't see them. My fingertips are still sticky with the strands as I press inside, and then time is sticky, too. I'm ten or eleven, being shown the secret way into the grove for the first time.

"Krummholz" is the word for this kind of vegetation I remember from one of Hap's lessons, a German term that means "bent wood." Over many decades, hard weather has sculpted the trees into grotesque shapes. The salt-rich north wind kills the tips of the branches, forcing them to dip and twist, swooping toward the ground instead of the sky. They're a living diagram of adaptation, of nature's intelligence and resilience. They shouldn't be able to keep growing this way, and yet they do.

In the grove, I feel a sudden, sharp ache for Hap. For all the loveliness he showed me, and the ugliness, too. For how he peeled back the world, over and over, trusting me to let it in. Being here makes me feel closer to him, and that much closer to the answers I've come for, the way I might put myself back together like a scattered, shattered jigsaw puzzle.

I close my eyes, trying to hold it all still—the spare sifting light, and the dense smell of moss. But the moment I do, a thought springs up as if on a blackened movie screen. A flash of afterimage, quick and dark. *This is a perfect place to bury a body.*

Cameron Curtis rushes to the surface of my mind, like heat. Like the blood tingling through my hands as I clench them. The wide brown eyes that have known difficult things. The stubbornly hopeful set of her mouth, and her long dark hair. It doesn't seem to matter that I've failed others like her and myself along the way. That it's probably too late already. She's here.

I'm almost stumbling as I duck back through the break and onto the headlands, walking faster and faster along the empty trail, to the edge of the bluff where the wind is so strong it almost knocks me sideways. Down below, four oily cormorants stud a ragged black rock, their necks tucked back against their bodies like hooks. The surf bucks around them, hurling foam. Farther out, there are black swells and green swells. A fishing boat rolls to the top of a crest, and then drops away, as if through a trapdoor.

I want Cameron Curtis gone like that, out of my consciousness for good. But not even the boat disappears. It springs out of the trough, small and white, clinging there. My ears have started to ring with cold, but I sit down anyway, cradling my knees tightly with my arms, holding myself together. My hair blows over my eyes and into my mouth, tasting of brine. Everything seems to swirl in a vortex, yanked back and forth, awful and beautiful. And I'm here with it, trying to remember how to live through unthinkable moments, how to ride out the wildness and the chaos and the fear.

Six

An hour or so later, as I make my way back to my car, I'm chilled to the bone but calmer in my head. As soon as I reach the parking lot, I stop in my tracks. Two striped police barriers half block the park entrance. Half a dozen uniformed officers are organizing near the rangers' board, with K-9 teams and walkies. This is a search party for Cameron Curtis.

Tightening the hood of my anorak, I make for my Bronco, feeling conspicuous, on high alert. I'm ten feet away with my keys in my hand when I hear my name. But I have to be imagining it. No one knows me here, not anymore. Speeding up, I reach the door just as a hand comes down on my back.

"Hey."

I whirl with my hands out automatically, ready for a confrontation. But nothing can prepare me for the face I see—so familiar, even with the intervening years. It's like swimming through vertigo, or waking up in a time machine.

"Anna Hart. I can't believe it."

I can only stare at him. Gray eyes, lined now but with the same light; his square jaw, and fine straight nose; the fringe of unruly red-gold hair bristling from under the brim of his hat. He's a phantom, a memory, a forever-ago friend. "Will Flood."

I go to hug him and bang my elbow against his shoulder, then back away, stepping on his foot.

"Ow!" He laughs. "What the hell are you doing here?"

I can't think fast enough to answer him. The last time I saw Will, I was eighteen and he was twenty-two, newly in uniform in the sheriff's office his father had run seamlessly for decades. Back then Will had big dreams, often talking of San Francisco, LA, Denver, Seattle, anywhere but in Ellis Flood's long shadow.

"What's going on here?" I ask, as if it isn't obvious.

"Missing girl. Two days now. Disappeared from her home in the middle of the night, no signs of forced entry."

"She a runaway?"

"Don't think so. Mom's Emily Hague."

"Emily Hague the *actress*?" I can hardly believe it. A movie star in Mendocino?

"What are the odds this falls on me? Family wants it all to stay out of the media. Dad tried to give me ten thousand dollars under the table to speed up the search. As if that works. Wave some money and the girl appears out of a hat."

"I hope you took it."

His laugh comes fast. "Listen, have a drink with me later."

"I can't."

"Like hell you can't. Patterson's at eight or I'll come looking for you."

I feel another spasm of vertigo and I wish I could blink and disappear. Be faraway and invisible. But this is Will. "I'll try."

"You'll be there." Then he's striding away toward the assembled team, giving orders as he goes.

I climb into my Bronco and start the engine as the team plunges out onto the main trail. I know it by heart, and the tough work that lies ahead for them, too. They'll be making a grid of each square mile, scanning for disturbed vegetation or shreds of clothing, anything that looks off or out of place. Some of the dogs will be search-and-rescue animals focused on Cameron's scent from a sweatshirt or pillowcase, something she's used often. Others will be cadaver dogs, trained to detect traces of human decomposition, a scent picture rising from the soil or hanging on the air.

In a case like this, when someone has simply vanished, the odds—at least at first—are just as likely that they'll turn up unharmed. It's possible Cameron has gotten lost in the woods somewhere, or that she's chosen to run.

It's not a crime to go missing, but there does seem to be a telling void here, a familiar dark shimmer that makes me wonder. She may have been coerced into leaving, or even complicit in whatever harm has befallen her. There's an old ghost story about that, I remember, how the devil steals souls by asking for them openly. He isn't a thief, but a master manipulator. The real danger, or so the story goes, isn't in the devil himself, but in not knowing you have a choice to turn him away.

That's the saddest piece as I see it, and have over and over. How some victims don't have even a whisper of *no* inside them. Because they don't believe the life they have is theirs to save.

Seven

All the way to the village, I feel like a shaken-up snow globe, sharp flecks of memory colliding head on. Will is still here. He's become the town sheriff, just like his father, and now what? How can I answer any of the questions he's likely to throw at me about my life and why I've come home? How can I avoid hearing anything more about his case, which is already pressing on me? And how will we avoid talking about the past? We aren't just two old friends with no baggage, after all.

All those years, from the time I was ten and Will was fourteen, we were part of each other's story. His father, Ellis Flood, was Hap's closest friend, and so we were often thrown together. But even if that hadn't been the case, in a small town like Mendocino, the kids ran in packs, building driftwood forts on Portuguese Beach, wandering through the woods behind Jackson Street, or playing flashlight tag out on the bluffs on moonless nights. Two more in our gang were Caleb and Jenny Ford, twins who had been living alone with their dad since their mother ran off years before for a man, wanting a life that had nothing to do with them.

I always felt drawn to kids with a story similar to mine, as if we were a kind of club, with an unspoken password. They were two years older than me, a gap that seemed wider with Jenny than with Caleb for some reason. He was smart in a way that was interesting to me, his head full of odd facts and stories about the town, which made him a natural fit as a friend. I'd always liked to know things too, not just history, but anything that was going on. Details about people and places, old stories and new mysteries, and secrets of every variety.

Caleb also happened to have the best hiding places for tag. One night I followed him when Jenny started counting and everyone scattered. A lot of the kids were lone-wolf types in tag, but Caleb didn't mind me coming along. I trailed him all the way out to the edge of the bluff, where he seemed to drop through an invisible door. When I followed him, I saw he'd found a small, perfect crow's-nest perch in a cypress tree. The forked branches held his weight, the whole tree embedded like a magician's trick into the side of the cliff. It was a genius spot, and also forbidden feeling. Technically we were out over the edge, but protected too—sort of. The limbs beneath us were just the right shape and size for two scrawny kids. The branches just bushy enough to conceal us—a cloaking device so effective that when Jenny ran up and looked right at the tree, her face spotlit and lemon yellow in the cone of her small flashlight, she moved on and kept searching.

All of this was still new and foreign to me, the night games and laughing bands of neighborhood friends: childhood. Caleb and I grinned at each other, self-satisfied, because we'd already won the game. Every game we might ever play. The night seemed to stretch out in every direction, made for kids like us, invincible—immortal—while far out on the bluff, Jenny shouted names, hoping to send someone running. We watched her for a long time, her torch bobbing and dipping through the black bunchgrasses, until finally the light she made was smaller than a pinpoint.

———

Back then, Will had a crush on Jenny, but everyone did. There wasn't a prettier or nicer girl in town. She had straight white teeth, like a breath-mint commercial, coppery freckles over the bridge of her nose, and long, brown hair that swung side to side when she walked. She had a beautiful singing voice too, high and haunting, like Joni Mitchell's. She'd play her guitar on bonfire nights, feet buried in wet sand, while other kids passed stolen beer around, only half listening. But I couldn't look away.

One night she sang a tune she'd written called "Goodnight, California," about a girl who feels so empty and lost she walks out into the sea and never returns. *Don't look for me, I'm no one,* the lyrics went.

On the beach, in red-gold firelight, she called up a feeling of such intimacy, as if I was actually watching her alone in her room, her body rounded over her guitar, all of her words about loneliness. In real life, Jenny never came across that way, but I knew that didn't mean anything. Any surface could hide sadness just beneath.

Because Jenny was two years older and hadn't invited me closer, I didn't know much about what her home life was like. But even if we'd been best friends, she might not have told me. There were a thousand different ways to be silent, I knew. The song spoke, at least to me, raising goose bumps along my arms and neck, landing dead center. *Goodnight, California. Goodnight, blue. The waves can tell my story now. All the words are for you.*

I was fifteen when Jenny Ford disappeared, in August of 1973. She was almost eighteen and had just graduated from Mendocino High. In the fall, she was supposed to go to UC Santa Barbara, to study nursing. In the meantime she was working forty-five minutes inland from the village, at Husch Vineyards in Philo, saving for a car and bumming rides home from anyone going her way. One night, she left work in the usual way but never made it home. For days, the whole town panicked, particularly Caleb. It was devastating to watch. There were whispers that she might have run away. Teenagers did that all the time, for all sorts of reasons. But Caleb insisted she wouldn't have—not without letting him know, or taking him with her.

As we waited to hear news, I felt an old, dormant fear come awake in my body. Those years in Mendocino with Hap and Eden had added up inside me, making me feel safe—saved. But now I knew for sure that what had happened to Jenny could just as easily have happened to me. Deep down, we weren't that different.

Eight

Will is sitting at the far end of the bar when I finally come through the door of Patterson's a little after eight-thirty, a nearly empty cup of coffee in front of him.

"I was starting to feel stood up," he says, hugging me with warm pressure.

I squeeze back, noticing that he's showered and changed into a fresh uniform. His hair is damp, combed flat, but I know where all of his cowlicks are, how wild it will look as soon as it dries. Except for the usual ravages of time, Will is eerily unchanged—same strong jaw and long eyelashes. Same energetic grace in his body, as if he's half man, half golden retriever.

"You surprised the hell out of me today," I say.

"Me too." He laughs a little and signals the barmaid over, a middle-aged blond woman with a soft jawline and heavily lined eyes.

I order a Guinness with a shot of Jameson, and then turn to Will. "Aren't you joining me?"

"Not on the job. I won't really be off the clock until I find this girl."

"Oh, of course. I don't know what I was thinking." The barmaid comes back with my order and I lift my beer glass to Will in a small mock toast. "I can't believe you're still here. You had so many big ideas."

"Did I?" He makes a face. "Where was I supposed to go?"

"A thousand places. Anywhere."

"Out of the old man's shadow, you mean?"

"Maybe. I think about him sometimes. Those impressions he did. Bugs Bunny."

"Yeah. He worked hard on that stuff. He'd practice for hours. He can be a son of a bitch in other ways, but he's funny."

"He's still around, then?"

"In a nursing home up in Fort Bragg." Will tents his fingers over his coffee cup, fidgeting through obvious discomfort. "Not quite all there, as they say."

"Oh, I'm sorry."

"It's okay." He lifts his shoulders toward his ears and then drops them, trying to release something. "He can still make my kids laugh."

"Kids? That's great. I'll bet you're a good dad."

"I try."

"Boy? Girl?"

"One of each, ten and twelve. Both of them too smart for their own good."

"And your wife, what does she do?"

"Beth. She teaches at the Montessori school up the road. She's been there a long time. She's wonderful with those kids."

"That's a nice picture." On instinct, I glance at his left hand. There's no ring, no indentation where a ring has been, and no tan line, either. Maybe he doesn't wear one, or maybe there's another story he's not telling me.

"What about you?" he goes on. "How long are you staying?"

"Not sure." I glance away. "Just taking things day by day."

"Married?"

"I married my work." It's a lie with oceans of truth in it.

"I've followed your career a bit. Project Lighthouse. You've done so well for yourself."

"Searchlight," I correct him. "But yeah."

"All those missing kids, it must be hard. I couldn't do it."

You are *doing it,* I want to say, but that wouldn't be fair. "How are you holding up?" I ask instead.

He shakes his head, looking weary. "I haven't slept since I got the call. The family wants answers, but I don't have any."

"Has the FBI stepped in?"

"I need evidence of kidnapping for federal attention, and I haven't got it. No evidence of any kind, actually, and no motive. No witnesses and no crime scene."

"But you think someone took her."

"It's just a feeling, but yeah. I do. There was that girl down near Richmond a few years back. Disappeared from her own front yard."

"Amber Swartz-Garcia."

"Similar age, right?"

"She was seven. There's a world of difference between seven and fifteen. Anyway, that was five years ago."

"Oh, right." He sighs. "Sorry. I'm forgetting you're on vacation."

"It's okay. My cop brain never really takes a vacation. Any reason to suspect the family?"

"Not off the bat. We're still conducting interviews."

"I'm assuming you're following up on registered sex offenders in the area? Checking in on probation and parole? Anyone who might have an affinity for this aged girl, this type of an offense?"

He gives me a funny look. "You really want to talk about this?"

"It's my only hobby." I shrug and take a pull from my beer. "Maybe she's being manipulated, somehow. Or gotten drawn into something dark without knowing it."

"Like drugs, you mean? She seems clean as a whistle."

"Could be sex. Someone might be controlling her."

"The mom's brother had rape charges thrown at him in college, but that was thirty years ago. Maybe it's Cameron's dad?"

"It happens." As I lean forward, I can't help but notice the strain around Will's eyes. He's desperate for a break, and I feel for him. I know exactly what he's carrying right now. How heavy it all can be.

"She's adopted. Maybe that means something?"

He's thrown out the detail as if it's just one more thing to consider, but it hits a little too close to home for me. Cameron could be struggling with classic adoption issues, testing her parents' love by acting out. Or she could have layers of emotional scar tissue, identity or attachment difficulties, boundary issues, or self-destructive tendencies. "Maybe," I say, working to keep my tone even, "if she's struggling. But you just said she's clean as a whistle."

"I know. Fuck." He exhales long and loud, then signals the barmaid to bring the check.

"I hope you get a lead soon," I say.

"Me too." He doesn't sound convinced. "I'll tell you something. I have new appreciation for my dad. The pressure he must have felt back then, when he couldn't make things right. And the sense of failure." His sigh carries generations inside of it, the way every shell holds the whole Pacific. "Everyone was waiting for him to make them feel safe again. But he never could."

He's talking about Jenny Ford. We've both been talking about her without mentioning her name.

"Have you seen Caleb yet?" Will asks suddenly.

"What? Caleb's *here*?"

"He came back almost a year ago, after his dad passed on. A stroke. Caleb inherited everything, sold all the paintings, too. That old bastard had millions."

"He did?" I conjure up Jack Ford, the eccentric hermitlike man I knew, always in the same paint-splotched jeans and flannel shirt, his hair ragged, as if he cut it himself with a kitchen knife. *A millionaire?* "I never liked him."

"Me neither. There was something off about that guy. He never remarried, you know."

"I'm not surprised. I don't think he had much use for people. How's Caleb now?"

"He's okay, I think, considering. I don't see him often."

"I would have thought he'd stay away forever. This town holds such pain for him."

"Us, too, I guess," he says simply. "But here we are."

After we settle up, I follow Will out of the bar and onto the quiet street, where the streetlamps seem to cast a supernatural glow over *Time and the Maiden,* as baffling and mesmerizing to me as ever.

Will stops in the middle of the sidewalk, blinking. "It's good seeing you again, Anna. This hasn't been the best year. I'm not gonna lie."

"For me either." I hug him quickly, surprised by the lump in my throat.

"Drive safe, will you?"

"You can't get drunk on beer," I say.

"Oh yeah? Tell yourself that all the way home."

His car is parked just down from mine. I know he still has work to do, but I feel him lingering anyway. Maybe it's just the anxiety of his case I feel radiating from him, or maybe it's pure loneliness. Those details about his perfect family might have been a lie. Or his marriage might have been completely fine, but he's gotten off track some other way. How quickly your own life can turn on you—that's something I know.

Unlocking my door, I settle behind the wheel of my Bronco just as Will steps closer, looking sad and unguarded. For a long moment, he holds my eyes, setting off a low buzz of apprehension. *Is he going to try to kiss me?*

But I've read him wrong. "I'm glad you're back," he says, "even if it's just for a while. In times like this, when the world feels so crazy, it's good to have friends around."

He's right, of course. I didn't come home for this, but he's absolutely right.

Nine

Five days after Jenny went missing, two fly fishermen found her body in the Navarro River, so waterlogged and disfigured, the coroner's office had to confirm her identity through dental records.

Hap took me into the woods to tell me. I'd never seen him lose his composure, but he was obviously struggling as he reached for my hands. "I'm always straight with you, aren't I, Anna?" he asked with a shaking voice.

My mouth went dry. The ground beneath my sneakers seemed to roll, but Hap kept talking, explaining how the fishermen had stumbled onto Jenny's remains on a little-used stretch of the river. How she might never have been found otherwise. She hadn't drowned, either. She'd been strangled.

The story was so sickening I wanted Hap to stop. But I knew he wasn't going to. If he was really going to protect me, he couldn't hold anything back. "Who did it?" My own voice seemed to bounce off the trees and into my lap like a stone, a small hard piece of the world.

"We don't know yet."

"Will Sheriff Flood catch him?"

"I believe he will."

"How could anyone do a thing like that?" I asked him, though I already knew the answer. I'd seen all kinds of people twisted by pain and circumstance. People who'd been hurt so bad and so deep they couldn't help but do the same to someone else. "Jenny was so young," I cried, hot tears running into my mouth. "She didn't even get to have a chance."

"There's death in life, Anna, things too impossible to bear. So many things, and yet we bear them."

I knew he was right, but I would have given anything to hear something else. If only Hap could promise me that it would never happen again, that I would never die, and that he and Eden wouldn't, either. That we would stay safe from harm together though the world was full of the most terrible things and people. People twisted up enough on the inside to murder a seventeen-year-old girl and leave her like trash in the river.

"How do we bear them?" I finally asked. "Those impossible things."

His hand was still and warm on mine, warm and steady and alive. He hadn't moved an inch from my side. "Like this, sweetheart."

In the coming days, I take to launching out from my cabin with a backpack and no real destination except to be in the woods. Long ago, Hap taught me how to read and follow a trail, even a little-used one, and also how to travel without one. There's nothing like it to quiet the mind. The beauty of the living world, damp ferns curled along the valley floor, lacy with moisture. Mustard-colored lichen and bearded moss splashed like paint against dark rocks and tree trunks. The canopy above like a map traced onto the sky.

One afternoon, four or five miles into a hike through Jackson State Forest, I cross an isolated county road and then come to Big River, which threads all through this part of the northern coastal range before spilling to the estuary at Big River Beach, just south of the village. The streambed is narrow and shallow, lined with mossy stones. I have a spool of lightweight line and a few fly hooks with me, and try catching one of the pale trout flicking in and out of the shadows. But they're too cautious, and soon I'm too hot. I give up, strip to my underwear, and wade into the pool. Above, through canted light, molecules of pine dust swirl like gold mist. The water plays over my skin like cool silk ribbons. I feel my heartbeat slow. This. This is what Hap meant by medicine.

On the way back, I head straight over the ridgeline, mostly for the effort of doing it. The terrain grows so steep in places I have to drop and scramble along on my hands and knees, through gray lichen and bracken and humus, my breath coming fast and sharp, my face filmed with pine dust and phosphorescent pollen.

At the top of the ridge, I stop for water, feeling winded and exhilarated. A hemlock has fallen up here and looks like a slain giant, its trunk like wet black sponge. Where the root ball has pulled up violently, I see three long scrapes in the earth and a length of animal scat that might be from a mountain lion. When I bend for a closer look, something flickers in my periphery, not an animal, but a solid form. Shelter.

Though the sun has begun to drop and a chill has settled between my shoulder blades, I plunge down the hill anyway, too curious not to take a closer look. I have to lean back on my heels to keep my balance on the decline. The soil is thin and full of deadfall. Dry bracken stings my hands and slaps at my jeans, but finally I reach the small compound. Someone's set up a hunting site like you'd see in a wilderness guide, propping a six-foot lean-to pole against a stripped Douglas fir, and then threading it with wire loop snares at intervals. It must be working. Around the base of the fir, pine-cone scales and other ground cover show trampling, the effort spent resetting the snares again and again. This is an effective kill site, elegant even. Whoever built it knows exactly what they're doing and is eating very, very well.

The shelter shows the same level of sophistication, and sets off subtle alarm bells for me. It doesn't look like a hunter's cabin, but a cone-shaped structure that reminds me of historical photos I've seen of indigenous peoples like the Pomo. They settled in small bands throughout Northern California thousands of years ago, and their homes looked much like this, rounded at the base with poles supporting the angled walls, tied together with reeds and overlaid with redwood bark and timber.

Who would go through this kind of effort to build a convincing replica of a Pomo shelter, though? And why so far from town, miles from anything like a road? Is this the work of a screwball survivalist who thinks the world is ending soon? Someone who's off the grid because they have something to hide, maybe? Or is this my cop brain reaching for dark possibilities when really it's probably just an outdoors type like Hap or like me, who needs the woods and the silence to feel whole sometimes?

"Hello?" I call out once, leaning in for a response, but only the quiet presses back.

I don't drive into Mendocino again until the first day of October, when I've reached the end of my supplies. The light has begun to change with the season, the way it always does, sharpening the angles and shadows and making you grateful for every sunny day. This one is chilly but clear, with a severe sort of freshness that feels good on my face. After I shop, I stash my groceries in my Bronco and decide to walk for a bit. In Rotary Park, a man and woman are camped out at the lone picnic table near a small, tattered pup tent. They have a medium-sized dog with them, shorthaired with a dark muzzle and reddish fur. He spots me and his head snaps up, as if we're friends. Then he trots over, falling into step behind me.

It's funny at first, how quickly he matches my pace. I stop, lifting my hand like a traffic guard—"Stay"—but he ignores me. I take a step and he takes a step. I laugh and he sits down. We're in a sitcom, suddenly, though no one seems to be watching, not even the hippie couple in the park.

I walk back to them. "Hey, would you mind holding on to your dog?"

"Not ours," the woman says. She might be thirty or fifty, with a sun-lined face and spiky blond hair resembling duckling fuzz. A Seahawks sweatshirt hangs halfway to her knees over a long print skirt. "Never seen it before."

The guy with her looks like he's been on the streets since the Summer of Love. A single graying braid hangs over one shoulder, loosely plaited but clean. One silver tooth winks as he says, "Smart dog, though."

"How can you tell? I've never kept dogs."

"It's all in the eyes," he explains. "She's listening, see."

"She?"

He flashes another silver-tipped smile. "You're not a dog person."

I find myself laughing suddenly, charmed by him. "Can you just hold on to her so I can get out of here?"

"No problem." He points to the ground once, and the dog sits, cued for his next command. When he flattens his palm, she drops to her belly. Over the back of his left hand I notice half a dozen *x*'s inside a circle.

"What does your tattoo mean?" I ask, pointing.

"Lessons." His pupils are so black they seem to bounce. "Things I shouldn't ever forget."

The woman beside him says, "Don't believe anything he tells you. Once he tried to say they stand for the men he killed in battle. Go ahead, ask him which one."

"Which battle?" I ask, playing along.

"Waterloo."

Ten

Eden was the first person I ever met who believed in past lives. Before then, I'd had a wild sampling of religion through various placements, from Mormonism to Pentecostalism to born-again Presbyterianism, without feeling persuaded by any of them. But Eden's universe was bigger and more complex than any I'd ever heard of, and far more intuitive. To her, the idea that we reincarnated was an obvious extension of the cycle of life. All life. Everything spun on a constantly moving wheel of birth, growth, and decay, the ocean around us and the Milky Way above, and all the galaxies beyond ours, numberless as the ferns unfurling along the side of the road. God wasn't up *there*, in some celestial kingdom, but here in the world, in dirt clods and dew, in the patience of the spider that lived behind the sugar jar, in the exquisite strands of her web. Death wasn't the end any more than a single shuddering wave on Portuguese Beach could stop moving. She'd made her peace with it, but I was still struggling.

After Jenny's body was found, an investigation stretched out for months. Ellis Flood and his team interviewed half the town, or so it seemed, trying to get to the bottom of the mystery. Her father and Caleb, all of Jenny's friends, and her coworkers at the vineyard in Philo. Jack Ford was a natural early suspect. He was an odd man and always had been, and everyone knew he drank too much. Besides his wife, who had left him suddenly when Caleb and Jenny were six, leaving no sign of her whereabouts, he wasn't close to many people, including his children. More than once I'd seen Caleb flinch when Jack called his name—but that wasn't evidence. Ellis Flood found nothing at all to incriminate him, and the search went on.

Jenny had kept a journal, it turned out, which was discovered when the authorities searched her room. The pages were primarily filled with cryptic poems and song lyrics, but there were a number of entries in the months before her death about wanting to leave home the way her mother had, by vanishing without a word. Things were intolerable. She couldn't stay. Couldn't take it anymore. That was the general tone of what she'd written, but there was nothing specific about pressures or fears, or why she felt so desperate now, on the verge of leaving home anyway, for college. Whether it made sense or not, the general theory was that Jenny had meant to run the night she vanished, but instead of a helpful ride, she'd crossed paths with her killer. As for who that person might be, there were no real leads. He might have been a drifter, passing through, or he might still have been here among us, hidden in plain sight.

Neighbors stopped lingering to talk on the street. Hap and Eden had never even locked their doors at night, but did now like everyone else. Hap's service weapon, the one he usually kept locked in his truck, regularly sat at the ready on his bedside while we slept. Did I feel safer for it? A little, maybe, but the surface of the world had shifted overnight, changing form—and not just for me. The sheriff's office began enforcing a nine o'clock curfew for anyone under eighteen. No one wanted to be out after dark in the village, anyway. Those days seemed gone for good, like the bonfires down at the beach, and flashlight tag on the headlands. Just when I'd started to believe I could count on them.

At the far end of Kelly Street, the Ford house is a weathered brown-shingled saltbox with a detached artist's studio, both buildings canted toward the headlands and the sea. Caleb once told me that it was built by one of the original founders of the village, and that one or another of his descendants has lived there since 1859, which isn't hard to believe, looking at the place. While he was alive, Jack Ford never made any effort to keep things looking nice, and now, so many years later, the effects of his neglect are still visible everywhere, in the peeling paint on the eaves and shingles, the battered-looking garage door, and the yard tangled with tall weeds and thistle. Almost as if he's still here, making sure nothing ever grows or changes or flies free of him.

Jack was always known as an eccentric in the village. A painter who worked on huge canvases in oil, he rarely left his studio. He didn't have many friends and seemed not to know how to talk to people civilly. Whenever I would show up looking for Caleb and find only Jack there, I got a strange feeling about him that was more than a little familiar. It wasn't anything he said, really, or anything he did. Just a heat he gave off that sent me backward, toward closed-off moments I'd left behind, people I never talked about.

Now as I walk slowly up Kelly Street toward the house, I don't know why I've come, exactly, or what I hope to feel. Maybe it's what Will said about crazy times and keeping old friends close. Or maybe I've never fully made peace with Jenny's death and need to stand at her door, one more time, even if she can't answer.

I've barely reached the edge of the gate, still whirling through things I might say to explain myself, when the studio door opens and a man steps out. He's tall and heavily built, wearing painter's coveralls splotched over with white. Underneath, his gray T-shirt exposes a tan neck, broad chest and shoulders, big hands. Nothing about him looks like the thin, brainy boy I once knew.

"Caleb?" I call out.

His head jerks up, eyes unfocused for a moment.

"It's Anna. Anna Hart."

He comes to the fence looking puzzled and then he recognizes me. "Oh my God. Anna. What the hell are you doing here?"

"Just visiting." I flush, feeling disoriented. The years between us seem to contract and expand. "I ran into Will Flood and he said you were back in town. You doing okay?"

"I am, yeah." He bobs his head. "Wow. Anna Hart."

"It's been a long time."

He shrugs, one ear dipping toward his shoulder. His hair slides boyishly over his forehead. "It has."

"Listen, you have time to grab a drink or something?" I ask without knowing I'm going to say it.

"Sure," he says hesitantly. "Let me wrap up here and meet you somewhere in a bit?"

"I could just grab a six-pack and wait for you on the bluff?"

"Sure," he says again. "Why not?"

Fifteen minutes later, we're sitting on the hard-packed ledge above Portuguese Beach, sipping cans of Coors. It's midafternoon and the light has slipped sideways. Fifty feet below us at the water's edge, sandpipers race back and forth on cartoon feet as the tide crashes forward and back. For some reason, I find it all reassuring, and somehow tender. When we were young, we sat here hundreds of times, sometimes with stolen beer. I miss those years. Those kids.

"I think you were still in high school when I left," Caleb says after a while. "I drifted for a few years, and then enlisted in the navy. I was happy to be out of here, even when I went to the Persian Gulf."

"Iran? That must have been tough."

"Some of it, sure. I was there in '79 during the Islamic Revolution. That was pretty intense, but the ocean was amazing. Super warm, not like this bitch." He smiles. "I learned to free dive there. Oysters the size of fucking softballs. And the reefs were fucking incredible." He takes a long slug from the Coors in his hand. "How about you?"

"I did half a year at San Francisco State, then dropped out and drifted for a bit. For a while I did Outward Bound trips in Yosemite."

"That sounds cool."

"It was fun, yeah, but started to feel like summer camp over time."

"You didn't want to be a ranger?"

"I thought about it, but police work felt more important. Once I entered the academy I gave it everything I had. I was interested in missing persons from the beginning. That seemed like the clearest way I could do some good. Never left the Bay Area."

"Missing persons, huh?" He sounds surprised. "So are you here to help find that high-school girl?"

"No." *Not yet,* my mind fills in, but I keep it to myself, uneasy about treading so close to old feelings. About conjuring up Jenny more than we already have. "I'm taking a break right now."

"Oh, good, then." He sounds like he means it. "Good for you."

"Thanks."

The sun is sinking fast now, staining the cloud line. Gulls draft over the chop below us, buoyed and free.

"This place," Caleb says quietly, as if he's read my mind.

"I know."

Eleven

One particularly bad year at Searchlight, when I'd dealt with three dead kids in a handful of months, Frank Leary sent me to a therapist. "It's not a punishment," he said. "Just protocol. You've been through a lot, Anna."

"I'm fine."

"Good. Let's keep it that way."

The therapist's name was Corolla, like the car. Her office was in the Embarcadero with a view of the Bay Bridge. Only a small, metallic sliver of the bridge was recognizable from her window, a toothpick-sized joke if you were going to charge for it. She had an Eames chair and red-framed Sally Jessy Raphael glasses, and a cashmere poncho that covered her knees, the triangle tip pointing at the conservative Persian carpet when she crossed her legs.

How was this going to work? I wondered. How could I possibly tell this woman in a poncho anything of consequence? And why would I want to? I was good at my job and had a strong track record. We hadn't saved these three, but that happened. We would save the next one. We would keep fighting.

"You have any trouble sleeping?" Corolla threw out. "Nightmares?"

"No more than usual."

"How about substance abuse? Ever worry you might be drinking too much?"

How much is too much? I wondered, but shook off the worry to shrug at her pointedly. "Listen, I don't really buy the whole talk-therapy thing. No offense. I'm here because I have to be."

"I've worked with a lot of clients who have trauma to process," she went on, unfazed. "My early training was with combat soldiers and shell shock. A lot of retired soldiers become cops. They think the stuff they saw and did back then is long buried, all in the past. They drown it. Numb it. Have bad marriages. Become alcoholics. But then something happens to trigger the trauma. And then boom, they snap."

"Why are you telling me this? I've never been in the military."

"There are other kinds of battlefields, Anna." She brought her fingertips together in front of her face, letting her point sink in. "On your intake form, you noted you grew up in foster care. You had siblings, too. What happened to them?"

"That has nothing to do with my job."

"Maybe not. It depends on how much work you've done to deal with what you've gone through. What you've already been carrying. What can you tell me about your parents? Do you remember them? Why couldn't they care for you?"

Her questions felt too rapid-fire, and far too loaded. I turned my body in the overly soft chair, wishing our hour were finished, but we'd barely begun. "I don't want to talk about this. And anyway, how will spilling my guts to you help me at work? I'll only feel worse."

"It might be a relief to talk, actually. Have you considered that?"

"No."

There was a long pause as she looked at me. "Humans are resilient, Anna. I have no doubt that you're incredibly adept at your job. You're holding it together really well. But maybe a little too well."

"What does that mean?" I'd begun to breathe heavily. My shoulders were tight and clenched.

"Just that sucking it up isn't a long-term solution. You might be thinking you can just go on this way indefinitely. But the things you've seen don't really go away. They build up inside you and start to take a toll. And then there's the older trauma you haven't really come to terms with. No one's bulletproof. Asking for help doesn't mean you're weak."

Weak? Where had that come from? "I'm fine. Ask anyone I work with."

Her eyes flicked over my face. "If you don't want to talk, we could explore other ways to help you process. Some of my clients do yoga or tai chi, or journaling. I'm just trying to offer you tools." She put down her notebook and then took off her glasses, balancing them between her hands. "When in your life were you the most at peace, the most yourself?"

"What?"

"Your happiest place?"

I had no idea where she was going with these questions, but Mendocino was the only possible answer. "My memories aren't all good," I clarified, "but it's home."

"Okay." Squeezing the frames of her glasses in her hands, she looked out at the city's grid, the sky. Then she closed her eyes. "Every day, I want you to picture Mendocino, to go there in your mind. Visualize it until it's complete, the whole place, just as you remember it. Then, when you have it all clearly, just as you want it, I want you to start building a house very slowly, board by board. A house big enough for everyone you've lost, everyone you haven't been able to save."

A chill sped through me. I stared at her. What kind of person *talked* like this? What kind of life had Corolla lived that let her sit in a room with a stranger and feel safe enough to close her eyes?

"How will this exercise help?"

"It's a way of integrating what's happened to you. A healing story."

Healing story? Had she read that in some therapist's manual? "There isn't a house big enough," I finally said.

"It's your house, your mind." The muscles in her face had softened. "It can be as big as it needs to be. Paint the rooms with bright colors. Let the light in. And when you have everything just right, picture them coming in together, Anna, together and happy and whole. All those children, the ones who deserved better."

Inside my chest, I felt something shudder and drop. If she would only stop *talking*, I could reset. But she wouldn't.

"It's not what you carry, but how you can learn to carry it. You need to heal yourself. Your child self too, Anna. Make room for her. Find a way to let her in."

Twelve

Back at the cabin after leaving Caleb, I heat up a can of stew and eat it over the sink, then pour two fingers of Maker's Mark into a glass, catching a glimpse of myself in the window glass. Haphazard ponytail and rumpled thermal undershirt, the jeans I haven't washed in weeks. Caleb was polite enough not to remark on it when we were together earlier, but clearly I'm having a *Call of the Wild* moment.

I stay up long past midnight, drinking and staring into the fire until I collapse at one point onto the scratchy plaid couch in the living room. Dreams come that I don't want. Haven't asked for. Are they even dreams?

I'm in the forest on a narrow trail with Eden. She walks ahead in one of Hap's heavy work jackets, her shoulders straight and solid. Not sick, then. Not sick yet.

"Look here, Anna. A medicine woman showed me this once." She points to a tree that's bent sharply sideways, as if it has a waist and is peering down at the thick, damp humus around it.

Wait. "You know a *medicine woman*?"

"It's a marker tree." Has she heard my question? "An arrow. The

Pomo sometimes did this to signal one another long ago. And see, we're just getting the message now."

"What message?"

Then Eden is gone, and Hap is with me instead, older than I ever knew him in life. Bent like the tree, nearly in half. Stooped on the trail.

"Just the old hip, screaming," he says aloud, as if he can hear my thoughts and knows I'm worried about him. "Come on. We can do it together. We're almost there."

Where? I try to step closer but am stuck somehow, glued in place. *I miss you,* I try to say. *I can't do this alone.*

"Almost there," he says again. But he hasn't moved.

Around us the fog is so complete that the trees drip with it. I see a banana slug on the path near my wet boot tip, fat and yellow-green, slick with dew.

"Everything's getting a drink today." He's listening to my thoughts again and laughs a little. "Here, now. Look."

It's the same marker tree, but the branches point down at a wounded doe. The creature's buff hide has been ripped open by something terrible, its abdomen chewed through so that I can see how its heart trembles, fist sized, black with blood. From its throat comes a noise not human or animal but both at once—a steady, deep sound of hurting.

Oh, Hap. Do something.

"I can't, but you can. She's just like you, honey. That's how you'll find her."

Then the deer is gone. The forest floor is cinnamon colored with redwood needles, cool and whole and still. Hap is nowhere in sight, but I can hear him, his words moving through me like original sound, the sea in a cupped shell, the whole forest in the branch of one tree.

"Don't be afraid. You'll know what to do. Just follow the signs."

What? No. Come back!

"Anna, honey. This is why you're here. Open your eyes."

I wake to a pounding headache, my tongue coated and thick. I've long been a vivid dreamer. All cops are, or eventually become that way. But this dream has left a hangover that has little or nothing to do with the Maker's Mark.

Starting the shower, I stand under the streaming water for a long time, waiting for the thudding in my head to subside, but it doesn't. A wave of nausea hits me and I drop to the floor, hugging my knees together while water rushes over me like a curtain of hot rain. I feel a strange dull ache in my lower back and belly, a sensation that confuses me until I smell a faint hint of iron. Notice the blood trickling from between my legs and down the drain, pale pink and diluted. My cycle is back.

As my mastitis has slowly healed and my breasts have begun to return to normal, I've tried to forget about my body, but clearly it remembers everything. How I screamed that day, sounding like a stranger. How Brendan kept telling me the ambulance was on its way, as if that made any difference. My neighbor Joan wouldn't leave my side. Her face was white and bloodless. *I'm so sorry,* she kept saying. But I couldn't answer her. Later the paramedics stood over me, my jeans clinging to my legs, wet and cold. I felt dead inside them. It was time for me to let go of the body, but I couldn't make my arms open. From far away, I heard a baby crying. One of the paramedics kept repeating my name, which sounded absurd suddenly.

Drenched and shaking in the shower, I feel it all with shocking immediacy, the weight of my guilt, the pain I've caused Brendan, Frank's doubt in me, the wreckage of my life in the distance, like a city on fire. I hoped Mendocino could help me heal and forget. Instead it's full of ghosts and clues, messages that have been waiting impatiently for me. Hap in my dream of the wounded doe. *She's just like you, honey. That's how you'll find her.* Cameron's haunted eyes in her missing poster. Her call for help, which I haven't stopped hearing for a moment, no matter how much I've tried.

I stand up, my knees knocking together so hard it feels dangerous to be in my body. I just got here. I'm not near ready for any of this, but it doesn't matter. In the fog on the bathroom mirror, a small circle has cleared, and my own face is centered inside of it. Every sign is the same sign. I'm supposed to find Cameron Curtis.

2

Secret Things

Thirteen

On the Fourth of July 1970, all the cruisers from our sheriff's department lined up on Main Street for a parade out to the bluff for fireworks. I was twelve that year, waiting for my share of the sparklers Ellis Flood was handing out to all the kids. He had a whole stash in his office, including smoke bombs and fountains and Red Rockets that said do not hold in hand after lighting on the side of the orange-and-blue box—as if we needed to be told. But maybe we did.

I'd never been very comfortable with holidays. Celebrating typically meant chaos to me, the grown-ups in charge even more distracted and erratic than usual, giving themselves permission to cut loose even more than they did every day.

On Christmas morning when I was eight, I woke up early in our apartment in Redding to find my mother wasn't in her bed in her room, wasn't home at all. In the living room, the plastic tree that we'd put up the week before had only a wadded-up bedsheet beneath it where the presents were supposed to be. The tree lights had been left on overnight and threw blinking rainbow-colored eggs across the wall and the carpet. On the coffee table, next to an overflowing ashtray, three red-and-white felt stockings that still had the price tags on them were half hanging out of a Longs Drugs plastic bag.

I was just starting to put all the pieces together when the kids came out of their room and I had to think fast.

"Did Santa come?" Jason asked. He was wearing his Captain Kangaroo T-shirt and no pants, his stuffed cheetah, Freddy, by his side.

"He must be busy this year," I covered quickly. "He'll probably come tonight instead."

"Where's Robin?" Amy pulled her thumb out of her mouth to ask the question, and then quickly plugged herself back in, looking all around the room as I pushed her gently from behind.

"Helping Santa. Come on, let's eat."

Jason and Amy were my half brother and sister, four and five that year. Irish twins, my mother always called them, though I had no idea what she meant. Their own mom, Trish, had always been a bit of a mess and hadn't come around for visitation in a long time. Our dad, Red, was doing time in county for armed robbery of a liquor store. He'd worn a ski mask, but had taken it off as soon as he was outside, and there were witnesses.

"What an idiot," my mother had said more than once after his sentencing. "He couldn't find his ass with both hands."

I'd learned to agree with her a long time before, and not to make anything harder. Thankfully she liked the kids even though they weren't really hers and she had never cared for Trish. I did most of the work anyway. We'd been on our own for months now, the four of us, and it was going okay. I had been allowed to cook from the time I was five or six and never had an accident or even burned a finger.

"You're a good helper," my mom said every once in a while, and when she did, it felt like the sun coming out from behind a large dark cloud.

——

That morning, I dragged a chair over to the stove to scramble eggs, pushing them back and forth in the pan with the wooden spoon until they cooked all the way through. Amy wouldn't eat them otherwise.

Amy had white-blond hair. When she was worried, she pulled the tips into her mouth and sucked on them at the same time as her thumb. She did it now. "Where's Robin?" she asked again.

"I already told you, she's helping Santa. Now drink your milk."

"I'm still hungry," Jason said. "Can I have a Pop-Tart?"

"You're fine." I had already looked at the food we had. Once, before the kids had started living with us, my mom had gone to the store for cigarettes and not come back for two days. I'd eaten cereal until I ran out of milk. For the kids, I would have to be more resourceful. "Here," I said, giving Jason the rest of my eggs. "We're going to get dressed and play a game outside."

"Aren't you going to school?" Amy asked.

"No, it's a holiday, honey. Now stop asking questions."

All that day we played in the courtyard of our apartment building, in the laundry room, which was perfect for hide-and-seek, and in the swimming pool, which had been drained at the end of the summer and wouldn't be filled again for months. We ate cheese sandwiches under a camellia bush and then built a fairy garden with rocks and clothespins and anything else we could find. That was good because it took a long time. Whenever one of the kids would ask when we were going back inside, I would tell them to be patient. That Christmas was late this year because of an ice storm at the North Pole and that was why Robin had to help.

Everything was moving along smoothly as a dream until one of our neighbors, Phyllis, walked by with her Chihuahua, Bernard, and stopped, eyeing us as if we were doing something wrong just by breathing. "Where's your mother?"

"Sleeping," I said, shooting a look at the kids that meant they shouldn't contradict me.

Jason nodded and then reached for Bernard, who skittered sideways, trembling.

That dog didn't like people, and especially not kids, but Jason couldn't help himself.

Phyllis scooped up Bernard's wriggling body with a disgusted look on her face and kept staring down at us. "On Christmas?"

Amy hadn't moved, but now she piped up. "What's wrong with that? She's tired."

Phyllis eventually went back into her apartment, but kept looking out through the slit between her drapes. Meanwhile I told the kids how good they were and that I was proud of them. And I was. Whatever worry I felt about my mother was balanced out by the lightness of the day, how easy things felt, except for the exchange with Phyllis, how free. Mom had "a lot on her plate," as she often put it. Even with food stamps, feeding three kids was no picnic. As erratic and moody as Red could be, he always had a way of making her laugh. Now that he hadn't been in the picture for a while, nothing stopped her from dropping down a deep well of a mood. She was lonely and tired, and life was passing her by.

Once, I found Amy in the hallway listening to Mom cry in her room through the door. She'd been in there all day.

"What is Robin so worried about?" Amy asked when I gave her a handful of animal crackers to distract her.

"A lot of things. You wouldn't understand."

Fourteen

Will's office is the same one his father had, I find. He looks up from his desk as I knock, surrounded by paperwork in a pool of fluorescent light, red-blond stubble flaring along his cheeks and upper lip, his eyes tired but expectant as soon as he sees me, and clearly surprised.

"Anna. Hey. What's going on?"

"Do you have time to talk?"

"Things are pretty intense right now. Can I call you later today?"

"Actually I'm hoping you'll let me help you with the case."

"What?" He blinks rapidly. "Are you serious?"

"Very."

He pours us coffee in stained ceramic mugs and tips in powdered creamer, the smell sweet and chemical, familiar. Everything is, the gray-beige industrial-wasteland cinder-block walls; the creased manila file folders spilling scraps and forms; the curled Post-it notes and half-used three-by-five notebooks; the scattered blue Bic pens with the caps bent and chewed. Behind Will's desk a sheet of butcher paper hangs with scribbled lists of names, dates, and times for Cameron's case. Just beside it is another missing poster, pinned at eye level.

KIDNAPPED
At Knife Point
Polly Hannah Klaas
D.O.B. 1/3/81
Brown hair—Brown eyes
4'10"—80 lbs
Last seen October 1, 1993, in Petaluma, Calif.

My eyes catch—snag—as everything speeds up. October 1 was yesterday. "Wait. What's this?"

He shakes his head as if he wishes he could erase the facts. "I know it's a lot to process. I've been on the phone since dawn. The suspect's still at-large." He hands over a composite sketch of a heavyset middle-aged man.

SUSPECT
White Male Adult 30–40 yrs.
Approx. 6'3" Dark/Dark Gray Hair
Full Beard, Wearing Dark Clothing
With Yellow Bandana Around Head
If you have any information on this man
CALL THE PETALUMA POLICE:
707-778-4481

A lot to *process*? I came here ready to do whatever I can to find one girl, and here is another. As if there's some kind of sick revolving door just out of sight. "How is this related to our case? Could this be the same guy who has Cameron?"

"I kind of hope so," Will breathes. "There are witnesses this time. There's a crime scene. Polly's two best friends were with her when he entered her room. They heard his voice. They saw his face."

As I let the details sink in, I feel more and more as if I'm treading thick dark water. We're in the deep end now. These were three twelve-year-old girls in the middle of a slumber party. Their Friday-night sleepover torn like a pink paper heart. Polly's kidnapper had blackened the bedroom door, threatening to slit their throats if they screamed. He'd put pillowcases over the girls' heads and had them count to a thousand. What had a thousand felt like? Nothing short of forever.

"There weren't any prints on the back door," Will is saying. "That's how he got in. The CSI team did find a print in Polly's room, but it's too smeared to run through the system. Apparently he came in with precut ligature and a hood he'd made, some sort of silky material, like a slip."

I reach for the sides of the bucket chair, smooth and solid. "One hood?"

"Right. The girls said he seemed disoriented to find three of them there. He asked which one of them lived in the house."

"Maybe he saw Polly somewhere else and zeroed in on her, not thinking or caring about who else might be there when he made his move. A house full of girls isn't exactly quiet. Where were the parents?"

"Mom was asleep and Dad was at his own residence. They're divorced."

"They might not have been able to protect her, even if they were both there and awake. Some predators stop at nothing once they're set in motion."

Will's eyes have gone slightly glassy, and I know why. For the last ten days, since Cameron's family reported her missing, he's been in a minefield, but now it's twice the size, with double the risk. "If this is the same guy who took Cameron," he says finally, "I mean, if he's actively on the hunt, there's no chance we're going to find her alive, is there? You can tell me."

But there isn't an easy answer. Seventy-five percent of murdered abducted children are killed within the first three hours of being taken. But Cameron isn't a child anymore. She's fifteen. And then there's this: In the slag heap of cases I've worked through the years, only once have I had a teenaged victim manage to escape her captor and come home, two years after she was abducted.

Usually even finding a body is a win. Whatever you can imagine, humans can do. And yet at the same time my cop brain knows that Cameron is probably dead, another voice, one that's pure instinct and intuition, is telling me not to give up.

"Listen," I say to Will. "We just can't know until we get more information. You've been in touch with the department in Petaluma?"

"First thing this morning. Eddie Van Leer is the lead detective with the Petaluma PD." Will reaches for the nearest notebook and rifles the pages. "Rod Fraser is the FBI special agent. You ever work with him?"

"Once, about ten years ago. He's solid. Not your typical FBI guy at all. Doesn't need to be the smartest guy in the room."

"Well, somebody's doing something right down there. Polly's face is everywhere already. It's a national case, when I've got nothing here. Van Leer tells me he's got sixty men on the job already."

"You can see why it's blowing up there, can't you? A twelve-year-old girl plucked out of her own bedroom on a Friday night? What parent hasn't had that nightmare?"

"Okay, but Cameron Curtis has been *my* nightmare for more than a week now. I'm over my head here, Anna." His voice catches and rings with strain. "I've had no help, no leads. The family is coming unhinged. And what do I tell them? *Christ*."

It is way too much, what he's been doing alone. It is way too much for both of us, but I'm not going to tell him that now. I put down my coffee and reach for his hand, rough and cool, before pulling back again. "Whoever took Polly Klaas might be our suspect too, but that's a long shot, Will. A serial offender has very specific patterns and preferences. Polly is prepubescent, and also young looking for her age. She doesn't have breast buds, doesn't excite the same kinds of appetites. Cameron may be emotionally young, but she looks like a woman, not a child."

"Okay, I get that. But opportunity comes into play sometimes, doesn't it?"

"Sure. Polly could have been the first girl who walked by when he'd been triggered and knew he would take someone. But think about his behavior for a minute, Will. This guy in Petaluma walked right into a full house with a knife drawn, leaving witnesses."

He nods slowly. Blinks against the unkind light. "And Cameron just vanished."

"That's how it usually happens, honestly, especially with teens. If you want to find someone like Cameron, where all the evidence is either absent or invisible, you have to study your victim to find answers. You have to live and breathe her. Dive deep. And then maybe, maybe, she'll show you where to look for her."

"You really want to jump into all this with me?" The hope in Will's voice is palpable, a tattered flag waving through smoke.

"As long as I'm not the face of anything. My name doesn't go down anywhere. Not on statements, not on payroll. I won't talk to the media and I definitely won't talk to the FBI. I'm here for you and those girls. That's it."

"Whatever your rules are, we can make it work. I'm just glad you're here."

I take a breath, and then feel for the cool, metallic edge of his desk, my shoulders already knotting with responsibility. "Me too."

Fifteen

On Tuesday, September 21, Cameron went over to her best friend Gray Benson's house to study after school, and then walked home alone, arriving at around six-fifteen. She and her mother, Emily, ate dinner, and then Cameron went to her room. Just after ten, Emily checked on Cameron. The two said good night and then Emily alarmed the house as usual, heading to bed and assuming Cameron did the same. But at seven the next morning, when she went to wake Cameron for breakfast, Emily found her room empty and the alarm deactivated. She didn't have time to think about why, if somehow it had malfunctioned or if she'd forgotten to turn it on. Her daughter was gone.

At 7:09 she called her husband, Troy Curtis, who was at their second home in Malibu. The call lasted three minutes. The second she hung up she called 911. Will's office had responded in minutes. Before 8:00 a.m., they were interviewing Emily and sweeping Cameron's room for clues. But there weren't any.

The property had a security gate with a video camera that held a week of film. On the night of the twenty-first, the tape showed only typical comings and goings. Emily drove in around six that night, and then there was nothing else until the 911 call and the arrival of Will's team. When they searched Cameron's room and the rest of the property, there were no signs of a break-in, and nothing significant was missing. According to Emily Hague, Cameron had always saved her allowance and had at least a few hundred dollars in her room, but apparently it hadn't been touched.

This is all I have and it's almost nothing. The simplest explanation is that Cameron chose to run. She disarmed the alarm and bolted sometime in the night, out the front door and through the woods, avoiding the main gate with its camera. It happens all the time, kids throwing off their parents' homes like shed skins, moving on to something or someone that promises freedom. One version of that freedom is black and permanent, like the bluff a hundred yards from Cameron's front door. She could have walked right off of it, her body carried away by the current or ravaged by sharks, erased with purpose, her escape driven by an inner pain no one could see or even guess at.

If she was suicidal or even just good and lost emotionally, her adoption might be part of that emotional equation. Cameron was surrendered to the state just before her fourth birthday, a particularly tender age, though in my experience they all are. Whatever her life was like before she was given up—whether or not she consciously remembered any of it—that time would still be with her, I know all too well, embedded in her nervous system, knitted into her singular blueprint. So would the whiplash of displacement. In a single day, a car ride with a social worker, her old family was erased, blotted out, and new parents appeared from nowhere—one of them a household name, no less. That part I can only imagine, but it had to be confusing and difficult for Cameron, as she got older and became more aware of the larger world, that her new mother was a world-famous movie star. Almost as confusing as how she could lose her family in one moment, because of a decision someone else made for her, probably without even trying to explain. With the signing of some papers, her story had stopped and restarted. The girl she had been was deleted along with her birth name, and all the rest of it. Siblings, pets, neighborhoods, toys, memories—whole years just gone.

Since looking at her file is like seeing a version of my own story, I know that even if Cameron felt lucky to have landed with the Curtises, as I had with Hap and Eden, she wouldn't necessarily be free of ghosts. No matter how resilient children can be, or how wanted, loved, and nurtured they are by their new parents, the original wounds of abandonment and rejection aren't just magically healed. Grit and inner strength don't altogether heal those wounds, either, because the parenting piece is primal.

Mothers and fathers are supposed to stay. That's the original human story, in every culture, since the beginning of time. Mine hadn't, and neither had Cameron's. All the scars I still carry, she carries, too. Trust issues, attachment trouble, identity problems, feelings of emptiness, isolation, alienation, and despair—cracks in the soul that can't be mended. I've seen it. I've lived it. How anyone with a hole inside them will search on and on, sometimes all their lives, for ways to fill it.

Sixteen

That Christmas when I was eight, my mom stayed gone. I was afraid, of course. Worried that she'd gotten into trouble somehow and couldn't call me. I tried not to think about how many ways she might have become stuck out in the world on her own while the kids and I piled into her bed to sleep together, giving Freddy his very own pillow. At some point during the day, the kids had finally stopped asking about Santa altogether, which felt like a small victory. As I dropped off to sleep, I had one hand on Amy's silky hair, and the other on Jason's T-shirt, and that helped quiet my mind somehow.

The next morning I let the kids watch TV while I raided the Folgers can in the kitchen and walked to the drugstore for bread and milk and eggs and peanut butter, since the grocery stores were closed. I passed Phyllis and Bernard on the way back, and she made a face at me like she knew what was what.

"Where's your mom *today?*" she asked pointedly.

"Sleeping," I said again, the first thing that had flown to my mind.

"Again?"

"Yeah." I hated her, suddenly, and her dog, too. "Hope you had a good Christmas," I said with false brightness. "See you later."

Even though Phyllis had rattled me, once I got home and shut the door, we had a great day. In fact, it was one of the nicest we'd ever had. There weren't any presents, but there was food and all the TV we wanted. We built a fort out of sheets and blankets in the living room and kept it up all day. When it grew dark, we turned off all the lights except for the tree and lay down on the carpet beneath it, looking up through the splayed branches as the rainbow bulbs blinked on and off, almost dreamlike. Then I got the kids into the bathtub and made sure they washed their hair and said their prayers. By the time we went to sleep that night, I was starting to believe we could just go on this way forever, even if my mom never came home. I knew how to take care of Jason and Amy. I could do it. We would be okay—or more than okay. We would be happy.

Very early the next morning, though, I woke up tired. Jason had wet the bed and we all got soaked. I had to put towels down on the bed after that but kept accidentally rolling onto the wet spot and waking up again. I was still worried about Phyllis, too, and wondering if we would run into her again, or if she would start making phone calls, even, to see where my mother really was. I was pretty sure she hadn't believed me.

I got up and went into the kitchen and started making breakfast for us, but kept checking out the window every few minutes to see if someone was coming. The kids had cartoons on, turned up too loud. I felt anxious and distracted and kept thinking I heard someone coming down the hall outside. Finally, I went and checked there too, looking both ways along the corridor. That's when I smelled the eggs burning. I had the gas turned up too high and the butter had blackened and begun to smoke. The second I realized what was happening, I shoved the pan off the heat with a skittering clatter, but the smoke alarm went off anyway, screaming and blinking

in the middle of the kitchen ceiling. I couldn't reach it, even with
the chair. The sound was earsplitting and endless as my heart
raced. Both kids started to cry and I was yelling at them to stop, but
they only wailed harder. I couldn't think. I didn't know what to do.
And then someone was pounding on the door, and I knew I'd made
a terrible mistake. We should have only had cereal. Cereal and peanut butter.

The cops pushed into our living room, two of them, heavy and
wide, scaring the kids with their uniforms and holstered guns, their
strings of questions. When was the last time I'd seen my mom?
What did she say before she left? Had she mentioned where she was
going on Christmas Eve? Did I know how to contact my dad? Was
there other family around? Mostly, I didn't have answers for them.
Jason and Amy were cuddled up next to me on the couch, pressing
hard against my sides. I kept trying to tell the kids it was going to
be okay, but I already knew it was far too late for that.

The Curtises live north of town on a secluded stretch of Lansing
Street, high above Slaughterhouse Gulch. When we pull up to the
security gate in Will's cruiser, he pushes a button, and someone
buzzes us through.

"It sure *looks* like a movie star lives here," I say as the wiper
blades rattle, sluicing back a thin film of rain.

"She's not a movie star anymore. She stopped working as soon
as they moved here four years ago."

"What is she like?"

"Before all this, you mean? I don't even know. The family hasn't
had anything to do with the rest of us. The husband commutes on
a private plane. They have all their groceries delivered. I'm surprised they let Cameron go to public school instead of hiring a
tutor or something. That must have been their one concession, a
stab at real life."

———

As we park and get out, the broad door opens and Troy Curtis appears, youthful and handsome in faded jeans and a sweater, blinking at the drizzle. We hurry toward him through the door he holds open, and that's when I see he's older than I thought at first, late forties, maybe, with small lines of tension around his eyes and mouth.

Will and I step into the entryway, where everything is spotless and almost surgically arranged. Recessed lighting and Danish-looking furniture all in white. Pale glossy flooring that we're dripping on.

"Let me get you some towels," Troy says, disappearing.

When he comes back, I rub myself self-consciously while Will introduces me, saying what we've agreed on, that I'm a criminal investigator consulting on Cameron's case, nothing more and nothing less.

"Any news about this kidnapped girl in Petaluma?" Troy asks. "Does this have anything to do with Cameron?"

"We don't know anything yet," Will says. "We're in close touch with the team there, though. As soon as we have news we'll share it."

Troy's nod is weary as he leads us into the living room and motions toward sleek, armless chairs. I'm still holding my towel and fold it under me, feeling out of place here, off-center. But that won't do. "Is your wife at home, Mr. Curtis?"

"Emily just went to lie down. The last few days have been tough on her."

"Of course," I say. "This has to be a terrifying time for you both, but I'm a little behind on this case." I glance at Will to make sure I'm not overstepping myself, but he's settled back in his chair. I have the lead, his body language tells me. I'm the one who needs catching up. "Can you walk me through the night of Cameron's disappearance?"

Troy looks drained, but agrees. "I wish I'd been here, but I work in LA and stay at our Malibu house during the week."

"What usually happens here on weeknights?"

"Dinner, homework. The usual stuff. I checked in with Emily a little before ten, Cameron was in her room. Everything seemed fine."

"And the next morning? What happened then?"

"When Cameron didn't come to breakfast, Emily checked her room, and that's when she called me. I told her to contact the police, then I got on a plane."

"Has your daughter seemed unhappy to you lately?" I ask.

Troy shakes his head. "Cameron's always been quiet. She's an introvert, more like Emily than me. But I wouldn't say unhappy."

"I understand she gets good grades and is sort of bookish. Not particularly athletic or popular. Did you ever think there might be more to her shyness or withdrawal?"

"What do you mean?"

I meet his eyes, which are cloud gray. "Some kids go inward, but really they're acting out secretly. Cutting or using drugs. Engaging in risky sexual behavior."

"No." His flinch is almost microscopic, but I've seen it. "Nothing like that. She's a good kid."

"I'm not suggesting that your daughter's not a good person, Mr. Curtis, or that she's done anything wrong."

"Teenagers can be hard to read." Will steps in.

"Sometimes they're struggling and no one knows," I add. "They're good at hiding what they feel."

"I'm not with her as much as I used to be," Troy says. "But Emily would have noticed if something was really troubling Cameron."

"Tell me a little about the adoption," I say, changing course.

"We used an agency in Sacramento, Catholic Family Charities. I believe they're still there."

I jot down the name in the notebook I'm carrying. "Open or closed adoption?"

"Closed. Why do you ask?"

"Just thinking out loud. It's not always the case, but some kids never get over the pain of being rejected. Abandoned by their first family. That pain can lead to certain types of behaviors and risks."

"I already told you, nothing like that."

"Did the agency reveal anything at all to you about her birth family?"

"Very little. We knew they had another child, quite a bit older. Also that there was some history of drug abuse and incarceration."

"That didn't scare you?"

"A little, I guess. Emily had very clear ideas of wanting to do some good, of helping where help is most needed." His gaze narrows and suddenly he's on the defensive. "Are you saying we did something wrong?"

"Not at all, I'm just laying out a few things to consider. Tell me, were there any older men in Cameron's life that might have shown a particular interest in her? A family friend, perhaps, or a teacher?"

"Not that I can think of off the top of my head."

"Steve Gonzales," Emily says from the base of the floating staircase. "Her English teacher." She's approached us without making a sound.

Seventeen

It's one thing to see Emily Hague as Heidi Barrows in her sitcom *Soho Girls,* her jokes and clothes and haircut known all over the world, and another to be with her in her living room in the middle of an all-too-real tragedy. She's more beautiful than any camera has been able to capture, and sad in a way that's far too familiar. For a brief moment, I wonder if I'm going to be able to handle being here, but then the deeper objective takes over.

I stand up. "I'm Anna Hart, a new agent on Cameron's case. I hope we didn't wake you."

"It's all right." Emily moves toward the couch looking guarded and delicate at the same time, as if she's nursing a physical injury instead of an emotional one. "Have they found the girl from Petaluma?"

"I'm afraid not," Will responds. "As soon as we have any news, we'll share it."

"I know how hard this must be," I say. "Can you tell me a little about Cameron?"

"What do you want to know?"

"Anything. Did you have a good relationship? Did she talk to you?"

"No one's asked me that yet." She crosses her arms over her chest as if she's cold. "I think so. I tried to let her know she could always come to me. But you know, mothers and daughters."

"Of course," Will says to be kind. "But beyond the normal sorts of tension? Anything seem to be going on with her lately? Any noticeable changes in behavior? Or new stressors?"

"We've been over this." Troy's hands cover his knees, the fingers clamped tightly together.

"I know," Will says. "But we need to catch Detective Hart up to speed. The more you both can cooperate, the more we can help Cameron."

"*Help* her?" Troy erupts. "We're just talking in circles. How about you get out there and *look* for her?"

"Troy," Emily says, trying to bring him back.

"What?" His face has reddened. Suddenly there's nothing at all handsome or composed about him. He's a cornered animal, lashing out defensively.

"I promise you we're taking action," Will says, stepping in. "My department has had every man on this since day one. We're hoping to get a fresh team from the U.S. Forest Service mobilized soon, too. Nothing's more important than finding your daughter."

"We all want the same thing," I add, trying to stay on top of my emotions. It's hard enough that I already feel too close to this case without Troy's reactivity. I'm not sure I trust him, or myself for that matter. "We need to focus more on Cameron right now," I say levelly. "Who she is, what she cares about, what her days look like, who she sees after school. Does she have a boyfriend?"

"No," Emily says quickly. "Never."

That surprises me. "A beautiful girl like Cameron? No interest from boys at all? Or men?"

"Men?" Emily looks pained. "Not that I know about. Not that she shared with me." She glances at Troy. "Us."

"What about this teacher you mentioned?" Will presses. "Do you know him? Ever see them together?"

"The school year had just started, but I met him at curriculum night. I don't think he was inappropriate or anything, but he did take a particular interest in Cameron. He told her she's a gifted writer and has been encouraging her poetry."

"We'll follow up," I say. "What about Gray Benson? Any romantic attachment there we should know about?"

"They're just good friends," she replies. "He's always been someone Cameron can lean on."

"Lean on when?" I ask. "For what sorts of things?"

"The usual stuff, I guess." Emily doesn't look at Troy, only re-anchors herself, taking a breath. "We've been having some problems. As a family."

"That's no one's business," Troy bursts in.

"Mr. Curtis." I stop him, keeping my voice as neutral as possible. "If Cameron was under stress at home, we need to know it. You can't hold back anything that might help the case."

"Troy, please," Emily says. "We have to be honest. Cameron has been affected by all of this. You know she has."

From the strain in Emily's voice I can tell how hard it is for her to let her guard down and show weakness. But that's true of most people in a situation like this. I've rarely encountered a family that could bear the scrutiny of an investigation without falling apart, sometimes slowly, sometimes all at once.

"We've been arguing a lot lately," Emily says.

"Everyone argues," Troy jumps in reflexively. "Marriage is no walk in the park."

"Cameron's always been sensitive," Emily continues. "I think she's been worried we'll split up."

"Sure," I say. "Did you try to reassure her?"

"I tried. Maybe not enough."

Will and I share a glance. We're only beginning to understand the family dynamic, but it's become obvious that Cameron has been under emotional strain. In that state she could have leaned on someone new or familiar, someone she thought she could trust to help. That need increased her vulnerability. It gave her contour as a target. Made her glow in the dark.

"Emily," I say, "at the risk of making you uncomfortable, Sheriff Flood mentioned to me that your brother has had criminal allegations made against him in the past. Has he had any recent access to Cameron?"

She blanches. "What do you mean by 'access'?"

"Is he still part of your life? How often do you see him?"

"Not as much as we used to. He and his wife, Lydia, live in Napa now. They bought a vineyard and make their own wine."

"He's retired, then?"

"He's done very well for himself." Her tone is stiff, defensive. But I hear something else, too. Survivor's guilt? Some sort of invisible alliance?

"Any reason the visits stopped?" Will asks.

"Just life, I guess. We've been busy here."

Busier now than when you used to work? I think to myself. Then I ask, "Do he and Lydia have children?"

"My nephew Ashton is in boarding school out east. Andover." She pauses, her expression darkening. "What are all these questions about? You're not suggesting Drew could have hurt Cameron?"

"I'd love to see Cameron's room," I say, closing my notebook. "Emily, would you show me?"

Eighteen

Will stays in the living room with Troy while Emily leads me down a long gleaming hall set with square windows at intervals. Inside each deep ledge, a perfect little bonsai tree arcs out of a terra-cotta pot like a work of art, pale green and sculptural. They don't look real.

"Do you have a gardener?" I ask. "A housekeeper?"

"A cleaning team comes every other week from town. I do everything else."

"That's impressive."

"Is it? Most women don't have help."

Most women aren't Emily Hague, I think.

We've reached the end of the hall, a closed door. Emily seems reluctant to step inside, so I go first, respectfully, sensing her strain. Dozens of men have already been here, turning everything over, dusting for prints. They've dug through her clothes and books and photo albums, opened every drawer. These violations are necessary, but hard to watch, particularly if Emily is carrying guilt and self-blame. Possibly years' worth, if my gut is right.

Cameron's full-sized bed is neatly made with a simple cream-colored comforter and sham, a small blue velvet pillow shaped like a rabbit. I wonder if she's the kind of girl who keeps everything neat and perfect all the time, or if Emily was the one to come straighten after the forensics team left, unable to stop herself.

"You were alone that night, just the two of you?" I ask. "Did Cameron seem okay?"

"Mostly. She hadn't settled into a routine with her sophomore year. She was moodier than usual, a little anxious, I guess."

"Did she say about what?"

"I tried not to pry. I have all these books that say teenagers need their space. Was that a mistake?"

"Teenagers are tricky." I walk over to the bookcase, gently touching the spines.

Little Women. A Wrinkle in Time. Tess of the D'Urbervilles. Catcher in the Rye. There are fairy tales and fantasy stories, graphic novels and poetry. Rilke, T. S. Eliot, Anne Sexton. This is the bookcase of a budding writer. "Where's the work you mentioned?" I ask. "The stuff her teacher praised?"

"I'm not sure. She's always been really private, even as a little girl."

"She sorted out her feelings on paper. Did she draw too?"

"Yes. More when she was young. How did you know?"

"Just a guess. If we could find some recent writing, we might have more clues to what was going on with your daughter." I reach under the lip of the bookcase and find nothing, not even dust. I open her desk drawer, and then feel under the edges of her mattress.

"She might have kept it all in her locker at school," Emily suggests.

"Maybe. I'm sure Sheriff Flood's team has collected all that, but I'll double-check. Just in case we missed something."

I cross to Cameron's closet, where half a dozen dresses have been pushed to the back. Mostly I see jeans and T-shirts, hoodies and plaid flannel. She likes black and gray and red, Converse low-tops, and high-necked raglan sweaters. Tomboy things. I reach for the hem of a red-checked shirt that looks worn and well loved. It's so intimate, being here among her things. I have the strongest urge to apologize to her.

Emily has come up behind me and gathers one of Cameron's sweaters into her arms, as if with enough warmth and attention she might bring it to life. "I'm trying to prepare myself for the worst, but it's killing me. If someone's hurt her, or—" She takes a gulping breath of air. "Do you think it could have been one of my fans? If it's my fault I just don't know how I'll live with myself."

"Let's try not to go there," I tell her. "If this is a gambit for your attention, more than likely there'd be a ransom note or some sort of message for you specifically."

"That makes sense," she says, seeming slightly reassured.

"There's still a lot we don't know, obviously. Let's just try to take this one step at a time."

"I keep thinking I'll wake up," Emily says, her voice full of knots. "That she'll walk through the door and I'll know it was all a nightmare."

"I know," I say quietly.

"What you were talking about before, the abandonment issues, I never really thought about that with Troy and me. Or maybe I did, and just pushed it all away."

I nod to encourage her.

"I should have been more open with Cameron, should have talked to her more. When I was Cameron's age, my father had an affair with someone from our country club in Bowling Green. In northern Ohio. That's where I grew up." She shakes her head, her eyes cloudy, full of unresolved feelings. "Everyone knew he was fooling around. It was horrible."

"But your parents stayed married," I guess aloud.

"My mother went off to a fat farm. When she came back we all pretended it had never happened. Six months of cottage cheese and peaches. My father gave her a sapphire tennis bracelet, but it slipped right off her wrist. She'd lost thirty pounds."

"And then you ran to Hollywood," I say. "You were how old then?"

"Nineteen."

"But you never really forgave your father." Again, I'm guessing, but would wager a lot on her answer. "What about your brother? Does he feel the same about your mom and dad?"

She drops the sleeve of Cameron's cardigan and begins to finger a loose tortoiseshell button she's noticed, frowning a little. "Drew has always taken care of Drew. He doesn't look back. We never talk about those days."

"Right," I say, having imagined as much. "When you moved here from LA, you stopped working as an actress altogether. Was that always the plan?"

She nods woodenly. "My work was taking up too much of my attention, and the paparazzi were always following us, to restaurants and family outings. We never had any privacy. I thought being up here would be better for all of us. Cameron would get a normal life, and I could finally devote most of my time to her." I watch her face crumple as she wrestles with the cruel irony of the situation, the guilt and remorse. "What if Cameron has been crying out for help and I just couldn't see it?"

The pain in her eyes is terrible. I have the urge to comfort her, and also to wake her up. There's work to do now.

"What-ifs will take you down a very dark hole, Emily. Cameron needs you to be strong. Will you help me?"

"I'll try."

"Emily, is your husband having an affair? Is that what you've been fighting about?"

Her face is glacier-still and poised, but I can feel fear coming off her body in stiff, solid waves. Inside, she's at war with herself over how much to reveal. "There's a woman in LA," she answers finally. "His assistant at Paramount. She's not the first."

"I'm sorry. I'll need her name."

"Why? You don't think she has something to do with this?"

"We have to follow up on everything at this point."

"It's just." She shakes her head. "Troy's going through a challenging time."

"Emily."

"Yes?"

"Enough of that. Enough of making excuses for him."

"I'm sorry. I don't even know I'm doing it."

"I know."

On Cameron's desk there's a red spiral class notebook with star-shaped doodles all over the cover. Emily opens it and tears out a blank page. Once she's written out the name, she folds the page twice and hands it to me.

"It might be hard, some of the things we're going to learn. Ugly, too," I tell her, "but I believe even the toughest kinds of truths are better than not knowing."

She looks fragile, full of doubt. "I hope you're right."

Tucking the page into my notebook, I cross to the large rectangular window that runs half the length of the north-facing wall. It looks out on the driveway and security gate to the left, the lawn bleeding into thick trees to the right. The blinds are made of sheer ecru-colored rice paper, pleated on a pulley system. When I gently push the dangling cords to one side, something catches my eye. Along the bottom of the screen there are tiny scratches, subtle enough to miss if you were looking for something else.

"Did Cameron ever sneak out of the house this way?"

"I don't think so." Emily comes over to look, strain clouding her beautiful features. "Why would she need to do that?"

When I press my thumb against the screen frame, it gives instantly, popping forward. Cameron's removed the screen more than once, or someone else has. "What's on the other side of these woods?"

"The coast road. Maybe half a mile away?"

"When Sheriff Flood's team combed the property, did they bring dogs in?"

"They did. What's going on? I'm confused. Are you trying to say Cameron ran away on her own?"

"I can't be sure, but that would explain a lot."

"Where would she go? Why?"

I don't answer her immediately, waiting to find the right words. Of course Emily's confused. She's been mostly blind to her daughter's pain, but also doesn't seem to understand her own.

She grew up despising her father only to marry a carbon copy of him. She pitied her mother but had become her. Had her flight to Hollywood accomplished anything in the end? She'd found stardom, yes, playing a role millions of people loved and identified with, but I wonder if what she'd really been after was an elusive freedom from what she'd left behind.

In my years as a detective and particularly with Searchlight, I've learned so much about cycles of violence in family systems. But cycles of silence can be just as dangerous—and they repeat through generations with startling consistency. A mother's dieting becomes her daughter's obsessive control over bonsai trees. Secret glaring infidelity becomes wordless assent and then emptiness. Cameron was exposed to all of this. Silver spoon or no, Emily had fed her powerlessness.

"I don't think your daughter was abducted," I say. My words are blunt, and I'm jumping to conclusions. But there isn't time for anything else.

"No," Emily says so thinly she might be saying *Yes*. The two words never live all that far apart, I've learned.

"If someone has Cameron now, I think she knows him. I think she went willingly."

Nineteen

"You okay?" Will asks when we're back in his squad car, sensing the precariousness of my mood.

I hand him the folded slip of paper. "Troy Curtis's girlfriend."

"I guess I'm not surprised."

"Me neither, but I wanted better. For all of them."

Moments later, we pass through the security gate, and the camera's eye pivots to follow us silently. I think of Cameron in her room, planning to evade that eye, a girl with a secret self, clinging to a hope she may have voiced to no one, and written nowhere.

"What do you think about Drew Hague being so nearby?" I ask Will. "Tell me more about him."

"He was nineteen when the rape allegation was made, a sophomore in college. Said it was a misunderstanding and the girl was drunk. I can't see how, but his parents made it go away. I'll bet it cost them plenty."

"How old was the girl?"

"Sixteen."

"And it went *away*? Let's interview him this week. Napa's really nice this time of year."

He smiles. "Agreed."

"Whether or not Drew's significant here, I think Cameron was complicit somehow. It's never as black and white as you think in these cases. Sometimes victims seek out their abusers just as intensely as they're pursued."

"What are you saying?"

I plunge ahead and tell him about the window in Cameron's room, and how it's possible she was groomed and manipulated by this predator, whoever he was. That he may have preyed on her insecurity and need. "The stickiest sorts of violence are often incredibly intimate, Will. They require trust. They take time."

"I don't know," he says. "If Cameron left the property voluntarily, she deliberately avoided the security camera. Why? Her parents were obviously going to figure out she was gone soon enough."

"You're assuming she meant to stay gone. What if she was just planning to sneak out for a few hours, but then the situation flipped? It's easy enough to avoid the cameras if she went through the woods to the coast road. All she had to do was disable the alarm. The remote was right there in her nightstand. She didn't even have to work at it."

"Are you saying this was a tryst? Like a date?"

"Maybe not. She could have only been seeking attention."

"From someone who could hurt her? Don't you think she'd know better than that?"

"No," I say. "She wouldn't." I can't expect him to be as tuned in to Cameron's vulnerabilities as I am. He's never been a throwaway kid. Never experienced the world in a woman's body, or a girl's. Never had a reason to confuse love with suffering. I've sensed that confusion almost electrically since the first moment I saw Cameron's missing poster, the woundedness in her eyes. "Maybe she never had healthy radar to begin with."

Will nods in a halfhearted way, and then falls silent. After a while he says, "What did you think of Emily?"

"I don't know. I want her to be stronger, I guess."

"She might be doing the best she can."

His words knock and spark, like flint on stone. Of course he's right. People almost always do the best they can. Sometimes it's enough, but more often it isn't.

"If Emily had had the guts to leave Troy the first time he cheated on her, that might have changed everything," I say.

"Could be. We'll never know now."

"What do you make of her?" I realize I have no idea what he's going to say.

He shrugs. "When the family moved here four years ago, I thought it would be so cool to have a movie star walking the streets, but they've really kept to themselves. I can't think of a single conversation I've had with either Emily or Troy, even in passing. And Cameron's just a face to me. It shouldn't be that way."

"It shouldn't." I have to agree.

"Listen." Will clears his throat. "Those things you said to the Curtises about being adopted, the identity stuff and the acting out, was any of that true for you?" He pauses, clearly uncomfortable. "I remember you as a pretty happy kid, but maybe I wasn't paying attention."

For a long moment I don't know how to answer him. Frankly, I'm startled he'd have the nerve to ask.

"You can tell me it's none of my business," he rushes to add, reading my face.

I fix my gaze on the horizon. "It's not," I say gently but firmly.

"Sorry." He clears his throat again.

We round the bluff, and the village flickers into view, sharp white rooftops, white fences, white spires. The storm clouds have begun to move off. In one place along the headlands, a blade of light breaks over dry grass and turns it deep gold. All my life this has been my favorite color. When I first came here, guarded and cynical, always on the alert for trouble, I felt sure that nothing would ever get better. But it had.

"It wasn't an act," I finally say.

"Good. I'm glad."

The gold grass ripples, bends. "Everyone deserves to belong somewhere."

Twenty

My mother died on Christmas, though it was a long time before I was able to put together the details. Everyone wanted to shield me, as if that wasn't making it all harder. The silence and the guessing, trying to read looks and faces, and eyes that never met mine. I eventually learned that she'd gone out on Christmas Eve after the kids and I were in bed, borrowing fifty dollars from a friend to get us presents. Instead she'd bought heroin and overdosed. They found her in her car in a parking lot of Long John Silver's on Christmas night and had come looking for us then, but we must have been asleep already. They might not have found us at all, I kept thinking for years after, in the magical way children think, if I hadn't burned the eggs.

As it was, the cops called social services to take over. I watched an older woman in a tired blue pantsuit sift through drawers trying to get the kids' things together. She wouldn't let me help, just kept shoving their clothes into pillowcases in a way that made me feel angry and embarrassed. I barely got to say goodbye before she put the kids in a car and took them back to live with their mom, who I already knew could barely take care of herself.

The last I saw of Amy, she had almost all her hair in her mouth, and her face was covered with snot. They'd put her light blue socks on Jason as if it didn't even matter what he was wearing. The way they both looked at me, I'll never forget, as if they were silently asking how I'd let this all happen. I was asking the same of myself.

Because Red was still in jail and because neither he nor Robin had any family around, no one knew what to do with me. I was taken to a safe house to wait for my first foster-care placement. The housemother was a young woman who didn't look much older than my mom had been—twenty-seven. She made her own clothes, she told me as she gave me a plate of graham crackers and a wedge of bright orange cheese that came in a huge block, the wax stamped in blue by the welfare department. "You've been through a lot," she said as I ate. "Do you want to talk about it?"

I didn't. Her skirt was brown with yellow flowers, like she was some sort of frontierswoman, a character in a Laura Ingalls Wilder book. There was no possible way she could understand my life, but pressure had been building inside my head. Words that I had to let out somehow. Not about my mother's death, which I had barely begun to process, or about how worried I was for my brother and sister, who were still so little and needed someone to pay attention to them and make sure they ate, but about a single moment in time. One flick of the dial of the range while a worry festered in my mind about Phyllis, who'd been harmless after all.

"I'm just so mad at myself," I said to the woman in the ruffled blouse, and started to cry. Until that moment, I had held the tears in tight.

"What?" she asked. "Why?"

"I was such an *idiot*," I said with the same inflection my mom had always used for my dad. "I shouldn't have cooked. That was so stupid."

The woman—I think her name was Susan—looked at me sadly. "You're just a little girl, Anna. You couldn't have taken care of your brother and sister. If you're going to be mad at someone, be mad at your mom. She left you alone. That wasn't right."

It was obvious that she meant well, but she didn't know the first thing about our family. My mom wasn't a very strong person. If she slept too much or cried too much or did drugs it was because our dad hadn't left her with much money and she couldn't handle it. "I was doing fine," I told her. "They're really good kids."

She gave me another forlorn look and shook her head. "We're going to find a nice home for you."

Suddenly the light in the kitchen shone right into my eyes. The graham cracker crumbs in my mouth had become sweet glue. She hadn't been listening at all. "I *had* a good home."

Silence fell. I think she was afraid to look at me. "I'm so sorry."

Twenty-One

Will's team of twelve has been working nonstop since September 22, just after Cameron vanished, canvassing and interviewing, going door-to-door in town and the surrounding area with her poster. Every day they've dug through databases, making phone calls to parole officers, hoping to find a name and a motive, a fit for this. I'm sure they're all good men and women, but I don't want to know them, or get any more tangled up in the nuts and bolts of this case than I have to. Will agrees. He tells me I can report to him alone and have as much independence as I want as long as I keep him updated.

"I'd like to interview Steve Gonzales," I tell him. "I also want to learn more about Cameron's birth family."

"Good. I'll track down Troy Curtis's girlfriend and get us more on Drew Hague. But first we talk to Gray Benson together?"

"I was thinking that, too."

It's a little after three o'clock when we head over, Monday, October 4. Gray lives two blocks away from Mendocino High on Cahto Street, a narrow residential stretch that borders Hillcrest Cemetery. There's no real room to park, but Will manages, steering his cruiser into the thick wall of vines and eucalyptus on the left side of the street, killing the engine while the last of the rain beads on the windshield, filmy on the inside with the humidity of our breath.

I know every stitch of Mendocino but haven't spent much time on Cahto. Only four houses run along it, counting Gray's, a simple shingled bungalow behind a plain low fence lined with trash cans. We get out and begin to walk up the street's slight incline, around muddy potholes and asphalt patches, over the word school painted onto the street in what's now a cracked, rain-slick yellow. The air smells heavy and sweet, like wet bark.

I'm trying to imagine Cameron here, to put myself in her shoes. The night she disappeared she studied first, after school, with Gray. She walked past these houses on her way home to dinner, thinking what? Did she already know she'd be meeting her abductor later that same night? Or did they somehow cross paths between Gray's house and home? Maybe he suggested a meeting then, promising Cameron something of value to her. But what?

"Did you canvass these houses to see if anyone remembers a suspicious vehicle?" I ask Will.

He nods. "Nothing."

"If Cameron was here a lot, you should look more closely at the neighbors. What about Mr. Benson?"

"He's out of the picture as I understand it. Moved to New Orleans when Gray was young."

"That must be another reason Gray and Cameron connect. Losing a parent changes you, no matter how it happens."

The front gate of the Bensons' house is open and tipped on its hinge from wear, with clematis vines clinging along the anchor post. In the side yard, I take in the messy vegetable garden sprouting from long planter boxes, neglected tomato plants bowing over wire stanchions, and think of how simple and real all this might have looked to a girl like Cameron, stranded on the bluff in a glass box while her famous mother pruned bonsai trees and pretended not to know what she knew about her husband's indiscretions.

Di Anne Benson answers Will's knock. She's plump and pretty, in her midforties, with crimped auburn hair. Behind her, the kitchen smells like jarred spaghetti sauce. "Sheriff Flood." She holds out her dish towel. "I wasn't expecting you."

"Sorry to bother you again. This is Detective Hart. Is Gray home? I promise we'll be brief."

She nods, leading us through the entryway and up a narrow flight of carpeted steps, a tan life-stained Berber. Lopsided botanical prints hang at intervals, the frames lightly painted with dust. Walking behind her, I notice the tag has flipped out of her loose-fitting navy sweater, and I resist the urge to tuck it back in.

"Gray?" Di Anne's voice stretches tentatively through the door before she opens it, moving to one side. Her movements have the feel of concern, I think. As if she knows her son has become fragile and wary. Vulnerable.

Gray sits half swallowed in a brown velvet beanbag on the floor, his long legs up like a shield. He has a sketchbook in his hands, which he closes, looking up, his red hair combed into a pompadour, like a 1950s heartthrob, or like Duran Duran's John Taylor in the poster taped to the inside of Gray's bedroom door, from their first tour—moody eyes, popped collar, and all. Gray's clothes are simple and everyday, though, a royal-blue hooded sweatshirt, soft khaki pants, and rubber-soled wool bedroom slippers. To me, he looks like someone caught between who he wants to be, and who he has to be.

"I don't have anything new to tell you." He fiddles with the closed sketchbook, not quite meeting Will's gaze or mine.

"That's okay," Will says, and then turns to Mrs. Benson. "We'll only be ten minutes."

"I'm Anna Hart," I say to Gray. "I'm one of the detectives trying to find Cameron."

"I've said everything I could remember."

"I know you have. I also know how hard it must be wondering every day what happened to her. I'll bet you're not sleeping. I'll bet you don't even know what to do with yourself."

He blinks. "I'm okay."

Lowering myself to the floor so we can be at eye level, I say, "We've just been to Cameron's house. Her parents have been going through a rough patch. Has Cameron talked much about that with you?"

"A little."

Will and I exchange a quick look. It's time to try another strategy.

"I'm just going to step out to make a call," he says. "Be back in a few minutes."

When he's gone, Gray looks at me warily.

"You like Duran Duran," I say. "'Ordinary World' is a great song."

I've surprised him. Maybe that's why he answers. "It's the best song on the record."

"Yeah, sad though. It's about David Miles, right?"

His pupils flare. "Simon Le Bon has never said that."

"He hasn't. That's why it's a good song. He's not giving everything away, but if you pay attention, you start to hear what he's not saying."

From Gray's face, I can tell he's following me. In that space, I decide to plunge ahead. "With the things that matter most, we guard them carefully. Sometimes we tell no one, and sometimes just one person, the one who knows us best."

"I guess so." Gray drops the sketchbook to the floor, and without it, his hands look empty and pale.

"Cameron's parents say she's been struggling lately. Is that how you would put it?"

There's a long beat as he wrestles with himself. Then: "There's been a lot of stress at home."

"Seems like it. Too much to deal with maybe for someone as sensitive as Cameron."

His gaze is still cautious, but he follows my lead. "It's always been sort of tough on her that her mom's this world-famous actress. And her dad's away a lot."

"Does his traveling keep them from being close? Emotionally, I mean."

"It's more than that." His pupils seem to twitch, his whole body subtly vibrating with the conflict inside of him. "He's been having an affair with someone he works with. Cameron's been mad at him, and worried about her mom."

I nod to encourage him, pretending he hasn't surprised me. "Do you think this is the first time he's cheated? Or maybe just the first time she's known about it?"

"Cameron says he's always been this way. But now it's worse. His girlfriend is pregnant and she's going to have the baby. Did her parents tell you that? Maybe I shouldn't even talk about it. I don't know."

I try not to overreact. *A baby?* How could that have not thrown Cameron over the edge? "You can say anything," I tell him. "There's no way to get in trouble here. Cameron is your best friend. It's natural that you keep her secrets and she keeps yours. That's what best friends do."

"The sheriff has come to talk to me a few times. I've been really confused."

"Of course you have," I say. "You want to protect Cameron. But, Gray, there might be things you know that can help us find her. Do you think you can be a little more open with us?"

I feel him tensing on the beanbag, wondering if he can trust me, if it's really okay to say what he's been holding on to. "Cameron had a lot of hard stuff coming up. Not just about her parents."

"Personal stuff," I echo.

"Yeah."

The door opens and Will is there. I feel myself deflate almost audibly. In an interview, it's rarely the first or second or third thing the subject says that's important. Real disclosure takes time. Takes patience in the unpeeling. And Gray has been close to telling the truth.

"Hey," Will says, taking a seat on the bed. "What did I miss?"

I glance at Gray and he nods almost imperceptibly. "We're just talking about Cameron's parents. Her dad's affair. Seems like the situation is more complicated than we thought."

"Oh yeah?"

I look to Gray again for some sign of assent before saying, "Troy's girlfriend is pregnant."

"Oh wow. That's a lot."

Gray says, "Please don't tell her parents I said anything."

"You have perfect anonymity with us," Will assures him.

"This is what I mean, Gray. This is how you can help Cameron."

Gray is quiet for a long time, his hands flexing in his lap. Finally he says, "Cameron was starting to remember things from before." The last word catches in his throat. "From when she was young."

"What things?" I ask gently.

"You really can't tell her parents." Gray closes his eyes and then opens them again, seeming to ready himself for the cost of the truth. I can feel his fear and worry. We're asking him to take Cameron's dark secrets out of the box he's kept them in for her. As her closest friend, he *is* that box. "You have to promise me."

We both nod.

"She wanted to go on birth control. She wasn't having sex or anything. Don't think that. Apparently it's supposed to be really great for your skin."

"It is," I say. "Lots of girls do it for that reason."

"Right. Anyway, she asked me to go to the free clinic with her. We took the bus to Fort Bragg after school one day a few weeks ago. It was like this racy grown-up thing."

"Go on," I urge. "You went to the free clinic."

"Right, but the woman there wouldn't just give her the prescription without doing a full exam. I waited for her, no big deal, but when she came out she was super quiet and shut down. I kept asking what had happened, but she wouldn't even tell me until we were halfway home on the bus. It was awful."

"What was awful?" Will asks.

"The nurse told her she had scarring." His face freezes and then crumples. It takes a minute before he can go on. "Like, inside her body."

I feel my gut twist. "Did she ever mention her uncle to you? Drew Hague?"

Gray shakes his head. "I don't think so."

"How about someone else? A man? Think, Gray."

"There weren't any men. Not that she ever told me about. After that day, she shut down again and wouldn't talk to me about it at all. That wasn't how we were with each other."

He's just a kid. Of course he's felt powerless, but so has Cameron. Otherwise she would have leaned on him, her best friend. She would have told him if she'd had the words.

"You're really brave for being so open with us," I finally say. "This could be important, Gray. I think someone hurt Cameron once. That person could have come back into her life, or she might have met someone new who's gotten close to her the same way. You can't blame yourself for not knowing how to make it better. There isn't really any way to do that. Do you understand?"

Gray's nod is almost nonexistent. I see him struggling to forgive himself.

"Can you let us know if you remember anything else? Anything at all?" Will asks.

I move closer to the beanbag, kneeling with my hands out. "And Gray?"

"Yeah?"

"None of this is your fault."

Twenty-Two

When Will and I get back to the car, we're silent. For the longest time, he doesn't even start the engine. Just outside my window, a eucalyptus branch stretches against the glass, making the clustered green-gray leaves look magnified, pearled with raindrops.

Hap had always called them gum trees. Once he told me there are seven hundred varieties of gum tree in Australia alone and that they can make their own fog, a blue haze that's created when their compounds vaporize in warm air. Seven hundred varieties of a single genus and counting, and yet human lives seem destined to repeat the same terrible patterns over and over, as if there is only one way the story can possibly go.

"Does this type of scarring for sure mean sexual abuse?" Will asks at last.

I'm not surprised he'd wonder, even after seeing how upset Gray became remembering the whole ordeal. "Not always. It's a controversial issue. A lot of providers will tell you scars like these are inconclusive. Others will tell you that most physicians either don't know what they're looking at or don't want to open that door. The most telling thing to me is Cameron's reaction."

"That she shut down, you mean."

"Right. My guess is she's buried this stuff really deep."

"I don't know what that nurse was thinking. It sure seems irresponsible to drop a bomb like that on a kid."

"Well, it's complicated. These clinicians see all kinds of things. Not telling her might have been more irresponsible."

"Is there a legal issue here? Shouldn't the clinic have alerted Cameron's parents?"

"You'd think so, but California doesn't require that kind of disclosure, at least not yet. I'm wondering what we should do with this information. Maybe just sit on it awhile, particularly since we haven't ruled out Troy as a suspect. What happened when you polygraphed him?"

"No discrepancies. Emily's results were more interesting."

"How so?"

"You know these things are fallible. I try not to take them too seriously unless I have nothing else to go on."

"Right." Something about his tone trips a faint feeling of unease in me. "What happened?"

"She failed."

Before I can respond, the radio in Will's cruiser screeches to life, startling us both. He picks it up, thumbing the receiver. "Flood here."

"This is Leon, Sheriff. We've just gotten a call from Gualala. Apparently a girl's been reported missing there. Seventeen-year-old Shannan Russo, last seen June second."

"June? Why is this coming in now?"

"Because of the others, I guess." The deputy sounds uncertain and also young, maybe not much older than Will was when he first began to work under his father.

"I'm on my way," Will says, and then rings off facing me, both eyebrows arcing toward the brim of his hat in pure bewilderment.

"Shit," I say for us both, wishing there were a way to press pause. If I could only step out of the car and into the woods alone, I might be able to think clearly. But Will is still looking at me. "Sometimes there's a waterfall effect," I offer. "A kid runs off and no one gives it a thought until someone like Polly Klaas becomes front-page news. Then the family decides it's time to panic."

"Maybe that's it." Will seems eager to believe me, though I haven't said much. "I'll send someone down to talk to the sheriff's department there. Or I might go myself. I know Denny Rasmussen pretty well."

"You want me to come along?" I suggest automatically.

"You've got enough to do. We'll meet up later and compare notes." He starts the engine and I lean back in the passenger seat, relieved to be given a pass.

These last few hours have drained me more than I want to admit, talking to Emily and then Gray, learning of Cameron's scars, how much she was hit with all at once. Too much for anyone, let alone a fifteen-year-old.

Almost as if he can read my thoughts, Will says, "That poor kid. Can you imagine being raped and not remembering it?"

"No," I say.

But I can. It happens all the time.

On his way to Gualala, fifty miles south, Will drops me in the parking lot of the high school. I let myself into the building, instantly colliding with the past, the teenager I was here, just a moment ago, it seems. The smells of floor polish and hormones are the same, the banged-up rows of lockers and cinder-block walls and greenish fluorescent lights. But was it really this small?

It's the end of the day, and the building's almost empty. I find the main office by muscle memory, where an administrative assistant directs me to Steve Gonzales's English classroom. I catch him putting the chairs back in order and introduce myself.

"Cameron," he says, and sits down hard, as if I've pushed him. Just that, the heavy way he's said her name, tells me he isn't going to be anyone of interest in our investigation. Tells me how much he cares about her.

Round shouldered and soft eyed, Gonzales wears wide-wale corduroy slacks and a cheap tan blazer he's probably put on every other day for years. There are threads of silver in his deeply black hair. He's been here a long time, I guess, and has seen every type of kid.

"Tell me about her work," I say. "What kind of student is Cameron?"

"A good one. I only had her for a month, but she stood out right away. The sensitive readers, they have a certain look. You can almost smell it on them, that they need books to feel okay."

"Emily Hague says you praised Cameron's writing."

"She wrote some poems and showed them to me. They weren't part of an assignment."

"Can I see them?"

"I gave them back to her, but I wish I'd made copies first. Maybe they'd be useful somehow."

"What were they like?"

"Really good, actually, but dark. It was a tricky moment for me. I'm supposed to talk about the craft of the poem, the imagery or a particularly good line, but in this case, the subject matter was disturbing, and I didn't know if I should say something about that. Young writers, they're almost always autobiographical, even when they don't mean to be."

"It says a lot that she would show you something so personal. She must have known she could trust you. What happened next? Did you get the feeling that Cameron wanted you to do something about it? That she was asking for help?"

Steve's dark brown eyes cloud over. "God, I hope not. I edit the school magazine. I asked her if she wanted me to publish the poems, and she said she'd think about it. Then she folded them up a bunch of times. It made me think she was embarrassed she'd shown me. I felt bad after she left, but then in class the next day she seemed fine."

"You love your job, Mr. Gonzales."

"I do, yeah. Though right now, I'm struggling." He looks down at his soft meaty hands. "The other students are still really scared. They can't focus, I've noticed. My colleagues say the same." I know exactly what he's talking about. When terror like this hits so close to home, it's common to see numbness, inability to focus, depression, and anxiety. Most grown-ups don't have the tools to deal with this kind of fear, let alone kids. It makes me feel for Steve, for all of them.

"The news about Polly Klaas has to have made things a lot worse," I say. "They must be feeling like it could happen again, to any of them."

He nods. "What can I do?"

"Be patient. Listen. Reassure them with your presence. Let them feel their feelings. Kids are resilient. They can heal with time, but first they need some kind of resolution. I hope we can provide that for them soon."

He gives me a long look. "Do *you* love your job, Detective Hart?"

The question catches me off guard. Once I had an easy answer, but not anymore. "I've always felt a need to help people. It gets to be too much, though, particularly when they're in real trouble and you don't know if you can make a difference, no matter how hard you try."

"Yes," he says. "That's how I feel right now."

Before I leave, I ask him to show me Cameron's locker, which is just a row over from where mine once was. Will's team has cut off the lock and taken nearly everything. Only her textbooks remain, *Algebra II, Beginning Latin, World History,* and a ragged paperback of *Jane Eyre.*

"We'd just started our unit on it," Steve Gonzales says beside me. Down the hall, a janitor rides a clunky floor polisher around and around in circles, the patterns behind him like glassy, disconnected bull's-eyes. "Girls like Cameron love Jane."

"I did too," I say, feeling a current of connection. "Jane has every reason to feel like a victim, but she's not. She's quiet, she's interior, but a fighter for sure."

I pick up the paperback to take with me, and then move the stack of books aside. In the lower-right corner of the back of the locker, somewhere only Cameron can see it easily, she's taped a blank postcard with a poem from Rainer Maria Rilke, the whole poem line by line in her steady, neat hand.

> I am too alone in the world, and not alone enough
> to make every minute holy.
> I am too tiny in this world, and not tiny enough
> just to lie before you like a thing,
> shrewd and secretive.
> I want my own will, and I want simply to be with my will,
> as it goes toward action,
> and in the silent, sometimes hardly moving times
> when something is coming near,
> I want to be with those who know secret things
> or else alone.
> I want to be a mirror for your whole body,
> and I never want to be blind, or to be too old
> to hold up your heavy and swaying picture.
> I want to unfold.
> I don't want to stay folded anywhere,
> because where I am folded, there I am a lie.

Twenty-Three

In Patterson's, as I wait for Will, I scan *Jane Eyre* feeling uneasy for some reason, as if I'm peering into Cameron's diary, or trespassing on sacred ground. Books can be incredibly personal to people, even holy. This one seems to be for her, worn soft and dog-eared, full of underlined passages and pencil marks—a coded map to her soul. I have the postcard with the Rilke poem, too, and copy it out in my notebook, circling phrases that feel meaningful. *I am too alone in the world . . . something is coming near . . . those who know secret things . . .*

The poem must be significant or she wouldn't have taken the time to write it out by hand, let alone keep it. In fact, I was guessing she recognized herself in all of it, that every word seemed to point like a burning arrow to who she was on the inside, and what she carried.

What I'd said to Will earlier, about not being able to imagine Cameron suppressing memories of her abuse, had been a lie. In fact, it's a common response, even endemic. The experience of being violated is often so overwhelming and annihilating, particularly for children, that the only way to survive it is for victims to leave their bodies. Not fight or flight, but complete dissociation.

If the abuser happens to be a caregiver, someone who is supposed to be safe and loving, the experience of shutdown can be even more dramatic and far-reaching. What we can't bear to know or feel, we often find a way to hide from ourselves, and hide well.

At whatever age Cameron was when the abuse happened, either once or repeatedly, her mind had likely stepped in to protect her. It wouldn't have been a choice she made, but something closer to basic animal instinct, the only way to get out of a thing too terrible to name or feel. She might not have remembered any of it until the free-clinic visit, a fluke occurrence, called it out of the dark.

I can barely stand to think about what Cameron must have felt that day, lying flat out on the exam table, already compromised and vulnerable, her feet in metal stirrups while the nurse practitioner donned latex gloves, unaware that she was about to detonate a lifetime's worth of secret pain. A tale Cameron's memory had swallowed but not her body. It was all right there inside her, written out in scar tissue.

Even if Cameron's memories hadn't been forced to the surface like this, the damage has been simmering for years and has no doubt found other ways to erupt, in feelings of shame or hopelessness, drawing her unconsciously to people and situations that echo or approximate the original pain. I've seen it over and over, how a trauma survivor's story finds a way to tell *her* instead of the other way around.

It makes me hurt for her, this girl I've never met but *know*. She survived violence, betrayal, and terror, the theft of her soul. She survived the smoking, buried shame and the silence, and years of forced amnesia. But can she survive what's happening now, inside and out? Can she survive the remembering?

Feeling overwhelmed, I shove the book and poem away from me on the bar top and order a quick shot of whiskey. The second it's gone, I push my glass forward, signaling one more.

The barmaid looks at me; her drawn-in brows shoot up. "You driving?"

"I'm fine."

"I'll tell you what. You hand over your car keys and you can have the whole damned bottle."

Suddenly I'm irritated. "Just pour the drink, all right? Why do you care?"

She stares me down. "Because someone has to."

Under her deadpan delivery, I see legitimate concern, but I haven't asked for it. For a split second, I feel an urge to throw my empty shot glass hard at the mirror behind her, just to do it, to make something break. Instead, I take a deep breath and let it out slowly. "How old are you?"

"What?" She snorts. "A hundred-some days. How about you?"

"Thirty-five. Thirty-five and a hundred-some days."

"Now we're friends?" Her teeth show when she smiles, but I can sense her trying to figure out what I'm up to and what I want from her. Is it just this next drink or something more? "I'll be forty in December."

"You been in this town a long time?"

She nods.

"Were you here when Jenny Ford was murdered?"

"I went to school with her. She was a few years younger. I've been thinking about her a lot lately."

"Because of Cameron Curtis? Me too."

She still holds the bottle. I can see her mind working out the puzzle of our talking. Of me. "Were you at Mendocino High? You look familiar."

"You would have graduated before I was a freshman. That was a long time ago." I draw a twenty out of my pocket and toss it on the bar. "I'm Anna. Sorry I've been such an asshole."

"I'm Wanda, and I guess I've seen worse." She picks up the bill and tucks it neatly into her bra just as Will walks up. "Speak of the devil."

Wanda and I lock eyes, laughing.

"What's so funny?" Will wants to know.

"Your face," Wanda says with a wink, and just like that I love her. The world needs an army of Wandas—strong, sarcastic, unafraid women who say what they think and act straightforwardly, without apology or permission. Women who roar instead of flinch.

"Hilarious," Will says flatly. "Just bring me a drink, will you?"

I brace myself for another round of Wanda's responsible-driving lecture, but she's obviously smarter than that, and wordlessly pours his pint, refreshes my drink, and then moves to the other end of the bar.

Will has clearly had a day. He downs his Guinness in two minutes flat, his shoulders looking sloped and weighted down. I have an urge to hug him but think better of it.

"What was the upshot in Gualala?" I ask.

"Depressing as hell. By all accounts this girl Shannan is trouble with a capital *T*. A habitual runaway into drugs of every kind, and sex, too. In sixth grade she got suspended for giving a blow job in the school bathroom, apparently for some kid's lunch money."

I can hear the recoil in his voice. The revulsion. Because I'm a woman, my filter is different. I live in a woman's body. Know the vulnerabilities acutely. All the ways you can get put on a table as a victim, or put yourself there. How sex can be weaponized from inside and out. "Go on. What else?"

"When Denny and I spoke with the mother, she couldn't even remember how many times Shannan has run away. Usually she comes back after a few weeks, thinner and dead broke. This last time she sent a note saying that she was leaving of her own free will and didn't want anyone searching for her. The postmark was stamped in Ukiah on June tenth. Sometimes Shannan talked about moving to Seattle, so Mom assumes she was headed there."

"Why call in the absence now?"

"You'll never guess." The bitterness in his voice doesn't suit him, but makes sense given the context.

"What?"

"She got a call from a psychic. A local woman named Tally Hollander. Anyway, this Tally finds Karen Russo in the phone book and calls to basically tell her Shannan's dead. I mean, who *does* that?"

I feel cold suddenly. If that's what happened, it does sound ruthless. "What did she actually say?"

"That Shannan had been murdered. Apparently she had a vision of a forest. She thinks Shannan's body might be there."

"What forest?"

"Beyond her extraordinary powers to narrow it down, I guess." He makes a disgusted sound through his nose. "She called me, too, right after Cameron disappeared and was just as vague."

"Really? Sometimes these people are legitimate, Will. I've had good experiences with a few, who were very helpful, actually. What did she say about Cameron?"

"That she'd been taken and was in some sort of tight space in the dark."

"Hmm. That's it?"

"Yep. She might as well have told us to look on Mars."

My thoughts click rapidly. It's hard to know what's next with so little to go on. "Shannan had a car, right? Has someone run the license-plate number?"

"I'm not sure. I could ask Denny, but the note was pretty clear. Shannan wanted to leave."

"Maybe, but she's still a minor, Will. We don't know that she wasn't in some kind of real trouble, or being coerced somehow. And what if she *is* dead in the forest?"

His look is sharp. "Tally Hollander is obviously a nutjob. You're not that gullible, are you?"

"Hey now," I push back. "This isn't about me, and you know it. If Shannan's alive, she needs our help. And if it's too late, she still deserves to be found. We can't just give up."

"This girl isn't Cameron, Anna. She's a runner who's been screwing up her life for a long time. And you heard what her mother said. Shannan doesn't want anyone looking for her. End of story."

"How can you even say that, Will? You're a parent."

"What does *that* mean?"

"We're responsible for this girl."

"*Why?* Why are we?"

"Because everyone wants to be looked for, whether they realize it or not."

It's a long time before either of us speaks again. The impasse is like a physical object between us, taking up space and air. Finally he notices the copy of *Jane Eyre,* his eyebrows lifting in curiosity.

"What happened with Steve Gonzales?"

"I liked him. He seems like a decent guy and a good teacher, and he obviously cares about Cameron. I don't think he's involved in this at all, but you can polygraph him to rule him out." *Wait.* My words catch up to me and seem to clang. In the cruiser, before the call about Shannan hijacked our day, Will had started to tell me something important. "Emily's polygraph," I remind him. "How did she fail?"

Twenty-Four

When I was first trained to interview suspects, I learned the Reid Technique of interrogation like pretty much everyone in law enforcement then. John Reid was a Chicago cop who came up with the method when in the 1940s and 1950s the Supreme Court outlawed beating, bullying, and threatening out confessions. Reid liked science. He was a polygraph expert and thought cops could be taught to detect lies, too, through a suspect's unconscious tics and gestures, repetitive speech patterns, stress responses. Through a series of escalating questions and steps, the interviewer was supposed to take more and more control while the polygraph did its work to register minute changes in heart rate, blood pressure, body temperature, and respiration.

Like Will, I've always carried healthy skepticism about the polygraph, considering it a tool, yes, but nothing to hang your hat on, let alone a conviction. An increase in heart rate might suggest guilty feelings or behavior, sure. But in a case like Cameron's, with a child's life at stake, a subject's emotions might *only* be hot and chaotic and bewildering. Unreliable. Also, in my experience, guilty people have no trouble passing polygraphs. Narcissists, psychopaths. People without a conscience.

"What happened, Will? What tripped her up?"

It's obvious from his look that he wants to drop this conversation, but finally he relents. "The question was 'Have you ever done harm to your daughter?' Emily's answer was no, and you're familiar with how this works. The question comes up a few more times, differently worded. Each time Emily says no, and each time, her heart rate spikes."

"That seems significant. Do you disagree?"

"I don't know. The discrepancy could mean anything. She might have spanked Cameron too hard once, or locked her in her room. Parents stew over that kind of thing for years." Will holds his pint between his palms and rolls the glass back and forth as if it might help him measure his words, help him persuade me. "It could be this case, for all we know. Her feeling of responsibility. That she couldn't protect Cameron in her own home."

Listening, I have to wonder if I'm jumping to conclusions. Or is he missing what's right here in front of us? Parental guilt can be a thorny and bottomless thing, I know all too well. But something *did* happen in Emily's home, and not just the night her daughter disappeared. Emily didn't protect her daughter when it counted, when Cameron was far too young to protect herself. That gap has widened with time, becoming the crevasse of this moment. In all the ways that matter right now, Cameron's past has created her present. "Will," I say, "we have to talk about the abuse piece."

He seems thrown. "What makes you think it didn't happen before she came to the Curtises, if it happened at all?"

I ignore his cynicism and plunge forward. "Statistically, onset of sexual abuse falls between ages seven and thirteen. Around ninety percent are targeted by a family member. And the victims, Will, they're quiet, troubled, lonely children. Girls like Cameron." An intensity has crept into my voice, telling me it's time to dial back, to hold myself in check, but somehow even the notion of self-control feels far away, beyond my grasp. "I think we should confront Emily and see what happens. We go to the free clinic with a warrant for Cameron's file and then push it right across the table at her."

Will looks shocked. "Christ, you're cold, Anna. Her daughter is *missing*." The word flares between us, sharp and spangled. "You don't think that garners Emily a break, a little benefit of the doubt? And what about Troy Curtis? Why does he get a pass? He might be the one who hurt her."

I'm suddenly aware of the heat in the room. The smell of fried fish wafting from the kitchen. The sticky bar top under my hands. Will's challenge isn't at all rhetorical. He thinks I'm over the edge, here. And I might be.

"I'm not forgetting about Troy," I say quickly. "But Emily was the one home alone with Cameron, and the primary caregiver. She'd stopped acting to be a full-time mom. And she's the one who failed her polygraph. I don't think I'm being cold at all, just realistic. We don't have time for kid gloves, Will. If Emily knew about the abuse, not only would that guilt light up the polygraph exactly this way, but also implicate her. Maybe she feels responsible because she *is* responsible. Maybe she closed her eyes when it was time to open them wide. Maybe she held her tongue when she should have shouted from the rafters." The barstool beneath me seems to vibrate with tension. My voice shakes, full of heat. "Maybe she protected her brother, Drew, instead of Cameron."

Will sits back, his expression shifting. "You seem awfully emotional, Anna."

"I'm fine," I shoot back, instantly on the defensive. "I just know I'm onto something here. Look, I found this poem in Cameron's locker. It might be important."

He takes Cameron's postcard as I push it his way and reads the lines silently. When he's finished, he looks up. "Shit. What fifteen-year-old reads Rilke?"

"A wounded one. 'I want to be with those who know secret

things or else alone.' Doesn't that say it all? Some violence is random, obviously, more about chance and opportunity. But sometimes it's very specific and in sync, like there's a hidden connection,
a vulnerability predators can sense in certain victims, even seeing
them for the first time. When the damage is there, it can come
through like radar. Almost as if the darkest part of someone's story
can speak directly through their body, alive in their cells. Do you
follow me?"

Will looks uncomfortable, his face pink. "Are you saying it's the
victims' fault somehow? That they're causing someone to target
them?"

"No, not at all. The *opposite*." I pick up the postcard again,
feeling frustrated. The right words seem beyond me.

"Then how? What actually happens?"

"I worked with a really smart psychological profiler once," I try
again. "He used the term 'bat signal' to talk about this sort of
thing, how victims unwittingly announce themselves to abusers.
We all come into the world with a pure bright light, right? We're
innocent, fresh as fucking heaven. Bright and pure and clean."

"I believe that," Will says, and the catch in his voice makes me
feel less alone. "Everyone's born with a clean slate."

"Yes." Emotion vibrates along an invisible string between us.
"But then for some kids—one in ten, maybe, though it might be
closer to one in four—really hard stuff happens to them, in their
own family, or by an acquaintance whom that family trusts.
Trauma, neglect, abuse, manipulation, coercion, exposure to violence. And they don't have the tools to process it, or the words to
talk about it. So silence follows. Forced complicity. Shame. Soon
what you've got is thick black tar, and when the light shines
through . . ." I let my sentence trail, knowing he's probably realized
I'm not talking just about my cases through the years, that some of
what I know, I've lived first.

"Bat signal," he says soberly.

"Yes. Big as the moon over Gotham City. And every psychopath, sociopath, sadist, alcoholic, narcissist piece of shit anywhere can see it and comes running. And when the two find each other, they click. They recognize each other on some deep level. It's like they speak two variations of the same language."

"Wow, okay. Jesus. That makes a little too much sense." He picks up the damp napkin under his glass and begins to worry it, shaking his head. "But how does the original abuse happen if everyone gets a blank slate? Why are some kids targeted and not others?"

"Cameron wasn't even four when her life was upended," I explain to Will as my thoughts ricochet back through decades, to my own childhood and Jenny's, and countless others', gathering charged momentum. "Think about how young that is to have your whole life turn on a dime. But old enough to not know who you are anymore, or where you really belong. Even if Cameron didn't seem lonely or scared to Emily and Troy, you can see how so much confusion and uncertainty could make her a little too trusting of others. She wanted love. She wanted to feel okay." The muscles in my throat feel tight and strange, my tongue heavy, but I force my way to the end of my point. "And if that wasn't enough, the scar of that early trauma might very well have drawn someone else her way. Another predator."

Will sighs. "That would be pretty fucking ironic. I mean, if Emily and Troy thought they were helping a needy kid and ended up causing the damage that led to her being taken?"

He *has* been listening. "You asked why I can't let Emily off the hook, Will? It's exactly that. What if everything bad that happened to Cameron happened *after* she was rescued? After she was supposed to be safe and secure and happy?" My voice cracks on the last word. My hands tremble on the edge of the bar.

Will has noticed all of this and more. I'm well over my head and we both know it. But he can't begin to realize how many other

forces are pushing me, why there's no way I can slow down now—
why I can't and won't lose Cameron, no matter what.

He pushes back in his chair to better face me, his brow a map of
concern. "You're smart about this stuff, and really experienced. I
know that. I also know your work in San Francisco took you
through a lot of things no one should have to see, Anna. Maybe
that's why you're back here."

I feel myself flush, unable to meet his eyes.

"If all this gets to be too much, you need to tell me, okay? I'm
here. We're a team." He reaches out for my arm and squeezes it for
emphasis. "Yes?"

"Of course." I swallow hard. "But, Will, someone has to save
this girl."

And it has to be me.

Twenty-Five

The next morning, October 5, I drive into town just as the sun is rising to meet Will at the GoodLife and grab coffee. Then we climb into his cruiser and head south along the coast toward Petaluma, skirting a single long gray fogbank that blanks out the sea and the horizon, everything but the road.

"Any news about the Russo girl?" I ask. I woke up thinking about her, as if I need another missing girl on my mind. "Did you run the plate?"

"I did. Nothing of note except the registration's expired. Her mother decided not to renew the tags probably. Why waste money?"

"What about an APB on the car? Just to be sure."

He shoots me a *here we go again* look. "On a psychic's claim?"

"Maybe," I say, holding my ground. "Maybe you don't believe in them, but they're not all crazy. Anyway, what does it cost us to follow up on this?"

He says nothing.

"Just because the girl's led a troubled life doesn't mean she's not worth our time. We shouldn't let anything go right now. The stakes are too high."

He tucks his chin, half a nod. I watch his face, waiting for more, and finally he says, "Okay."

An hour later we come into Petaluma through olive groves, cattle land, a rural patchwork of farms and fields. I've forgotten how like New England this part of California looks and feels.

"It's *Our Town*," I tell Will as we roll along Petaluma Boulevard, past historic adobe buildings and vintage façades. There seems to be only one bar, and the sign reads saloon.

"We used to call it Chickaluma." Will points at the poultry-processing plant. "Can you believe we're forty-five miles from San Francisco?"

It's too close. I have a spiking irrational fear that all my pain and regret might get louder at this distance. "Crazy," I say thinly, focusing on the tidy storefronts and sidewalk, the savings bank with a giant smiley-face sticker in the window. Nothing seems out of place, not even a jaywalker. "A town like this feels so safe and apart from the outside world. You start to wonder if it's dangerous."

"The fairy tale of it, you mean?"

"Right. False security. You stop looking over your shoulder, because the picture feels real. Nothing bad can happen when there's a moat around the whole town, right? Battlements. Guards at the gate. But the dragon shows up anyway."

Will glances over. His look is loaded. "You know what this place reminds me of?"

"Yeah," I say. "Mendocino."

The Petaluma PD is just north of downtown. We park, sign in, and wait at the front desk until a junior officer appears to lead us back to a string of offices.

"This is Sergeant Barresi," he says, stopping at an open door.

The sergeant is a big guy with a sallow face and slicked-back hair. As he stands up from behind his desk, I'm reminded of a lot of commanding officers I've worked with over the years, right down to his beige suit, so new it looks shiny. For the press conferences, I guess. Ready or not, he's PR now. It's already clear that this case will be high profile. Polly's age and the way she was taken, so brutally and from her own home, have triggered widespread fear and concern. The entire nation will be watching this one unfold.

"I thought we were supposed to meet with Ed Van Leer," Will says.

"He'll be along shortly. We're co-leading the case. Tell me what I can do for you."

"We've got a missing girl up in Mendocino," I jump in. "Cameron Curtis. I'm sure you've heard. Now there's another missing report filed in Gualala. Shannan Russo, age seventeen, last seen early June. Just trying to see if any dots connect."

"We're not even sure what our own dots are," Barresi says flatly. "Crime happened late Friday. We're only at Tuesday morning, here. I've got FBI everywhere, from Washington and San Francisco, more agents than I've ever seen in one place. But that doesn't mean I can find my ass."

I know the pressure he's under to get this case right. Everyone watching. The last thing he needs is something else to think about, but I have to try just the same. "Listen, we know your time is valuable," I tell him. "If you could just take a minute to lay out the case for us."

"Van Leer said there was a handprint at the scene?" Will presses.

"Too blurry for the computer," Barresi replies. "If we had a suspect we could make it work."

"Any other witnesses besides Polly's two friends?" I ask.

"There was a renter on the property in a garage apartment. He had a friend visiting. The two were watching TV with the door open when the unsub came up the driveway and approached the back door."

Will sits forward, his question echoing my own silent one. "They weren't suspicious?"

"Apparently the guy just waltzed up as if he owned the place. The back door was unlocked. Maybe it's a friend of the family, he thinks."

"Still, that's damned bold when you know you've been spotted," Will replies.

"There were witnesses on the street, too," Barresi adds. "A warm Friday night. People in the park. Lots of foot traffic."

It's easy enough to picture what the sergeant's describing, the kind of person who doesn't care about witnesses or time of day or repercussions or risk—who, once triggered, would take Polly no matter what.

That kind of reckless confidence is partly why some perpetrators are able to pull off abductions in plain sight, even in broad daylight. In 1991, in the small mountain town of Meyers, California, near Lake Tahoe, a car approached eleven-year-old Jaycee Dugard as she walked to her bus stop. Several of her classmates watched as Jaycee was attacked by a stun gun and pulled into the car. Her stepfather witnessed the kidnapping, too, and set out in pursuit on his mountain bike, but he couldn't keep up. The car had sped away. A massive search effort had launched immediately, but Jaycee had vanished.

Two years and three months later, she's still gone, but very much on my mind in Barresi's office, even as he changes gears and begins to talk about Polly's family.

Eve recently split from her second husband, who fathered Polly's half sister, Annie, just six. Was it possible that there were tensions between the two, or that Marc Klaas wasn't happy with the custody arrangements? Barresi was grasping at straws.

"The suspect didn't knock or hesitate," he's saying. "That could mean he knew the victim, had access to and knowledge of the house."

I know the odds as well as he does, that less than five percent of the time is the perpetrator a stranger. But I already have a feeling this case is going to buck the odds, maybe lots of them. "Time will tell," I offer. "Anything else you can share?"

"You can go on over to the scene if that would help. We've cleared the perimeter. You can't screw anything up."

"Thanks," Will says. "How are the other girls doing? Polly's friends?"

"Those are some brave little girls. They've done nothing but co-operate with us since late Friday night. We've got officers posted at both their houses. I imagine they won't be ready to go back to school for a while."

"I'd never go back," I say.

"Normalcy helps sometimes," Barresi explains.

I nod, not wanting to contradict the sergeant in his own office. But inwardly I'm thinking the only thing I can think. For those girls, just like the classmates who saw Jaycee Dugard attacked on the street in front of them, just like Gray Benson, who watched his best friend vanish into nowhere, normalcy was going to be off the table for a long time, maybe even for good.

Twenty-Six

Eve Nichol's house is part of a sleepy and serene residential neighborhood about a mile from the town center. The block has been roped off, so we park nearby, crossing through Wickersham Park under leafy elms and plane trees. I can picture it as it should be, full of shrieking children on the lopsided jungle gym and swing sets, mothers gossiping on the wooden benches and at the picnic tables. Today, there isn't a soul anywhere.

Police tape has been strung through the picket fencing surrounding the small blue-gray bungalow in the center of the block, cute and kept up, but otherwise indistinctive, with white trim and a large bay window. Potted flowers droop on the front porch. The mailbox is stuffed with Safeway circulars. It's any house in any small town in America, except it isn't.

We don't need to knock. The door stands wide open, two uniformed officers from the Petaluma PD posted just beyond. Will flashes his badge and drops Barresi's name. He's called ahead for us, which makes everything easier. Apparently Eve and daughter Annie have gone to stay with friends nearby. A humane decision, I think. Two CSI officers are processing Polly's room—still or again.

The kitchen has been turned into temporary headquarters for the FBI team, led by Rod Fraser.

"Good to see you, Anna," he says, grabbing my hand with his, warm and solid. He's heavier than I remember, and his hairline has receded. Ten years can do that. "Wish it could be under happier circumstances."

"Me too," I say, though truthfully "happy" is relative in our line of work.

In Eve Nichol's kitchen, there's a strange feeling of suspension, of normalcy disrupted. Polly's report card on the fridge under a Hamburglar magnet, a vacation photo of Polly and Eve curled at the edges, both of them in bright dresses, squinting at the sun with the same bold happiness, Eve's springy hair blown over part of Polly's smile. Every object in the room gives off a charge of intimacy and exposure. The jar of Oreos on the counter next to an envelope full of coupon clippings. The cat clock over the fridge with its tail swinging back and forth.

"I got here the night of, just after midnight," Rod says.

"The girls were still here?" Will asks. "Polly's two friends?"

"Allison Palmer and Erin McGrath. They're our main witnesses. Mom was sound asleep and didn't hear anything. Neither did Annie, Polly's sister."

"That's a blessing, I guess," Will says, while inwardly my heart breaks for her. When this monster had come for her daughter and held a knife to her throat, Eve had been unconscious, incapable of coming to Polly's rescue.

"Mom and Annie went to bed around nine-thirty," Rod adds. "The girls were having fun all night, playing dress-up and board games, putting makeup on each other. At ten-thirty or so, Polly went out to the living room to get the girls' sleeping bags, and the guy's in the hall with a knife drawn. Big guy, heavy and bearded, middle-aged. He's got a duffel bag, too, with rope and a hood inside. All premeditated, obviously."

"Where was the print you found?"

"On the top bunk bed." He points. "It's just a partial, and pretty smeared. We'll see if we can use it."

"Why didn't Mom hear anything?" Will asks.

"She had a bad migraine and went to bed early. She probably couldn't have stopped him anyway," Rod goes on. "She's a slender woman, and he had the knife, remember?"

"Barresi mentioned that he asked the girls which one of the three lived in the house," I say, jumping in. "That seems to suggest a stranger, right?"

"Not necessarily. I've seen custody issues where the parent hires someone to snatch the kid and make it look like a stranger."

"Right," I say. "But in this particular family, the parents are amicable, it seems. Six years in and no court orders or restraints in place. No domestic disputes."

"Not that we know of," Rod adds. "But apparently he told the girls, 'I'm just doing it for the money.' Then when Polly offered him fifty dollars from a box on her dresser, he ignored it."

"That's odd," Will says. "Though I guess if he's a gun for hire as you say, he could have gotten stressed out or disoriented. Afraid of getting caught."

"Why would he ask which girl lived in the house?" Will wants to know. "If he was a family acquaintance, he wouldn't be confused about that."

"Maybe," I allow. "Or maybe he *is* a stranger. A sociopath who says whatever occurs to him in the moment." This is where my mind is headed, though it's a long shot. Only one percent of the time does a missing child involve a full-on predator, true, but the usual markers for family drama don't seem to be obvious here. Also, the details we do have, like the silk hood and ligatures, feel too specific to be props.

If the guy who took Polly really *was* paid off, as Rod is suggesting, he wouldn't have taken any more risks than necessary. He'd have waited until much later at night. He'd have thoroughly scoped out the place to make sure the family was asleep first, and that Polly was alone. But another type of guy, with no motivation but the sick story in his head, wouldn't follow any clock or care about being recognized. Once he'd decided to attack his victim, he wouldn't be able to stop himself. Risk wouldn't matter. Nothing would, just the girl.

"Can you walk us through the rest?" I ask Rod. "What happened next?"

"He ties them all up using the ligatures he brought, plus cord he's cut from the Nintendo game. The whole time, though, he's telling them he's not really going to hurt them."

"Sick bastard," Will mutters, and I have to agree.

"He gags them all," Rod goes on, "puts hoods over their heads, and tells the other two girls to start counting. Then he carries Polly away. The girls hear the front screen door creak and know he's gone. It takes them a few minutes to wrestle free of the bindings and wake Eve. Then she calls 911."

"What's the tape like?" Will asks. "Anything unusual?"

"Not really. Mom's a little groggy and confused, as if she can't quite believe this is happening. The call goes on and she starts to crack. To break down."

I feel a tingling of unease as the story he's telling veers too close to mine. Eve's grief and mine blurring, colliding. "Have you heard about Cameron Curtis?" I ask Rod, deliberately changing course.

"The actress's kid?"

"That's right. Fifteen-year-old girl disappears from her own house sometime after ten p.m. a little over a week ago. No sign of forced entry, no leads, no obvious motive, no reason to think she ran. Just poof."

Rod turns to me, thumbing the rim of the coffee cup in his hand. "What are you thinking for this, Anna? Any reason to believe it could be the same guy?"

I'm still trying to collect myself when Will jumps back in. "This girl's not a runner. And I don't think we can ignore the geography piece. Sometimes these violent offenders have territories, right?"

"Sure. But the behavior doesn't really line up, let alone the victimology. Twelve and fifteen look completely different, particularly to a predator. And you have to think about the zone of control. Where these girls would be allowed to go. Who they might run into inadvertently."

"Do you remember the hitchhiker murders around Santa Rosa in '72 and '73?" Will goes on, as if he hasn't heard Rod, or doesn't want to. "That killer struck often and very specifically before he went underground, always within the same hundred-mile radius."

"That was a long time ago. It would be pretty atypical for a guy like that to strike again in the same area after being dormant for twenty years."

"I guess so." Will leans back against the kitchen counter, but his muscles stay tensed. "I just can't stop thinking there's some sort of precedent here that we shouldn't ignore."

Fraser's eyes move from Will to me as I think of how to safely weigh in. I'm still rattled about Eve, but more than this, I feel pressure coming from Will to agree with him about the possibility of a serial predator. The stakes are high, and this is the first chance he's seen at getting some outside resources. Rod has reason to trust my instincts, too. If I tell him I see a link between the two cases, it might convince him to take a risk and send some of his own men our way. But pressure or no, I have to be honest.

"I don't see it," I finally say. "No way it's the same guy."

As Fraser bobs his head, I feel confusion and disappointment radiating from Will's body. His mouth is a tight line. The tips of his ears are almost fuchsia.

"Someone took this girl," he snaps. "I need some *help* here."

Rod crosses his arms over his chest, clearly uncomfortable. He has a big heart, I know, and will be feeling for Will and the whole situation, whether or not he can act. He's not callous, hasn't over-spent his compassion along the way. "I don't know what I can do," he finally says. "I'm at my limit and then some."

Will's sigh rattles. He cups his forehead with one hand, squeez-ing his temples, the headache there. The strain. "Maybe you could just make a call and remind the Bureau that we've got another missing girl up here. Possibly two. The Gualala PD has just posted a missing persons report for a seventeen-year-old who vanished in June."

Clearly Fraser hasn't heard. "Gualala?"

"Shannan Russo," I jump in. "We have a psychic who says this is related somehow to the Curtis girl."

Rod's eyebrows shoot up. "A psychic called here, too. Wonder if it's the same woman."

"Did you get her name?" I ask.

"Barresi did. She said she wanted access to Marc Klaas's apart-ment in Sausalito, something about sensing Polly's *vibrations*." Rod's look dismisses her credibility and closes a door simultane-ously. Even if I do plan to interview Tally Hollander, now's not the time to bring it up.

"You know how it is, Rod," I offer finally, working to shift us back to sounder footing. "We don't want to get confused here, thinking everything is connected, but we don't want to miss any-thing, either. Whatever's between those two things, that's the line we're trying to walk."

He nods, hands on his hips, saying nothing. He knows the terri-tory all too well. He's one of the good ones—the best. But that doesn't mean he can solve his mystery, or ours.

Twenty-Seven

As I'd told Will, women like Tally Hollander aren't unknown to me. Searchlight has used them occasionally, with some success. And then there was Eden.

She was "sensitive"—her word—able to see the future in dreams and visions that arrived when she could sense someone was in trouble, doubled over the bathtub after a bad fall, or under a truck at the side of the highway, trying to remove a flat. These were real people, as I understood it, but almost always strangers. She was simply at the receiving end of an image, a flash of telegraphed panic, as if her unconscious was a kind of cosmic phone line. Occasionally she intervened or tried to, when the events in question were to happen nearby, to people she could identify, not too far in the future or the past to be useful. Never, ever, was she in her own visions, which she found a relief.

"I don't want to know what's going to happen to me," she explained once. "I don't know anyone who does."

"What if you could stop the future, though? Do something different?"

She shrugged almost imperceptibly, her head bent over the bowl where she was kneading dark studs of raisins and pecans into pale bread dough. "It doesn't work that way."

"No one can change anything? Like fate, then?"

"No, I don't mean fate, Anna. I mean character. We do what we do because we are who we are."

Her words dropped through me like polished stones. "Do you dream about me?"

Eden's eyes glanced up. I caught the edge of a troubled thought before she cleared it away, like drawing a broom across a corner of the room. "Sometimes."

I was afraid to ask my next question. It hung there, weighted, while I looked at her.

"What do you want to know, Anna?" Her voice was tender and patient.

"Nothing." Without moving, I wrestled with myself. "Just . . . do you think I'm a good person?"

"What?" She shook the bowl upside down over the oiled pan, which caught the dough with a satisfying thump. "What kind of question is that? Of course I do, honey."

Suddenly Lenore made a strange sort of noise from her chair, almost a growl, and it rattled me. It was one of those moments when I thought the bird knew too much, could sense things. "Never mind," I retracted.

Eden opened the oven and put the pan inside, then she came over and sat next to me at the kitchen table, untying her apron so that it hung over her lap. Particles of flour fell to the floor like dust, but she ignored them. "Are you thinking about your brother and sister, Anna? We can try to find them if you want. You must still worry about them a lot."

Lenore flapped her good wing out and began to preen, separating and rearranging her feathers with her beak. It seemed a calculated gesture to me. As if she was pretending not to listen, but in fact had begun to pay even closer attention. "They're probably fine, right?" I threw out.

"I don't know," she said softly. "They're how old now?"

"Eight and nine."

"Ah. Well, there's one way to find out. Let us call Linda. Maybe you could even visit them. I'm sure that kind of thing gets arranged all the time."

A sharp pinch came at my side, just below my rib cage. "I don't think I want to visit. Not right now. You can ask, though. Call Mrs. Stephens. I'd like to know if they're okay."

"Sure, honey." She reached for her apron strings and cupped the loose bundle in her hands, thinking for a moment. Then she said, "I don't know anything about those kids, but I can tell you they don't blame you for what happened."

"*How* do you know?" I couldn't look up.

"Because it wasn't your fault."

I felt heat in my cheeks, and pressure. More than anything, I didn't want to cry. Not in front of Lenore, who would never forget it. "Well . . . anyway."

"No, listen to me, Anna." She sat forward and reached for my hands. "This is important. Sometimes grown-ups fall down. Your mom was probably in a world of hurt. I don't know for sure. What happened to your family might be because she felt too much pain, or because the world got to be more than she could handle. Or hell, any number of reasons. But not because of you, sweetheart. You didn't do anything wrong."

I desperately wanted to believe her, but it was hard. The way her palms were folded around mine, she seemed to be offering to carry something for me. If only I could let it go. "Do you dream about Hap sometimes?" I asked. If I didn't change the subject, I really was going to unravel.

Her eyes passed over me so gently, full of love and acceptance. "Too much. That's something I'd change if I could."

"But you can't." I wanted her to know how closely I'd been listening to her from the beginning.

"I can't."

"But you can make bread."

"That's right, Anna." She squeezed my hands once, twice before letting them go. "That's something anyone can do."

Twenty-Eight

When Will and I step back onto Fourth Street, he's fuming. "Would it have killed you to back me up? Jesus, Anna. You know what kind of pressure I'm under."

I stop him with my hand. "I *do* know. I'm sorry. But it wouldn't have been right to get Rod's team involved when the MOs don't line up."

He releases a frustrated noise, his mouth tight and closed, but he'd heard everything I had. Polly's abductor broke into her house on a warm night, with lots of activity on the street, and took Polly at knifepoint in front of witnesses. How could that be the same guy who somehow lured Cameron out of the safety of her home, and probably manipulated her beforehand? She went willingly, like a farm girl in one of Grimms' fairy tales who gets lured deeper and deeper into the dark forest by shiny trinkets dropped on the path. Looking up only when it's too late, when she's lost and afraid, far too far from home.

"We're going to figure this out, Will," I say, "but you have to trust me."

"Do I?" His eyes blaze.

"Anna! Wait up," Rod Fraser calls suddenly from Eve's porch. He's motioning me back.

I ask Will to wait and hurry over. "What's up?"

"I just wanted to say how sorry I am."

"Don't worry about it," I reply without thinking. Then it hits me. He doesn't mean our case or his own. He means me. The funeral and investigation.

"I should have sent a card." His eyes are dark with emotion. "My heart really went out to you."

"It's okay," I say dumbly.

"I guess you must feel ready now. To be back on the job."

"Almost." It's the most honest word I've spoken all day. "Thanks, Rod."

"Of course." He clears his throat. "Listen. There is something I can do for you guys. It's not much, but we've got a helicopter patrolling night and day now, with a photographer shooting anything that looks out of place or notable from the air. There's so much ground to cover. So many places this girl could be."

"Ours too."

"That's what I'm thinking. It wouldn't take much to send the crew higher and wider, down to Gualala, too. As you said, we wouldn't want to miss anything."

"That'd be great." I reach for his hand, and then hug him impulsively instead, leaning into his barrel chest and neck for one beat longer than the moment warrants, missing Frank Leary and my partner. Missing Brendan, as complicated as that sounds. But most of all missing Hap. I've never needed him more.

"If Shannan Russo's dead, her remains might be hidden in the forest somewhere," I tell Rod. "Just a tip we got. And keep an eye out for her car, too. I'll get you the plate number."

"Sounds good," he says as I step off the porch, feeling the smallest flicker of promise. Rod hasn't offered much, but sometimes you have to start there, with almost nothing. And hope for everything anyway.

Twenty-Nine

"A helicopter can cover a lot of territory," I relay to Will as we walk toward his cruiser. "That will help make up for the men we don't have."

"I'd rather have the men," he says without looking at me.

Wickersham Park is still eerily silent. We pass by an empty teeter-totter traced with shadows. "I know you're mad at me. Let's talk this through."

"What's the point?"

When we reach his vehicle, he slides behind the wheel, his body language all barricade. "You heard everything Rod said," I try again. "Let's use our energy to learn more about Cameron."

"Did it ever occur to you that you could be wrong about all this? What if there *is* a connection and you're missing it, Anna? Have you never made a mistake?"

I hold my tongue, looking into the splayed shadows along the street. "What if we go to Napa to see Drew Hague?"

"Maybe." The tension in his body shifts microscopically.

"We're less than an hour away from there. What do you think?"

"It can't hurt."

It's only been an hour or so since we left the downtown area for Fourth Street, but it's clear as we head back in that direction toward the highway that something has accelerated. Kentucky Street, one block west of Petaluma Boulevard, is bumper-to-bumper with media trucks now—local, regional, and national. *Dateline, Primetime Live, America's Most Wanted.*

"Must be a press conference," I say.

"Another one?"

Since October 2, the day after Polly Klaas's kidnapping, media attention has been growing exponentially, and local volunteer efforts, too, Sergeant Barresi explained before we headed to see Rod Fraser. These aren't experts, just ordinary townspeople—getting involved with the search effort on their own initiative, going door-to-door, spreading the word about Polly. As Barresi told it, he's both impressed and a little in awe at the size of the response. A local business owner donated empty retail space for the Polly Klaas Search Center, and the phone banks are already up and running. Someone else has divided the town and surrounding area into a grid of seventeen locales, and over six hundred townspeople are conducting daily searches of the fields, creeks, and farmland around Petaluma. They aren't waiting to be told what to do, or how to be useful. They're acting.

Every restaurant and storefront already has Polly's missing poster in the window. Apparently the owner of a small downtown print shop has rolled out thousands of copies and challenged every other business in town with access to a printer to do the same. A mailing effort is underway sending flyers to hospital emergency rooms and police departments all over Northern California. Truck drivers and bus drivers are being given boxes of flyers to distribute on their routes, widening the net even farther.

"I've never seen anything like this," I say to Will as we move slowly back through town.

"Me neither. Four days in, she's America's Child. How does that happen?"

"The town feels responsible for her. That's rare. Do you really think they know her personally?"

"Maybe yes, maybe no," he says. "They care about her. That's what matters."

"What is there to learn here?" I ask him.

We've come to a long stoplight, and he stares at me. "That the word 'kidnapping' has a shitload of power."

"Emily should go public with a plea for help," I say. "I know why she's terrified of a media circus, but she still has a voice when most don't. Millions and millions of people know who she is. Think of what that kind of attention could do for Cameron."

"We can't force her. She's not ready, Anna."

"This isn't about *her*." I hear my voice pitch sharply. My heart has begun to thwack off rhythm. "We're wasting so much *time*. We should have had a search center and a phone bank up from the beginning. We should have been printing flyers like crazy and sending them everywhere. If we had, Cameron might be home now."

"Are you saying I fucked up?"

"Not at all," I rush to say. "I blame the family. They're the ones who begged you to keep all this quiet. Emily shouldn't have a choice to hide away."

He sighs heavily and stretches his neck to one side, trying to unknot some of the tension there. "Maybe you're right about the keeping quiet part. I should have trusted my gut on that. But you have got to back off Emily a little, okay? She's not perfect, but she's also not the enemy, Anna. She's just a mom."

"I know."

"Shit. Her life just got smacked *sideways*."

I *know*. Deep in my chest, my breath catches on a familiar jagged hook. But Cameron is what matters now.

"Maybe we don't have witnesses or a crime scene," I finally say, "but you and I both know Cameron's life is just as much at risk as Polly's."

"Not every kid lands on the milk carton," Will replies flatly, his voice seeming to come from very far away. "Some just vanish."

I can hear him hanging on to his anger about Rod and my disloyalty, but I don't care suddenly. I'm angry, too. "That's right, Will. But I'm not ready to be okay with that. Are you?"

It's taking us forever to get through the center of town. Traffic is standing still for no reason that I can see. It's the middle of the day, too early for rush hour, as if there's such a thing in a small borough like Petaluma. We're all but creeping.

Then I see why. "Will, stop the car."

Strung between two streetlights in the middle of Petaluma Boulevard, a banner has just been erected. Large work ladders still straddle the sidewalk. A dozen or more kids and their parents spill into the street looking up. A block ahead of us, the central traffic light changes to red, and we watch a woman in jeans and an open trench coat climb out of her VW Beetle. Then others follow, killing their engines to stand in the street, staring up at the bulging, colorful bubble letters: please send polly home! love p.j.h.s.

"Oh Jesus," Will says. He puts his cruiser in park and we get out, now part of whatever this is, a spontaneous gathering, a voiceless prayer.

These are Polly's classmates from the junior high school. They've painted hearts and flowers, birds and clouds, six feet high and forty-five feet long, sweeping over the street. No matter what happens next, it's amazing what they've done. Even if the sign gets forgotten one day soon, faded and abandoned in Polly's shuttered rescue center. Right now, past the puffy hearts and flowers and balloons, past cheerful hope and sweetness, innocence is a *demand*. Her seventh- and eighth-grade classmates have written a letter— sky-high and bright and *loud*—to Polly's abductor.

Thirty

Leaving Petaluma, we follow directions that Will's deputy, Leon Jentz, has passed along to Will over the radio, skirting the Petaluma River along 116 before cutting farther inland, through lush farmland and then into wine country. Emily said her brother had done well for himself, but as we drive through the more commercial, kitschy part of town, over the Napa River and onto the Silverado Trail, it becomes obvious that Drew has done much more than well. Extravagant estates glow like jewels next to big-name wineries like Stag's Leap and Mumm, their tasting terraces etched into the hillsides with million-dollar views. "Scenic" isn't the word. This is paradise, with a staggering price tag.

Will whistles as we roll through the gated entrance to Provisions, Drew Hague's private vineyard. Leon did some research for us and learned that Emily's brother and sister-in-law don't bottle or distribute their own wine, just sell the grapes in and around the valley. Their product is widely respected apparently, even prized, but it's obvious that their money was made well in advance of their success here. The curved drive carries us past sculpted cypress trees toward a Grecian-looking manse with high columns surrounding a central courtyard. It's like Tara, or the Parthenon.

"You've got to be kidding me," Will says with a chuckle.

The struts and pediments on the main house seem borrowed from the Greek Empire. Creamy-looking stucco goes on and on in every direction, much of it strung with ivy. Near the vast marble entryway, two slender deerhounds doze, barely noticing our arrival, as if like everything else they're strictly ornamental.

When we ring the bell, an assistant in a striped suit with a lapel mic lets us in, looking like a security guard crossed with a marketing director.

"Wait here, will you?" she says, depositing us in a thickly carpeted library. Custom cherry shelves gleam from floor to ceiling, filled with hardbound volumes and cataloged sets that appear to have been arranged by color. In the hearth a grand fire blazes, though it's barely October. I can feel it from across the room, and begin to sweat.

After what seems an unreasonably long interval, Lydia Hague arrives in a plain yellow T-shirt and the kind of overalls you'd buy at the local Farm & Fleet. I do a double take and watch as Will does the same before he introduces us. Whatever we've been expecting, it's not this.

"It's harvesttime," Lydia says, as if that explains everything from her unkempt silvering hair to her shoeless state, her white athletic socks plain and bright on the rich carpeting. Since she doesn't seem embarrassed, maybe it does. "My husband will be tied up for the rest of the day, I'm afraid, and into the night, too. We pick our whites after dark a lot of the time, to keep the sugar levels stable."

Her niece is missing and she wants to talk about sugar levels? "Cameron's in real trouble," I say, feeling annoyed. "He'll need to make himself available."

I'm ready for an argument, but Lydia only nods soberly and then reaches for the house phone. "Drew's on one of the tractors," she says once she's hung up, "but Janice will try to reach him."

Janice is the stripe-suited assistant, I assume.

She gestures to the seating area in front of the fire, plush and oversize. "Of course we're worried sick about Cameron. How can we help?"

Will and I share a look before sitting down. It's hard to get a bead on Lydia or this place. There's a glaring disconnect between how she looks and the palace she lives in, between her initial distractedness and her steadiness now. What's the story?

"Can you describe your relationship with your niece?" Will asks her once we're settled. "Would you say you're close?"

"We were a lot closer when she was young. Our son, Ashton, is two years older, so they grew up together, at least at holidays. We moved out here five years ago."

"Before Emily and Troy relocated to Mendocino," I fill in.

"That's right. The idea was to see each other more, but that hasn't happened as much as we'd like. We're so busy now, and Ashton is out east most of the year."

Her tone is steady, but her body language has changed and stiffened. I have a sense she's holding something back. "When did you see Cameron last?"

"In July, I guess, for Emily's birthday."

"How did she seem then?"

"Cameron? A little checked out, actually. She seemed to be going through something, but the whole day was sort of a train wreck."

I study Lydia, feeling beads of sweat pearl on my forehead. Now that I'm closer to the fire, it seems even more ridiculous and overpowering. I lean back, blotting the perspiration with my sleeve. "Would you say you and your husband have things in common with Emily and Troy?"

Lydia's brows lift. "Not really. They've made certain choices. . . ." She lets the rest of her sentence drop.

"Choices?" Will prompts.

"Emily hasn't had a typical life, I know. I try not to judge."

"But?" I encourage her.

"But we've never really understood why she stays with Troy, honestly. He's incapable of being faithful, even when they were first dating. A man like that doesn't change, and Emily should have so much more, should have her pick of anyone. It's never made any sense."

Will catches my eye. I've said as much to him about Troy's infidelity, but the pattern is a lot clearer to me now that I know Emily's family history. "What about Cameron?" I ask, shifting focus. "Has the tension in her parents' marriage changed her in your opinion?"

"Maybe," Lydia says thoughtfully. "But honestly, she's been changing for a while. Or that's how it seems to me."

"In what way?"

"More sensitive, I guess, and easily upset. Harder to get close to."

"Guarded?" I throw out.

"Maybe that's it." Her gaze darkens. "When she first came, I thought it was going to be a good thing for all of them. Emily had wanted a child for a long time. And she was always so overwhelmed by her career. *Hollywood*." Lydia says it as if she's named a virus.

"Then what?"

"I don't know exactly. At some point, Cameron seemed to shut down and go inward. Honestly, I've been worried about her for years now. Not that there was a lot of room to say that to Emily."

I sit forward, suddenly far more interested in Lydia. Will seems to agree.

"Worried how?" he presses. "About what exactly?"

"I thought she might hurt herself or something. Don't girls her age do that sometimes, cut themselves or act out self-destructively?"

"Did you ever offer her any help?" I ask.

"I tried. In July she seemed like she was barely there. When I asked, she said she was fine, but later we learned she'd just found out about the baby. Troy's assistant, no less. What a nightmare." Her look is barbed. "You know about that, I assume."

"We do," Will says. "How did Cameron find out?"

Lydia's mouth tightens irately for a moment. "His girlfriend called the house and she answered the phone. Can you imagine?"

I can't. "Troy's girlfriend told *Cameron* she was pregnant? That's cruel."

"Cruel but effective." Lydia shakes her head. "Actually it's inexcusable. Cameron was probably reeling, but we had this completely stiff birthday lunch. Crab salad and flourless chocolate cake. Emily didn't let anything slip, not a single sign that anything was wrong. But that's Emily, right?" She sighs meaningfully. "Drew and I haven't spoken to Troy since."

At the sound of Drew's name, I'm jolted back to reality. With all this talk of Cameron, I've nearly forgotten why we came. Maybe Will has, too, or maybe he's just been biding his time.

"Cameron disappeared on the twenty-first," he says. "What was going on for you and Drew that night?"

"We'd just started harvesting the pinot," Lydia explains. "We were out in the vineyards until two or three, I think."

It's obvious she means a.m. "Together?"

"That's right. It's all hands on deck from August through October. No one sleeps."

"And you started working when that night?" I ask.

"Just after dark. Around seven."

My heart sinks at the detail, not because Lydia has just given Drew a strong and verifiable alibi, but because she seems believable. Neither of these things lines up with what I want right now, which is one solid lead.

Eventually we hear a commotion in the hall, and Drew comes into the library. He takes off a dusty straw cowboy hat and drops it on an end table before shaking hands with both of us. The hat has dampened his sparse mousy hair in a silly-looking ring, pressing it flat. His face is reddened and there are flecks of silt across the bridge of his nose. He's been working hard, not playing farmer as I supposed, and I feel resentful more than relieved. I want his guilt to be glaring. For this whole scenario to be an obvious sham.

Will stands. "Mr. Hague. I'm Sheriff Flood from Mendocino County, and this is Special Agent Anna Hart. We're here about Cameron."

Drew sits without flourish. Janice has brought in iced tea on a scrolled silver tray, and he reaches for a glass, draining it in one go. "Horrible business," he says as he finishes, the cubes clattering like crystal. "And now the other girl, too. In Petaluma." He frowns.

"Your wife tells us you were harvesting the night Cameron disappeared," I step in. "Is that right?"

"Yes. This is our busiest time of year. Otherwise we'd be doing more to help."

"Have you had much contact with Emily or Troy since that night?"

"No, actually. I . . ." He flexes one of his hands over the other. "I haven't known what to say."

"We feel a little embarrassed, actually," Lydia adds. "Tension and disagreements shouldn't matter at a time like this. A family should stick together."

As Drew nods uncomfortably, I find myself looking at him, his damp hair and sweat-lined collar. At his hands, too, which are large and strong. Does he seem like a man who could hurt a fifteen-year-old girl? Or one much younger? My gut is saying he might, regardless of his alibi. It's just a feeling, completely unfounded maybe. But it's there.

"I'd like to polygraph you both," Will says. "Just standard procedure."

"Oh?" Drew looks surprised. "If that's the way you do things."

He glances at Lydia. "It might be a little difficult to schedule right now. We still have a few weeks left in this harvest."

"We don't have *weeks* here, Mr. Hague." I glare at him. "You must have staff who can pitch in if you need to be away for a few hours."

I expect him to back down right away, but he doesn't. His eyes are blue and unwavering. Emily has gotten all the beauty in the family, but Drew has something else. Even in his farm clothes, I can see he's used to wielding power. Authority. And that he's rarely challenged.

"If anyone on my property is working, you can bet I'm going to be there. It's a code we swear by around here. I hope you understand."

"Your work ethic is honorable," Will says, lingering over the word. "But we don't have time to be flexible right now. I'll expect you at my office tomorrow." He looks at Lydia. "Both of you. How's eleven a.m.?"

Drew's expression sharpens. He's angry.

"Of course," Lydia says without looking his way.

Janice appears at the door, and Drew leans forward, grabbing up his hat. When he stands, he presses into my body space for just a moment, and I feel a crackle of physical power coming off him. It's over in a blink, but I have a strange sense that the move is intentional, that he means to lean too close to me—to flex. My muscles read his subtext instantly, tense and on guard. I can't help thinking of that rape charge during his undergrad years, and how violence against women is almost never about sex, but about domination. About crushing a woman's autonomy with total control, driven by hate.

When he's gone, Lydia walks us to the door. "We've been watching the news from Petaluma. I even have a few friends who are volunteering at the search center for Polly Klaas. If getting something similar started for Cameron is a matter of money, we'd like to contribute. Drew and I have already discussed it."

Will and I exchange a look. Maybe she's feeling guilty or ashamed for not doing more right away, or maybe this offer is a veiled attempt at an apology of sorts, repayment for what her husband has done, or who he is. Some wives of sexual predators are silently complicit, while others—a very few—openly collaborate, serving as a kind of pimp for their husbands' appetites. And then there are those who know and suspect nothing, even when the abuse happens under their own roof, and not because they're ignorant or lack insight. Many offenders have the uncanny ability to show only what they want others to see. There's a level of duality—a firewall between discordant parts of their personalities. From our brief visit, there's no way of knowing where Lydia falls on the continuum.

"Good of you to offer," I tell her.

"We can discuss it more tomorrow," Will adds. "Thank you for your time."

Thirty-One

"What the hell was that?" Will asks when we're back in the car.

"Damned if I know. I don't like him, though."

"I can't tell what to think. He's got the whole midcareer Clint Eastwood thing going. But then you also get the feeling he's been in a lot of boardrooms swinging his weight around and signing big checks."

"And that stuff about no one on his property working if he's not there? Is he for real?"

Will shrugs, starting the engine. "He's got an alibi either way."

Unfortunately, I can't argue. I take one more glance at the house, the stately disproportionate front entrance where the two deer-hounds sit in profile. They haven't moved an inch since we first arrived, as if they've been glued in place. An operation like this needs lots of hands to make it run smoothly, but I don't see anyone around. Maybe they're all well back in the vineyards, or in the out-buildings, occupied with the crush or whatever goes on by day, but it's still an odd picture, like an enormous beehive, perfectly constructed and full of honey, but utterly empty of drones.

"I still wouldn't rule out Drew for the abuse piece," I say. "He wasn't on a tractor back then."

"Good point," he agrees as we head back down the long, manicured drive. "What did you make of her?"

"Lydia? I don't know. A few things she said about Cameron seemed pretty insightful. But if she does care, why hasn't she reached out to Emily and Troy since Cameron disappeared? You'd think she'd be camped out in their living room like families do for one another. None of it fits."

"Even if it's the *harvest*," he says pointedly. "They don't need the money."

"Exactly. And if they're pissed at Troy, why not show up and make a stand? Did you hear what Lydia said about Cameron having a change in personality from when she first came? She's been worried, okay. But why keep that to herself?"

Will grumbles his agreement as we pull back out onto the main road, where the vineyards run in long lines, on and on in a symmetry of red-gold light. Strings of colored tinsel flicker from wires above the vines, there to keep the birds away, but beautiful in their own right. This is why tourists come to wine country, not just to get tipsy from tiny pours of Cabernet Sauvignon, but to be inside this world, where every surface mirrors back the sun.

I try to get comfortable for the long drive home, but my shoulders still feel tense and weighted. Will's radio is tuned to his own department's air. One of his deputies comes on to report a 10-15, a domestic disturbance. Will leans forward, listening intently until another deputy is dispatched. Only then do I ask him what's been on my mind for a while. "What are the chances of getting a warrant to unseal Cameron's adoption file?" I ask Will.

"Why? What do you think you might find?"

"I'm not sure, but I'm still stuck on when Cameron's abuse might have happened. If it was Drew, interviewing her birth family might help us eliminate the earlier part of her life. Or who knows. Maybe someone from back then has found her here? Stranger things have happened."

"I can try. What did you think of Lydia offering to help with a search center?"

"If she's serious, you should have no problem taking her money. But even a big fat check might not help us get the town involved. That's what's really working in Petaluma."

"We've been over this, Anna. I can't compete with 'kidnapped at knifepoint.' Nothing here pushes those same alarm bells. And Polly was clearly a very special girl. You saw. Those people feel personally invested. You can't fake that and you can't force it, either."

"No," I have to concede. "But we can work to give people more of a sense of who we're trying to find. You've said yourself that the Curtises have always kept their distance from the community. That has to be part of the problem. What about calling a town meeting and asking for support, just flat out? Do a big shout-out to the media first to get them there. Tell them we have breaking news."

"Do we?" Even in profile, his eyes on the snaking road, Will looks annoyed.

"Maybe we will by then, and if not, we show them our turnout, the whole town coming out for Cameron. We put pictures of her everywhere, and then you stand up and say her name ten times. Twenty times."

"It can't be that easy."

"What else have we got?"

He doesn't answer. For a long moment the vineyards clip by, green and gold and deep purple. Dusk light is like a soft warm animal lowering its body over the round yellow hills and live oaks.

"I can reach out to Gray," I try again, "and Steve Gonzales, too. The kids at the high school have all been traumatized. This might help. They could feel more active and empowered. We can't just leave them wrestling with those feelings. You know how bad it can get. They need to *do* something."

"I guess it's worth a try. Troy and Emily might not like this angle, though."

Screw them, I want to say but manage not to. "Maybe they'll come around."

It's dark when Will drops me off at the GoodLife. My legs feel rubbery from being in the car most of the day, and the waistband of my jeans has gouged ridges into the flesh of my still-soft stomach. I decide to walk off my anxiety instead of taking it to a barstool at Patterson's, and the moment I do, I feel rewarded. The wind picks up as soon as I reach the end of Lansing Street, scrubbing over me with every salt-filled gust, rinsing off the day.

At the edge of the bluff, I look down at Big River Beach and know immediately that it's the setting of my nightmare, the one with the girl running through kelp and driftwood, being chased or hunted. The night is cloudy and the way is dark, but I can see the first few earthen steps leading down the grooved, sandy bank ahead of me, and start down, ignoring the little flares of warning. I'm isolated here if I fall, or worse.

And yet I don't stop. I know this path, or my muscles do, remembering how to drop low and feel along the cliffside for handholds, clumps of bunchgrass, like fistfuls of hair. The last few steps have been washed away, but I scramble past the treacherous spots on my butt, pushing off with my hands to drop the last three feet into damp sand. It gives with a soft wet sound, and I catch my balance, feeling triumphant for a moment. Then: *How will I get back up again?*

As my eyes adjust, I can see the beach is empty. Low tide has left a long ragged string of kelp. I can smell it decaying wetly as I make my way to the water's edge, the sand seeming almost phosphorescent in the gloom, the feel of it loose and creamy under my boots as I skirt pieces of twisted white driftwood. As a girl, I always thought they looked like human bones, and I have to admit they still do.

Out across the water, the mast light of a night fisherman flashes red. Farther out, another light answers—but that's just how it looks from here. In truth the boats are at least a mile apart. Neither knows the other, probably. They can't hear each other either except through their VHF radios, through the static.

"You okay down there?" a deep male voice shouts from the top of the bluff.

I jump, startled. Above, his hulking silhouette is faceless, completely without contour. It's hard not to feel cornered. I look up and down the beach pointlessly, and then call out, "I'm fine."

"You look stuck."

"No, I'm good," I shout back at the figure.

He doesn't answer, just makes a noncommittal wave, his shadow breaking up and then retreating, thankfully. When I'm alone again, I feel safer, but still have to find a way out of here. The jump I made getting down doesn't work for up, obviously. Feeling stupid for my predicament, I pace back and forth along the cliff wall, looking for a better way, but there isn't one. No handholds or well-placed gouges. The wind has picked up and I'm shivering now, too. If I have to sleep down here, I'm going to freeze to death.

"Hey!" The voice comes again. He's back.

Shit.

"Watch out, I'm throwing down a rope."

Thirty-Two

Even with the rope, the climb is a struggle. The fibers are rough and feel like woody splinters, eating into my palms as I inch my way along the cliff face, banging up my elbows and knees. The muscles in my back contract, and my thighs begin to burn. Why does this look so easy in action movies, I wonder, and who is this guy anyway, some well-meaning neighbor or passerby, or a full-on villain? And how the hell did I end up here, letting a stranger hold my body weight, with no choice at all but to keep going?

When I finally reach the top, he gives me his hand and pulls me, breathless and full of adrenaline, over the ragged lip of the bluff and onto the path. It's the Summer of Love hippie guy from Rotary Park. The street behind him is empty, the storefronts flat and dark.

"I remember you," he says, dropping the length of rope at his feet. "Not too safe down there, you know."

I glance up and down the path we're standing on, weighing my options if this goes bad, and then back at his face and body, trying to read him. He's a big guy, big enough to snap a girl's neck in two without difficulty. Big enough to take me out if that's where this is going. "I'm fine. I know what I'm doing. Thanks, though."

"Last month, a rogue wave took a guy right out to sea. Happened at Devil's Punchbowl. They come from nowhere."

His speech is odd and clipped, the sentences coming in sharp little fragments. But he also hasn't moved toward me or said anything particularly threatening. "I'll keep that in mind."

"I'm Clay LaForge. My girl and I were just sitting in the park when we saw you go by a bit ago. When you didn't come back through, she sent me to check."

"Oh." I can hardly believe what he's saying. Most people don't give a damn about anyone who doesn't directly touch their lives. "That's . . . nice of her."

"We all got to watch out for each other, that's what she's always saying. What were you doing down there, anyway?"

"Nothing. Just thinking, I guess. Did that person drown? The one out at Devil's Punchbowl?"

"For sure," he says almost cheerfully. "Tourists. Think they know things they don't."

It's not just his way of talking that's unusual, I realize, but everything he's saying. He's like a character from a storybook, a wizard trafficking in metaphors, or a hermit holding out three magic beans—or, in this case, a rope. The whole encounter is odd, but unless I'm missing something glaring, he doesn't seem dangerous to me. In fact, he could be useful. He's not a tourist, but something more than a local, even. He sleeps in the park, or so I assume from the tent I saw the other day, where he can watch everyone the way he's just watched me—like a TV show he can turn on and off by rolling over.

"Has anyone from the sheriff's office come and interviewed you and your friends about the missing girl, Cameron Curtis?" I ask.

"Why? Because we're the closest thing this town has to a criminal element?" He might be winking a little as he says it. Even under the streetlamps, the light isn't good. Either he's amused or I've offended him.

"You're outside most of the time." I try to elaborate. "You know everyone who lives here by sight. I'm thinking you'd catch it if something was off. Or someone."

He nods, his features muddy. "Lots of kids come by the park on their way to the beach, smoking sometimes. Every once in a while one of them asks us to buy beer or a fifth of Four Roses. But not that girl. I'm not sure I ever saw her come through. If I did, she didn't stand out."

"Do you think this is a safe town? You guys camp out, right?"

He shrugs. "Sometimes outside feels safer than inside. You know exactly what you're up against."

It's the sort of thing Hap might have said. "How long have you lived here?"

"Couple years. My girl always wanted to live by the ocean. I said sure, let's try it. We were in Denver before. The sun shines every damned day there, right through the snow sometimes. But Lenore said the altitude turned her upside down."

"Lenore? That the woman I met the other day?"

He nods. "She doesn't like people all that much. I'm surprised she talked to you."

"My family had a pet raven named Lenore once."

"What, in the house?" He shakes his head, frowning. "You can't tame an animal like that. Bad luck."

"She was a rescue animal. One of her wings didn't work." I don't even know why I'm telling him the story, or why I can still see her scuttling around the house after Eden, begging for raisins and blueberries and pellets of dog food. She could talk, too, but only had one phrase, something she'd pulled from her life before, *Don't you, don't you.* "She scared me to death," I find myself saying to Clay. "I thought she could read my mind."

"Of course she could," he says without faltering. "All birds are telepathic."

As odd as Clay is, I can't help but like him a little, this sort of transient hippie outcast, living under a tarp in Rotary Park but thinking of the mountains, or Waterloo, not totally in this world or any other. "Where's your Lenore tonight?"

"Back at the tent. I should probably go let her know you're okay. She's a worrier."

"The surf isn't really what's most dangerous right now, Clay. Whoever took this missing girl might be walking around among us."

"Wouldn't surprise me if he was. Small town like this one. Anything can be happening right next door and you'd never know."

It's the second time in minutes he's reminded me of Hap. "Who would you look closely at, then? As a suspect?"

A look moves over his face that's hard to read in the darkness. But then I place it. I'm taking him seriously and he's flattered. "Everyone, I guess. I don't think it's like the movies. Some *Friday the Thirteenth* thing. I'll bet he looks like us on the outside. All the really scary stuff's on the inside, where probably no one's ever seen it."

It's a good insight. "You should have been a detective," I say.

"Maybe I'm undercover," he replies, grinning. Then he looks over his shoulder, past the circle of light thrown by the streetlamp overhead, into the length of the dark street. "Here she comes now."

"Lenore?"

"No, your dog."

Thirty-Three

I was sixteen when Eden got sick, at the beginning of my sixth year with them. Her symptoms were confusing at first, nausea and dizziness and night sweats. Her doctor told her it was menopause and would pass.

"Menopause my ass!" Hap burst out at dinner one night, while Eden picked at her plate. "You've lost forty pounds!"

He rarely raised his voice, because he never had to. Eden became visibly upset, and so did Lenore. "Don't you, don't you!" she warned from her chair.

I knew ravens could be as smart as parrots, but Lenore was more than smart. She seemed to read our moods easily, and to smell fear. I looked back and forth between Hap and Eden, wishing I could sense what was happening in Eden's body, or that she could. That for once she could appear in her own dreams.

"I'll go back in," Eden promised Hap. "I'll make him give me something."

"I'll go with you," he said, not remotely mollified. "We'll see if that doctor has the nerve to ladle out that same vague horseshit when I'm in the room."

But he had.

———

It was a full year later before we knew Eden had endometrial cancer. On her last good day, we went to Point Cabrillo, and looked for whales. We brought lawn chairs, hot coffee, and blankets for our laps. It was fiercely windy that afternoon, with wind hammering a million divots in the surface of the bay.

"If I were any kind of water," Eden said, staring out and out, "I'd want to be this ocean."

You already are, I wanted to tell her. *You're everything I can see.*

Those hours together seemed to last for ages. We counted six humpbacks.

"Six is the number for spirit," Eden said.

We saw wind flap over the kelp beds, flags of green and gold. And then the sunset, and the first evening star flickering awake. And then the moon rose like a pearled shard of beach glass, fractured and whole all at once.

Three weeks later, Eden died in her sleep under a pink afghan, small as a child by then, and incoherent from morphine. When Hap came to tell me she was gone, his face buckled. I'd never seen him cry, and he didn't then, just hovered on the edge of what he couldn't bear, but had to somehow. One day I would know this exact state with horrifying intimacy. In that moment, I could only stand by numbly while he went back to the bedroom they shared and closed himself in to be alone with her. No one was going to rush him to call the coroner. Not for this woman, his life for more than thirty years. Not until he was good and ready.

My own goodbye seemed impossible. I wasn't ready to lose Eden. I couldn't. In a kind of trance I made for the woods, barely feeling the hike. Miles from town, trekking straight down Little Lake Road, I reached the Jackson State Forest and left the trail almost immediately, plunging up the side of a steep ravine and down again, forcing my way through wet ferns and spongy undergrowth. There were signs of fire damage, the hearts of trees burned black and gutted.

By the time I broke into a stand of old-growth redwoods, my muscles were spent and my clothes were damp with sweat. The trees were hundreds of feet tall, toweringly still. Hap had told me once how trees as old and big as these only took one breath a day. How if I really wanted to understand them or even a single tree, I had to be there in the moment it breathed.

"Really?"

"Sure. Oceans breathe, too," he said. "Mountains. Everything."

I dropped in the center of the ring of trees, down into the litter of needles and dust and lichen. It wasn't prayer, exactly, but something Eden had emphasized over the years. When things got hard and you felt shaky, she liked to say, you could hit your knees wherever you were, and the world would be there to catch you.

I'd had too many mothers, and not enough mothering. Eden was the closest I'd ever gotten to feeling like a real daughter. And now she was gone. I stilled myself and waited for faith to come, for some sign of how to go on without her, but nothing arrived. Nothing except waves of chills from my own cooling sweat, and a sadness that seemed to settle into the spaces between the trees, between the trunks and branches, between the needles and leaves, between the molecules. It climbed inside my body and curled up tightly under my ribs, like a fist made of silver thread.

Finally I stood on weak legs and began the long walk home. It was well past dark when I got there, no porch light on, and all the rooms dark. When I went into the kitchen and turned on the lights, Lenore flinched. She'd somehow clawed her way up onto Eden's chair at the table, and as I stepped closer she flared, her feathers plumping around her neck in an angry collar, as if she was protecting the space.

"You hungry?" I asked.

Glaring silence.

I found the bag of dog food and put a few pellets out for her on the lip of the chair anyway, but the minute my hand drew close, she flapped out with her good wing, neck feathers bulging, just missing me.

I hit her without thinking. Her body was far more solid than I expected, thick and unbending as something carved of wood.

She struck back instantly, stabbing the flesh near my thumb with her beak, both wings up now, even the broken one.

"Stop it!" I raised my hand again, knowing I'd crossed a line. No one was supposed to hurt animals, ever. Eden would have hated to see us like this, but I found I couldn't help myself. I couldn't back down.

"Don't you," Lenore warned, the same phrase as ever, but it made sense, finally. She was talking to me about now, about us. The look in her eyes was so cold my heart turned over.

I lunged for her, grabbing up her thick body and catching her off guard. She churned against my chest horribly, thrashing and fighting, trying to get free while I pressed her tighter. Opening the front door, I threw her into the yard and then slammed the door behind me fast, locking it. Then I hurried to my room and slammed that door, too, lying facedown on my bed, roiling with hatred and guilt and shame and who knew what else.

Oh, honey, Eden would have said. *Who are you really mad at?*

You. But that wasn't right, either. Nothing was right. My eyes burned. My heart was on fire with emptiness.

After half an hour or so—I had no idea, really—I got up and moved quietly through the house to the front door. I opened it, expecting her to be on the mat or the front walk, but Lenore had gone. I panicked, rushing to find her. But she wasn't under the hedge or around to the side of the house. She wasn't cowering near the garage or between the trash cans. I grabbed the boxy flashlight, big as a thermos, which Hap kept in the front hall closet for stormy nights when the power would cut out, and pointed it into the inky night, whispering Lenore's name over and over instead of shouting the way I wanted to. I was afraid to wake Hap, or Eden, maybe, wherever she was now, up near the stars, or down the ragged coastline, searching and patient, an unhoused beam of light.

Eventually I gave up and came back into the kitchen, collapsing into the chair where the whole nightmare had started, next to the abandoned pile of dog-food pellets. I'd done something terrible and on purpose and I couldn't take it back just because I felt sorry. Sorry wouldn't find her. Sorry was maybe the loneliest feeling of all, I understood, because it only brought you back to yourself.

Thirty-Four

As the dog trots up to us, Clay LaForge's smile is wide, as if the universe has just cracked a joke. Maybe it has. "People always say elephants have great memories, but I'd put a dog up against an elephant any day."

"I can't take care of a dog."

He keeps smiling that mysterious smile. "You know we don't actually keep them, right? They choose to stay or they don't. That's any animal, mind you."

I'm still thinking of Eden's Lenore, so the words tumble out of me, unfiltered.

"I've made mistakes."

He only stands there, nodding as if to say *Of course you have.* Then he snaps his fingers, and the dog's attention shoots to him instantly. "I get the feeling you can't screw up here. See the markings in her face and her reddish color? She's got Belgian Malinois in her. Not many breeds smarter or more intuitive. That's why they make good police dogs. They partner with humans to make a team."

"How do you *know* all this?"

"I was a trainer once, in another life. I'd put her age at four or five. She's lost muscle from living on the streets, but seems healthy otherwise. You'll want to get some raw protein in her and not just kibble. Salmon oil is good for her coat and vision."

"Clay . . ." I'm backpedaling, fumbling for another argument, but his attention is back on the dog. Kneeling at her side, he runs a steady, knowledgeable hand from the top of her skull to her tail and back while the dog submits to his touch.

"Yep," he says quietly, still bent over. "Some breeds are hard-wired to know what we need before we do. She's good and sound. Strong, too. Can't imagine asking for a better partner."

I don't need a partner, something in me wants to insist, but even I know how thin the excuse is. How blatantly untrue. "I can't believe this is happening," I say instead.

"Yeah." Clay chuckles. "Life's funny that way."

He walks with us as far as Rotary Park, where his girl, Lenore, waits at the picnic bench in the same outfit as before, Seahawks sweatshirt long as a skirt, her hair like a dense blond scribble above her lined forehead.

"Oh, good," she says in a low voice. "You're okay."

"Thanks for sending Clay to look for me."

"I thought maybe you ran into trouble."

"No. I'm fine." I look back and forth between them feeling inexplicably grateful for their presence. We don't even know each other, and yet we're here.

"What's your dog's name?" Clay asks me.

"Good question. Too bad she can't tell me."

"Oh, she can. Just not in English."

I reach Mendosa's Market only minutes before it closes, leaving the dog in a down-stay just outside the door while I look quickly and in vain for salmon oil. They have only tinned sardines and anchovies. I buy both, plus a fillet of salmon, almost luridly pink against the white butcher paper as the clerk wraps it, and dog food—wet and dry.

My items are rolling down the conveyor belt when I notice Caleb, his arms full of groceries.

"Hey." His eyes flick over my purchases. "You have a dog?"

I feel flustered for some reason, almost embarrassed. "I've rescued her. I must be crazy, right?"

"I always wanted one, but my dad was allergic," he says offhandedly, but not quite. Just beneath the remark is a shadow of emotional accounting. A tick mark in the column where life has shorted him—or not life per se but Jack Ford.

As we move outside, there's a dance of sorts as Caleb and the dog say hello.

"She's really pretty," he says. "Looks smart, too."

"So I've been told."

We drift toward my Bronco, where I load the groceries, and then the dog jumps into the back seat as if she already knows her place. My back is still turned when Caleb says, "I ran into Will yesterday. He told me you're helping him with that missing girl."

I spin to face him, more than a little surprised. Will and I agreed to my being incognito. "My role isn't official or anything."

"I see. I thought you were just passing through is all."

"Me too." I close the tailgate with a thump. "Are you really doing okay, Caleb? You can tell me."

His eyes flit toward mine without landing. Then he says, "I don't really talk about those days, Anna. It's just way easier not to."

"No, of course. I get it. Listen, do you want to grab a drink or something? My treat."

"Nah, I have to get home." He hefts up the groceries in his arms like a prop, an excuse. "Rain check?"

"Sure, yeah. I'll see you soon."

———

On my way out of town, I roll down the window and turn up the radio, Bob Seger's "Against the Wind" filling the car, which feels more solid somehow with the dog stretched out across the back seat as if she owns it. I assumed there'd be a big adjustment period for both of us, but the dog at least seems totally relaxed and unconcerned.

Back at the cabin, she finds a place by the woodstove and waits patiently for her dinner. I cook half the salmon for myself, searing it for a few minutes on each side in a hot skillet as the oil pops. We eat together and then she stretches out near my feet, while I sit up with Cameron's copy of *Jane Eyre,* looking for clues in the passages she's underlined and dog-eared. *I have little left in myself— I must have you; The soul, fortunately, has an interpreter . . . in the eye; He made me love him without looking at me; Are you anything akin to me, do you think, Jane?*

The book seems to be a puzzle like everything else about Cameron, but can I solve it? Is the key to her dilemma and her pain here in the pages of her ravaged Penguin Classics paperback, or am I looking in the wrong place, for the wrong thing, grasping at straws?

I put down the book feeling my eyes burn, and watch the dog instead. The tip of her dark nose lightly touches the wall as her belly rises and falls rhythmically, as if whatever life she's had before now doesn't take up space or trouble her in the least. She sleeps so peacefully it makes the whole room feel lighter, and warmer.

Thirty-Five

"We've got this," Will tells me the next morning before the polygraph technician arrives from Sacramento to interview Lydia and Drew Hague. "You said you were going to talk to Gray and Steve Gonzales about drumming up support for the search center, right?"

"They'll be in school all day. I can help you here."

"We've got enough hands on deck. Get some rest and we'll connect later?"

"*Rest?*" I ask incredulously. "When we've got two missing girls, and maybe three?"

His look tells me to drop it. "It's just a few hours. I'll check in with you later." Then he turns on his heel and leaves me wondering if he's punishing me for Petaluma and Rod Fraser. Maybe he's still fuming over missing resources and manpower or maybe it's some deeper thing, our disagreement over Emily's polygraph results, or what he said at Patterson's about my getting too emotionally involved with this case for my own good. Whatever his reasons, he seems to be drawing a clear line, with me on the other side.

I climb back into my Bronco feeling irritated, held in check. "Do you want to rest?" I ask the dog when her head pops up from the back seat.

She shifts her ears forward, widens her eyes, listening.

"Yeah, me neither."

First we drive toward the patch of the coast road that abuts the Curtises' property. Since my conversation with Emily, I haven't let go of the theory that Cameron might have disabled the alarm and slipped out her window and through the woods to meet someone waiting there. Someone who'd promised something valuable to her—love, maybe, or freedom from the pressures and upheaval in her home. Someone she mistook for a life jacket when she felt she was drowning inside.

The stretch of road is far enough from town to be isolated, just past a large undeveloped meadow a few miles from Caspar, where only a handful of residents live. The houses I do see as I park along the verge are well concealed behind privacy fences. Even if Cameron's abductor had idled here at the roadside, waiting for her to appear, it would have been late and dark, with little chance of anyone spotting him, let alone noting the make and model of his car.

I get out with the dog at my heels and look for signs anyway—trampling, oil stains, tire marks, footprints. We comb both sides of the road carefully, and then backtrack through the meadow and woods, scanning for anything off-key. He could have overpowered her immediately and dragged her somewhere nearby. He could have discarded her body in the ferns, or buried her in a shallow grave. The grim possibilities roll through me, because this is my job. I'm looking for a body, knowing we might never find one. And then there is the irrational part of me that can't let go of the possibility that Cameron is still alive. The two sides of me are in constant battle. My mind believes she's gone forever. My heart can't accept that. Won't.

It's almost noon when I finally stop, my jeans damp at the cuff and my feet tired. I walk back to my car and just sit behind the wheel for a long time, wondering where to go next. And then it hits me, the psychic.

Tally Hollander isn't hard to locate. I find her name in a phone book in town and then drive to the address in Comptche in less than twenty minutes, finding the driveway marked with a large painted sign that says abundance farm: alpaca wool and milk sold here. Most of the psychics and mediums I've worked with over the years have been unassuming, even frumpy. But an alpaca farmer? Who knew you could milk one anyway?

Up the curving drive stands a modern farmhouse with a wide wraparound porch and sloping corrugated metal roof. To one side, a shiny Airstream trailer sits with a red-and-white awning stretched over the entrance. A chalkboard is propped there, spelling out the names of her animals and the prices of various items, milk and cheese and wool, honey and jam and fresh flowers. I'm beginning to think you couldn't make up a woman like this except as a character in a movie.

I climb out of my Bronco and the dog follows, ignoring the animals like the trustworthy sidekick she obviously is. A woman walks out onto her front porch in a long linen dress with an apron over it, double tied at the waist, and gray felt clogs. Her hair is cut in an edgy crimson bob, with quirky asymmetrical bangs.

"Can I help you?" she asks.

"I hope so. I'm Anna Hart, a detective working with the Mendocino sheriff's department. Do you have a few minutes to talk?"

"Of course." She rests her hands on her hips in an open, sunny way. "And you brought a friend. Why don't you both come on in?"

Tally's kitchen is cluttered and cozily dim, an L shape that traces the line of the wraparound porch. Along her wooden countertop, jars full of herbs sit squeezed between a collection of books that don't seem to belong to a single reader, let alone in a kitchen, a volume on climate change next to Agatha Christie next to the poems of Alexander Pushkin.

She lights the kettle and brings a ceramic bowl full of tangerines to her round kitchen table, where I sit, watching her putter, the dog at my feet. She's fifty or a little older and pretty, with fine lines around her mouth and eyes that show me she's spent time outdoors, in the sun. The way she's dressed and carries herself seems much more typical of a painter than a psychic to me, but that's probably Northern California. Everyone's a painter here, or a potter, or a jewelry maker, or all three.

"I'm sure you know there are several missing girls in the area," I say. "Your name came up recently in relation to Shannan Russo."

"That's right." She sits across from me, resting her hands on the table, palms up. It's an unusual gesture, but the main thing I notice is that she doesn't seem nervous or put off by my being here. "I phoned her mother. I felt I had to."

"Shannan's been missing since June, Tally. Why call now?"

"I woke up with her name in my mind and the strong feeling that she'd been murdered."

"Is this typical for you? This sort of vision?"

She blinks at me thoughtfully. "I've always had the gift if that's what you mean. When I was younger, I didn't understand the messages or what I was supposed to do about them. It's not always clear how I can help, but lately, the feelings and images have been very strong. Not just about Shannan, either. I reached out to Sheriff Flood to try and talk to him about Cameron Curtis almost two weeks ago, but he didn't want to hear what I had to share."

I sit forward, remembering the conversation I'd overheard in the café my first day back, the two men arguing about this very thing, and whether or not Tally was a con artist. They must have heard the story from Will or someone in his office. If she is a con artist— and she might be—I can't see her angle just yet.

"Do you think Cameron's still alive, Tally?"

"I do, but she won't stay that way if you don't stop him." She looks at me levelly. "There's a lot of mystery in the universe. I don't pretend to understand everything that comes through me, but I do my best not to be afraid of it, either."

"What did Karen say when you called?"

"She cried. She feels it's all her fault, that she pushed Shannan away."

"Really? Will Flood got the impression Karen washed her hands of Shannan a long time ago."

"Maybe that's a defense mechanism for guilt. When Shannan was little, there were a lot of men around, a lot of instability. Violence. She has a good deal of regret."

"Karen said this?"

"People tell me all kinds of things, Anna. They seem to need to. I think it helps them feel less burdened."

"So she believed you?"

Tally's eyes are clear as museum glass. She doesn't blink or pause. "Yes. Maybe she'll be able to grieve now, and find more peace. Everyone deserves that, wouldn't you agree?"

Along the floor at my feet, the dog stirs. I inch my leg closer to her body, warm and solid, but still feel uneasy, as if Tally is talking about my life, not Karen's. "Anything else from the dream?"

"Shannan was wearing a rabbit-fur jacket, short waisted with a zipper. Very soft, soft as anything."

"Does the coat mean something? Was she wearing it when she died? Is there evidence in one of the pockets?"

"Possibly. I'm only a conduit, Anna. You're the detective. If anyone can solve these mysteries, it's you." Her tone shifts, sharpens. "Do you believe in the other side? In life after death?"

A muscle between my shoulder blades tenses. Wherever she's headed with this, I don't want to go there. "What else do you have to tell me about Cameron Curtis?"

"I dreamed about her just after she went missing." She doesn't seem fazed that I've changed the subject midstream. "What's that? Ten or twelve days ago now? She was alone and in some sort of tight small space. Badly hurt, too, but definitely alive."

"Alive" is a powerful word, even when the source isn't necessarily reliable. "Somewhere nearby? Did you recognize anything?"

"I don't think so." She studies her teacup, the moss-green ceramic curve of it between her fingers. Then she says, "You don't trust me. That's fine, except some part of you does, or wants to. In your heart you hope I can help you get to Cameron."

Her sudden intimacy makes me uncomfortable. What could she possibly know about my heart? "Have you done this sort of thing professionally before? Worked with law enforcement?"

She nods. "When I lived up in Oregon, outside of Portland. I've only been here a little more than a year now. I forgot how small towns work sometimes, how nervous folks can be about things that aren't exactly rational. But I believe any sort of insight comes with responsibility. I think I can help you find her, Anna."

"Me? Why not go back to Will Flood? Maybe he'll listen to you now."

"You know he won't." She picks up her saucer and sets it down again. "We're all just energy, you know, me, you, this table, this town. All moving at certain frequencies. When we pass from this life, our essence keeps going, keeps moving."

The airiness of her vocabulary is irritating, or maybe it's more than that. "What's your point?"

She bats away my hostility without effort. "There are things that change us fundamentally on this side, too, like loss and trauma. Just think about it. We know trauma changes the brain. Why wouldn't it affect our energy? Of course it would. It does. You're the right person to help now, Anna."

"What do you mean? Why?"

"This is your life's work for a reason. The things you've lost have drawn you to help these children and young women. I think you know that already, but you can't see what I can."

My chest feels tight listening to her. I don't want to know more, except I do. "What?"

"The ghosts of the kids you've helped, they hang on you like stars. They're all around you, even now."

Like *stars*? The image feels almost ludicrous. Spangled with loss. Despair. "What do you want from me?"

"You came to see me, if you remember." She pauses, looking at her chapped pink hands. A workingwoman's hands. "I'm just the messenger here, Anna. I don't know who took Cameron, but I feel a lot of darkness and chaos coming from him. He doesn't really want to kill her, but he doesn't know if he can stop himself. He's trying to fight his own demons, but they're powerful. I don't think Shannan was his first victim, Anna. And Cameron won't be his last, either, if he's not stopped."

I hate everything she's saying, even if I haven't quite made up my mind about believing her. "*Can* we stop him?"

"I think so."

Against my legs, the dog twitches, flexing in a dream of running or hunting. The warm side of her body rises and falls, with a small wheezing pause between the two.

Tally looks down at her, too, her expression softening. "She sounds like a cricket, doesn't she?"

She does, I think, before refocusing. "We're running out of time, Tally. With every day that passes, the odds grow slimmer that we'll find Cameron alive."

"Learning more about Shannan might bring you closer."

"That's what my gut tells me. We have aerial surveillance going, looking for her car. But we're talking about a thousand square miles of wilderness. It's like a needle in a haystack."

"Some people find those needles, though, don't they? I think it's going to work out somehow. You were drawn here after all. The universe doesn't do random."

"Who *are* you?" I ask again, a faint roaring in my ears.

"I told you, I'm just the messenger."

Thirty-Six

"What's the story?" Will asks when we meet in front of Patterson's later that day. He eyes Cricket. It wasn't in English, as Clay had predicted, but with a little help from Tally, she'd managed to tell me her name.

"My new partner."

That wins me a real smile if a small one. "You get some rest today?"

"A little," I lie.

As it turns out, Wanda speaks dog and won't hear of letting Cricket sit outside while we eat, even though the cook releases a string of epithets, shaking his fist. She waves him off and brings us the lunch special, fish sandwiches and coleslaw with a vinegar tang. Then Will fills me in on his morning with the Hagues.

"His polygraph didn't turn up anything suspicious, and neither did Lydia's. I had Leon do some more digging for us, too. He interviewed some of the staff at Provisions and a few of the neighbors as well. Apparently Drew's alibi checks out for that night. He was working with his crew, lots of witnesses. Plus, it turns out the rape charge wasn't black and white. The girl was seventeen, not sixteen, with a police record no less. A few months before, she solicited an undercover vice agent with an offer of a 'date.' After that, Drew seems to have cleaned his shit up. You saw. He's the emperor of Napa Valley. A model citizen."

"I saw." I can't keep the skepticism out of my voice. "But there was something else, too, when we met them yesterday. I don't know. I just had a feeling he doesn't like women. That he's threatened by them."

"Based on what?"

"Just a sense I got."

He waits for me to say more, but I don't have more. "Well, Troy seems to like women too much."

"His assistant, you mean? The girlfriend?"

"*Former* assistant," he clarifies. "Indiana Silverstein. She's twenty-two and not talking. I got the details from another woman who used to be his office assistant at Paramount. She requested a transfer two years ago after just six months at Troy's desk."

"Let me guess. He made advances."

"And big promises. As I understand it, most of the administrative team is made up of young hopefuls trying to be discovered."

"What a pig. But at least this one didn't give in to him. Did she have anything to say about her replacement?"

"Only that Indiana is keeping the baby."

"Can we find out if he's tried to pay her off?"

"Not without a warrant, and we have no reason to seek one. Not yet anyway. Maybe it's not out of the question that he really has feelings?"

I push the coleslaw on my plate with the tip of my fork. "Oh, please. I don't believe that for a second."

"Maybe I don't either," Will says, "but so what? Does being an asshole philanderer mean he could have hurt Cameron?"

"It still could be Drew Hague, couldn't it?" I race to fill in. "Just because he has an alibi for the twenty-first doesn't mean he wasn't the one to target her back then. Maybe you could bring him in again for questioning and widen the frame?"

"Okay." Will twists the napkin in his hand as if it's a tourniquet. "But even if Drew did abuse Cameron years ago, his alibi clears him on the night she disappeared. Which means it's someone else entirely. Maybe a family friend, or a neighbor, or a teacher? In LA, maybe, before the family moved up here?"

"Maybe." I feel an inward sputtering. We're short on leads and even shorter on time. And I've been hoping to see my hunches line up. Now what? Now *who*? "I need to think."

"Well, while you're thinking, chew on this. At 3:02 p.m. yesterday, Marc Klaas's phone rings in Sausalito at his place. He answers, and a little girl says, 'Daddy, it's me.' "

"What?"

"The call lasts less than a minute. She says she's at a hotel but doesn't know where. That a man took her, that she's scared and hungry. Then click."

"Klaas believes it was really Polly?"

"Says he'd swear by it, but here's the thing. There was no trap trace on the line."

"Holy shit," I blurt. "How'd that happen?"

"The girl resides with her mother. The trap is there, on Eve Nichol's line. Seems no one thought that far."

"If it was Polly, why would she call Dad and not Mom?" I can't help asking. "It's Mom she lives with most of the time."

Will shrugs. "Maybe the call had to be local? She's in San Francisco? Anyway, we won't know now. Not unless she calls back."

My thoughts race to Rod Fraser. A mistake like this isn't just fodder for the media, but potentially lethal for his career. And then there are the personal ramifications. The self-blame that will no doubt be louder and more punishing than anything anyone else could aim at him. "Poor Rod. Jesus."

"I know. Can you imagine missing something this big? When the media catches wind, that town will lose their fucking minds. Maybe we're glad we don't have that kind of circus here after all."

"It's the risk you run when you play big." Over the bar, the TV is tuned to a soccer game in Argentina, but a news banner scrolls beneath with the latest on Polly's case. Her name and face are known all around the world, and yet aside from this missed call, no one has seen or heard from her in a week. It makes me feel more anxious than I'd like to admit about our own case. "Anything happening on the town meeting?"

"I reserved the community center for Saturday and have a request in for taking over the building full-time as a rescue center. The *Mendocino Beacon* has agreed to mass-produce Cameron's missing poster for mailings."

"Saturday's good," I agree. "We'll get better attendance, maybe some tourists, too. That room should look full." I scan the tables around us for confirmation. These are the very people we want on our side. "I'm going to talk to Gray right after this, and then Emily. We need to have pictures plastered everywhere for the cameras. Images move people. Seeing Cameron's face at different ages will make her more real. Those missing posters might as well be invisible."

"I get that," Will says. "I wish we had stronger language before we run the new printing. Obviously we can't say 'Kidnapped' without being misleading."

"And borderline unethical," I add. "What about something like 'Foul Play Is Suspected'? That might hit a good middle spot and get us a little more attention. Today is the sixth. We're two weeks in without a single solid lead. I don't like the way the odds are shaping up."

He nods soberly just as Wanda comes up with a plate for Cricket, a hamburger patty she's broken up into bite-sized pieces. "Shh," she says, flicking her eyes at the kitchen window before running to grab our check.

Though I know it will probably lead to an argument, I say, "Why did you tell Caleb I'm on this case, Will? I thought we agreed I was totally off the record."

"What? It's Caleb, not some journalist."

"So?"

"I'm sorry. It just came up when we were talking. I guess I thought it would make him feel better."

"Better how?"

"About Jenny. That the two of us are on it. That we won't let it all happen again."

What he's saying has already crossed my mind. As a story, it's too much for anyone to live through once, let alone twice. And not just for Caleb. Pretty much anyone over twenty-five was here when Jenny was murdered. That's why things have to turn out differently this time—for all of us.

Thirty-Seven

An hour later, I'm squeezing down bumpy, narrow Cahto Street in my Bronco to find Gray on his way home from school, shoulders hunched beneath the straps of his backpack, his red hair lacquered into a pyramid or some sort of protest flag.

"I hope it was okay, what I told you the other day," he says once I've parked and caught up with him.

"It's all okay. Your help means a lot to us, Gray." We've stopped in the middle of the street, but it doesn't matter. There's no traffic, no noise at all, not even birdsong—as if the whole world's on pause for us. "Girls who have gone through a lot of tough stuff like Cameron has can often have a hard time getting close to people. But the two of you have proven that's not always the case. What you have is special. It also makes me feel optimistic for her once we bring her home. Meaningful relationships can change outcomes. Can change everything."

I can see from the way Gray looks at me that he's grateful for my certainty. Not *if,* but *when.* Also that what I'm saying about trust is registering in a deep way. He has probably come to need that closeness just as powerfully as she has. "Have you thought any more about who might have had access to Cameron? Anyone she might have mentioned. Anyone you spotted together, even once, that gave you an off feeling."

"I've been trying, but I just don't remember. We were together all the time, almost every day. We told each other everything, too. If she'd met someone, I think I'd know."

"Okay. Keep racking your brain. And in the meantime, I have a big favor to ask. Saturday night we're going to have a town meeting at the community center to talk about Cameron. I want to make a sort of collage of her life so that people know who she really is and what she cares about. No one's closer to her than you, Gray. Will you help?"

"I can try." His expression is tentative, but I also know he'd do anything for her.

"Great. Think of everything that makes Cameron Cameron. What she loves. What's special about her. Make lists of her favorite things, and get some great pictures of her photocopied to share. This doesn't have to be professional, just come from the heart."

"I only have a few years' worth of things. We didn't start spending a lot of time together till the end of seventh grade."

"That's okay. Two years is a long time when you're really close to someone."

We start to walk again, toward his front door. He's nodding to himself, still processing what I'm asking of him. To do this right, he'll have to dive back into all sorts of painful feelings. Stepping up will hurt, maybe a lot.

"Who was her best friend before you?"

"Caitlyn Muncy, in sixth and seventh grade. But she's sort of a bitch."

"She might be, but I'll bet she'll help anyway. She holds a piece of Cameron. Get her to show it to you."

"How do I do that?" He stops in place, pulling on the straps of his backpack as if it's just grown heavier. All of this has been too hard already. "What if I screw it up?"

I recognize the signs of panic whirling through him. He reminds me of myself at so many moments. Whenever the stakes have been high, and I've cared too much. Like right now.

"You won't," I tell him gently. "You love her. All of this is about love."

My next stop is the Curtises', to get them on board somehow. Troy happens to be away for the day, an emergency meeting at Paramount, Emily explains after she's buzzed me in and offered tea. I feel irritated with him but not surprised. The greater emergency in his own home is probably too much to take without some sort of escape hatch. Plus his life has been exploding for some time. His doing, yes, but it makes sense that he wants to be somewhere else as the pieces continue to fall.

"Do you have anything new to share?" she asks from one side of the pale marble island in her kitchen, chrome and glass gleaming all around.

"Another girl has been reported missing, down in Gualala. We don't know yet if this has anything to do with Cameron. No one's seen her since June."

Without moving, Emily seems to falter. "All this waiting and not knowing. I don't know how I can keep doing it."

"Just try to take it one day at a time if you can. Sometimes it helps to find an outlet. You can talk to Cameron, or write notes to her. Let her hear you."

When she looks up, Emily's eyes have filmed over. "Okay."

"We went over to Napa to talk to Drew and Lydia."

Her breath catches audibly. "You did?"

"We polygraphed them both. It's standard to interview any family members," I say without tipping my hand. "I also spoke with

Steve Gonzales. We don't believe he's involved in any wrongdoing, but he did share a little about Cameron's writing. It seems she showed him work that was pretty dark. He wonders if it might have been autobiographical."

"Was she really so unhappy here?" Emily's voice sounds small and wounded. "I should have been paying more attention."

"We're holding a town meeting to drum up support," I say, shifting the focus back to Cameron. "On Saturday evening. You and Troy should be involved. A public statement could get more eyes on the problem and a lot more bodies in the field, too. We need to increase involvement, Emily, and not just locally."

"Reach out to the media, you mean . . ." Her voice trails. "Troy and I have talked about it and think it's a mistake right now. For us. You can imagine the kinds of stories that would run. Sensational, exploitive. Those people are monsters."

"I've seen the ugly side of publicity in my work, too. I wouldn't begin to say their motives are always virtuous, but ours can be. We can control the message."

"You can't, though. That's just it." She sounds diminished, physically and literally, as if she's receding when I need her to grow, to *reach*. It makes me want to shake her. To show her there are much-bigger monsters in the world than TV journalists. One has taken her daughter.

I take a deep breath and try something else. "Right now, Cameron's just a name on a missing poster that no one's even paying attention to. But if people are moved, they act. They come forward to help, make phone calls, offer time, money."

"*We've* offered money. We did that right away."

"I know you did, and trust me, it will be put to good use as the search continues. But I still think your presence could galvanize the community. I get why you've been reluctant to be a real part of this town, Emily. Celebrity has made you wary. It must feel strange to try to open up to people as yourself, and not some character. But this is important."

Emily looks away as I finish my sentence and seems to spiral inward. Beyond her, through a massive window, the afternoon is hazy, the sun only an idea behind low, loose clouds. Between us, the silence becomes its own weather system, a pressurized feeling. "Whatever you think, I love my daughter. She's the most important thing in the world to me."

"I believe you," I say, and I want to. I can see her struggling just to stay upright. So much has gotten away from her. There are things she would have done differently. Things she *will* do differently if she can just get Cameron back safely. We all make those bargains, offering anything, everything, for one more chance.

"Do you have children, Detective?"

The question is simple. I can't answer her.

Thirty-Eight

At Searchlight, my supervisor, Frank Leary, is a seasoned veteran. He looks like Karl Malden from *The Streets of San Francisco*, with a bulb nose, enormous gray caterpillar eyebrows, and a slanted, sideways smile that's nothing like Hap's but often reminds me of him anyway. For thirty years, he's been on the job, and it's almost miraculous how sane he is.

He and his wife, Carole, live in North Beach, in the same neighborhood where Joe DiMaggio grew up. Theirs is a gently sagging Victorian with a wraparound back porch and a grill the size of a small car. On Sundays, Frank cooks for his three married daughters and eight grandchildren plus husbands and neighbors and anyone at all who happens to be hungry. I was there one Sunday just a few weeks after I started seeing Corolla.

"How's therapy going?" he asked, clipping off the *h* so that the word came out more like "tare-apy."

"Fine," I said, opening another bottle of Heineken. "It's not really my thing. How come you don't see a therapist, Frank?"

He chuckled a little, and then used his grill tongs to point at the yard, his kingdom. The yellow roses and the big garage full of power tools. The sloping lawn where four of his granddaughters were playing on a massive blue tarp like a homemade Slip 'N Slide. The girls were all between five and seven, shrieking and tumbling in bright two-piece bathing suits as Carole squirted them with the fizzing end of a garden hose. "This is my therapy."

I smiled, knowing he was completely serious. But it wasn't an uncomplicated solution. In the yard, I watched one of the girls split from the herd to run back and forth on the lawn for some reason only she understood, her body a blur of color. The picture of innocence, of vulnerability. "You must worry about them a lot."

He lowered the lid of the grill and faced me, hands on the hips of his kiss the cook apron. "Some days are tougher than others. I'll work a case that gets in too deep, and then I want them all to move in, like a bunker. A bomb shelter. But they have their own lives, and that's as it should be. I get this gripping feeling when they leave sometimes. Like an elephant is sitting on my goddamned chest."

"And then?"

"And then the feeling passes and I clean my grill and put the toys away. I go to bed and kiss my wife good night, and when Monday morning comes, I go to work. When you love someone, there's risk. You can't avoid it."

I nodded and swigged from the beer, so cold it punched the back of my throat going down. Lately Brendan had been pressuring me to get pregnant, and I was having a hard time justifying my reluctance. I had told him early on in our relationship about how my mom had died, obviously, and that I'd grown up in foster care. He knew I had baggage, but I'd kept some things hidden. How I'd screwed up with Amy and Jason. How I'd lost them. I knew it wasn't rational, but on some level, it almost felt as if I'd already had my chance at kids and botched it, badly.

I still checked in on Amy and Jason from time to time, which I also didn't share with Brendan. Almost the first thing I did as a cop was search for their names in the database, trying to piece together from a scattering of home addresses and workplaces and speeding tickets whether or not they'd really made it through their child-hood. Whether they were truly okay.

The last time I'd looked, just a year or so ago, Jason was a day laborer living in Daly City with a dodgy girlfriend who had a long list of priors. Mostly small-time stuff. Jason had no criminal rec-ord beyond shoplifting, traffic violations, and one DUI, but he was a frequent visitor at a methadone clinic, a detail that made me feel sucker-punched when I read it. Amy was still in Redding and had been married twice, as far as I could tell. I'd asked a colleague with ties in the area to do a little more digging, discreetly, without ex-plaining my relationship with her or why I needed to know how many kids she had and if they were from different dads, what kind of neighborhood she lived in, and how long she'd been a manager at the Burger King where she worked, and if she looked happy.

I could have driven there myself if I'd had the courage, of course, and knocked on her door. I had imagined that reunion thousands of times, but had never made it past the moment in the script where she slammed the door in my face for failing her. The closest I'd come in real life was sitting in my car one day watching Jason rip shingles off the roof of someone's tired-looking garage with a few other shirtless guys. Then he shotgunned a forty-ounce in the front seat of his dusty two-tone El Camino while I thought about that damned stuffed cheetah of his, how he couldn't sleep without Freddy pressed right against his face. I never knew how he was able to breathe like that, but as he cranked up the Beastie Boys and peeled away from the curb, I found myself wondering, instead, how he breathed without it now. Without me.

But it wasn't just the way I'd failed Jason and Amy that rattled me when I thought about becoming a parent. It was my DNA, too. My mother hadn't lived to see thirty. My father had been shot and killed in 1989 in a domestic dispute over a woman that sounded like a seedy episode of *A Current Affair*. If that weren't enough, I'd had half a dozen foster parents who had made me seriously wonder if any grown-ups had their act together. It wasn't until I came to Mendocino that I saw some actually being that, grown-up, doing more than just getting by. Hap and Eden had a stable marriage—another first for me. They said what they meant. They were patient with my moods and outbursts. They asked questions and seemed to care what I had to say. They gave me a real childhood when I'd long since stopped hoping there was such a thing. And all I had to do was be myself.

All of this—the presenting evidence on each side of the decision I needed to make—seemed far too complicated to try and wade through with Brendan. He didn't have any ambivalence at all about starting a family. He was part of a sprawling Irish brood, with five brothers and sisters who were loud and cheerful and always in one another's business. When I saw them with their kids, I could *almost* see it—that messy, happy version of domestic life we could have, *maybe,* if everything lined up just right.

"You wouldn't do anything different?" I asked Frank as he manned his grill tongs, turning over peppers and onions with a satisfying hiss.

"Maybe go to dental school instead?" He smirked. "Nah. I like my life."

"How do you know when you're ready?"

His laugh was a snort, as if I'd asked the funniest question he'd ever heard. "No one's ever ready, kid. You just gotta leap."

Thirty-Nine

Crayoned sun drawings with goofy, large-headed stick figures splayed beneath. A chameleon on a cloud and the words *Dear Mom, I have been missing you!* A spelling test from second grade with "100%" circled in red, with stars by two extra-credit words, "parallel" and "integrity." A glittery purple beanbag lizard with loopy plastic eyes. A Strawberry Shortcake tea set. All of this in one large plastic bin in the attic—fragments of a girl, a childhood. One white roller skate with slightly battered wheels. Tucked inside, a pair of rainbow suspenders like Robin Williams wore in *Mork & Mindy.* Four pastel My Little Ponies with a collection of tiny pink hairbrushes for their manes and tails. I never had a box like this, but I recognize I'm looking at treasure. Somehow these things add up to Cameron. I need to find her so she can get back to who she was. Who she *is.*

There are photos, too. In one she looks five or so, standing on the beach—Malibu?—holding a pearly pink seashell in her hand, bare feet half swallowed by sand. Several feature a preteen Cameron next to a girl about the same age, but fair where Cameron is tawny, with a heavy blond ponytail next to Cameron's glossy black curtain. In some, both girls have the same hairstyle as if they were looking for ways to get closer. Closer to being the same person. That's what young friendship is, I remember. You meld, and it feels wonderful. Like you'll never be separated.

"That's Caitlyn," Emily says from the door with fresh mugs of tea in her hands, tendrils of steam rising like flame. "They were best friends from the time we moved here until the end of seventh grade."

I look back down at the photo, at Caitlyn's wide smile and glinting metal braces. The earrings she's wearing, pink enamel hearts. "Then a falling-out?"

"I think so. Cameron wouldn't talk about it. I was worried about her, actually. She seemed so sad. She told me no one sat with her at lunch. She didn't seem to have any friends at all, and then Gray came along. Thank God."

"Misfits find each other."

She looks taken aback. "What do you mean, 'misfits'?"

"It's not a criticism. Some people feel out of place when they're young, not because anything's wrong with them, but because there's something special that sets them apart. Something they haven't figured out yet."

"Figured out? What are you saying?"

I can feel her confusion palpably and decide to tread a little more lightly, leaving my suspicions about Gray out of it. "Well, with Cameron it might be about identity. She had another life behind her, like turning the page of a book. Maybe she'd begun to wonder about that. About where she might fit."

"She fits here," Emily said defensively. "She belongs with us."

"Of course. All I mean is that when hard things happen for kids, they often think they did something to cause it. That it's their fault."

Emily is wearing an oatmeal-colored cashmere sweater and soft suede loafers, her tawny hair held back in a tortoiseshell clasp. Everything about her is neutral and refined, smoothed to perfection. But her eyes have grown clouded. "We tried to show her every day how much we loved her."

"I believe you. But someone gave her away, Emily. It's hard to get over that, even into adulthood."

"Maybe," she says. "But I had two parents who stayed married and I can tell you that was no walk in the park, either. And Troy's parents weren't much better. He's from West Virginia. He likes to say he was raised by wolves, but I'd trade places with him in a second. His parents were simple people. They didn't have much, but there's no shame in that."

The word hangs there for a moment. "What *is* there shame in, Emily?"

"What?"

"What would you have changed about your own family?"

I watch her shoulder muscles clench and then settle. Some great weight either landing there or letting her go. "Everything."

It isn't hard to follow the shadows in her gaze back to Ohio, to long muffling winters and short, hot summers, taffeta formals at the country club. But of course I'm guessing. Emily is the only one who really knows how big *everything* is, what it contains, where it still clings.

"One thing."

"The politeness, I guess. The civility. Ironed linen napkins at every meal. My father had this phrase, 'Mail your envelope,' meaning your napkin should be in your lap. 'Mail your envelope, Emily.'" Her voice vibrates with held emotion as she imitates him. Rage, probably, and much more.

It's a big jump, where my mind goes next, and yet I have to ask. "Did he ever beat you?"

"No." She doesn't seem surprised that I've opened this door. She might even be relieved. At a certain point, once they get tired enough of holding it, most people want to put down their stories. "Not that."

"Tell me a little about your father."

"There's not much to tell. He worked all the time and lived at the club on the weekends. When he drank too much he'd call me over to the bar and show me off to his cronies. Not the best time."

"Did you ever ask him to stop?"

Her chin bobs with a kind of fierceness. "I wasn't raised to acknowledge my own feelings, let alone stick up for myself like that. That's movie dialogue, not real life."

"Maybe it's why you got into acting. So there'd be room to actually say things."

She shakes her head. Her eyes blaze up. "Do all detectives sound like psychologists?"

She has me there. "A lot of them, yeah. People are interesting."

"Why are we talking about me instead of Cameron?"

It's the right question. But the answer is so complicated that it takes me a moment to weigh how much to tell her. "Family systems are revealing. That's something I've learned from this line of work. The more you talk to people, the more you see how generations repeat patterns. Everything fits together, even when it seems not to."

"And the adoption? How does that work with this theory about families?"

"I see it this way. Your biological parents give you their genes, the map of your physical self. But whoever raises you makes you who you are, for better or for worse. Family dynamics are acted out, not built in, though someday scientists might prove otherwise."

"The tension with Troy," Emily says. "I wish I had been able to keep that from her."

"Maybe that would have helped. Or maybe Cameron needed the opposite . . . more talking through things, not less. Who knows, really? When she comes home, you can ask her."

Emily's face contorts, her eyes shining. "If I can just have *one* more day with her—" She can't finish the sentence.

Emily and I are different women with entirely different stories— but I need to see the thread between us. How we've been to the same war.

I've spent time faulting her for not keeping Cameron safe enough, not protecting her when she couldn't protect herself. But what does it all add up to? What is all the suffering for if not so we can see how alike we are, and not alone? Where will the mercy come from, if not from us?

3

Time and the Maiden

Forty

Will makes good on his promise and soon we have a warrant to open Cameron's adoption file. He offers to send Leon Jentz to Catholic Family Charities in Sacramento, but I can't let anyone else go. I don't want to see a fax or copy. Whatever I might find, this is personal—and I'm okay with that. Maybe *too involved* is exactly the way to find Cameron. Maybe the moment I decided to come back to Mendocino, this was always going to happen. All of this, just the way it's unfolding.

The drive to Sacramento takes four hours, long enough to feel grateful that Cricket is a model traveler. I stop near Clearlake to give her a bathroom break, and then we set off again on Interstate 5, past a checkerboard of parched-looking farms and fields, the median thick with white oleander. Once we reach the patched asphalt parking lot, I don't feel great about leaving her in the car, but she's not an official service dog—not yet. So I park in the shade and crack the window to give her plenty of fresh air.

"I'll be back in half an hour," I tell her while her ears tip forward, listening. And then I hear myself and have to smile in disbelief. In forty-eight hours I've become someone who thinks dogs can tell time?

Inside, Catholic Family Charities has the feel of a government building and houses fewer nuns than I expected. Mostly I pass drably dressed clerks in polyester skirt sets and flat shoes, and lots and lots of filing cabinets. Once I find my way upstairs, I talk to a secretary who pushes me through to another, and finally to the cramped office of the on-staff attorney, a pantsuited woman with a helmet of inky-black hair who asks only a few questions before handing over a copy of the file and asking for my signature. The flat look on her face tells me she's overworked and underpaid. Cameron means nothing to her, and how could she? The metal cabinets behind her are full of cases, each file a complex story, a life. I thank her and head back to the bank of tired elevators in the hall. And then it hits me that I now have Cameron's documents all to myself. It's as if I've robbed a bank.

I push the button for the first floor and step inside alone, almost dizzy with the instant privacy, the anticipation. As soon as the door closes, sealing me off from everything else, I open the file and notice Cameron's childhood address. Ukiah. Emily and Troy were living in Malibu when they adopted Cameron. In 1989, four years ago, when their daughter was eleven, they moved to Mendocino, to the glass house on the bluff. And if you drew a line from that bluff almost straight east over the coastal range, Ukiah was just thirty miles away. With a closed adoption, neither family would have had any idea. But some force had pulled them close anyway. Thirty miles between Cameron's before and after lives? It was crazy. It was *fate,* Eden might have said.

Stepping out into the main lobby, I spot a pay phone and pause in front of it, digging for quarters to call Will. But then I stop. I have the names and address of Cameron's birth parents right here in my hands. I'm close—so close—to learning more about her early life. Maybe a key piece to the puzzle of her disappearance is nearby, too, with her first family.

For a long moment, I feel myself teetering on the brink of something, pulled in two directions. Will would want to be involved in the interview, but part of me doesn't want him there. Doesn't want to share, or wait for him to join me, or to have to jump through hoops of any kind. I don't even want to ask for his permission. Going alone is a maverick, shortsighted move. What if I miss something? What if I screw it all up?

I pocket the quarters and open the file again. Clipped just inside is a photo of two children in dress clothes against a swirling blue background, the kind you'd get done in a Sears Portrait Studio in a shopping mall. The boy must be Cameron's brother, about ten in the picture, with a starched white collar, jet-black hair, and slightly crooked front teeth. But it's three-year-old Cameron I can't look away from. Brown eyes like saucers under dark, feathery brows. Her face round and brave, and so precious it's hard for me to breathe right, looking at her. The fierce set of her chin, as if she's challenging not just whoever stands behind the camera but the whole day and everyone who's part of it. Her hair in a fountain held off her face with a white plastic butterfly clip. Her dress made of white lace and cotton, and her smile wide open. Her light right *there,* pure and bright as the fucking sun. No victim sign. No bat signal. Just a little girl, Lisa Marie Gilbert, born March 20, 1978, the first day of spring.

Forty-One

Driving fast in a straight shot up Highway 101, Cricket and I hit Ukiah just after four with all the windows down. Hap had always called Ukiah a cow town, too small for culture and too big to have any kind of charm or quaintness. I never corrected him, nor did I tell him what I remembered from living here myself, twice, in two short placements, each less than a year. My memory of that time was frayed, even then. Just small shreds of images, a first-grade teacher who wore dark flesh-colored nylons and drank Tab at her desk, a mother in a filmy yellow nightgown, on the couch drinking peach schnapps from a coffee cup all day long, a February afternoon when some kids on the bus jeered and told me my brother smelled like pee. He wasn't really my brother, and I was the one who smelled, actually, but I'd only slid down in the seat with my book and disappeared.

I come off the freeway to a string of fast-food restaurants next to check-cashing places, a Walmart Supercenter, and the Bartlett pear factory, recognizing nothing, thankfully. The section of town beyond Ford Road where Cameron spent her early years stands between the freeway and the fairgrounds. I pass Vinewood Park, a chunk of dry grass ringed by low-slung ranch houses, most of which have seen better days. The park looks thirsty and dejected, the squared-off playground studded with one of those climbing gyms made from recycled tires, and a badly oxidized swing set.

Cameron would have played here, though, as Lisa, the same way we played in a drained swimming pool and thought it was wonderful. She wouldn't have seen any of the dinginess, because no one ever does until they're on the outside of a place, looking in.

Even with the address in my hand, I have no way of knowing if any members of the Gilbert family still live here, at 3581 Willow. The surrounding streets are named similarly—Mimosa, Acacia, Fig— pastoral words that clash with the blistered, derelict lawn furniture strewn over the yards and stoops, the sagging clotheslines strung up between carports. I park in a dusty pullout as a shorn-headed boy in a Hulk T-shirt roars a three-wheeler around in a wide circle a few hundred yards away. He's staring at me as if I must be lost. Possibly I am.

Climbing out of my Bronco, I pocket my keys and approach the long, slim ranch house with Cricket at my heel. It's done in rust-colored siding with silvery aluminum trim that throws off spears of light. A lopsided TV antenna dangles from the roof. Before I even reach the three plywood steps, the front door rocks open and a short, thick-shouldered man stops me like a bulwark. I feel Cricket's energy change instantly, and put a hand on her collar.

"Help you?" he asks, but really he means *Go away*. His right eye is lower than the left and red rimmed, giving him a mournful look. The rest of him is all sledgehammer, thick biceps, unshaven double chin, wide jaw clenching as he sizes me up.

"I'm looking for Ruben or Jackie Gilbert. They're not in trouble or anything. I just need some information."

"They don't live here no more." Obviously he's spotted me as a professional, badge or no. He coughs, waiting for me to back away.

"Are you a relative?"

"That family moved on. I don't know where."

"I'm working on a missing persons case in Mendocino, a fifteen-year-old girl named Cameron Curtis."

"Never heard of her."

"She's in real trouble, Mr. Gilbert." The name tips out and I let it fall, fishing.

His big body heaves as he takes in a deep breath. Then he says, "Get the fuck out of here. I don't know anything about no missing girl."

I flinch back before I can stop myself. He's a big guy and could mess me up pretty bad if he had a mind to. Maybe coming alone has been a terrible idea. "Listen, I don't want to hassle you, I just need to fill in some missing blanks."

"I don't talk to cops."

"I'm not a cop, I'm a detective, and anyway, you're not in trouble. This is about Cameron. You haven't seen the news?"

He coughs roughly, throws back his shoulders. "No."

"She may have had a connection to this place, a long time ago."

No response.

"There are several girls missing in the area, actually, but I'm just here about Cameron. Can't we go inside and talk a little, please?"

His chin dips, his good eye seeming to bulge. "I told you. I don't know shit about no missing girl. Now get the hell out of my way. I gotta work." Then he stares me down, posturing, until I have no choice but to step aside.

I stand in the yard and watch him climb into a maroon Ford Taurus, feeling almost nauseated because I've blown it. Cameron lived here. Somewhere nearby are missing pieces, maybe, ones that might show the whole of her. And what now? I can try to canvass the neighborhood and pray someone is here who either still remembers her or has anything to tell me about the Gilberts that will help in some way. But I'm not feeling overly optimistic.

The Taurus accelerates through the turn from Willow onto Fig, nosing dangerously close to a stand of mailboxes, and then the kid on the Big Wheel is back, coming around for another lap on his circuit, his gaze on Cricket. Kids always seem to zero in on dogs.

I give him a small wave, but his eyes are stony. They graze right over me, and then he brightens. Behind me, the door has opened silently.

"Hey Kyle," a voice says.

"Hey Hector," the kid says. "Can I come in for a while? My mom's not home."

I look back and forth between the two, too surprised to say a word.

"In a minute, okay? I gotta talk to this lady."

Forty-Two

Familiar shag carpeting stretches through the living room and into the tiny kitchen, threadbare and pea green. A table and chairs and a tired-looking sofa with a dark stain across the back are the only furniture. Cricket parks herself at my side while Hector stands with his hands on his hips, studying me studying him. I'm guessing he's twenty-one or -two, with muscled, tattooed forearms under his faded blue work shirt. His neck is inked, too, a band of interlocking shaded bubbles, like python skin. Dark, cuffed jeans hang from his waist over black steel-toed, ass-kicking boots.

He's a rough-looking character, and yet I don't feel threatened. Instinctively I believe he'll at least listen to my questions. His age and coloring make him a good bet for the boy in the photo or another sibling of Cameron's. Plus he opened the door.

"Hector, my name is Anna Hart. I'm trying to find a missing girl from Mendocino."

A shadow passes through his dark eyes. "What happened to her?"

"We don't know for sure. She vanished from her home on the night of September twenty-first, and no one's heard from her since. I'm worried that someone might have taken her."

"I heard about that other girl in Petaluma. She's not mixed up in something like that, is she?"

"I don't know. I wish I did."

"I heard you say she was fifteen, huh? I have a sister who would be that age."

I don't even breathe, hoping he'll go on. And he does.

"I was eleven when they split us up."

"The girl I'm looking for was adopted in 1982. What was your sister's name, Hector?"

"Lisa."

Something twists hard in my throat, then relief rushes in. Hope. "Can you tell me about it?"

He sits down heavily on the couch and reaches for a pack of Camels on the floor next to a blue glass ashtray, lighting up. "My folks probably knew social services was coming to take us, but they didn't say a word. Isn't that the most fucked-up thing you've ever heard?"

I take the chair across from him, and Cricket follows my cue, lying down while I register the tension in Hector's face and hands. "What happened then?"

"I don't know everything. My dad was mixed up in a lot of shit, I think. Drug stuff. The cops came a few times, and then one of the neighbors made an anonymous call about *negligence*." He nearly spits the last part.

"Was that your father I talked to?"

"That piece of shit? That's my uncle Carl. My dad went to San Quentin a long time ago. Still there, for all I know."

"Why wouldn't Carl talk to me?"

Air comes in a puff from Hector's nose. What I've asked is ridiculous.

"But *you're* talking to me," I say.

"I got nothing to hide. Plus I just got a feeling that you were here for something important. You ever get those feelings?"

Yes, I want to say. *Like right now, all of this.* "Your mother, where is she?"

He shrugs, his forehead bunching. "She skipped town a while back with some other loser. I'd be surprised if she was still alive. She was working pretty hard to kill herself even then."

"Why did you guys get split up?"

"I don't even know, really. I came home from school one day and Lisa was gone. There were social workers here." He scratches his shoulder hard as if the memory itself is right there at his fingertips, a sting or an ache. I know that instinct. The ongoing futility of it. How you can never quite reach the place that hurts.

"Did you get adopted, too, then?"

"No. I was too old, I guess. I got taken to a foster home, but I ran away." He still has half a cigarette left, but reaches for the pack on the table and squeezes it for comfort. The cellophane whispers against his palm. "I ran away five or six different times, then went to a group home when no one else would take me. When I was eighteen I came back here, but my parents had left. Carl doesn't like me much, but he hates everyone. You saw."

"I'm so sorry." I know my words sound just as meaningless now as they did when strangers said them over and over to me when I was growing up. Language fails sometimes, but I *am* sorry for Hector. He's old enough to remember everything. The battle wounds of his childhood. The loss of his sister, the confusion, the displacement. The pain. He's me, and Lisa is Amy or Jason. Both. But now more loss has come. More tragedy.

"They should have told me they couldn't take care of her," he goes on about his parents. "I would have done it myself. We could have figured out something. At least we'd be together." His pupils bloom black, dilating with emotion. "They brought her home from the hospital and that was the best day of my life. Before that, it was just me and these crazy people. But after? I took care of her."

I want to cry listening. Instead I nod.

"We slept like puppies, on this mattress on the floor. I kept my arms around her like this." He lifts his hands to show me. "We were always together. Anyone even looked at that girl and I was *there*. You know?"

I do know. The savage loyalty in his voice takes me all the way back to that Christmas alone with Jason and Amy. Those hours and days, which felt suspended in some sort of bubble, when nothing could touch us. "You protected her."

He draws hard on the Camel, the paper collapsing with a hiss as he wrestles with the past. "I tried. Our parents were really messed up, but everyone is, right?"

Not everyone, I want to say, but also know he has no reason to believe me. "What kind of kid was she? Quiet?"

"Lisa?" His laugh chops out, hard and spontaneous. "That girl never stopped talking or dancing. She sang in the bathtub, running down the street. She would sit down under the mailbox and play with nothing. With *rocks,* you know? And she'd be *singing.*"

Suddenly I can see her, that girl. He's called her up, and it makes me feel gutted. How can it happen in one life, to be stolen twice? "Do you remember anything ever happening, before you guys got split up?" I ask him. "Something that changed Lisa's behavior? Did she ever get real quiet, or cry for no reason, or seem afraid?"

"Why? What are you thinking?"

"I'm not sure. I want you to look at something." From my pocket I draw out Cameron's missing poster and unfold it in front of him.

"Shit," he whispers and puts his cigarette down. "That's gotta be her." He pulls the page near him, shaking his head back and forth, his eyes glistening. "I can't believe it. She's so pretty, so grown-up. You have to find her."

"I'm doing everything I can. What else do you notice?"

He studies the page for a long moment. "Those are her eyes. Lisa's eyes. But she looks so sad here. Right?"

"I think so too, and I want to figure out why. Life is hard,

Hector. You and I both know that, but I can't see *this* girl sitting under a mailbox singing at rocks."

I can feel him trying to process what I mean. He grips the paper more tightly, his thumbs whitening around the nail beds, as if he wishes he could climb inside of it somehow and touch her. Help her.

"My Lisa was a fighter," he finally says. "Man, that girl was *stubborn*. You try to take a toy from her or get her off the swings before she was ready and you had a tiger to mess with. She'd ball up her fists like this." He holds one hand up, makes a face that tells me he sees her right now, close enough to touch. *"Fierce."*

"So what happened? That's what I want to know. That's why I came here, to see if I could figure it out. Do you have pictures around from when you were kids?"

He shakes his head. "Nothing like that, sorry." Looking at the poster again, he says, "Can I keep this?"

"Of course. I'm going to give you my number, too." Flipping the poster over, I write the digits for Will's office and my name beside it. "You think of anything useful, let me know. And if you want me to keep you in the loop, I can do that."

"Yeah." He digs in his pocket for a wadded receipt and scrawls his phone number for me, passing it over. "If there's any way I can help, let me know, okay? You got people looking for her, right?"

"We do."

"Good."

He walks me to the door as Cricket trails us. At eye level on the nicked jamb, there's a tarry black smudge the size of a handprint. The doorknob looks plastic. This place feels so cramped and dingy and hopeless I have a crazy urge to take Hector with me, to throw him in the back of the car with Cricket and run for the hills. But he stopped being a child a long time ago. And anyway, he's not asking to be rescued.

Forty-Three

It's late when I finally reach the village. I drive past the sheriff's office, hoping to find Will still at work, and catch him getting into his car to head home. He rolls down his window as I pull alongside him. Before I can even squeeze in a hello, he says, "Where in the world have you been? I've been looking for you for hours."

"I told you I was going to Sacramento."

"Even with red tape, I thought I'd hear from you by two. What gives?"

"Do you want to grab a drink?" I backpedal. "I can explain."

His expression doesn't soften. "Come inside. It's been a long day. There's a lot to catch you up on."

With Cricket trailing me, I follow Will to an empty conference room with bad fluorescent lighting. He plunks down in the nearest chair. "Well?"

"I just got excited, I guess." I take a seat across from him, feeling increasingly as if I've been sent to the principal's office. "When I opened the file, I found the address for Cameron's birth family was in Ukiah. Isn't that eerie? What are the odds?"

"So you went to Ukiah? Was the family still living there?"

"The parents are out of the picture now, but I met an uncle and

Cameron's brother, Hector. I'll tell you, it's heartbreaking the way these two kids were split up by social services, Will. Hector never even knew where they took his sister. He got blindsided, and then shuttled through foster care. You can see it's really messed with him."

Will's face remains flat and expressionless. "Did you interview this guy or run a group therapy session?"

I feel a spear of shame. "Why are you being so hostile?"

"You don't know?" He takes off his hat and drops it between us with emphasis. "You've been gone all day without checking in, making decisions that concern this case without prior authorization, and now you come back with nothing but a script for a made-for-TV movie."

I swallow back more embarrassment, his words knocking me further off-balance. "I'm sorry. I should have touched base first. I just had a feeling I should go alone."

"My department doesn't run on *feelings,* Anna. And this investigation doesn't, either. I should have been there, or one of my deputies. Then at least we'd have had two sets of eyes on the situation. How do we know this Hector's not a suspect?"

"He's not. I know it."

"You know *how?* Did you check to see if he had a criminal record? What about the uncle? You get license-plate numbers for me? Aliases? Alibis for the night of September twenty-first?"

No was the answer, but he was missing the real point. "You sit behind a desk too much, Will. Instinct is fifty percent of the job at least. And shit. Hector probably *does* have a record after the number the county did on his childhood. But he cares about his sister and wouldn't have done anything to hurt her, even if he had access to Cameron, which he didn't."

"Hold up. I'll ask again, Anna. How are you coming to these conclusions? First you're *sure* Drew Hague is the guy who abused Cameron, and we've got nothing. Then you tell me Steve Gonzales isn't a suspect based purely on some feeling you have. Thankfully you got lucky on that one."

My face has grown hot. "Why are you giving me such a hard time? If you don't trust my judgment, what am I doing here?"

"Hang on. Can we deescalate for a minute? I'm just doing my job, Anna. Trying, anyway. You're a great resource, and I'm really grateful you're here. But the questions I'm asking you, I have a right to ask you. Okay?"

I look at my hands. "I should have called you from Sacramento. I can own that. But I'd bet my legs Hector Gilbert didn't take Cameron Curtis."

"I'm sure you're right. Let's just follow protocol and run a background check—see what we're dealing with. And we should bring him in for a polygraph, just standard procedure. Same with the uncle, and same with Steve Gonzales. We have to cover our bases."

"Cover your ass, you mean," I say without thinking.

"Anna." His warning chimes.

"Sorry." I roll my shoulders up and back, trying to release the knots there. "It's been a challenging day."

"Yeah, here too. . . . Now I need you to watch something with me. You've missed a lot."

Forty-Four

In one corner of the conference room, a TV and VCR sit stacked on a wheeled metal AV cart. Will crosses over and clicks on the set, pushing the play button. It's tonight's taped episode of *America's Most Wanted*. A pretty blond journalist I don't recognize is interviewing Erin McGrath and Allison Palmer. Maybe she's not even a journalist. The show isn't exactly hard news.

As the interview begins, the camera zooms in on the two girls sitting side by side on a narrow studio couch. They look brave and poised and very, very young to me. Which they are.

"We thought it was a prank at first," Erin says. She has shoulder-length brown hair with a straight center part, a button nose, and wide-set brown eyes. "Polly could do stuff like that sometimes. She was a good actress."

I can't help but notice she's using the past tense, and feel it like a needle prick. "We'd already been goofing around a lot," Allison adds, tucking a dark blond strand of hair behind her ear. "Talking about Halloween and trying to scare each other. We put white makeup on Polly and she did her eyes like a ghost and painted her lips black."

"Then what happened?" the interviewer urges.

"She went out to get sleeping bags for us," Allison continues. "When she came back there was a guy with a knife and a duffel bag standing behind her in the door. He was older. He didn't look scary or anything, not at first. That's why I thought Polly might be kidding."

"It didn't feel real," Erin is quick to add. "That's what I was thinking. And he was really calm, the way he was talking. He said he wanted money and Polly showed him her jewelry box. She had fifty dollars. That's when he changed. His voice got harder and he told us not to scream or he'd slit our throats."

"Then he started to tie up Polly and she was crying," Allison says. "He took pillowcases off the bed and put them over our heads. He tied us up after that. I said the cords were too tight and he loosened them a little and said he was sorry."

"That's when he said if we counted to a thousand, Polly would be back," Erin finishes for her.

"But that didn't happen?" the interviewer prompts gently.

"No," Erin replies. "We heard the screen door slam and then we tried to get out of the cords he tied us up with. Allison was stumbling around and trying to wake up Polly's mom who was asleep next door."

"We were both really scared," Allison says.

"Of course you were. Your friend had just been kidnapped. I think you're very brave. And everyone in America is looking for Polly's kidnapper from the description you were able to give the police. Millions of people watch this show. Everyone is trying to find Polly. Everyone wants her to come home." Her face is the picture of somber hope, her eyes pointedly soft. "What can you tell America about who Polly was? How was your friend so special?"

"She's really funny," Erin replies, almost smiling for a split second. "Her favorite color is purple and she eats cinnamon toast every day after school."

"She wants to be an actress," Allison adds. "She's madly in love with Mel Gibson. There's a poster in her room with these two black-and-white cats and a Dalmatian that says don't be a copy cat. That's her. There's no one like Polly."

After the interview, the usual number rolls across the screen for tips, then the tape goes black. My eyes shoot to Will. Even though I'm numb and hungover from our talk, my mind has begun to whir.

"This is exactly why we need this town meeting *yesterday*," I say. "Cinnamon toast. Almost no one in town knows anything about Cameron. You can't care about something you can't picture."

"Okay, sure. But listen. You know the actress Winona Ryder? Seems she's flying to Petaluma tomorrow on Harrison Ford's jet. I talked to Fraser and it seems she's collected donations from a bunch of A-listers for a private reward if Polly's found. Anna, it's two million dollars."

"What? That's crazy! Even if they can get that kind of money together, why spend it on Polly? Why is Ryder so invested anyway?"

"She spent part of her childhood in Petaluma. She and Polly even had the same drama teacher. Apparently she's been watching the news and decided it was time to act. She just called today. Talk about a media circus."

"So we go back to Emily. She's got two million dollars, easy."

"Money isn't the issue, Anna, and you know it. The problem is we have no evidence. The FBI thinks Cameron's a runaway. You don't get *America's Most Wanted* coverage for that. I'm not sure we have a prayer of getting even local media right now, despite Emily's help. Everyone will be covering Ryder's visit."

"I think we have to try anyway. We can't control media interest, but we can fucking show up, right?"

"Maybe," he offers. "Anyway, there's something more."

"Did Polly phone again?"

"No. Fraser's pretty sure now that call was a prank. But Silicon Valley is jumping in. Some computer systems hotshot has been watching the news and had the bright idea to scan Polly's missing poster into a computer. A bunch of network companies have donated equipment. They're faxing thousands of posters all over the world and using the Internet, too. Someone told me that ten million people in half a dozen countries have seen the poster."

"Holy shit. That number."

"I know. It's a brave new world, right? Can you imagine where we'd be if we had something like this ten years ago, or twenty?" His eyes flash with meaning. *Jenny.*

Just like that, her face shimmers up. Her laugh. Her walk. Her voice out on the headlands, flickering through the dark and then gone. Since her disappearance and long before, missing children and teens were seen on blurrily reproduced posters taped to telephone poles or tacked up in post offices. What would be different if the Internet had existed in 1973? Crisply faxed likenesses of Jenny generated and shared everywhere in a blink? Maybe nothing, or maybe everything. Maybe the entire thrust of our lives.

"Can we do something like this for Cameron?" I ask. "Shannan, too?"

"I've already made some calls."

"What do you think of me going to talk to Shannan Russo's mother?"

"To learn what?"

"If there's something that links the two girls."

"Personally they seem like night and day to me. If you didn't see a connection with Polly, why would you look here?"

"Promise you won't laugh?"

His look is noncommittal.

"I saw Tally Hollander."

"The psychic? Oh brother, now I really am worried about you, kid."

"C'mon. Bear with me for a second, Will. Some of the things Tally said about Shannan and the way she grew up made me think the two girls share some emotional DNA. I just want to check it out." I grip the table in front of me, cool and flat and real. "This isn't a *vision* I'm talking about. When Tally called Karen, she opened up and shared all kinds of things, how there was a lot of upheaval in Shannan's childhood, men coming and going, exposure to violence. I know she was hard as nails with you, but if I can get Karen to talk to me, we might learn a whole lot more about how Shannan may have crossed paths with a psychopath."

He sighs and I see how tired he is. We're both running on steam. "Okay."

"Okay?"

"It's a long shot, but honestly, all the breadcrumbs matter, I guess."

"That's right. They do."

Forty-Five

Early the next morning, I head to Gualala to Karen Russo's workplace, a dated-looking salon called Rumor's All About Hair. She's leaning against the front desk when I walk in, a pretty if slightly hardened brunette in a dark smock over belled jeans and high cork-bottomed wedges. I put her in her midthirties, which means she probably had Shannan at eighteen or nineteen.

As soon as I introduce myself, Karen's eyes flatten. She's had enough of cops and reporters. Maybe I should have brought Tally with me, I think too late.

"I'm working here, all right?" she throws out.

"Just fifteen minutes for coffee?"

"I don't have much to say."

"That's okay. I'll be waiting across the street at the coffee shop. I only have a few questions."

Forty-five minutes later, she finally turns up. I've had three cups of coffee, all watered-down diner coffee, but my palms are clammy anyway, my optimism waning.

"I have someone at eleven," she says. "A regular client. I can't be late."

"Understood. I just want to get a clearer picture of your daughter if possible, Ms. Russo. What can you tell me about Shannan's habits, before all this, I mean?"

"She was bored, in trouble a lot."

"She was a senior in high school when she went missing, am I right?"

"She never cared about school and I gave up trying to get her there. Honestly, I gave up a lot of things. I know that sounds shitty. Shannan didn't want a mother. She didn't want anyone to care about her."

Karen's toughness may be a defense, as Tally suggested, but it's a formidable one. "That must have been hard, her pushing you away."

She squints, her lashes thick with inky mascara that's so black it's almost blue. "I had plenty of time to get used to it."

"Tell me about the last day you saw her." I flip through my notes. "June second. Did she go to school that day?"

"Your guess is as good as mine. She was dressed and out of bed, but she could have been going anywhere. She had lots of friends who weren't friends, if you know what I mean."

"Men? Are you saying your daughter was prostituting herself?"

"Maybe." She pulls a patterned cigarette purse from the pocket of her jacket and holds her lighter to the tip of a Marlboro Light, inhaling and then waving away the smoke in a practiced gesture. "I don't know how she made her money. I didn't help her out, I can tell you that. I knew she'd drink whatever I gave her, or whatever else she was snorting or shooting. I stopped asking."

"These friends. Did she ever mention anyone by name?"

"Not that I remember. At least one of them had money, though. She brought home a new Nikon camera once. And someone gave her a coat, a nice one."

That gets my attention. "Can you describe it?"

"It was short and brown, some kind of animal fur. Maybe it wasn't real, but it sure looked that way, and expensive. She certainly didn't buy it from around here."

"Was she wearing it that last day?"

"Maybe. I can't remember."

It's clear I'm getting almost nowhere with Karen. Whatever the trick is to get her talking openly, I don't seem to know it. "The psychic who called you, what did you think of her?"

"What *could* I think?" Karen makes a troubled face as she exhales again, smoke fanning out like a screen of poison. "Shannan always did exactly what she wanted. If someone killed her, she probably asked for it."

The harshness of her words silences me for a long moment. I've known women like Karen, flinty and shut down. But I also understand that anyone with a shell like this has come by it honestly. She's had good reasons to protect herself, and still does. "Ms. Russo, I really do want to help find Shannan, but I'm going to be honest with you. My primary case is Cameron Curtis. You've heard of her."

"Sure, the movie star's kid. I watched that show for years. Never thought I'd have something in common with Heidi Barrows." She shakes her head.

"We have very little to go on with Cameron, but she had a lot of disruption in her childhood. Violence, too. We think that might have something to do with her being targeted." I look at her meaningfully. "That's why I'm here asking questions about Shannan when she was young. It could be the same guy. I'm looking for threads."

She seems unmoved, at least on the surface. Glancing at her watch, she says, "I've told you what I can."

"We've still got a few more minutes. Where's Shannan's dad? Has he ever been involved?"

"That piece of crap?" Her lip curls. "He took off when she was still in preschool. Haven't gotten a dime from him since."

"It's hard to be a single parent."

She flicks her eyes over me, seeming to wonder if I'm being straight with her, if I have some ulterior motive. "Yeah, it is."

"Was it always just the two of you?"

"On and off. I've had boyfriends over the years. Probably not the best thing to have around a kid."

"Boyfriends in general, or these particular guys?"

She gives me a barbed look. "Meaning what? You questioning my choice in men?"

"I don't know your life."

She looks at the wall, a swirling pattern of gold Formica. Harvest gold, from the 1970s, when everything was either gold or avocado green. "Well, I can tell you I probably didn't make totally great decisions all the time. I mean, who does, right?"

Unfortunately she's right. Not for everyone, but for many of us. "Do you have a picture of Shannan?"

"Nothing recent." She puts down her cigarette and digs through her pocketbook, fishing out one of those little photo keepers that sometimes come with a wallet. The plastic sleeve is yellowed and dog-eared but filled—all school pictures with cloudy blue backgrounds, Shannan as a gap-toothed five- or six-year-old leading the parade.

I take the book from her and flip through it feeling more and more saddened. Maybe the girl was trouble, but she didn't start out that way. Wasn't born trouble, but sweet, pure, original—like anyone. "She's really pretty," I say. "What did she want to do with her life? When she was little, I mean. Any big fantasies?"

"Does Disney princess count?" Karen's mouth tightens, deepening the feathered creases on her upper lip. Then she says, "She did have the shiniest hair. I used to fix it for her in a fishtail braid down her back. That's not easy to do. It takes at least an hour, but she'd sit real still and not move."

I meet her eyes, trying not to blink or break the moment. It's the most unguarded she's been with me, the most human. "I'll bet she looked really beautiful."

"Yeah, she did. Beautiful wasn't the problem."

Forty-Six

Sometimes snatches of the past floated up like shredded paper and caught me off guard, things I was sure I'd forgotten. My mother sleeping on the couch, on her side with her knees curled up like a child, a crocheted afghan over part of her face. A day that seemed like a fantasy when I was six or seven and the kids were toddlers, taking turns holding someone's pet rabbit in our laps on a patch of grass. When it was my turn, I touched the ears, which were warm, felt the rabbit's frantic heart and tensed muscles, how it wanted to run but didn't. A few days later, three cop cars showed up at our apartment with a warrant for my father. They took him off in handcuffs while my mother yelled at them to stop. She threw an ashtray that bounced hard off the wall. Threw a lamp to the floor so that the bulb shattered. I watched everything from the darkened hall, all the bedroom doors closed, the kids hiding in a closet where I had put them and told them to be very quiet. A charged, stifling feeling in the air around me and in my body. After that, my dad became a stranger to us. It was only a few years later that my mother would leave to borrow fifty bucks and never come back.

But there were other memories, too, softer ones, like bits of webbing. Memories of Hap and Eden and Mendocino, how when

I was ten, I found I could crouch down inside the bunchgrasses on the headlands above Portuguese Beach and *be* grass. I could be the sun setting, smearing light like wild honey over everything it touched. I was the Pacific with its cold blue eye, the crow in a cypress tree, flapping, talking to itself about the world. For as long as I could remember, I'd had reasons to disappear. I was an expert at making myself invisible, but this was something else. I was part of things now, knitted into the landscape. And not overlooked at all, but cared about.

The community center stands on the corner of School Street and Pine, next to the ball fields, now yellowed like everything this time of year. I meet Gray and his mother Di Anne there just after noon on Saturday to work on the bulletin board that should help personalize Cameron for those who don't know her, and honor her for those who do. Will's petition to use the space indefinitely has just been approved by the city council. A temporary sign hangs outside until a banner can be made, with cameron curtis rescue center in red block letters.

"Red is Cameron's favorite color," Gray explains. He and Di Anne made the sign together and have been at the center for hours, I can see. The bulletin board is already more than half filled with photos, postcards, and drawings. In one corner, Gray has pinned the album jacket for Madonna's *The Immaculate Collection,* the record that's been the soundtrack of their friendship over the past two years. He found and talked to all of Cameron's teachers, some of whom have saved copies of papers and poems. One from fifth grade was called "Ginkgo Leaves":

Flat balloons. Parachutes.
Each leaf like something burning.
A dream taking flight. I stand
Under the yellow tree and think

about yesterday. Does yesterday
think about me?

I read the lines feeling my throat grow tight. It's more than good
writing; it shows a vulnerability I wouldn't have dreamed of revealing when I was her age, particularly about the past. I wasn't that
brave then. I still might not be, not in that way.

"She's special, right?" Gray says from behind me.

"Yeah, she's special."

With Gray and Di Anne's help, I work in the things I've brought
with Emily's permission, the crayoned drawing of the chameleon—
Dear Mom, I have been missing you!—the Malibu beach picture
with the pearly pink seashell, and several more, including one of
Cameron and Caitlyn Muncy, each wearing a single roller skate,
their hair done up in tight high ponytails that tipped to different
sides, as if they completed each other.

"Gosh, they're sweet," Di Anne says as she pins up the picture.
"I don't remember Cam at that age."

Cam.

"I talked to Caitlyn Muncy like you asked," Gray says. "She
wasn't a bitch at all. She cried."

"Cameron must mean a lot to her, too," I tell him.

"She gave me this." Gray holds up a VHS tape. "Is there a way
to play it?"

We dig around in the back room and find a cache of AV equipment, slide-wheel projectors, an old reel-to-reel, a Betamax player,
and then bingo. A VCR.

Plugging it in, the three of us gather to watch on an old Magnavox in the tiny kitchen. Nearby, along the windowsill under
skewed venetian blinds, there are grayish drifts of dead moth
husks. A dry sink is filled with cracked pieces of Fiestaware. Then
the TV set hums to life, and none of it matters. The room disappears.

Cameron and Caitlyn are singing "Under the Sea" from *The Little Mermaid* into Mr. Microphones, giving it all they have. The ponytails are in full force, Cameron's nearly to her butt. They have the half-formed look of preteens, not yet grown into their faces. They have pimples, braces. They're radiant.

"This is perfect," I tell Gray, feeling emotional and overwhelmed.

"I don't know if she'd want us to play it for a bunch of people."

"Why not?"

"That was a long time ago. And I don't know, she seems so innocent in the tape."

"Innocence is a gift, Gray," I say, hearing my voice dip emotionally. "Look how beautiful she is. Whatever pain she felt, however she'd been hurt, she doesn't show it here. She let it go, even for a minute. Kids can be so resilient. I never stop being amazed."

"I haven't thought about it like that."

As the tape ends, the machine crackles, then whirs. Gray hits rewind and then Di Anne puts her arm around him, pulling him close, and we watch it again. Sunlight pierces the venetian blinds, throws a single slash of light over the wall just above the Magnavox. Then the singing: *Just look at the world around you / Right here on the ocean floor / Such wonderful things surround you / What more is you lookin' for?*

Forty-Seven

Will and I have arranged to meet at six-fifteen that night to go over his speech, but by then people have already begun to arrive. Someone has set up a long table under the far wall, and it's loaded with food. Potluck dishes, a crockpot full of barbecued meatballs, cheese and crackers and piles of rolls, plastic cutlery, paper napkins, pink lemonade, and a tower of Styrofoam cups. For a moment I'm thrown, but then I remember how it is in small towns, where any public gathering means food. Plus eating always brings people together, gives them something to do with their hands.

Soon, the chairs begin to fill. Wanda has been passing out flyers and has done her job well. The village has shown up, finally, each person here because the time has come for this, for arriving and surrendering, for saying yes to the truth and just going there, to that place, where we already are.

As the hour draws closer, I see Steve Gonzales arrive with a short, pretty woman who must be his wife. He has a hand on her shoulder, nodding at me and then heading off to sit near a group of young people who are obviously from the high school. A few minutes later, Clay LaForge comes in with Lenore, both of them a little shy, or seeming so as they slide into a row at the back. Lydia Hague arrives and subtly waves hello. Then I notice a tall, striking woman come in, with a dramatic line of silver through wavy black hair. She has a boy and a girl with her, one at each side. I watch as Will reacts. This is his family; this is Beth with his children.

"Go over," I tell him.

"I will in a bit."

My guess about their split might be right, I realize, and feel terribly sad for all of them. Will's daughter with her bleached jeans, ripped at the knee, his son with his same thick auburn hair, the same strong chin and gray eyes. And his wife, whom I don't know, but feel close to anyway. In a time like this, they need to be together. People in crises always do.

When it's time for Will to speak, only two reporters have shown up, and neither of them has brought a camera crew. Will guessed right to think every news station from here to San Francisco would be covering Winona Ryder's visit to Petaluma instead of us. A rumor had flown through Will's office all day about the actress going out into the fields with a search party, calling Polly's name with a megaphone for hours.

But I'm not going to let myself feel disappointed. Whatever is happening down there for Polly, something else is happening right here, right now. The town *has* shown up. Twice as many bodies as I had let myself hope for. Tally is here, and beside her sitting in a motorized wheelchair is a dark-skinned man I don't recognize. Patterson's has closed and all the employees have come, many still in uniform. Clerks I see all the time from Mendosa's Market, the guy who pumps my gas at the station in Little River, the woman who runs the post office and has for twenty-five years. And Cherilynn Leavitt, who answers the phones in the sheriff's office, with her shaggy musician boyfriend, Stewart, who plays folk sets at a few of the better hotels. And Gray and his mom, and Caitlyn Muncy and her father, Bill, who runs the *Beacon,* and even Caleb, I see, and almost want to cry, because I know how much it has cost him, what memories might be dredged up, already too close to the surface.

When the room is quiet, Will moves in front of Cameron's bulletin board where the microphone is waiting and holds up the new missing poster with the word FOUL PLAY SUSPECTED blazing out in red like a slap.

"I know most of you," he says, "and I know what you're capable of. Where your hearts are. On September twenty-first, Cameron Curtis went missing from her home in the middle of the night. We have reason to believe she was coerced to do so. Two other girls have been reported missing since then, as you no doubt have heard, both within a hundred miles of us. There's no way of knowing if Cameron's disappearance has anything to do with them, but I'll tell you this. All of these girls need us now. Everybody in this room and all over the county, up and down the coast. I'm asking you to sign on to help with the search. You're working. I get that. You have lives, but maybe you go out one afternoon a week with an organized search party. Maybe you send out flyers from your kitchen table. You answer phones, you go door-to-door, you spread the word.

"Some of you know Cameron, but many of you don't. Her mom and dad are private people, and they've kept to themselves. But even if you're just seeing Cameron for the first time on these posters, I want you to take a good look." He turns to the bulletin board. "Someone's hurt this girl. We don't know who, but it's our problem now. She's a kid and she deserves better. Let's make sure she gets that, okay? Let's bring her home."

In the charged applause that follows, Troy Curtis stands up and comes to the front of the room. I barely recognize him. He looks ten years older than when I last saw him, ashen and wooden as he reaches for the microphone. For the first time, I don't note any arrogance in him.

"Cameron is a special person," he says, clearly working to keep his voice steady. "She came to us that way when she was four years old. It seems impossible that anyone could ever want to hurt her. Any crime like this against a child is an outrage. Any child. She's an innocent girl. Please help me find her." His voice cracks with strain. "I know she's got to be alive somewhere. I can feel it." Overcome with emotion, Troy passes the mic to Will and returns to his chair as hands begin to go up, and the questions start coming. I scan the faces nearby for Emily, but she isn't here with her husband. She's not ready after all.

By the time the room begins to empty, it's late. I'm standing by the front door about to go and check on Cricket when Caleb passes me on his way out. I reach for his arm, feel how stiffly he holds his body. His shoulders seem to be made of stone, but that makes sense. He must be holding back so many memories, so much pain. "I'm glad you came," I tell him.

"I almost didn't. Looks like you got drawn into the case after all, huh?"

"It seemed too important not to. Get in touch sometime soon, okay?"

"I'd like that," he allows.

When he moves off, Tally appears. "My husband, Sam," she says, her face warm and open.

The man beside her in the wheelchair is younger than she is, thirty-five or forty and Native American, with his long black hair in a neat ponytail, and warm dark eyes. When I visited her in Comptche that day, I assumed she was single, but now it seems obvious she wouldn't be.

"This is the detective I was telling you about," she explains to Sam.

"Thanks for the work you're doing," he says. "I can help by answering phones or whatever, but I was also thinking I could maybe make my yoga studio available for anyone who wants to come in and just be quiet for a while, and breathe. The kids from Cameron's school. Anyone."

"That's so generous. Thank you."

"I got into it after my accident, and it's changed my life. Now I work with a lot of vets, spinal cord injuries, people who have trouble with the mind-body connection."

"I don't know what that is."

He squints one eye at me, his look gently chiding. "Mind. Body. Connection. Which part's confusing?"

"Sam." Tally laughs. "Behave."

"It's okay. He's funny."

"That's how he works his wiles," she says. "He can be very persuasive."

"Come to one of my classes," Sam throws out.

"See?" Tally laughs again, a musical chime.

I say, "Is it that obvious I need some help?"

"I think you'd like the people I work with," Sam answers. "They've been through some amazing things, and they're so resilient. They just keep doing it."

"What?"

"Trying."

Forty-Eight

I'm already halfway to my car when Will catches me, asking if I'll follow him home for a drink. I've never been to Will's place, so I feel confused when he drives out of the village and south along the coast road, not stopping until we arrive at Elk, fifteen minutes later. The town isn't much more than a speck on a map. In its early logging history it was a boomtown, but now fewer than five hundred people live here in a clutch of houses around the Elk General Store and Queenie's Diner, where Hap and Eden used to bring me for breakfast on weekends sometimes.

Will parks to one side of the store. Whitewashed steps lead up to a narrow door with an apartment number.

"I didn't know anyone lived up there," I say on the darkened street, letting Cricket out of the car.

"I haven't been here long," he says. "Should warn you that I haven't cleaned up in a while."

I follow him up the stairs with Cricket just behind me, watching the space between Will's shoulder blades. The moment feels a little too intimate, or maybe just intimate enough, depending on how the coin lands. For the moment, it goes on flipping inside me, spinning like a top without arriving at an answer. He opens the door and clicks on the light. It's a studio apartment, simple and spare. No bachelor squalor in sight. Then again, he isn't a bachelor.

"When did you move out?" I ask, looking around. There's one sofa, a coffee table, a small dining table with one open chair, the other loaded down with files.

"A few months ago. Beth thought it was better for the kids."

"I'm so sorry, Will."

He shrugs resignedly.

Watching his face, I realize that I haven't been much of a friend since I arrived. He obviously isn't okay, but I've never made an effort to ask him what's been happening in his marriage. I've barely felt capable of dealing with my own crises, let alone inviting his in. But that hasn't been fair, or generous. "Do you want to tell me about it?"

"I'm not sure I have the energy, frankly. . . ." His forehead crumples for a moment before he shakes off the thought or feeling and turns to the icebox, taking out a lean bottle of vodka. After the night we've had, it's probably not the best idea to start drinking straight liquor. I also know I've been leaning on alcohol a little too much lately, but for some reason I can't quite bring myself to say either of these things out loud as he comes over with our drinks, two stiff pours over ice.

"What came of your trip to Gualala?" Will asks.

"Not much. Karen was pretty guarded with me, too, but I still think the two girls have more in common than it looks from the outside. Remember when Karen told you and Denny how Shannan started acting out sexually in what—sixth grade? That's a glaring sign right there. No one at that age gives a blow job in the bathroom by choice, Will. Desire has nothing to do with it. Sex has nothing to do with it. She was working out some kind of emotional garbage, whether she knew that or not."

"You're thinking she was abused, too?"

"She might have been, but there are lots of other ways Shannan could have gotten messed-up boundaries. If she saw her mother beat up, for instance. If there was too much dislocation, or negligence. Karen might have been so distracted by her own problems, she couldn't really bond with Shannan, or consider her needs. And where's the dad in all of this? He must have abandoned the family, and that's another strike against her. Another hole to fill."

He sits forward, swirling his glass until the ice cubes rattle. "Okay, let's say you're right, and that they're both sending out these bat signals, both of them the same kind of not-quite-okay gorgeous girl. What then? What kind of guy preys on that? Who are we looking for, Anna?"

"I don't know yet, but it's all I can think about." With a snap of my fingers, I call Cricket over and rest my hands on the warm back of her head. It's amazing to me how quickly I've adapted to having her nearby, how much she means to me already.

"Did you ever wonder why we're both here right now?" Will asks.

"Because you wanted a drink?"

I was hoping for a smile, but he's all business. "I mean here in Mendocino. With all this going on."

"Bad karma?" I try again.

"Very funny." He clears his throat and moves closer to me on the couch until our knees are only a few inches apart, near enough so that I can feel his body heat bleed into the space. "It does feel like karma sometimes, though. What's the saying about life giving you what you can least handle?"

I manage a hollow laugh. "We're not the luckiest two people."

"No." He takes a long pull on his cocktail, draining the last of it without effort. It's a move that's very familiar to me. The faster you drink, the faster you can try to erase whatever needs erasing. "Can I show you something?"

I steady myself on the glass in my hand. "Sure."

Forty-Nine

The apartment is one long vaulted space partitioned off at the back with drywall to form a bathroom and bedroom. I expect a bedroom, anyway, and wonder worriedly if I've missed some signal and this is a romantic ploy. But when Will opens the door and reaches for the light, I see only storage chests stacked in the center of a bare room.

"Where are you sleeping?" I have to ask.

"On the sofa. It's fine. I don't sleep much anyway."

I think of Hap. His habit of nodding off in the living room, a blanket pulled up over his chin—resting, thinking, and chewing over the problems of the world. Glancing around at the file boxes, I'm about to ask what it's all for, but then it hits me. Beth's decision to split. His insomnia. The way he can drain a glass of vodka as if it's water. They're all rooted in a single problem, a single obsession. "This is about Jenny."

"Not just Jenny, but yeah." He opens the lid of the first box and pulls out a grainy photo of a pretty teen. Button nose, straight teeth in an openmouthed smile, eyes with a downward turn but still bright, still open to whatever waited. I don't recognize her but think I'm supposed to. "Yvonne Lisa Weber," he says, reading my look. "One of the victims of the Santa Rosa hitchhiker killer."

"Wait," I say, remembering how he'd brought this up with Rod Fraser in Petaluma, grasping for connections. "What's going on here?"

"Just a project of mine. A lot of these girls went missing the same year Jenny disappeared."

"You think they're related, then." I exhale, surprising myself. I didn't know I'd been holding my breath. "There was never any connection made. I remember that from when we were kids."

"That's right, but I've always thought the authorities missed something. That my dad dropped a thread, or that no one really looked close enough."

I can see from his body language how wired he is, how none of this is theoretical or remotely casual. But I can't imagine faulting him. My own obsessions have driven my career from the beginning and are still here, perhaps louder and more insistent than ever. "Do you think these cold cases have something to do with Cameron?"

His eyes bounce from the box to my face and back again. "Not necessarily. I just can't let go of the idea that I might still be able to figure out what happened to Jenny. A clue might be here." He reaches for another photo, of Yvonne Weber's best friend, Maureen Louise Sterling. "They disappeared together in February of 1972, after leaving a roller rink well after dark. They were thirteen."

I almost don't want to hold the two pictures when Will offers them side by side. The paper they're printed on is light as a feather and impossibly heavy. The girls could have been sisters, they look so much alike. Brown eyes. Button noses. Dark straight hair parted in the middle and falling over slender shoulders. Their eyes pull me in and in. "When did you start working on this?" I finally ask him.

He shrugs. "Since Jenny died."

Shit. "What have you learned?"

"That it'll fuck you up good to obsess over anything for twenty years."

"Oh, Will." My heart flutters. How well I knew. "I'm sorry."

"It ruined my marriage."

"Tell me about it. Tell me about Beth."

He looks away, smoothing his hand over a glassine sleeve filled with old news clippings.

"Please?"

"She's a saint."

"No one's a saint."

"She's close enough for me, then. We met just after college, up near Mount Shasta. I was there with some buddies, camping. She and some friends were in the next campsite. That was pretty much it."

I have to smile then. "Love and s'mores?"

"And a few cases of Coors Light. Yeah." He reaches into the box again and pulls out more photos, notebooks, and index cards wrapped in crackling dry rubber bands.

"Besides Jenny, these girls hit me hardest. There were seven victims over eighteen months, including Jenny. But these two were the youngest. The only ones taken together. One watched the other die first. Can you imagine? They were best friends."

"Twenty years is a long time for one murder to go unsolved, let alone seven of them, Will." I let the words float. "Does Beth really not understand why you need to keep pursuing this? She knows your history, right? How close you were to Jenny? How could she just give up on you?"

"She didn't. She never did. I gave up on me."

I don't know what to say.

"I haven't opened these boxes in a while. A year maybe?" He scratches his head and sniffs, trying to hold back tears the way that men do, by pretending to have a cold. Sinus trouble. It's something

I've always found endearing and maddening, but in Will's case mostly endearing. I feel for him.

"Why now?"

"I don't know. Maybe it's Cameron and the other girls, all within a hundred miles. Maybe it's the Internet. We've never had a tool like this before, not anything like it. Millions and millions of people are out there, reachable with a few clicks of a button, and at least one of them knows something."

He's right. A whole new day is dawning. A chance to take another crack at this case and so many others, thousands and thousands of searches that had grown cold, enough to fill a yawning morass.

"It can't be a coincidence," he continues. "We were both here back then, and we're both here now. Doesn't that seem like a sign or something? We're supposed to pick this all up again and solve it."

I'm almost dizzy listening to him. A big part of me would give anything to finally put away Jenny's murderer, for all the same reasons Will has, plus my own. But he means the others, too, a massive undertaking by anyone's standards.

Will isn't waiting for my answer or for anything, the momentum inside him building like a wave. "In Petaluma the other day, Barresi mentioned something when you went to grab coffee. The FBI is working on putting together a national database connecting crime labs all over the country. You know how slow everything is now, how disjointed. Once the new database is up and running, a semen sample from a rape kit in Seattle could be matched with a sentenced perpetrator in Philly or DC. Think about all the cold cases that could get new life, Anna. It blows my mind."

"Exciting stuff for sure. But how does it help us right now? Why did you bring me here tonight?"

Some complex feeling shears over his features. He takes a deep breath and lets it out. "I brought you here because I hoped you'd see it, too. That we're supposed to solve Jenny's case, too. All of them."

His expression is so intense. It's taken a lot for him to show me the files. "Maybe someday," I say, finally, afraid to promise more. "When all this is done."

Somehow he's begun to move closer. I can smell his Barbasol shaving cream beneath the vodka we've been drinking. I can smell his nervousness, his need.

"Will," I say. But he's already leaning to kiss me. A kiss that has taken forever, plus weeks of full-on crises and chaos. His lips are warm and insistent. His mouth tastes like forgetting.

I'd be lying to say I don't want it. Not just the sex but also the distraction from all of this, shutting my eyes and tumbling into his arms. But after it was over, wouldn't I be right back where I started, only with guilt in the mix, and regret, too? I've already hurt Brendan enough. Even if he never found out, I've already broken too many promises to add infidelity.

Will's lips press harder, his tongue opening my mouth.

"Please don't." I stumble backward. The look on his face kills me. He's hurt, confused. Decades' worth of disappointment gather in his eyes like a storm. He's already been kicked out of his marriage. And then all this pressure from the town, an impossible job to do for anyone. It's not sex he wants at all, but a lifeline. A raft to keep him afloat in the godforsaken nothingness, or even a single piece of driftwood, as long as the two of us could cling hard to it, together.

The phone rings from the other room and I jump. A shrill burst of sound.

"Let it ring," he says.

"No. Answer it."

"Anna."

The ringing seems to go on for an eternity. Cricket barks once, high and sharp, from the living room, and finally Will goes to get it. Almost shaking, I find the door to the bathroom, shut myself inside, and look into the mirror hard. *Don't do this.* My eyes meet hers in the glass, reversed. I think of Brendan, think of the woman I was not so long ago. I've made terrible mistakes, yes. And maybe my work has taken too much out of me, and I haven't been able to truly be there for him and our family. But that doesn't mean I don't love him. There is a part of me that hasn't given up hoping I could still win back his trust and go home again. But I'll never have a chance at that if I turn to Will now, no matter how comforting his arms might feel in the moment.

I hear Cricket at the door coming to look for me but stay a moment longer, splashing my face with cold water, and then using Will's towel. Even that feels too intimate. The right thing to do is clear. I still know where true north is.

With Cricket trailing me, I walk down the little hall to the living area, trying to find the words that will let Will know I've always cared for him, which is exactly why I have to leave now. That I can't give what isn't mine to offer. That we can't stay broken on that raft, not even for each other. Not for Jenny. Not for anyone or anything. We have to let go and swim like hell, alone, because that's the only way to any shore that matters.

He's just disconnecting, the heavy plastic receiver in his hand looking alien and incomplete. "They found a car that might be Shannan Russo's. The Sonoma County helicopter spotted it late today. Denny's crew is heading up at dawn to check it out."

"We have to be there."

"I agree. We'll leave at six. Dress warm, okay? It might be a long day."

"Will . . ." I say, needing to settle where we've been, to move through instead of around it. We owe each other that.

But he cuts me short. "Get some sleep. We've got an early start."

Fifty

In a remote section of Montgomery Woods, an hour southwest of us, Shannan's Firebird lies hidden in a stand of trees beyond a little-used dirt service road. It looks as if gasoline was poured over the hood and interior, or some other chemical that intensified the blaze enough to incinerate the seats and melt the paint, the tires, the mats and steering wheel. The windows exploded at some point, sending glass out in a mortar fan, over the ring of burned vegetation and beyond.

When we arrive, Denny Rasmussen and his men are on site, along with a medical examiner and a team of forensics people who have already begun to process the car, which is scorched, collapsed. I'm disappointed to see the extent of the damage. We need fingerprints or hair or fibers, anything that can provide essential information, but the car is little more than a blistered husk. It's hard to imagine any evidence surviving the incineration.

"You okay?" Will asks.

I can't tell from his tone if he means okay with the look of the scene, or something more personal, but either way I don't have time to answer him. The crime scene specialists have moved around to the trunk, which seems to have been more protected than the rest of the car. We join them as they manage to pry it open. And then silence falls. The smell hits us like a wall, a thick and heavy rot. Her body is curled fetally and her eyes are open, sunk back into her skull like jelly. Her mouth gapes, a ring of teeth jutting from a seeping hole.

I steel myself, pulling down a layer of emotional armor so I can focus on the work at hand. But it isn't easy. Her arms have been wrenched behind her body, her hands bound with skinny electrical wire, probably an extension cord. The trunk has shielded the body from the blaze, but it's also held in moisture and heat. Her fluids have puddled, as if she's suspended in a lake of herself, while maggots writhe like foam, a moving tide.

"Mother of Christ," Denny mutters. He's muscular and fair-haired with the legs of a cyclist, thick calves stretching against the fabric of his khakis. Physical stamina won't help him here, however. His face has gone white. Mine has, too, probably. No matter how many times I've seen the remains of a murder victim, it never feels like less than a rape of the psyche. The human mind wasn't built to make sense of this.

And yet we have to. Have to see everything with investigative eyes. Have to admit that as awful as it is to find a body like this, at least she's no longer missing. That's a win. A shitty win but a win nonetheless.

The medical examiner, Robert Lisicky, scans the victim silently for several minutes before pushing at the nose of his wire-rimmed glasses with a gloved hand. "Caucasian from the hair. Here a few months, I'm guessing, based on the state of the body. But let's seal this up. We've got to get the car to an enclosed space so you don't lose evidence. Can you bring in a flatbed?"

"Sure thing," Denny says, and peels away to make the call. One of his deputies steps back as if to follow him, and then rushes toward the woods, where he heaves and then vomits.

I glance at Will, wondering how he's managing. He's a professional, but even so, this will be new for him. And men always seem to have a more difficult time compartmentalizing at these times than women, I've found. Women are stronger because they have to be.

I watch him wobble a little next to me and then right himself again as Lisicky takes two baby food jars out of his pocket and carefully collects specimens from the blossom of bugs on the body. An entomologist will be able to help us determine how long she's been here, hopefully. The autopsy report will too. For now, the trunk is dusted for fingerprints and then sealed with crime scene tape, and the car is photographed from every angle.

One strange thing is that the fire didn't spread beyond a large scorched ring surrounding the car. It doesn't make sense. Summer is the dry season up here. The flames should have taken acres if not more, half the damned park, but they didn't.

Will has noticed too. He points to the bald, blackened vegetation under the wreckage and then above to the tree line. "If this guy's an amateur he got lucky."

"Maybe he knew exactly what he was doing," Denny says, chiming in. "He could be a ranger, couldn't he?"

"Shannan didn't have any reason to be in these woods," I add. "She wasn't camping, she was carjacked and then lured here. Her killer's familiar with these roads. He knew the car wouldn't be found right away."

"We'll start running a list of park personnel through the database to see if there's anyone who looks right for this," Denny says. "Usually the Forest Service does a thorough background check before hiring, but I don't know. Somehow he was able to stop the blaze from spreading after setting it. That's not easy unless the weather turned."

"I don't remember rain up here in early June," Will says. "But we'll confirm with the National Climatic Data Center right away."

"Did he kill her here or just need a place to deal with the car and body?" I ask, though I know I can't get an answer. We won't know anything until the autopsy and crime scene reports come back—and maybe not even then.

"Let's move to sweep this whole area," Denny says. "There are rangers' cabins in these woods, and huts for hikers. If he drove Shannan here in her car, how'd he get out unless he had a vehicle here waiting? Or lives somewhere on reserve property?"

"He could have had an accomplice," Will throws out. "That's one of the theories with the Klaas girl. That there was a driver too, someone who stayed in the car while the other went in to take Polly."

"It's possible," I have to admit while, inside, a louder voice tells me, *No*. That this is one guy with strength enough to lift a body into the trunk, and skill enough to control a serious fire in woods he knows well. Maybe he is a ranger, as Denny suggested. Either way, if he's the same guy who took Cameron in late September, he waited four months before hunting again. Could Cameron be in these woods, too, I can't help wondering, hidden somewhere nearby? Is her harrowing ordeal still unfolding, or are we already too late?

I look at the car again, a last stand, unwitnessed. Think of the photos in Karen's wallet, her story about the fishtail braid. Nothing in the trunk looks like the girl who once wanted to be a Disney princess. But this is Shannan, I know it. And she was tortured before she was destroyed.

Fifty-One

I haven't been in Montgomery Woods since I was a teenager. It was late spring and warm, one of Hap's rare days off. He drove us out of Mendocino along the Ukiah-Comptche road, one hand on the wheel, the other out the window. Several miles shy of the state reserve, on runty, narrow Orr Springs Road, he pulled his Suburban onto the berm and killed the engine. Then he grabbed a daypack from the tailgate, slugged a little water from his hiker's canteen, and led us straight into the forest, where there wasn't a trail for miles.

The going was hard, just the way we both liked it. I scrambled after him, twigs stabbing through my jeans, attacking my hands, spiderwebs catching in my hair and stretching across my face. But after a while, I was able to match his stride. My legs had been growing stronger year by year, and my skills had improved exponentially. If at ten I was Hap's cautious shadow, by fifteen I was deft and capable.

The mountain laurel was at the end of its blooming season, white and pink star-shaped clusters that came apart in filmy layers, covering the ground like spent confetti. Through a dense grove of them, we dipped into a small valley where the vegetation shifted to the ferns and vines of riparian meadow, and gave off a boggy scent. Heading south along the meadow's green rim, we walked for another half mile or so until we came to a thick tangle of alder and then a wide, still redwood grove. At the center was a towering giant that made my neck pinch as I looked up to see how high it reached.

"Some will tell you this is the tallest tree in the world," Hap said. He was in his weekend uniform, blue flannel shirt and jeans and a brown felt Stetson. His sweeping, silver-tinged mustache moved when his mouth did. "There's another one up in Humboldt could be taller."

"How tall is it?" I asked.

He glanced up along the surface of the trunk, which was lightly furred where the fibers pushed out like tufts of hair, red and brown and almost human. Half to himself he said, "Is knowing so important? If something makes it this far, through everything the universe has thrown at it, maybe we should just say thank you."

As usual, he had a point. I followed the arrow of the trunk to the distant scrap of sky, a mandala of pale blue and deep green and rust.

"Do you know where you are?" he asked quietly.

"Montgomery Woods?"

"What do you hear?" That's when I knew we'd begun one of his survival tests, just for fun but also completely serious.

I strained, then stilled. "The trees sound like they're whispering."

"Can they tell you how to get back to the car? Have you been paying attention as we walked?"

"I think so."

"Let's say you're lost, and I'm not here."

"But you are."

He smiled. "I'm not. What do you do?"

"Look for the trail again," I offered. "Look for water."

"Which?"

"The trail."

He didn't say yes or no. Growing up in strangers' houses, I was adept at reading faces and guessing feelings, projecting myself into others, but this never worked with Hap. He was too deep and too quiet, too inside himself. What was that song about people being rocks and islands? Hap was neither. He was his own wilderness.

"What time is it?" he asked.

I looked up through the canopy to fix the angle of the sun. We'd left the car around three, I guessed, and had walked for an hour or a little more. "Four-fifteen. We have plenty of time before dark."

A rare smile. "Maybe we do."

I closed my eyes and felt outward with my other senses, not moving until I began to hear things that hadn't been there a moment before—the tremor of a leaf blown into a spiderweb, water moving underground in a trickle that pushed and sighed. There was more, too. Beyond all of this, beyond what I could actually hear, if I was going to parse it rationally, the sound of an engine, machinery. Civilization. "I think I know the way."

He let me lead from there, out of the grove and through the red alder, following signs that showed me where to go subtly, almost invisibly. Some of the spaces between the trees looked different from others, jogging my memory, alerting me to landmarks in the white slashes of mushrooms, in lichen, and in moss. There was the brackish smell of the meadow, the wet-feeling air as we neared the fern forest, the mountain laurel blossoms in a translucent pink carpet. A few times I got off track, but Hap didn't say a word. He wasn't going to help me at all this time, and it wasn't out of stubbornness either, but out of love. He wanted to show me that I could do it. That I was competent and resourceful. That I could trust myself as much as he had learned to trust me.

When we finally reached the car, I watched Hap load his daypack back inside. The steady movements of his hands, and his quiet concentration. Here was the tallest, straightest tree I would ever know. When he turned back around, I said, "Thank you."

Fifty-Two

The next day the examiner calls with the autopsy report. Manner of death: homicidal force, strangulation. A fractured hyoid bone and soft tissue damage in the neck confirm it. The ligature marks suggest protracted binding.

"When the Curtises hear, they're going to lose their minds," Will says once he's filled me in. "Of course they're going to wonder if Cameron is next."

We're in his office, both jangling from the ongoing stress and too much caffeine. The last twenty-four hours have been so exhausting and upsetting, I can barely remember the kiss in his apartment. It's as if it never happened, and that's a relief. We have enough to deal with.

"Strangulation is almost always a power thing," I say to Will. "So much force is required to finish someone that way. You can see their eyes and smell their breath, knowing that you can stop the train at any moment and spare them. Or not."

"Jesus," he says heavily. "I never thought this could happen on my watch. It nearly broke my dad. I don't think he was ever the same kind of sheriff again. Maybe I'm not strong enough, or good enough. I mean *shit*, Anna."

I know what's filling his head right now. The trunk. The body. It's all with me too. "Try not to think about it," I say gently. "You can do this. We're in it together."

"Yeah," Will says, clearly unconvinced. "What do you think of Denny's ranger theory?"

Hap's profession has always been sacred to me, but I have to admit the idea sounds plausible. A ranger would be local and familiar with the area, comfortable in the outdoors. "Could be a firefighter, too," I add, "or military, or someone in the National Guard? All those guys learn how to handle fire, and they're physical."

"True," he agrees. "By the way, did you notice Drew Hague didn't show up at the community meeting? He seems pretty comfortable in the outdoors, too."

I had noticed. If Emily couldn't bring herself to come, with all she's dealing with, that's one thing. But Drew has no excuse. Not a plausible one anyway, unless there's a story. "I think there's something he's avoiding. How did the follow-up polygraph go?"

"The technician had to cancel at the last minute. We've rescheduled for Wednesday."

"That's two days from now."

"You don't have to tell me, Anna. But what am I supposed to do? I've always had to call in techs from other counties, and Polly Klaas's case is still sucking up a lot of resources. Anyone with talent is working there. Her tip line is still going crazy, and it's only going to get more crazy now."

"We're going to have to call Rod Fraser right away and share everything we know. This guy could be the same one who took Polly, right? We just don't fucking know."

He stares at the center of his messy desk for a long moment, obviously overwhelmed. Then he says, "Let's go back to the ranger idea for a minute. If that's who we're looking for, how would he have made contact with Shannan up here in the woods, particularly if she was on her way to Seattle? She wasn't outdoorsy."

"Could he have run into her socially somehow, in a bar or something? Even dated her for a while?" I tap two more packets of Sweet'N Low into my coffee, hoping the rush will help me think. "Maybe it was an accident, even. Say he and Shannan hooked up one night and went somewhere quiet to have sex in her car. But then something flipped. He got violent and strangled her, and then afterward there he was with a body. He'd go somewhere he knows, right? He'd burn the car and bury his tracks and try to forget about it."

"June to September, that's four months," he adds. "So maybe he's successful for a while or thinks he's kicked it. But then Cameron Curtis appears. Why her and not someone else? What do she and Shannan have in common?"

"They look a little alike," I try. "Both girls have long dark hair parted in the middle and brown eyes. Both are more than pretty, too. They're stunning. They'd stop you on the street."

"I can see that. But he definitely didn't run into Cameron at a bar. By then something had shifted. He sought her out."

"He'd have to." I sit forward in my chair, feel the hard plastic pressing into the back of my legs. "She's not out in the world all that much, just school and home and sometimes to Gray Benson's." My temples have begun to throb dully. "It's a crazy idea, but what if Cameron sought him out instead? Remember that poem from Cameron's locker? The one that goes, *I want to unfold. I don't want to stay folded anywhere, because where I am folded, there I am a lie?*"

"Shit, you've memorized it."

"Oh, stop. Just hear me out a minute. Cameron's not just any fifteen-year-old. Her life has been a pressure cooker these last few months. The silence and lies at home, between her parents. And that's only going to get worse, right? A baby's coming, maybe her parents are divorcing—or, worse, *not* divorcing but just going on this way. She'd be desperate for a way out."

"How about the free-clinic thing?" Will sounds as if he hasn't quite caught up. To be fair, the theories have been flying pretty fast. "Where does that fit in?"

"I don't know. Maybe the appointment was about independence, or started out that way at least. Maybe Cameron was just trying to carve out a life of her own. Having Emily for a mom can't have been easy. It wasn't all that long ago when she stopped taking film and TV roles. And even then, she stayed recognizable. Once she was even voted one of the fifty most beautiful people alive, right?"

"I've thought about that. I mean, we think those magazines are stupid, but Cameron probably wouldn't. Most girls would never feel special enough with that to measure up against."

"If Cameron wanted to break out somehow and make her own mark, how would she try and do that? What does that kind of *unfolding* look like, and how would that put her on a path to meet the kind of guy we're looking at, a forest ranger or a military guy? With something to offer her, an escape route out of that glass box?"

"I don't see it," Will says.

"Yeah, me neither." I feel the oxygen in the room dip. Feel us both spinning our wheels. After a while, I say, "Somehow there had to be enough trust built up between them that Cameron agreed to meet him late at night. How did that happen? What would it take for this particular guy not to scare her off but draw her closer? That's the magic question."

Will makes a sound of agreement. "Emily said she'd never even had a boyfriend, remember?"

"Exactly. Shannan might have been someone he hooked up with, but I'm starting to wonder if his attraction to Cameron could be something else. If she's some sort of ideal."

"Meaning what?"

"I've seen this come up a lot in profiling," I say, reaching for language that will help him understand my line of thinking. "Guys who are outsiders and can't get close to people sometimes fixate on an innocent as a chance to redeem themselves. Or that's the story they want to believe."

"Wait. So he's not a psychopath?"

Clearly I haven't succeeded. "Maybe he is," I try again. "But even the most twisted minds want love and connection. Maybe the reason we haven't found Cameron's body yet is because he thinks she can make everything bad inside him feel right again. Fix the ways the world has hurt him."

"I don't know," Will says doubtfully. "That's a pretty big hypothesis, Anna. Why are you assuming this guy has been wounded?"

I stare at him, feeling frustrated and out of sorts. This day has been too long, and way too hard. This week, and month, and year. "Because that's how you make a predator."

Fifty-Three

One year Frank Leary gave everyone at Searchlight a copy of a book called *Sexual Homicide: Patterns and Motives* and told us to treat it like the Bible. The writers were two FBI criminalists and a psychiatric nurse specialist who organized and conducted dozens of interviews with convicted killers and torturers, psychopaths, sociopaths, pedophiles, and sexual sadists, trying to understand the criminal mind in a systematized way they could share with professionals as a teaching tool.

It was provocative stuff, to be sure. The agents had gone into maximum-security prisons all over the country to sit across an interview table from Charles Manson, David Berkowitz, Edward Kemper, and thirty-three others, hoping to learn from them. Not the facts of their cases or convictions, and not whether they could ever be rehabilitated, but what they were thinking in the moments before, during, and after the murders they committed. How and why they selected certain victims, what their triggers were, where their violent fantasies began, and what the most exciting parts of the crime were—basically how these brutal killers thought and what they felt around all aspects of what they'd done.

No one had ever tried to look so deeply into the criminal psyche before, let alone compile and catalog data so that law enforcement officers like myself could more accurately profile and identify suspects, and more readily solve cases. And though the depth of the fixation on warped minds was disturbing to me, and the way the writers sometimes lingered over gruesome, sensational details, as I read something clicked for me and opened a larger question about the connection between victims and perpetrators.

I remember trying to talk to Frank about it over drinks near our offices one night, the dim bar seeming to bend around us on our stools, and the whiskey to flicker. "When you read a book like this, the violence starts to feel like a movie. The crimes feel like sick plots, not real life, and all the details are so lurid and specific. But it *is* real. And the victims, who just come through as names with thumbnail photos, just targets, we don't know them at *all*. We never get the whole picture, how they got drawn into the story in the first place, how certain sets of experiences made them vulnerable, and not just in a general way either but to the particular predators who targeted them. That book would be fascinating, wouldn't it? That's the stuff I want to know." I stopped there, catching my breath. Feeling everything I'd said and meant.

He looked at me for a long time. "Well, maybe you'll have to write it one day."

"Right. That's going to happen."

"Why not? These are good questions, and no one's asking them. Not yet, anyway. This is obviously your lane, Anna. I've seen how involved you get in your cases, how much you care about the victims, how you try to understand their side of the story. It's how you're built, I guess. So why not feed it, and see what happens?"

What Frank didn't know that day—because I'd never been honest with him—was that I wasn't just involved in my cases, I lived and breathed them. If my level of dedication made me a good detective with a high solve rate, it was also ruining my personal life. Those questions Corolla had asked about sleep, about drinking too much. I hadn't told the truth that day. I had nightmares consistently and often woke in the middle of the night feeling as if my whole body was buzzing, set on high alert. The minute I walked in the door after work, I had to pour a stiff drink or three just to come down from the intensity of the day. But even when the edge was gone, I couldn't quite land in my body. I was always thinking about a case, trying to crack an interview or tease out a complex lead, canvassing witnesses in my mind, even in the shower. When Brendan would complain or get mad at me, I would go on the defensive. The truth was I didn't have any control over my obsession, nor did I have the energy to fight with him. I would never have said it out loud, but he wasn't my priority.

Then things got worse. I had just come off ten weeks of maternity leave when Frank gave my partner and me a particularly tough case—an infant. The father had called it in, thinking drug dealers had kidnapped the boy. They lived in a rough neighborhood. It wasn't out of the question. Meanwhile the boy was only six months old, and he had seizures, the family reported, something to do with a difficult delivery. He was still on medication and could die without it. Time was ticking as we searched for him, and the stress was getting to me. I kept having dreams about children screaming on the other side of a brick wall. Whole families under water and no way to reach them. During the day, I was edgy and distracted, and Frank noticed.

"I think you need more time off, Anna. I pulled you back in too soon."

"No, no. I can do this," I raced to reassure him. "It's just hormones or something."

"At least go back to that therapist," he suggested.

"It's not necessary."

"Asking for help doesn't make you weak, Anna."

"I know that."

"Sometimes I wonder," he said, clearly unconvinced. "Baby doing all right?"

"The baby's fine." I forced myself to sound cheerful. "We're all fine."

"Let's keep it that way."

Days later, my partner and I found Jamie Rivera's body in the basement of his family home. We discovered him by accident almost, under fifty pounds of processed venison. The freezer was one of those old Whirlpool chests that open like a coffin. The compressor had been wheezing as we searched the space, giving off a chemical smell. We'd already opened it, but my instinct told me to go back and recheck. He was all the way at the bottom, under strange red bricks that had once been living creatures. We threw them to the floor—and then we saw the boy. A glaze of frost stiffening his eyelashes. His small blue hands.

4

The Bent Grove

Fifty-Four

Once Shannan Russo's remains have been identified, media trucks set up camp in Gualala, in front of Rumor's All About Hair, and on Lansing Street in Mendocino, where our case is finally gathering steam. I don't watch the looping clips of Karen Russo because I can't bear to see her face. Instead, I focus on the new momentum and direction Shannan's discovery has created. Finding her body has helped us begin to compile and refine a profile for her killer, which might also aid in our search for Cameron. The torture and strangulation Shannan endured and the controlled incineration of her car don't immediately seem to dovetail with the details of Polly's abduction, but Rod Fraser is being briefed on every significant finding, and on the profile we're still building, bit by bit.

For the moment, we're looking for a federal- or state-level parks employee, a firefighter, or a military guy, single probably, and somewhere between the ages of twenty-seven and forty-five, given statistical averages and the physical strength he's already demonstrated.

The media likes to sensationalize psychopaths and evil geniuses like Charles Manson and David Berkowitz, but in real life, people who commit serial murders are typically of average intelligence, and rarely show an obvious degree of mental illness, at least not on the surface. In this case, there's even more reason to believe our suspect blends easily into his environment. He probably first encountered Shannan in a public place and hadn't frightened her or given her cause to be alarmed, not enough to make any kind of scene. The same had probably been true with Cameron, if my instincts are on track. Because of her age, he would have needed to move slowly in getting close to her, and also have had something to offer her, some opportunity or possibility she didn't see at home. We only have to find out what that is, now, and comb through tens of thousands of records, hoping someone jumps out.

The discovery of Shannan's remains in our county has given us greater traction in the search for Cameron overall. We've always been missing evidence and hard clues. Now that it seems more and more likely that the two cases are linked, we finally have more manpower and equipment, not to mention volunteers. Reserve land is being searched mile by mile, plus the estuaries and the coastline, with particular emphasis on any cabin, shed, or structure in or near Montgomery Woods. Most serial killers have a comfort radius and a clear anchor point they hunt from, a narrow range of territory they're intimately familiar with. All things being equal, Cameron is probably no more than thirty miles, give or take, from her own home and where we found Shannan's body. This is our most plausible grid.

The Cameron Curtis Rescue Center begins to run twenty-four hours a day. Local business owners donate postage, phones, and fax machines. Everyone does what they can to help with the mailings, stuffing envelopes, pasting flyers all over the area, and answering the phone. Calls begin to come in by the hundreds, some just to say that Cameron is in their prayers, some offering ten dollars, twenty dollars, kids wanting to donate birthday money and allowances. Most of the calls are from women reluctant to give their name. "I know who he is," one says. "I dated him in college."

Patterson's hosts a fish fry for all of the volunteers. A team of counselors is sent into Mendocino High as well as the elementary and middle schools, to offer support and comfort. Some of the older kids in the community start doing afternoon shifts, going door-to-door, organized by Gray Benson. Clay LaForge and Lenore spend hours a day addressing envelopes to hotels and restaurants, gas stations, laundromats, anywhere someone might have seen Cameron since she disappeared. In each mailing—Lenore's idea—there's a handwritten note asking whoever receives it to place Cameron's poster in a prominent location and not let it be taken down or covered over. It's a small touch, personal and direct.

Wanda volunteers to be in the center late nights. "I'm a night owl anyway," she explains when I find her there, alone at a long collapsible conference table, stuffing envelopes. She perks up to see Cricket, the two falling on each other like old friends. And then the door swings open, and Hector walks in, blinking against the yellow fluorescent lighting.

He wears a denim jacket that seems to jut at the shoulders and the same ass-kicking boots I noticed in Ukiah, but the look on his face is tentative. Uncertain. "I read about that murdered girl," he says. "That can't happen to Cameron. Tell me what to do."

I soften just looking at him. Cricket trots over to refamiliarize herself with his smell, and Wanda says hello, seeming to know there's a story here, one she can learn some other time.

"You can help with the mailings or in the field," I throw out. "We've got four or five different groups going out every day. Come tomorrow morning. We'll be here."

He nods and takes in the room, heading to the bulletin board, our shrine to Cameron. I watch his eyes move over the images, the poems and drawings, each a new part of her he's never had a chance to know.

Moved, I go over and stand next to him. He's staring at a photo I don't recognize. Gray must have brought it in recently, maybe just today. In it, Cameron is almost unrecognizable. Her hair has been gathered into a low, sleek ponytail and pulled over her left shoulder. Her eye makeup looks professionally done, with winged liner that makes her look not older exactly but wiser, more confident and experienced. There's also an imitative quality to her pose and expression—I don't know how else to explain it to myself—as if Cameron was acting for the camera, somehow, pretending to be someone else, someone not just beautiful, but famous. Her black blouse has draping sleeves and bares her midriff. Her black skinny jeans look painted onto her body above low-heeled black boots. I stood in her closet and didn't see anything like this. Are they even her clothes?

Hector is still staring. "Where was this taken?"

I step closer. The background is wooded and lush. Cameron leans against a tree trunk that's deeply textured, curved like a body, its color almost mauve with shadows. The light is eerie and familiar, I realize, and the shapes of the trees, too. Suddenly I feel a jangle of dread, like a premonition that's come true. This is the krummholz grove.

Fifty-Five

Before seven the next morning, I'm headed back to Cahto Street, my mind a hive of questions. Is the krummholz grove just a random place Cameron and Gray decided to hang out one day, or is it connected to our killer's territory? Did I miss a sign of him when I hiked into the grove? Was he nearby then, or when the photos were taken? Had he brought Cameron there some other time? And whether he had or not, why is she so unrecognizable in the picture?

Di Anne answers the door in her bathrobe and slippers, looking rumpled but tender somehow without a trace of makeup. Offering coffee, she leads me into the kitchen, where Gray stands packing his lunch for school, cheese and apples in a brown paper bag, a Dr Pepper, a Hostess cupcake, all of it so ordinary and uncomplicated, I almost hate to ask my questions.

I hold up the photo of Cameron. "Did you take this, Gray?"

"Yeah." He seems confused by my intensity. "We did them when we were bored one day over the summer. Just screwing around."

Really? Cameron doesn't look like she was killing time to me. She had a purpose of some kind, even if I can't yet identify it. "I think they're good. She doesn't even look like herself."

Gray brightens. "I did her makeup. I got a new camera for my birthday. She shot some of me, too."

"Why did you choose this place? Had you been there before?"

He shakes his head. "It was her idea. I thought it was creepy at first, but the light was supercool."

"The shoot was her idea, too?"

"I think so. I don't remember how it came up."

"I don't recognize that outfit on Cameron, do you?"

"She brought it over with her. She'd just been to a thrift store."

"Gray." I put my coffee down, needing his complete attention. "These don't look like thrift-store clothes. And even if they were, if she brought them over, it's likely she had a clear objective in mind."

"I don't get it. Why?"

"That's a great question. Had she ever talked about the grove before? Do you remember what she said when she suggested it?"

"No." His forehead wrinkles. I can tell my questions are scaring him. He clearly hasn't registered the possible significance of this day in Cameron's disappearance and now is worried he missed something important, a chance to help me, a chance to find his friend.

"It's okay," I say, trying to ease his mind. "Tell me, did Cameron ever talk about wanting to do modeling?"

"She wasn't tall enough. She knew that."

"I don't mean the practical side of her, Gray." As I fumble for the right words, Di Anne sits down, closing her robe with her hands.

"Honey, I think Anna's asking if Cameron ever dreamed about that kind of life for herself. You know, the way kids your age do, wanting to travel the world, be famous, meet interesting people? Do something wonderful."

Gray blinks, his eyelashes spiked with mascara, the makeup subtle, almost invisible, but not quite. "Sometimes we both talked like that, sure. Her mom was always so negative about Hollywood and being beautiful, a celebrity, but sometimes Cameron and I talked about how cool it would be to be discovered like Emily was. To have money enough to go anywhere we wanted together. Doesn't everyone want that, though?"

"I've never met anyone your age who doesn't have some sort of fantasy they like to imagine," I tell him, "no matter how impossible it feels, how far away. The tougher the real world, the more important that dream becomes. Do you know what I mean?"

"The stuff she was struggling with? Her parents lying to her all the time, and the bits of memories coming back."

I nod, encouraging him. "That would make sense, wouldn't it?"

There's a creak as Di Anne shifts in her chair. I can see from her expression that Gray hasn't told her anything about Cameron's situation at home or her abuse, but she doesn't pull back or away. Maybe she's intuited the darkness Cameron carries.

"Dreams can tell us a lot of things," I go on. "They're a kind of map of the inner life. Sometimes thinking of who we might someday be is the only way we can get through the reality of who we actually are."

Di Anne's look is soft. "Like not quite fitting in in a small town where no one looks or thinks like you, honey."

I can't help but admire her. She's a single parent. Gray has never mentioned his dad, but Di Anne seems to be doing okay on her own, at least in one way. She's trying to meet her son where he is, accepting him as he finds his way, loving him.

"I guess so," Gray answers quietly.

"Dreaming is brave," I say. "Sometimes it's all we have."

A short while later I'm out at Jug Handle, hoping to find even a fragment of the answers I need in the krummholz grove. Hiking in, Cricket rushes ahead of me as if she's long known the way, through the break in the trees with her nose to the ground, already getting down to business. Morning sun comes through the canopy in spears. Light catches dozens of spiderwebs, turning them into diamonds. Some are the size of maple leaves. Others are tiny and pearled with dew, like fairy hammocks or swings. It's the kind of place that can make you believe almost anything: that whole civilizations can live under mushroom caps; that the usual laws have never fully landed here, or mattered.

While Cricket explores, nudging under low, tortured branches, I do my own slow reconnaissance of the area. Way too much time has passed for physical clues to be likely, but I'm searching for something deeper and more subtle—something I might not see as much as feel. My eyes flick from branch to branch. Was it here Cameron stood that day? Or here? And when she looked out, her best friend behind the lens, what did she want? Who came along to trigger her hope? And how did he reach her in the first place?

It's hard for me to imagine the hook coming out of nowhere, someone stopping Cameron on the street, after school maybe, and asking her if she'd ever wanted to be a model. Even if her boundaries were bad, and her desperation was high, wouldn't she have told Gray what she was thinking of doing? And anyway, even if this was the method her predator had used to draw her in and then dangle large promises, could the kind of guy we've been looking for lately—a ranger or parks employee with access to and knowledge of reserve land—also have encouraged Cameron to think she had this kind of shot at being successful, or even famous? How do those two elements connect, if at all? Are we wrong about the ranger angle, and am I on some ludicrous tangent right now? Following a false lead to a place that signifies nothing?

Talk to me, Cameron, I think. *Please.* But only Cricket stirs, her coat flecked with sunlight while fine pollen motes float all around us, never settling.

Fifty-Six

When Eden died in September of 1975, we buried her in Evergreen Cemetery in the Strater family plot, next to Hap's mother and father, grandmother and grandfather, aunts and uncles, the dates on stones going all the way back to the 1850s.

Hap didn't deliver her eulogy or speak more than a few words at her service. He didn't want people gathering at the house, passing along words of comfort, and didn't want to wear his suit a moment longer than necessary. He just wanted to be in the woods.

Afterward, we went to Van Damme State Park, just the two of us, into the fern forest, walking without talking much. What was there to say? We hiked for an hour or more, not resting until we reached a shaded area along the river. There, we sat on a large flat rock, side by side, just looking at the water.

"Did I ever tell you the story about the boy I found once who had accidentally shot his brother?" he asked after a while.

I shook my head. He hadn't, but I would have told him no anyway. I would have done anything to keep him talking. Any story would do. Any lesson at all. I needed all of them.

The boys had been sixteen, he told me, Jake and Sam Douglas. Twins. At first, he only knew they'd been reported missing after a day hike. Their mother had dropped them here, at Van Damme State Park, and then panicked when they didn't return to the parking lot three hours later.

Hap's team had gone out before dark that same day, but came back empty-handed. The next morning, he pulled more men and went back in. The park was eighteen hundred acres, with ten miles of maintained trail along the Little River. The boys' mother had insisted they wouldn't have any reason to go wandering, but they didn't turn up along any part of the trail. Not in the pygmy forest, where the soil was spongy with fresh rain. Not in the groves of stunted cypress and rhododendron and dwarf pine.

It wasn't until late afternoon the second day when one of Hap's rangers spotted a bright blue shirt inside the camouflaging hollow of a redwood trunk, a small cave where the root system had opened like a secret door. Inside, crouched in that narrow space, Sam Douglas was found mute and dumb and completely disoriented. Beneath him, his brother Jake was bleeding from a gunshot wound to the thigh that had nearly ripped off his leg. The two boys had apparently been target shooting with their grandfather's contraband pistol. The gun had gone off in Sam's hand. Ashamed, he'd dragged the body into the cave of the tree, hiding there all day and night, unable to face what he'd done.

"Did he die?" I asked Hap by the river, feeling sure the answer was yes. Someone always died in his stories.

"Actually, it was the damnedest thing. Jake had lost consciousness and probably would have bled out if Sam had gone for help. The weight of his body made a tourniquet."

"Wait," I said. "He didn't know his brother was still alive?"

"That's the most interesting bit as I see it. He thought he'd passed beyond forgiveness, but that was just a story. A terrible story, but believing it saved his brother's life." He looked at me to make sure I was with him. This was the important part. "You know, we don't always understand what we're living inside of, or how it will matter. We can guess all we want and prepare, too, but we never know how it's going to turn out."

I struggled to take in his meaning. Was he still talking about the boys, or was he trying to tell me something more, about us and now, about Eden and how we could possibly go on without her? I wanted time enough to ask him and hear his answer, wanted years, decades—an eternity. But he'd rested enough and was ready to hike again. The lesson was over.

We had one more year together, just the two of us on our own, then I went away to college at SFU. Hap drove me down himself, the back of his Suburban crammed with boxes and bedding. I should have been excited to start this new adventure, but I was already homesick. And I hadn't even gotten out of the car.

"I'll see you at Thanksgiving," I said later, when we'd unpacked everything and it was time for him to go. I was trying and failing to keep my voice even, to be strong when I felt the opposite.

"Take care of yourself, sweetheart," he said, closing his car door. His hand lingered for a moment on the open window gasket. "Be good."

Two months later, in the early hours of November 12, 1976, one of Hap's junior rangers found his pack seven miles beyond the trailhead in Russian Gulch State Park, but no sign of Hap himself. No one had seen him since the previous afternoon, when he'd gone off on a recreational hike alone. An extensive search turned up nothing, even with K-9 units. He'd vanished into thin air.

When Ellis Flood called, he reached me at my dorm, through my RA. I sat on a hard chair in her room, looking at a painted cinder-block wall, a laminated poster about teens and stress. As Ellis Flood talked, I could barely take it in, plunged into confusion and disbelief. What would have caused Hap to leave the trail without his provisions or even water? He was a consummate professional in the field, intimate with the challenges and dangers of any wilderness area. It didn't make sense to me that something terrible could have happened to him. Not with his skill and experience.

"Obviously we're going to keep searching," Ellis reassured me, "but, Anna, it's possible that grief could have caused him to lose focus. You and I both know he hasn't really been the same since Eden died."

He was right, but I didn't want to admit it. Instead, I began to cry as the sheriff went on gently, trying to explain his thinking. Hap could have made some critical error and gotten lost, or contracted hypothermia. He could have miscalculated his footing and fallen into a ravine. He could have become disoriented and drowned, or been attacked by a bear. These things happened all the time, even to those who knew what they were doing. As for the body, it must still be out in the woods somewhere, too well camouflaged for the searchers and dogs to find, or dragged off by a bear or mountain lion. Ellis wasn't giving up hope, just wanting me to at least begin considering that we might not find him.

The next few weeks were hell as I waited for any kind of news. I couldn't focus on my classes or homework, could barely eat, in fact. Every few days, I'd check in with Sheriff Flood. Finally, near Christmas break, when not a single sign had appeared in more than a month, he said, "We're still going to keep looking, Anna. But some part of me is starting to wonder if Hap meant to leave the trail that day. He might have been trying to take his own life."

I was on a pay phone in the hall of my dormitory. As Ellis went on, I wedged my body into a corner and shook, not caring who saw or heard me. If Hap *had* wanted to die, this was the way he'd do it, of course—in the woods alone, on his own terms. No drama or fanfare. No goodbye. As much as I wanted to believe he would never abandon me, no matter how unhappy he was, I was eighteen now, and no longer his ward, at least as far as the state was concerned. He'd fulfilled his promise to me.

In the corner, as tears streamed, Ellis's words continued to echo through the phone, stealing the air from my lungs. "Will you have a funeral?" I managed to ask him, feeling strangely hollow.

"In cases like this, it takes many years until someone is declared dead by the state. But there's talk of a memorial service. I'll keep you posted so you can come home for it."

Home. Somehow the word had altered completely in a single moment. Without Hap and Eden, Mendocino was just a place—anyplace—or so it seemed as I tumbled through grief. "Sure," I said, then thanked him and hung up. I never went back.

Fifty-Seven

When I leave the grove, I head straight for Navarro Beach, south of the village, to meet up with a team of searchers. The little beach parking lot is at the end of an overgrown road that takes me past an old inn, here since the lumber boom in the nineteenth century. Back then the coast was pocked with dogholes, as they were called, tiny shipping points where millworkers sent boards down rickety flumes to the transport schooners that waited. Later there were whalers, rumrunners, women of ill repute. For seventy-five years or more—an entire generation—this area had grown and flourished, supporting saloons and little subsistence stores and homes that were more like camps. Now there's just this haunted inn to show for it, a broad spread of beach full of driftwood, and twenty or thirty searchers readying themselves in the parking lot.

I get out and, putting Cricket in her harness, notice a group of women nearby, zipping windbreakers over exercise clothes. One of them is Emily, and I feel proud of her. Surprised, too. This is a big step for her. Seconds later I spot Hector stamping his boots as he waits, as if his feet are already cold. More likely it's anxiety he's feeling, at the idea he could find his sister, too late. Or not find her at all.

It's strange to see him and Emily standing less than twenty feet apart. In Cameron's fifteen years of life, they've shared her in a blind and disconnected way, knowing utterly different versions of the same girl, versions that have never touched. But just now, they almost do.

The organizer is Bill Muncy, Caitlyn's father. As he splits the party into smaller units, I quickly say hello to Hector, and then pull alongside Emily so that I end up in her group. I haven't seen her since before Shannan's body was found, and want to know how she's doing.

She seems relieved to have something to do with her fear this morning. I feel the same as the party fans out from the parking lot. Our group has been assigned to the northernmost section of the beach, where most of the driftwood is localized. The tide brings it in and leaves it here in sun-bleached piles, where for decades teenagers and artists and free spirits have scavenged through the pieces to make castaway-looking shelters and strange, elaborate sculptures, all cobbled together naturally, anchored in the sand.

I've always found the structures beautiful, but today the wind is cold and the sun is hidden, and we're not here as tourists, but to look for a body, or a murder site.

"You found that girl," Emily says as we begin to walk. Her voice is brittle, fragile sounding. "What does this mean for my daughter?"

"We don't know yet, unfortunately. But in a way this might be good news, Emily. The FBI is helping us now. We have a lot more hands on deck and more resources. I'm really hopeful something will click soon. We're going to find her."

When she doesn't respond, I follow her eyes to a long pile of driftwood, where there are hollow places, shadowy areas that someone will search today, carefully, and even painstakingly. From the tension in Emily's body, I can guess what she's thinking, that "finding" Cameron doesn't necessarily mean bringing her home alive.

Subtly I turn us north, where the beach is wide open, bounded only by a rocky black cliff face at the far end, and a small estuary that's already been dredged. Not that Emily needs to know this. I keep it to myself as we walk side by side, the wind at our backs, gusting in small pushes that feel almost like human hands. The sand courses by, glinting, giving the air a body, one made of glass. My hands are cold and I shove them deep in my pockets.

"Did you know Cameron wanted to do some modeling?" I ask her, deciding to open up a little, to share my thinking, whether or not it's a good idea.

"What? No. Cameron didn't even wear makeup. There was nothing girlie about her."

"Not outwardly, maybe." I draw out the photo, handing it to her.

She stops midstride, as if she's seen a snake. "It doesn't even look like Cameron. When did she do this?"

"At the end of summer, just before school started. I think she was working on a modeling portfolio. She never mentioned her interest at all?"

"I would have said no."

"Why?"

"Because she would have just gotten her heart broken."

Getting your heart broken is the privilege of being human, Eden used to say. I didn't know what she meant then. My heart had been broken lots of times, and I was supposed to say thank you? Now, all these years later, I'm at least starting to see that she was really talking about the whole journey. That it's impossible to be alive and not get hurt sometimes, not if you're doing it right.

"She's so beautiful," I tell Emily. "She might have had a shot."

"The world is full of beautiful girls."

"Even if she had been disappointed, that would have been her choice, right? Part of her figuring it all out."

She doesn't answer.

We're a hundred yards from the lip of the estuary now, a shallow trench of seawater with a foam-pocked shore, a hundred and fifty yards from the tide line. Something in the expanse of flat water catches my eye, a rock levitating or a scuba diver, I think, but really it's a seal surfacing at the edge of the estuary. We watch as it hoists itself out of the cloudy water, its front flippers, its sleek brown head in profile, nose pointed at the surf. This is where it needs to go, inch by inch—back to the sea. No one can help it get there.

Emily says, "Why are you bringing this up now? What does it have to do with the case?"

"I'm just trying to understand Cameron's dreams."

"Why?"

For some reason I can't stop following the seal with my eyes. The way the animal struggles along through loose sand, throwing its body forward like a seesaw or like a bag of rocks. It wasn't made to move like this, wasn't made for the earth at all, but for water. And yet it keeps going.

"Sometimes our dreams can be the most revealing things about us. Who we are when no one's looking, who we believe we're truly supposed to be, if we can get there."

She flicks her eyes at the photo again, and then stares at me, confused or angry or both. "Are you saying this Cameron is more real than the girl I saw every day?"

"Not the makeup, Emily. That's not what I mean. The wishing. The wanting to be more."

As she shakes her head, I can see she's not following me at all. Maybe it's because I'm barely following myself. This might be the wrong conversation completely.

Before I can censor or second-guess myself, I say, "Emily, I don't mean to hurt or shock you, but I have reason to suspect your daughter might have been sexually assaulted as a child. Do you know anything about that?"

She freezes so fast it's like I've punched her. But of course I have. "Why would you even *say* that?"

All I can do is keep talking, hating every word. "Some evidence has come forward from a health clinic Cameron visited about a month ago. I can't share more right now, but the exam showed internal scarring."

"What?" The word rips through the air between us. The sand at our feet feels treacherous, full of knives. Of all the questions Emily's fighting with now, about why Cameron had gone to the clinic in the first place and hidden it from her, only one issue has the power to kill her a little. Or a lot.

Me too. "Can you think of a time when Cameron was young when her personality seemed to change? When she started to have bathroom accidents at night? Or asked to sleep with the light on? She might have been having nightmares or acting out suddenly, becoming more emotional for no reason?"

"I don't know. I can't remember anything like that." She shakes her head, thinking, her honey-colored hair whipping past her face.

"Lydia says that Cameron used to seem lighter somehow. Does that make sense to you?"

"I don't know," Emily says again. "Maybe. There was a time when she started having a lot of stomachaches. I thought it was just nerves about tests or whatever. She's a sensitive person."

"How old was she then?"

"Eight or nine?"

"Were her symptoms worse in the mornings? Or when she'd try and do her homework?"

I can see Emily traveling backward fast in her mind, searching for certain memories that are changing as she reaches for them. "She always seemed fine about school, actually. Her grades stayed good. Homework was easy for her, except one year. That would have been fourth grade. For one whole term she stayed home with me."

"A whole semester? Why?"

"She had mono. We thought that was a little funny, actually. That she'd get the kissing disease when she was so young."

"They did used to call it that," I say carefully, because we're finally getting somewhere. It takes effort to speak slowly, to weigh every step. "But mono is really a suppressed immune system. That can happen with stress. Do you remember what was going on at home around that time? Was there any new adult in Cameron's life? Someone who took a particular interest in her?"

She blinks at me, poised to fly apart. "What are you really asking?"

"Emily, I need you to think. Who could have hurt Cameron when she was too young to protect herself?" *When you weren't there,* I almost say. But that won't get us anywhere. I need to build a bridge for us now, not a wall. "When she was vulnerable?"

Emily is so still, and so afraid I can barely look at her. It's all catching up to her, cracking her open. She starts to cry quietly, and then raggedly, her face contorting, ugly and honest. "Why?"

"It happens." *Terrible things happen in a life,* Hap echoes from inside my heart.

"Think, Emily. Think about what you just told me. She had mono in fourth grade. Bad stomachaches before that. What was new at age eight and nine for Cameron? The when might tell us who."

"You must think I'm a terrible mother."

"I don't," I say, and mean it—maybe for the first time. The way I've been judging Emily feels cruel now, given this conversation. Maybe I've been unfair with her from the beginning, seeing her in a mirror and hating myself. She's been struggling to do the right thing, even when her own hurt has made that harder than it should ever be. "You've done your best."

She shudders in place. "I've tried."

"Think back." I press as gently as I can.

"We were still in Malibu then."

"Any new babysitters or neighbors? Family friends?"

"No."

"You never left her alone with anyone?"

"No," she says again, but the word clicks, whirs like a timepiece. "Wait." Blood flushes into her cheeks, the hot bloom of difficult feeling. "Cameron's third-grade year was when my family first came to the beach house for Christmas. We'd been going to Ohio with Cameron, but that year Troy said it was bullshit to suffer through snow if we didn't have to."

I can see how hard this territory is for Emily, a land of memory that's shifting violently as she looks at it. Nothing will ever go back to the way it was. Because the way it was was a lie. "Then what? What was different?"

"We always shared a room in Bowling Green. Cameron slept on a trundle bed in our room. She was afraid of the dark."

"But in Malibu she had her own room."

"Yes." Her voice wobbles, vibrates. "Oh my God."

I say nothing, giving her space to put the pieces together. To see what she couldn't see back then.

Her mouth is a tight line, white where her lips press together. Then she says, "Everyone came for a whole week that year. Lydia and Ashton had the stomach flu and spent most of the time in bed. I remember being so mad at them for exposing us to their germs." She falters, her thoughts clearly racing. "My dad had never taken that much time off. He didn't even play golf."

Again I'm silent. For a long moment I just stand beside her while everything gathers and rushes. Sand flies by us like a million mirrored surfaces. On the beach, the waves lunge at the shore where the seal has finally reached the tide line. Strangely I want to cheer for the animal for not giving up or turning back.

Then something snaps and shines. Breaks in. Emily starts to vibrate, and then to shake. She cries out, covering her face with her hands, doubling over.

I place a hand lightly on her back, wanting her to know she's not alone. But I can't really help her. Not for this.

When she stands, her face is damp and raw. Mascara clouds her cheeks. She's breathing hard. "What kind of monster would hurt a little girl? My own *father*?" She shudders, repulsed. "Or my brother, even. It's so awful."

"How many years did your family come to Malibu for Christmas?"

"Three. My mom couldn't travel after that because of the dementia. And then we moved here, and Drew started hosting."

"Drew was at all of those holidays, too, then?"

"He was. I hate thinking this way. I *hate* it."

"I know. I'm so sorry, Emily." We're standing a foot apart, the same bitter wind at our backs. I can't make anything easier for her. I can't take her pain away. All of these questions hurt. The truth has teeth and won't let go.

"What age was Cameron when things started to shift?"

"When we came north. We thought it was the mountains, the fresh air. She started to seem more like herself again. Then she found Caitlyn, and everything seemed really great for a while."

"That timing lines up with the bigger picture, Emily. The abuse might have stopped then anyway. She was getting older. More likely to tell."

"My God. It's so *sickening*. What are we supposed to do now?"

"Keep looking for your daughter. We'll need to rule them out as suspects, of course. And someday, when this is all over, we'll investigate and try to get a conviction."

She meets my eyes, a fresh wave of dread moving through her. "My mom is so fragile now. The news about Cameron has been hard enough. This would kill her."

"Have you spoken with your father lately?"

"A few days ago. I've been updating them when I can. You don't think he's the one who has her now?"

"Is that possible? Have he and Cameron remained in contact? Would she have gone to him?"

"No. I really don't think so. He never leaves my mother alone now. It's sort of ironic." Her glance hardens. "She can't travel anymore. It's why they haven't come out."

"I'll have the sheriff's department follow up, just to be sure we're not missing anything."

Emily says, "Why didn't Cameron ever tell me what was happening?"

I wish I had a simple answer for her, but there isn't one. "It's possible she didn't remember," I manage to say. "It happens a lot. Her subconscious probably forced it away to help her endure it. And even if she did remember, she might have been too ashamed to tell you. Most of the time, abuse victims blame themselves for what's happening to them, as if something they did caused it. It's one of the hardest pieces to understand. The saddest, too."

"I didn't protect her." Emily's voice sounds small and gutted, undone. "I let her down."

I reach out for her arm, wishing there was some way to turn back time for her and for Cameron. And for me, too. I feel the grief grow huge between us. "You never meant to hurt her, Emily. You just didn't see. Maybe you couldn't. You had your own scars after all. Everyone does." Tears spring to my eyes, and I let them come. "There's still a chance to help. You can start from here."

She sags against me, surrendering to something. Maybe everything. Over her shoulder, far out on the beach, another search group shouts to one another over the wind. Hector out in front, striding purposefully. The sea is stormy, black water terraced in white lace. "Okay," she says, gulping breath.

"Okay," I say back, and we stand there, inches apart, together and alone.

Fifty-Eight

It's hard to leave Emily at her door after the day we've had, but Troy is home, and I know they need time to talk.

"Call anytime," I say.

"Thanks, Anna. None of this feels good right now, or even *doable*." Her voice trembles like fine wire. "But I know you mean to help. That you care about Cameron."

"I do."

I'm just heading back toward the village when Will's cruiser passes me going the other way. I see him in my rearview, turning in to a dirt pullout, and find a spot to park myself, walking to meet him halfway.

"I've been looking for you all over, Anna. One of the patrol teams up in Montgomery Woods found some items of Shannan's, one of her shoes, a bracelet, her pocketbook with money inside, a few hundred dollars. So this wasn't theft, but we knew that."

"Any fingerprints?"

"Unfortunately, no. There was a camera, too. No usable prints, but we processed the film inside and might have something to go on from the time and date stamps."

Pressure materializes at the base of my skull, as if actual hands are squeezing there. I try to ignore the feeling. "Where are they now? Can I see them?"

"Sure. I'll make you a copy. I'm headed back to meet Drew Hague and the polygraph technician if you want to follow me."

"I'll do that, but I should tell you that I had a long talk with Emily this morning. Seems like her father also could have been the one to hurt Cameron."

"You told her about your suspicions, then?"

"I did."

"How is she now?"

"Pretty shaken up. Make sure the technician asks Drew about holidays in particular. Christmases in Malibu. The father's name is Andrew Hague, Bowling Green, Ohio. Emily says he's not traveling these days because her mom is so sick, but we have to rule him out anyway."

"Understood. Let's check in later. And you should get some rest if you can. You look awful."

"I don't care how I look, Will. I just want those photos."

He seems reluctant to back down. "I don't suppose I can insist?"

"Not a chance."

As soon as I have the photos from Shannan's camera in my hand, I spread them out on the floor of my cabin, looking for signs or clues in the images. Most are silly, spontaneous throwaways—Shannan's bare feet with a gnarled dandelion between two of her toes. A six-pack of beer on a patch of grass. A blurred nature picture that could be of anything, shot almost anywhere. Part of Shannan's bare leg, the shutter having clicked the picture by accident, maybe.

As Cricket paces around me, I feel frustration build. Foolishly, I thought something would jump out immediately, but each shot seems equally innocuous, even the one of her in what appears to be the mysterious rabbit-fur jacket, her hair loose and tousled, her eyes narrowed cynically. The date stamp is from May of this year, almost a month before she disappeared. There's no way of knowing who took the photo, though, if it was the same guy who gave her the camera and coat, or any of it. Maybe she stole them both. Maybe this is all a dead end, and the pictures mean nothing to anyone, even Shannan while she was still alive to care.

With Will tied up all day, I decide to drive to Comptche to talk to Tally. It will probably be a waste of time. She doesn't have a crystal ball, obviously, and might not have more insight than I do into the pictures. But right now, I just need to be moving somewhere, following a lead, even if it's pointless.

Cricket and I arrive after two and find her in her garden tying back vines, readying them for winter. Her face is pink and wind-chapped above the collar of her green fleece jacket.

"I don't really know why I'm here," I say candidly as she approaches me and takes off her thick work gloves. "Do *you* know why I'm here?"

She squints, smiling. "I must not have scared you off last time. I wondered."

There are two wide wicker chairs on her porch, and we sit side by side while she looks through the pictures.

"Does anything jump out at you?" I ask after a moment. "Is that the coat from your dream?"

"I believe so." She leans forward. "That poor girl. It makes me hurt to think of what she lived through."

"I know. I feel the same. But if we can figure out who did this to her, it might lead us to Cameron. My instincts still tell me the girls are linked."

Nodding, Tally says, "Mine, too, or maybe that's just hope." She shuffles through the pictures again, more slowly. "Now that I see the coat, I'm wondering if it's just something really personal to

Shannan, something she loved, and that's why it came through to me? I can't be sure."

"It's all right. I'll keep thinking. Maybe something will click."

Before I leave, she asks if I want to follow her out to the barn to check on one of the newborns.

Cricket trots ahead of us, through the yard and then the enclosure pasture, tall grass threaded with asters and deep-blue campanula, the last flowers of the season. The barn is old but solid. Pushing open the big door, Tally sends pigeons wheeling high in the rafters. Slanted light comes through cracks in the weathered siding, piercing down through the hayloft in molten shafts.

"What an incredible space."

"Isn't it? My grandparents had it moved here from Idaho, board by board," she says, leading us toward a set of wooden stalls. In the nearest one, a mother alpaca stands facing a corner, a harness and lead around her sloping brown neck. Cricket looks through the metal slats curiously, and then sits to see what we'll do.

"She hasn't gotten the hang of nursing," Tally says. "It happens sometimes. I'm just going to help her along."

I follow her in, watching as she kneels under the animal, stroking her thigh and talking softly. Little by little, the animal seems to relax. "You're good with her."

"She doesn't like people that much. I have to go slow with this one."

She seems to be talking about the process as well as the mother alpaca. I watch the milk run into a bucket, thin streams only slightly cloudier than water. After five minutes, Tally has collected only a small amount of fluid, less than half a cup.

"Will that be enough for the baby?" I ask.

"Hope so. This is mostly colostrum. The cria is going to need it."

In a stall nearby, the newborn is still damp. Tally has lifted him onto a large heating pad and now takes some of the colostrum into a syringe before lowering herself to the ground. "Here, Anna. Can you lift his head for me?"

"I'm afraid I'll do something wrong. He's so small."

"He's tougher than he looks."

Kneeling in the loose hay, I reach to support the baby's neck. His coat is like warm, wet carpet. His pulse taps against my palms, and I feel my heart turn over. The vulnerability in his body is almost too much to take. "Will he live?" I ask, afraid of her answer.

"He's had a rough morning, but I think so. Here." She hands me the syringe. "Place it right at the base of the tongue. There you go. You've got it."

I feel a tug as the cria latches on to the soft plastic tip, see his eyelashes flutter as he looks at me, suckling. An old ache floods in, rushing through all my doors like water, or like love actually.

"Not so different than bottle-feeding a baby," Tally says. There's a long, quiet space, then she says, "I was thinking about forgiveness today. You know, so many people get confused about what it is, binding it up with guilt. Feeling ashamed about things they never had any control over in the first place. I don't believe forgiveness is something we have to kill ourselves trying to earn. It's already here, all around us, like rain. We just have to let it in."

My arms have gone stiff under the cria's head. I shift them a little as I wonder what Tally is getting at. Why she's brought this up. "It's not that simple."

"Maybe not. But I do think that the bigger and more impossible something is, the more it needs to move through us so we can keep living."

I look down at the cria, sated now, his eyes closed, and the syringe empty but for a small bit of froth. "Why did you bring me here today?"

"I thought you might need to hold something, that's all."

My eyes sting, film over. All I can do is nod and hand back the syringe.

Fifty-Nine

That evening, Will and I sit in front of the fire at my cabin, a bottle of Jack Daniel's and Shannan's pictures between us. We haven't been alone like this since that night in his apartment, and though the moment feels years away now, and not at all threatening to me, I can't help but wonder where he's at with it, since neither one of us has said a word. Maybe he considers the kiss a moment of weakness or bad judgment, or maybe he's still attracted to me but trying to shut off the feelings—as practiced as I am at ignoring difficult emotions and hoping they'll go away.

"What are we missing?" I ask him about the photos.

"Hell if I know. Whatever happened to her in that car, there's no hint of it here. I don't see a suspect in any of these."

"Me neither." Exhausted, I reach for the sleek photo of Cameron, straining to sense how she's connected to Shannan. Besides her beautiful face, her center-parted dark hair, there's nothing to grasp at. Nowhere to look next. "What happened with Drew Hague's polygraph?"

"His results were all over the place. I think he's starting to crack a little."

"Did you ask him about Shannan?"

"We did. Nothing there, seems like. But Cameron is a hot point. Denny was in the room, too, and he agrees."

"Is Drew's alibi still holding?"

"Unfortunately, yes. Whatever guilt we're looking at is more likely from the past, but how far back?"

"Most sex offenders have years or even decades of unreported behavior before they're identified by authorities. *If* they're identified, that is. I just don't know how we can get a full disclosure from him unless we have Cameron as a witness or someone else comes forward."

"Lydia?"

"I wouldn't hold out any hope that she'd betray him, if she even knows. We just have to keep moving forward with what we have."

"We're getting a few more bodies tomorrow and a herd of ATVs to do another sweep of the area around Montgomery Woods."

"That will help, but here we are in the middle of October, Will."

The firelight has drawn shadows around his mouth and eyes. He looks years older than he did only weeks ago. "We can still get to her on time, though, can't we? It's not impossible."

"Not impossible, no." But so unlikely.

It's almost midnight when Will leaves. From her place by the fire, Cricket stretches with a groan and stands up. *Let's go to bed*, she's clearly saying, but how can I even try to sleep when everything feels so nebulous and grim? Even though the fire is mostly spent and the light is patchy, I stare at the two photos, Cameron in the krummholz grove and Shannan in the rabbit-fur jacket, trying to step back and see them objectively, one of Hap's old tricks, avoiding the blind spot, the place where being too close hides what matters most.

I know Cameron was modeling for Gray that day in the grove,

but still don't know why for sure. What she'd planned to do with the photos from that shoot, or whom she was trying to impress with those clothes and that hairstyle, the look in her eyes. As for Shannan, I haven't seen any other images of her except the ones Karen showed me in Gualala, from when she was young. Her expression in this one is shrewd and cynical, her brown eyes narrowed in some sort of challenge, her mouth set, lips closed. No smile. No invitation or openness. If Cameron was trying to feel seen for the first time, Shannan had been seen far too much, had been used for her looks and also traded on them herself for a long time, way too long to feel anything good could still come of it. It's almost ironic to look at the girls side by side this way. Factoring in face shape and hair and body type, they're more alike than not—and yet their relationship to hope, to possibility, is stark in contrast. Black and white, as Will has been saying from the beginning, two sides of a tossed coin that won't quite land.

At some point, I give up, the fire burned down to a low red smear. The dog curls next to me, warm and steady, doing her work, which is just to be here, by my side. I still don't understand how I deserve her, or how she's come to me, but I'm grateful anyway, for her body, her even heartbeat. Especially now as the night moves in, pressing heavily.

A dream tugs me under, strange images rising thick and moist, like the breath of an animal. I'm in a roundhouse, partially underground, a structure like the Pomo once built for rituals and ceremonies. Some sort of purification rite is taking place around me, elders in deerskin capes and robes, their chests bare, chanting with everything they're made of. As if they're singing through the pores of their skin.

I can smell burning sage. Gray smoke climbs the earthen walls and widens upward like a spell.

"Where does it hurt?" I hear a familiar voice ask me.

Everywhere, my mind answers.

It's Hap. I can't see him through the smoke but recognize the solid, spreading warmth of his skin and his smell, which has always been exactly like this, the scent of trees becoming wise.

I can't do this, I tell him with my mind, meaning solve the case, unpuzzle the clues, find Cameron. But suddenly I mean everything. My whole life—heavy with loss. Jason and Amy. My mother in that awful parking lot, dead on Christmas Day. Jenny's murder and Eden's cancer. Hap's disappearance. My daughter's accident. The dark abyss of my work and how it connects in an awful and yawning way to everything else.

"It's okay." Hap speaks into my ear. "It was all a long time ago."

No. I feel small and powerless beside him, as if I'm ten again. Twelve. Eight. Sixteen. All the ages I've ever been. There's a sound like a ringing phone coming through the wet smoke around us, but it's too far away, and I can't reach it. *Where did you go, Hap? I wish you could have said goodbye.*

"Life is change, Anna. We don't get to keep each other."

I let you down. I'm not who you think I am.

"Hush."

I have to tell you what happened. What I've done.

"Be still, honey. It doesn't matter now."

But it does. *Help me, Hap. I can't live like this,* I plead as the dream spins on.

The elders are turned away from us, drumming over hot stones. The roundhouse seems to be breathing like a lung, taking in grief and letting it go.

Hap says, "I'm so sorry, honey. I know it hurts, but we never have to do anything alone. I've never left your side. Come look at what I brought you."

I gaze up and the roof has disappeared. The sky is dazzling and boundless, sparks flickering on and off and on again.

"We can't always see them," Hap says, meaning the stars, "but they're always with us, sweetie. Don't give up."

Help me move on, Hap. I need to find Cameron.

"You've already found her, Anna. See? She's been here the whole time."

Sixty

When I wake, my eyelashes are sticky and damp. I've been crying in my sleep. Remembering, reliving. Replaying the trauma in my body, where it's been all this time.

I dress numbly, forgoing a shower while Cricket paces, reading my mood. I'm out of coffee, out of food, too. Shoving my feet into boots, I drive into town, barely feeling the steering wheel under my hands, the air on my skin. Little flashes of the roundhouse dream wriggle through the emotional fog, Hap trying to reassure me that I'm not alone. But I sure feel like I am.

This case is getting away from me, and from Will, too. What he was saying in his office the other morning after we got the call from the medical examiner, that he might not be strong enough, or good enough. I wonder if he might be right—about both of us. Maybe we're not ever going to solve this. Maybe Cameron will stay lost, and her abductor will go unnamed, and history will repeat itself.

Leaving Cricket in the car, I walk into the GoodLife and feel bombarded by the cheerful chaos, bright light and noisy conversation, and the smell of milk becoming sweet foam. I order coffee and a breakfast burrito and then head over to the message board by habit, to wait for the food. Cameron's missing photo is still here, plus the new one with the words foul play suspected screaming from dead center. The rest is innocuous, including a posting for Sam Fox's free community yoga class, but something has struck me suddenly. A high bell has begun to ring steadily in my inner ear, a warning sound, because *this* is how Cameron's abductor could have reached her. Exactly this innocuously—hidden in plain sight.

My eyes flick over the board, across the top and down the side, a feeling of dread and inevitability rising. And then I see the posting I'm looking for, in the lower-right corner, simple and spare, printed on Kelly-green copy paper:

ARTIST'S MODEL WANTED
No Experience Necessary
Will train if other requirements met

It was here three weeks ago, when I found the listing for the cabin, but I didn't register it. Haven't even remembered it until now. The phone number at the bottom is local and repeated in a fringe of tear-off tabs, no name. All but two of the tabs are gone. artist's model wanted . . . will train. Twelve words, three lines, all without heat or persuasion or intensity—which is why the posting is so potent. It's like the kill site I saw in the woods that day, simple and incredibly effective.

I take Shannan's photo out of my jacket pocket feeling sick to my stomach, all the hairs on the back of my neck vibrating. It's not the coat I'm looking at anymore. The coat doesn't matter, only the heavy-souled girl who's wearing it. Her cynicism, her world-weary look. Her bat signal flashing out past her wounds.

Everything Shannan has lived through is here in her eyes—the day her father skipped town and her mother stopped trying, all the fights she heard from her bedroom at night, the sound of a fist against the wall, against her mother's face. The way she tried to mute it all in the school bathroom, her knees on the tile, some boy's hand on the back of her neck, pushing too hard. The times she ran and found nothing. Came back and found nothing. Left again. Of course I'm stretching, filling in the blanks. But in another way, it's no stretch at all, but incredibly familiar.

Shannan isn't me, or Jenny. She's not Cameron either, but I can also see how we all line up behind one another, making a version of the same shape in the world. Trying to believe in people or in promises. Trying to be enough. Trying—always trying—to be free somehow. To unfold.

I pull the tack from the corkboard, feel the needle prick as it finds the fleshy pad of my thumb, a tightrope feeling coming over me. The number at the bottom of the posting in my hand is his number. A thin piece of paper, trembling in my fingers, everything zeroing to a single pinpoint, a freckle of my own bright blood.

Careful to touch only the bottom portion of the posting so I don't disturb any valuable fingerprints or sweat residue, I ask one of the cashiers working the register for a large ziplock bag and tuck the posting safely inside before crossing to the pay phone at the back of the café to call the sheriff's office. Cherilynn Leavitt picks up.

Through her voice, warm and cheerful, the bell keeps ringing. "Hey, Cherilynn," I manage to say. "It's Anna Hart. Is Will around?"

"He's in the field. Want me to get him on the radio for you?"

"No, that's okay." My voice sounds glassy. I take a breath. "Listen, can you get me a reverse phone lookup on the fly? I'll hold."

"Sure thing," she says.

As I wait, I'm barely in my body. My thinking is jumbled, nonsensical. Finally Leon Jentz comes on the line.

"Hey, Anna. I have the information you wanted. What's up?"

"Hard to say yet." Again, the disembodied feeling, and yet somehow I keep talking. "Just following up on a lead. What did you find?"

"That number is registered to the Mendocino Art Center."

He's right here, blocks away. Of course he is. "Do you have a name for me?"

"No name. The artists' studios have phones and this is one. The residents shift around a lot, I guess."

"Do we know which studio?"

"Number four. What do you think you're onto here?"

"A new witness, maybe." I pull the lie from thin air effortlessly. "I'll let you know if anything turns up. In the meantime, can you get a message to Will to meet me at the Art Center as soon as he can get away?"

"You got it."

Sixty-One

Minutes later, I park, leaving Cricket in the back seat, and approach the cluster of outbuildings that has been here since the late fifties. In the largest of the outbuildings, there are twelve numbered apartments that function as living quarters as well as work space for instructors and artists in residence, six above and six below, with a bowed industrial-looking staircase between.

Number 4 is blank and quiet. In the dusty window to the left of the entrance, a piece of stained glass throws blurred color onto the concrete walkway, red and blue and yellow spheres.

I knock and get no answer, then test the knob to see if the door is locked, and it is. I try to peer in the windows, but they're filmed over with dust and spiderwebs, flyspecks.

The studio gallery where tourists come to buy hand-painted windsocks and blown-glass ashtrays isn't open yet. No one's around except a gardener on his knees dividing a hosta plant with a sharp spade—an older man I don't recognize. He's wearing overalls and a ball cap, with tufts of his silver hair poking from underneath.

I head over, pointing back behind me. "Do you know who this studio belongs to? Number four."

"Been empty for a bit, but a new intern's coming from Portland at the end of the month." He rests his soil-stained gloves on his knees. "Who are you looking for?"

"The artist who left."

His glasses are cloudy, but his eyes are sharp. His shoulders square. "His lease is expired, but all the paperwork is in the office. Why? What is it you need to know?"

I can tell I've awakened his suspicion. I probably look more than suspicious, actually, my hair wild, and my clothes rumpled, careless. I'm out of breath, too. But as much as I know I need to slow down and reassure him that I'm not a threat, I can't stop thinking about getting through that door. The man who killed Shannan and then took Cameron might be just inside. His prints might be on the phone, or his name on a receipt or a business card, or a piece of art.

"Who's your supervisor?" I ask the man, and then crouch to meet him at his level. "I need to get into that studio. Who has a key?"

"I'm the supervisor. Stan Wilkes. What's going on here, anyway?"

It takes me several long minutes to explain myself and convince Stan to let me take a look inside. Finally he nods, moving with a tortoise's slow swing, and stands up, brushing off his knees. After eons, he reaches into his hip pocket and produces a skeleton key, small and rounded on top, hanging from a piece of red string.

We go over together, and he opens the door, his big shadow thrown onto the lintel and jamb.

"Go right ahead," he says.

I step inside just as it strikes me for the first time that even at his age, Stan might be who I'm looking for. He's a large man, still capable of doing harm. Without breathing, I whirl on him.

He stumbles back, startled. In his widened eyes, I see his age become obvious. It's in his hands, too, and the shine of his fore-head. He's just an old man, and I've scared him.

After Stan leaves, I close the door behind me for privacy. The room is a chilly rectangle, maybe twenty by twenty-five feet. Cracks and dark stains mar the concrete floor. Splotches of oil paint. Along one wall, a wooden workbench appears similarly scarred, battered from long use.

The switch for the overhead fixture doesn't work, but above there are three bubbled Plexiglas skylights. They throw light down in milky cones, where dust motes swim, seeming magnified. Granular. Though the room is bare, there is the sense of residue everywhere. The almost medicinal tang of linseed oil and gouache emanating from the walls. The blackened mouth of the empty kiln. The easel leaning in the corner, one of the support legs dangling as if it's a broken limb.

I can't help but wish the space could talk to me, tell me its story. Has Cameron been here, modeling or preening? Begging for love, or for her life? Did her abductor use this yellow slimline phone against the doorjamb to call her? The one with the snaking twisted cord? Is this where she first reached him? Where he first began to draw her into his tormented fantasy?

I'm still fixated on the phone when I hear a fluttering behind me. No one's there when I turn, but the sound continues, like a small soft hammer on the wall or the pipes, coming from a closet at the back.

Cameron, I think and cross to the door. It's not a closet at all, but a dim cinder-block storage space. The walls are gray and po-rous and smell of damp. The air feels thick and moist enough to drink. To swallow in pieces. In one corner, above a small rusted utility sink, a small bird drops down from the rafters, startling me as it thrashes against the wall violently. The gray-white wings are a frantic blur. It's come through a broken transom window and can't get out.

I feel its struggle as if it's hammering at my chest instead of cinder block. All of its panicked energy and hopelessness pointed at me. My pulse jumps as it flails against the concrete and then the rafters, looking futilely for the sky. Finally it stops on one of the cobwebby joists, its heartbeat thumping visibly. And then I notice several canvases have been stacked nearby, resting between the joists like rungs on a ladder. Almost instantly, I forget the bird and find a chair, careful not to disturb anything that might have fingerprints on it. It takes some effort to hoist the canvases down without falling, but when I do, I'm stunned; they have Jack Ford's telltale swooping signature in the bottom right-hand corner. They must be worth hundreds of thousands of dollars.

My first thought is that Jack must have had some connection to this studio, which has been here for more than thirty years. He could have painted here, or simply used this room for storage. Then it occurs to me that dozens of artists must have used this space over the last few decades, and that any one of them might have been a collector of Jack's work, and inadvertently left the canvases here. The level of dust on the paintings and the fact that they've been left here when the rest of the studio is swept bare leads me to suspect that they likely don't have anything to do with the present, with Cameron or her abductor. But he *was* here, and she may have been as well. Obviously we'll have to get a team in immediately to sweep for prints as well as fiber and hair samples, particularly in the storage area, which with the thickness of the walls and high inaccessible transom could easily have been used as a captivity cell. If Cameron had managed to discover a loose stone or some other object, she might have broken the window as an attempt to get someone's attention. Maybe that's why her abductor had moved her from this place, so no one could hear her scream if he took off her gag.

My thoughts are still spinning on possible scenarios when I hear Will call my name from the main room. He looks flushed, as if he's scrambled to get here, and it feels surprisingly good to see him. To know I can get through to him when I need to, and that he'll find a way to come.

It takes me a while to explain my message-board theory once I've shown Will the posting, how it could have been used to target Cameron and possibly Shannan, too. Then I lead him to the storage area, where I've left the paintings propped against the wall, not wanting to handle them further in case they're useful somehow to the investigation.

"These are Jack's?" Will asks incredulously.

"Crazy, right? It could be a total coincidence that they're here."

"Or they're Caleb's and he's involved somehow," Will jumps to add.

"Caleb? Why would you think that?"

"Because all of Jack's work belongs to him."

"Exactly. If he knows about their existence, I mean if he himself has a connection to this studio, wouldn't he have sold them like he sold everything else? He must not know they're here."

"Maybe. Or it could be that his complicated tie to his dad would make him want to hold on to these, right?"

I shrug to acknowledge the possibility as Will calls Leon on his walkie, explaining to him that we have a potential crime scene to process, and that he should alert the team.

Then he turns back to me. "Do we know who was in here last?"

"All the files are in the gallery office. It's not open yet, but the caretaker's name is Stan Wilkes. He's the one who let me in. I could be totally off base with the message-board angle, but I don't think so."

"If you *are* right, he could have reached other girls this way. Maybe he's already got another victim in his sight lines."

"I know. These postings could be all up and down the coast by now."

Will nods, and then stoops to take a closer look at the front-most canvas, still propped with the others against the wall of the storage area. The lighting is bad and the painting's surface is aged and covered with dust, but the image is visible for all that. It's abstract and almost primitive looking with a limited use of color, just black and white and blue. The shapes are dramatically angular, and suggestive of something I can't quite place until Will points it out.

"I think this is supposed to be the carving above the Masonic Hall."

"Oh, shit. You're right," I say, wondering why I didn't see that right away. "It's *Time and the Maiden*. What about the others?"

He pulls his shirt cuff over his hand to preserve any prints and carefully tips the canvases forward. There are four altogether, and they're all versions of the same tableau, with the same color scheme. A bold white V shape, suggesting wings. A black slash approximating death's scythe. The maiden's face round and blotted, her hair a grouping of watery white squiggles. The background rough and thick in each, a dark blue—even through the film of dust—that seems to have been spread like frosting with a palette knife. "Creepy," Will says.

The obsessiveness *is* creepy, I have to agree, though painters often return to subjects again and again. Monet and his lilies, or Degas and his dancers. The difference here is that the object that so clearly fascinated Jack Ford, at least for the period in which he painted these, has also fascinated me all my life. "I hate to admit it, but they're sort of beautiful," I say aloud to Will.

"Hate to admit it because Jack was an asshole, you mean?" His expression tells me he agrees. "Anyway, we should check these out. Maybe Caleb can help us ID them. I'll send one of my deputies over to bring him here."

"I can go. It won't take me five minutes. In the meantime, get Stan Wilkes to let you into the office."

"Okay, sure. Just be careful, all right?"

"I'm always careful."

He gives me a sideways look, as if to say, *We both know that's not true.*

Sixty-Two

The distance to Caleb's house from the Art Center is only a few blocks away, so I walk there, my thoughts quickly returning to the posting, and to the photos I've been staring at for days, of Cameron in the grove, of Shannan with her weighted gaze, her guardedness. I'm still far from understanding how all the dots connect, but finding the studio has to be some kind of break. Even if the artists at the Center typically move around a lot, Stan Wilkes should be able to give us a list of names to run through our database. The crime lab techs should also be able to lift prints from the posting fairly easily if the paper hasn't been overhandled or moved. And then we have the paintings, which hopefully Caleb can help us place.

I pass through the front gate, noticing that the light is on in the garage. Inside, I see Caleb's large shape crossing in front of the square window. When I head over, tapping on the door lightly, he's standing in front of a suspended easel with a large canvas on it. From what I can see, the image is abstract, full of dark undulating curves. Somehow it's escaped me until this moment that Caleb is an artist too.

"Anna," he says, opening the door for me. "What's up?"

"Sorry to barge in on you like this." I step inside and see he's very much taken over where his father left off. Large-scale pieces. Bold and almost savage lines. "It's just that we found some signed paintings of your dad's over at the Art Center. Maybe you can come over and ID them for us, or even help us know who they belong to."

"Oh wow." He rubs his hands on a rag he's holding and then drops it into a nearby five-gallon plastic bucket on the concrete floor without looking down, as if he knows right where everything is. The space behind him is spotlessly organized. Brushes and tubes of color are neatly and even chromatically arranged on his work-table. In Jack's day, when he painted here, the space had always looked as if it belonged to a hoarder. Now everything is startlingly in its place; the floor swept bare. "What were you doing over there?"

"Just following up a lead on the Cameron Curtis case. The paintings were a total surprise." I drift a little closer to his easel, and subtly see him move his body in front of it.

"The Art Center. Why would you be looking there?"

I glance at the canvas again, registering something decidedly female in the shapes at play, this time, the curves and dimensions. "Oh, a random tip we got."

"Interesting." His eyes flick coolly, electrically, over mine. I recognize the change in his energy, which is almost reptilian now. He's reading the air between us the way a snake does with its tongue. Reading my mind, or trying. "You're sure they're my dad's?"

I know I can't hide what he's already seen. That I'm putting the pieces together. Figuring out what I've missed before. What's been right in front of me. All I can do is play out this game. "Definitely. They're all of *Time and the Maiden*. Do you remember seeing anything like that when Jack was alive?"

He frowns a little and shakes his head. "I don't think so. Let me lock up and I'll meet you over there."

"It's fine. I don't mind waiting."

"Oh, sure." His pupils flick over me again. He seems to be enjoying this. "I just have to grab my wallet and I'll be right with you. Hang on."

He locks the garage as we step out into the driveway, and then heads for the house while I stand there, quietly exploding. Can he really mean to follow me over to the Art Center? Is he that bold? And if so, is there a way to let Will know I suspect him once we get there? My mind tumbles on and on as several raindrops hit my face. When I left the cabin this morning, it was chilly and clear, but the sky has gone dark and spongy. I glance quickly toward the house to see if Caleb is coming, and then step toward the locked garage door, peering through the window. I want another look at the canvas again, to confirm my impressions. But this time my eye catches on something else. A photograph pinned over Caleb's workbench. Black and white and old-fashioned somehow, as if it's been cut out of a history book.

I lean closer to the glass, on the edge of recognition, when I hear a car start, and then see Caleb pulling out from behind the garage in a white Toyota pickup. Adrenaline flares as I jump out of the way, wondering if he means to run me over. Instead, he slams on the brakes long enough to shout through the open window, his eyes hardened, almost ceramic. "If you follow me, I'll kill her."

Then he punches the gas and fishtails away.

I'm paralyzed for an instant as it all lands, everything that's escaped me, like a bomb detonating in my mind. How Caleb's profile is a perfect fit for the kind of man who might flip violently, becoming a killer, a monster. A childhood fractured by abandonment and chaos, his father a tyrant and an alcoholic. The way he'd lost Jenny, the person he loved best in the world, completely powerless to save her. Then the case going unsolved, her killer never found. That piece alone would have been enough to set rage loose inside him, altering him fundamentally, twisting him at the root, as Hap had explained long ago in the krummholz grove.

Somehow I haven't been able to recognize the tortured quality in Caleb, his woundedness—even when we sat side by side on the bluff that day. Maybe I've been stuck confusing his story with my own, or confusing his past with his present. Or maybe I've simply forgotten Hap's cardinal rule, about keeping my eyes open all the time, my trust withheld until it's earned. Either way, regret is a luxury I don't have time for. I can't lose Caleb but don't have a way to follow him. And every second counts.

Just inside the garage door, there's a heavy black rotary phone. I kick the doorframe hard, just above the knob, and it clatters open. When I dial Will's office, my hand twitches, every muscle tense and jangling. Cherilynn picks up.

"We have the suspect," I tell her. "He's headed east out of town, maybe toward the highway. He's driving a white Toyota pickup. The license plate starts with H46. I didn't get the rest. I'm at Caleb Ford's house on Kelly Street."

"I'm sending someone over for you," she says before she clicks off. "Stay put."

I feel almost dizzy as I hang up, praying that it's not too late to stop Caleb before he reaches Cameron. His threat to me, that he'll kill her if I follow, is terrifying. But now that he's on the run, chances are that he'll do that anyway, as fast as he can.

From Main Street, I hear sirens begin to wail. I'm headed out the door to meet the unit when my eyes catch again on the black-and-white photo over the workbench. And now I know why it looks familiar. It's of a Pomo woman in traditional dress with a baby laced into a woven basket, breasts loose under her garment, a mound of gathered acorns nearby. Her home is cone shaped, made of bark and reeds, and planks of redwood. Just like the shelter I saw in the woods that day.

I race through the door, into the driveway. The rain is falling faster and the sky is nearly black as I take in the lit-up cruiser speeding toward me, desperate to see Will inside, or in the second car just behind it. They both screech to a halt, doors flying open. Will's face the only one I look for as raindrops pelt sideways into my face and neck.

"He's gone back to the woods," I shout, though I know it won't make sense to him yet. "Back to kill Cameron."

Sixty-Three

"Can you lead us there?" Will demands to know once I've explained everything, still out of breath, my body shaking terribly. "You remember the way?"

It's not just Will that I have to convince, but all of the state and local officers that have been newly dispatched, dozens of strained faces all pointed at me. The APB has gone out wide with a description of Caleb's truck, but by now he's most likely had time to stash it somewhere and start hiking toward the Pomo shelter. I've only seen it once, on that long hike from my cabin, and that was miles from where I'd first set out and who knew how far from the nearest road. Can I find it again? Do I actually know where it is?

"Yes," I make myself say.

Will radios for help from the ranger station and works to assemble every available man for the search-and-rescue mission while I study the map with sickening stabs of self-doubt. There's an area north and east of my cabin, deep into the green swath of reserve land, that might be right. But is it? Did I cross a service road that day? Is the river that far from the highest ridgeline? Is the elevation right?

"You have the coordinates?" Will asks from behind me.

"Here." I point at the area I've found, hoping to God I'm not mistaken. "The county road will get us within a few miles, but the rest we'll have to do on foot, splitting into teams with walkie-talkies. Each team will need a photocopy of this sketch I've done of the Pomo shelter, along with the coordinates and the plate number of the white Toyota pickup truck registered in Caleb's name."

"Got it," he says. Then his eyes narrow. "You okay?"

"Of course." I try to breathe. "I'm ready."

Within half an hour the convoy sets off in silence from town, dozens of vehicles churning up mud along Little Lake Road toward the main entrance for Jackson State Forest, the rain spattering the windshield. With each winding turn, I feel a similar twist deep inside, wondering if we're already too late.

Will and I ride together without speaking. The sky is so dark it might as well be night by the time we reach the service road, the end of the line for vehicular travel. From there we connect with the rest of the team, all of us in black ponchos that become slick before we've even switched on our walkies to set off on foot. I take the lead, trying not to think at all or to let my anxiety cloud my instincts, hoping that my body knows exactly where it's going and can take me there by feel. But the stakes are so high now it's hard not to let panic slip in.

We hike for a mile, two miles, twenty-five searchers in a line or sometimes a tight V until the terrain makes that impossible, all of us soaked to the skin. Even when we pull out our flashlights, the heavy atmosphere makes visibility a challenge, the vegetation dripping in one thick mass around us, the hills and valleys growing more and more slick and steep, impenetrable in places. Each time I come to a fork in the trail, I look desperately for landmarks, any sort of sign that I'm on the right track, but it all looks different in the rain. I can't be sure I've ever been here at all, but fight to keep my fear and doubt from showing. The team needs to believe I know the way. I need to believe it even more.

The temperature has dropped and the sky looks black, though it can't be much past two o'clock. I can see wisps of my own breath beyond the dripping hood of my poncho as I wonder if I've gotten us hopelessly lost. I'm exhausted by all of it, the self-doubt and the exertion, the building pressure and the dread. The voices in my head telling me I've failed her already, missing the most important clues and signs.

And then it happens. I look up and know I've found the right ridge. I scramble through clinging brush and mud to the top, and there's the Pomo shelter, down below, past shadowy wet deadfalls and bracken, beneath pines and hemlocks heavily drooping with rain—there. The teams behind me make too much noise arriving, drawing their firearms, and I feel myself tensing to the breaking point.

I touch my Glock through my jacket to be sure it's still there as Will double-checks his safety. "I think he knows we're coming," I tell him.

"What makes you say that?"

"The way he told me not to follow him, as if he knew I could figure it out."

"You were alone that day, when you saw the shelter. You're probably the only person in the world who could put this all together, even with the photo in his garage."

"Right," I say, feeling no better about our odds. "I guess we'll know soon."

When Will gives the signal, we move down the rise through drenched brush and foliage, a small army trying to keep surprise and stealth on our side, and most likely failing. Maybe one man should have gone alone first, I think. Maybe we should have posted snipers above on the rise—but it's too late to wonder, and then too late entirely.

When we get there, the shelter has been destroyed, or nearly. The whole site looks as though a cyclone has come through. The support poles and pieces of bark are scattered like kindling. No sign of Caleb.

"Cameron!" I shout, but she's not here. Inside on the soaked earthen floor I see only traces of her struggle, smears of blood on a tangled sheet that looks like a lurid watercolor painting, and lengths of shredded, sodden ligature. A bucket on its side smells like a latrine. A stained plywood bed looks like an altar and probably has been exactly that as he's raped and tortured her these weeks she's been his captive.

Will signals to most of the team to spread out and keep searching. Then he radios out to have the park entrance blocked. When he turns back to me, his expression looks grave, driven. "He's taken her somewhere. What are you thinking? Where would he go?"

"I'm not sure," I say, trying to focus through my fear. Through the very real possibility that no matter how close we've come or how hard we've tried, we haven't been able to save her.

Sixty-Four

Jackson State Forest occupies fifty thousand acres of reserve land, and is as black in the current storm as an uncharted planet, a nightmare coming true minute by minute. In his dozens of stories over the years, Hap had described every type of challenge in these woods, predators and bad falls, hypothermia, lost hikers. If Cameron has gotten free somehow—a wild, unlikely thought—she could be in terrible danger even without Caleb. But at least she's in these woods and not anywhere else. I know this territory in my cells, my nerve fibers. If Cameron is here, I believe I can find her.

The remaining teams split up and fan out from the site, shining flashlights into bracken and deadfalls and spongy, hollowed-out redwoods, communicating by walkie, calling Cameron's name. The rain is easing to a cold, intermittent spatter, but the sky stays dark and swollen, making shadows out of everything, cold black air and tree bark, rock and ravine, the going more and more treacherous. The number of potential directions feels dizzying and endless, trails almost nonexistent. At one point, I find myself waist deep in gummy ferns, the ridgeline so murky it feels like I'm swimming instead of hiking. I lurch forward, hearing Will just behind me, and wait for him to catch up.

"I'm going to head down into this valley," I say, pointing to the slope to our left. "If she's trying to hide from Caleb, she'd stay off the ridge and stick to dense, lowland areas."

"Good thought. I'll go first."

"We'll cover more ground if we split up," I insist. "We can't have much light left anyway. If you head that way," I point to the opposite slope, "the valley runs east to west for about half a mile. I'll be hiking in the same direction and meet up with you before the next rise. We'll use our walkie if we need to."

"Okay, but Anna? Be careful."

I promise him I will before I test my footing, and start inching my way down sideways. Within minutes, he's gone from sight and I'm deep into more ferns. They slap at my poncho and cling to my hands as I try for a safer angle on the slope. Then before I know what's happening, the ground goes utterly slick and I'm tumbling down the hill at alarming speed, curling to protect myself while wet black branches pelt me from every angle.

When I finally reach the valley floor, I'm winded and bruised. I've fallen two hundred meters or more, almost vertically. "Will!" I call, and then strain for his response.

Nothing.

I start to reach for my walkie, but then do a quick triage of my injuries first. My hands are cut up, and my right hip throbs. I touch the stinging back of my head with my fingertips and feel my own wet blood. Gouged and bleeding this way, to any nearby predator I know I smell like dinner. And then there's Caleb, who could be anywhere, in any of these shadows that drip and shudder. Having Will beside me wouldn't necessarily protect me from Caleb, though, not if he's intent on killing me. And I'm not *that* hurt from my fall. I decide to walk a bit farther on my own, feeling grateful that at least I didn't drop my flashlight on the way down.

Slowly, I begin to move haltingly forward, the valley floor water-logged as marshland. Minutes later, my torch seems to hiccup as if it's beginning to lose battery power. I shake it in warning, and then trip on a root and fall again, slamming my right knee hard into the muck. From my hands and knees, I see something darting off to my left, a black wing of movement, as if I've startled an owl or something larger.

I freeze, listening with my whole body. My heart thrashes thickly. My throat feels knotted and closed. Left at thirty degrees is where I saw movement. I dig for my dropped light, and then make myself stand up again. Pressing forward through a spongy traverse, I feel the forest floor rise up underfoot like a soft black mouth. I'm terrified of what I might find, or who.

Above, the canopy seems to have knitted closed, and the sky is a memory. I have the sense that I've fallen through the world into a void. That even if I called Will he couldn't reach me here. This isn't one of Hap's tests, either, not some game of survival. It's my life, and maybe my death, too. I think of all Hap tried to teach me about the wilderness, how it demands respect no matter how much knowledge you have. His own disappearance proves that. He knew more than anyone, had more patience and reverence and respect. And still it took him—nature—but it can't take me. Not if I'm going to have a hope of finding Cameron. That's what I have to focus on now, not my fear, but my reason for being here. Because that's what survival means.

I push on through the heavy undergrowth, leaves and twigs tugging wetly at my clothes. Then a clearing opens, a stand of old-growth redwoods. I can smell them, can almost hear them breathing. They seem to be here as witnesses, but of what?

Then something moves again. I hear a small choked-sounding gasp. And then my flashlight blooms over a figure. Bone thin and painted with mud, more animal than girl.

She's half crouching in a tangle of branches, her hair knotted and wild, trying to camouflage herself. Her eyes are huge and they're staring right at me, her expression haunted and fierce. "Cameron!"

I'm hardly breathing as she takes a step toward me in her ragged flannel shirt, legs pale and frighteningly thin. Her feet are bare. "Who are you?" she croaks before she trips and falls, either too weak or full of shock to stand.

I rush to her side, drop to my knees. She's trembling as if she might break apart.

"It's okay, Cameron. I'm a detective and I'm here to help. I've been looking for you a long time."

"Where is he?" Her voice is frayed, terrified.

"We're still looking for him, but you're safe, I promise. No one can hurt you now. I won't let them."

"I want my mom," she cries. Something deep inside her snaps and releases. "I want to go home."

Before I can answer, I hear brush catch and rustle from behind us in the clearing, a body on the move. I spin to meet the sound, ready to fight to the death if I have to. But it isn't Caleb. It's Hector.

I can't even imagine how he's gotten here. Maybe he followed the search party from town, not willing to leave it to the authorities. Or maybe he's simply materialized by magic? However it's transpired, right now he looks as if he's seeing the resurrection. In his hands, his flashlight trembles, light staggering over his drenched clothes and face, the impossibility of it all. The grace.

He doesn't say a word, just drops his flashlight, still illuminated, and races to us, scooping up Cameron into his arms. She must weigh nearly nothing by now, but I can see that it doesn't matter what size she is. He's going to carry her anyway.

I thumb open the channel on my walkie. "We've got her. She's alive, over."

A crackle flares, and then Will's voice. "Anna? Oh, thank God. What about Caleb?"

"No sign of him."

"Do you know where you are?"

"I think so. I have help here, too." I glance at Hector, leaving the full explanation for later. "We're going to find a road and I'll reach out to you from there. Get an ambulance, all right? And no media. Not yet."

"Roger all that."

In the stillness that follows, I tell Cameron she shouldn't be afraid. That Hector is safe, a friend. Then I lead us out of the clearing, a flashlight in each hand, the valley dense and inky around us, my heart so full I think I could fly if I needed to.

Ahead in the distance, I can hear the Big River, engorged from the storm and running fast. I point us that way, directing the light through the underbrush, while behind me Hector's breath comes with effort, his steps falling heavily. I don't hear Cameron at all after a while. Maybe she's unconscious, or maybe she trusts she *is* safe in Hector's arms. To her, he's only one of her rescuers, a man strong enough to hold her body weight. That she doesn't know he's her brother somehow makes the thing twice as beautiful.

Sixty-Five

We rush Cameron to the hospital in Fort Bragg, where Emily and Troy are already waiting in their car. I've told Will no media, but the networks have somehow gotten wind of the rescue anyway. The parking lot beyond the ambulance bay is clogged with vans and mobile floodlights and video stands. Emily has to pass through them to get to the room in the emergency wing where Cameron is being treated, but she does it.

"I know you want to see your daughter right away," I explain after I've led them to a private room for debriefing. "And you will see her. But right now we need to let the doctors do their job. And then we'll need a statement from her. She's safe and alive, though. That's the main thing."

"That monster who took her is still out there somewhere," Troy says with force, as if he hasn't heard me at all. "You let him get away. What kind of incompetence *is* that?"

"Listen, our sheriff is on this, and the FBI, too. An all-points bulletin has already gone far and wide, north and south, across state lines, to the moon if necessary. We'll find him."

Troy's face has turned lavender as he builds up steam. I can see he needs to blame someone, but I've had enough. "If you can't pull your shit together, you'll have to stay outside. I'm not kidding. Your daughter's been through hell. Do you get that?"

His eyes flash pure disdain. "How dare you."

"Troy." Emily's voice is unexpectedly firm.

His jaw flexes, full of knots that might never fully release. His guilt unaddressed. All the things he's done but won't ever ask forgiveness for. But finally, grudgingly, he steps backward, dropping the argument.

When it's time for me to begin my initial interview with Cameron, I leave the Curtises with one of Will's deputies, who can answer any questions they might still have, and head toward Cameron's room. On the way, I see Hector arguing with a nurse, trying to get information about his sister. His boots are still caked with mud, and his face is terrible to see, gripped with every emotion.

"It's fine," I tell the nurse, to let her know I've got this.

"Where is she?" he demands once she's gone.

"Just sit down for a minute."

Hector's eyes dart past me, scanning up and down the hall as if he can't wrap his head around anything but Cameron. He brought his sister here, carried her until his arms cried out with fatigue, but now he's a stranger again. No one knows who he is except me.

"How did you end up in the woods, Hector? I was pretty shocked to see you there."

"I've been going crazy lately, not knowing how to help. I was in my car across from the sheriff's office when I saw all the patrol cars light up and race out of town. So I followed you. I guess that's not cool, but it turned out okay, right? I got to her in time."

"You did," I say, knowing exactly how much those words mean. "She's been through a lot, but it could have been so much worse. Her ribs are badly bruised, and she has torn ligaments in her shoulder. She'll need surgery, but I'm sure she'll come through just fine. She's a fighter, right?"

He nods, and then his pupils narrow to pinpoints. "Did he . . . *hurt* her?"

From the pressure he's put on the word, how he can't quite make himself say what he means, I know he's asking if Cameron was raped. I wish that there was some way to spare him the truth, but it's too late for that. All I can do is nod slowly while his face contracts. Raw pain becoming fury and then despair.

"What can I do for her?" he asks in an anguished way.

"Oh, Hector. I'm so sorry. Right now we have to let the doctors take over. You'll have to be patient, if you can. The healing process will be very involved for her. But if you really love your sister, and I know you do, you won't get in the way or force your own feelings on her. In time, though, she should know who you are. You hold all those memories. You can give back that part of her life to her."

His eyes glass over and he swallows hard. "That guy who took her, he's still on the loose."

"He is. But we're going to catch him."

"You can't expect me just to sit here." He's clenching his fists so tightly they whiten at the knuckles. "Not while he could turn up here or hurt someone else."

"He can't get to Cameron here. We've placed armed officers outside her room, and no one is going to leave her unprotected for a moment. I promise you that."

He just sits there, his whole body seeming to tick. I recognize what's driving him now, that if he doesn't take some sort of action, he's going to fly apart.

"Listen," I say. "Do you think you could do a favor for me? My dog is at the sheriff's office in Mendocino. Can you get her and make sure she has food and water, and bring her here for me?"

"Oh." Some heaviness shifts from his eyes as he sits up straighter. "Yeah. I can definitely do that."

———

When I open the door to Cameron's room, the blinds and privacy curtains have been pulled closed. In her bed, Cameron sits propped against pillows, her knees drawn up beneath the blankets as if she's trying to become smaller while a nurse swabs the lacerations on her hands and wrists. Butterfly tape marks her right cheekbone and the center of her chin where she's had stitches. Through all of this—wounds and bruises, invisible and otherwise—she's beautiful. She's alive.

Cameron looks at me. "Your name's Anna," she says weakly.

"That's right." I step closer. "Anna Hart."

She closes her eyes and opens them again. "You saved my life."

The nurse looks back and forth between us, registering the emotion. "I'm just going to step outside for a minute. I'll be back soon."

When she's gone, I take the chair she was occupying, just a few inches from the head of Cameron's adjustable bed, the bland white sheets. "You saved your own life," I say as my throat tightens with feeling. "You did everything."

She looks at me unsteadily, as if she might cry, too. "Thank you," she says in a small voice.

"You've been through so much, but I'm going to have to ask you just a few questions. Do you know who took you? Would you recognize a picture of him?"

She looks away.

"Can you tell me what happened, Cameron?"

She shakes her head, still facing the wall.

"Do you have any idea where he might go?"

No answer.

"I know this is hard for you. But it's really important if we're going to stop him."

Again she says nothing.

I take a deep breath, trying to meet her where she is, which is utterly shut down. "It's okay. We can talk later. Are you cold? Can I get you another blanket?"

The bruised side of her neck twitches. Her beating pulse. Somehow I have to find a way to reach her, but now is not the time.

"I just want you to know that there's nothing you could tell me that would make me think less of you. You're very brave, Cameron."

She half turns to look at me. "I didn't have a choice."

"You did, though. You could have given up."

Will is in the hall when I come out of Cameron's room.

"Anything?" he asks.

"She's not ready."

"I get that, but this is a manhunt. Caleb could be on his way anywhere right now. Across the border to Canada, or already working on another victim."

"You think I don't know that?" I glance toward Cameron's door, then lower my voice and lead him toward the nurses' station. "She's fragile. Think of what she's been through. The trauma she's endured. A lot of what's happened to her will be unsayable, Will."

He sighs as my meaning lands, and then nods.

"She has to know she's our priority, not the information. She's earned that."

"Yeah, she has." He rubs his eyes with his fingertips, looking spent. Behind him at the nurses' station, there's a whiteboard with Cameron's name on it, along with scrawled red notes from her caregivers about IV fluids, vital signs, meds administered. At the top is today's date. October 14.

I stare at the numbers disbelievingly. Between my leaving San Francisco and today, an eternity's worth of changes have come and gone. Both of us broken open and transformed, linked forever, whether or not there are words for any of it. And yet only three weeks have passed. Not even a single cycle of the moon.

Sixty-Six

All that night and into the next day, the manhunt for Caleb continues. Dogs are brought in and more field teams, more men. Every county in Northern California signs on to help with the search—and it feels as if we have an army, finally, a rising human tide. Rod Fraser sends his helicopter our way again, to sweep the coast. He's shown Caleb's picture to Allison Palmer and Erin McGrath, and neither of them thinks this is the man they watched kidnap Polly. Still, the media is going crazy with speculation. More news teams arrive to flood the village, trying to get close to Cameron and her parents, hounding Will for statements and updates.

When the all-points bulletin for Caleb goes out over the Internet, it reaches thousands and thousands more within hours, and the army expands. The next morning, October 15, Caleb's Toyota pickup turns up near Galloway on a little-used county road, spotted by a woman who recognizes the license-plate number from the news. She calls Will's office, almost shouting.

We send dozens of men there, combing the area for places Caleb might be hiding. But even with this important find, we have no way of knowing how long his truck has been abandoned where he left it, or how many miles he can walk in a day. Or how carefully and completely he might be able to disappear, or for how long.

As the search continues, Will and I and a small team of men, some of them FBI, work to turn over every inch of the Pomo shelter, and the storage room at the Art Center, where other victims might have been held captive or even killed. We get a warrant for Caleb's house, which will take a long time to go through, even with the additional bodies.

Stepping inside feels strange and unsettling, as if time is spiraling backward. As if I could walk down the long paneled hallway and find Jenny in her room, playing her guitar or listening to Simon and Garfunkel on her hi-fi.

The first door off the hall to the left is Caleb's. I was last here as a teenager, lying on the brown shag carpet and eating peanut butter crackers while Caleb talked about famous shipwrecks or other obscure facts. The room is the same, feels almost time-stopped, as if Caleb never really finished growing up in this house, because Jenny couldn't either. The checked bedspread is navy and maroon, boyish. Two walls are lined with stuffed bookshelves. Over his desk and all along one wall are dozens of photographs of girls, all adolescents with long dark hair, brown or black, all beautiful, all targets or objects of obsession. Prey.

Shannan is here in three portraits side by side, looking painfully strung out, her eyes numb and haunted, as if the series is a triptych of her spiral into nothingness. And then I see Cameron, both in color and black and white. There are also pencil sketches of her face and shoulders, her neck and wrists, every nuance and fragment painstakingly captured with layered strokes and shading. Tenderly attentive and meticulously controlled.

I continue to scan the room, feeling more and more on edge. It's as if I'm standing not in a bedroom, but in a laboratory. This—all of this—is the inside of Caleb's mind. How he thinks. What he wants. What's been driving him these last months, if not years. I have to believe there are probably other victims, too, in the places he's lived before, even the Persian Gulf. That he's been doing this a long time. That he'll never stop if we don't catch him.

When Cameron's out of surgery and comfortable in her private room, Will and I begin to interview her, slowly and with care. One of the hardest things about earning her trust is that we're part of the problem, making her think about things she wants desperately to forget. We have an obligation to find and stop Caleb. Otherwise, she might never be safe again. But more than this I know that if she can find a way to speak even a portion of her tragedy, reconstruct some of these memories, they might begin to leave her body, and make more room inside, so she can slowly reclaim herself.

It's a complicated process, and not just because of her shaky physical state. The trauma of her ordeal has affected her memory and her ability to focus. One moment might seem clear in the telling, while the next splinters apart. She repeats certain details, but changes others. Sometimes she can't talk at all, only cry. Other times she seems almost emotionless, blinking in her hospital bed, as if we're complete strangers. She never says his name. But every once in a while, I see something come through the grief and numbness. A fierceness, small but present. What can't be broken.

The time line of the last few months is one of the trickiest things to cobble together, but little by little we begin to see, in small, sometimes-fractured pieces, how Caleb managed to reach Cameron in the first place. In early August, she'd seen his ad on the message board for an artist's model. She was with Gray that day, just grabbing a snack at the café after some time at the beach, but when she tore off the number and slipped it in her pocket, she did it secretly. She phoned him in private, too, from her room one afternoon when her mom was out, setting up a first meeting at the Mendocino visitors' center on Main Street.

"A public place," I remark, listening to her. It was a key move on his part, meant to build trust. The location was a smart choice, too, filled with tourists, not locals. They most likely wouldn't be spotted by anyone who knew them, and if so, they were only talking outside at one of the picnic tables in the shade, a nice day at the tail end of summer. "You felt safe to go alone."

"Yeah." She nods. "I guess that was stupid."

"Not at all. He could have been completely legitimate."

"But he wasn't."

"You didn't know that."

She looks up with eyes still deeply shadowed from her ordeal, her body painfully thin. "He looked normal."

"What did you talk about that day?" Will asks. "Do you remember?"

"He wanted to see my modeling portfolio, but I didn't have one. I was embarrassed I didn't even think of it before."

"Is that when you asked Gray to take those pictures in the grove, Cameron? You wanted to bring back something professional looking."

She nods. "When we met again, I showed him the photos. He said they were nice but not quite right for him. He was going to be doing sketches and wanted someone who looked really natural. I guess I was wearing too much makeup or something."

"Then what happened?" Will presses gently.

"He told me he would think about it and get back to me, but that if it worked out, he had a lot of contacts in the art world, in fashion, too. I guess I fell for it all." Her eyes flit away as shame drops down.

"If you did it's because he manipulated you," I tell her, wishing I could carry some of this for her. Her impossible burden. "He drew you in, catching you with your guard down. You didn't do anything wrong."

"I should have told my mom or Gray. Someone."

"You just wanted something for yourself. That makes so much sense given how stressful things were at home."

"I guess so." She doesn't sound convinced.

"The things that are really important to us, Cameron, a lot of the time we don't tell anyone because we can't. What you did was natural. And you're only fifteen, you know."

In her silence, I hold her eyes with mine. Try to speak to her without words. *You fought for yourself. That's why you're still here.*

Over the coming hours and days, we learn more. How by early September, Cameron began going to Caleb's garage studio to sit for him once or twice a week, after school. He didn't ask her to pose nude for him, or do anything that would have set off alarm bells. At every turn, he had behaved almost passively, which ironically increased his power with her. In other words, all his snares had worked.

Maybe things had escalated quickly between them because other things had already transpired, things that no one could have predicted. Cameron had gone to the free clinic and been confronted with all of that buried trauma. She'd also picked up the phone one Saturday to find Troy's assistant on the other end, calling to drop a bomb on her family. It's hard to say what might have happened without those factors, but soon she was sneaking out to meet Caleb, either because she had grown to trust him more and more, believing that she could have this dream of being a model if she worked hard enough for it, or because her desperation had built up to the point that she wasn't thinking clearly at all. Either way, Cameron obviously didn't have any idea of what she was really inside of, until it was too late. Until the night she went out to meet him and didn't come back.

"Why that night?" I ask.

"He said he had an art friend from LA who I should meet. He was only going to be in town for a few hours."

"So you waited for your mom to go to bed, and deactivated the alarm. Had you done that before?"

"A few times. I thought it would be fine. I believed him. But when I got to his truck where he was waiting for me, something was different."

"He seemed agitated?" I guess. "Not himself?"

"Yeah. He was nervous, and talking to himself. Like, whispering. It was really weird."

"Did you ask him to take you home?"

"I didn't know what to do. Then we came to the stoplight heading into town, and he went the other way. He wasn't going to the studio at all. There was no friend."

"And then what happened?" I ask her as gently as I can.

"I tried to get out of the car. I was going to jump out. I was really scared." Pulling up her blanket, she clutches at her arms beneath her cotton gown. I can see goose bumps under her hands. "He slammed on his brakes and screamed at me. He started to choke me and slammed me against the side of the window. I think I passed out."

"And that's when he took you to the shelter?"

"No, he took me someplace else first. A small dark room, sort of mildewy smelling. My hands were tied. I thought he was going to kill me right away, but he didn't." She turns toward the window, her body clenched as a fist. "He told me he loved me."

There's a long, charged silence. We bring her water. I ask one of the nurses for another blanket for her, a heated one, and notice my own hands are freezing in sympathy. My chest aches.

"How long were you there?" I ask, wondering why I hadn't

heard her the day I hiked near the Pomo shelter, why she hadn't heard me.

"A week maybe? He kept giving me some sort of pill to put me to sleep."

I glance at Will and our eyes catch. The forensics specialists have found traces of blood with luminol in the storage room at the Art Center, but none of the samples are large enough to match and type. They've collected more unidentified bits of evidence, too—nail shards, miscellaneous fibers. Some of the hair samples appear to match Cameron's, but there are others that don't.

"Did you see any signs that he'd kept anyone else either in the room or at the shelter before you?" Will asks Cameron.

"I don't know. I don't think so."

"Did you ever see another model with him?" he goes on. "We've found a lot of photographs of other girls. One is Shannan Russo, a seventeen-year-old who was murdered earlier this summer, but most we haven't been able to identify yet. It appears he's been doing this a long time."

From Cameron's expression, I can see she understands what we're saying. That she's lucky to be alive.

"How did you finally get away?" I ask.

She blinks slowly, heavily. "I'd been in the shelter for a long time, mostly alone. He'd come back every few days to feed me and . . ." She swallows the rest of the sentence, unable to even think about what came next, let alone say it. Clutching her blanket like a shield, she says, "I hadn't seen him in a while. I started to think he was going to let me starve, but then he came back and that was worse."

"What was different?" I ask.

"He seemed freaked out about something. He was tearing around grabbing stuff, talking to himself, really unhinged. He had a knife in his hand, and I thought for sure it was all over." Her voice falters and sticks.

"And then what happened?"

"He cut my hands free and I don't know. I had this thought that I didn't have a choice except to fight. That it was my last chance."

"Had you ever fought him before?"

"Not really. He's so much bigger than I am. The knife was right there, but I didn't think I could try for it. Instead, I just started throwing things, whatever I could grab. He got off-balance and fell against the wall and then things started crashing. I made it to the door and kicked it open, and then I heard something. He heard it, too. Someone was coming."

"And that's when you ran?"

"Yes."

"Do you have any idea where he might have gone?" Will asks. "Did he ever mention other places, wanting to get away?"

"I don't think so. He likes it here, likes the ocean. I don't think he'll go very far."

"The ocean?" I ask. "What about it?"

"Everything. He told me about diving for pearls in Iran." She lifts her gaze to meet mine. Her eyes seem very clear suddenly. Sad but clear. "He didn't always sound crazy."

No, he didn't, I think. And then we let her rest.

Sixty-Seven

On Halloween, though I don't feel remotely celebratory, I stand in front of Patterson's and watch neighborhood kids trick-or-treating up and down Lansing Street, ducking into the businesses that all have their doors open and their lights blazing long past closing time. There's an inflatable bouncy house in Rotary Park, and a table set up in front of Mendosa's where kids can get silly face tattoos. But all I can think as I see ghouls and witches and superheroes stream by, parents just behind them at a respectable distance, is that everyone—the whole town—should be home with their doors shut tight.

Wanda comes out from behind her post at the bar to talk for a while. She's dressed as Pippi Longstocking, with wire hangers suspending vivid yarn braids out over her shoulders. She's got a big stainless-steel bowl of mini–candy bars in her arms—Three Musketeers and Crunch and Special Dark. "How's Cameron doing?" she asks as she reaches down to lavish her usual affection on Cricket, balancing the bowl on her hip.

"Better every day. She went home last week."

"That's wonderful." She's only half listening as she rubs Cricket's face and ears, the two of them having a moment.

Just then I spot Will and his kids round the corner onto Ukiah Street, Beth nowhere in sight. As I watch them, two preteen girls stop in front of us, saying hi to Cricket while Wanda drops an entire handful of candy into each of their orange plastic jack-o'-lantern buckets. They grin as if they've won the lottery, both dressed like Little Red Riding Hood.

When they've walked off, capes waving like flags behind them, I say to Wanda, "If it were up to me, I'd keep her in the hospital until we find Caleb. It's safer, I think. Easier to monitor than her home."

Her usually unruffled stance calibrates as she listens to me. "Are you okay, Anna? You wanna come in and have something to eat? The soup is good tonight."

"Thanks. I'll be all right, I guess. I just wish these kids would get off the streets. You know?"

She follows my eyes with her own. So much innocence on parade. So much fragile human life. "I see where you're coming from, but I also think it's sort of brave to be out trick-or-treating tonight. Not just for the kids, I mean, but the parents as well. As if they're saying, *You can't take this, too.*"

Cricket leans against my leg as if she agrees with Wanda's point, but I don't.

"He could if he wanted to, though, Wanda. He could take it all."

After a while, I decide the best place for me is home, and head out from town with Cricket in the back seat, along the pitch-black juddering road. In my current mind state, the forest seems to distort beyond my headlights, single trees jumping out like hooked black shadows. I keep spinning on how many victims Caleb might have had over the years, how many targets of obsession. In the dozens of photographs in his room, at least, the girls all bear a striking resemblance to one another. Same long dark hair and gently rounded face shape. They also suggest more than a passing physical connection to Jenny, as if Caleb has been searching for variations of his own sister.

It's a disturbing thought, but one I can't help mulling over as I pull into my own shadowy driveway and kill the engine. The night is chilly and utterly silent here in the woods. No owl sound, no coyotes, no moon to light my way. Cricket trots ahead of me and up onto the porch, stopping once to mark her territory. I unlock the door, my thoughts still on Jenny and her tie to all this. With serial violent offenders, *who* they come to target is a crucial piece of understanding *why*. For Caleb, the complex series of triggers in his past have to include his sister's violent murder. But his relationship with Jenny would have been heightened long before by other factors, his mother's abandonment, his father's neglect and alcoholism. Losing a sister doesn't turn everyone into a killer, obviously. Something had already begun to twist Caleb at the root so that Jenny's death had done more than plunge him into grief—it had broken him.

Whatever the specificity of his wounds—and I can only hazard educated guesses just now—at some point they became too pressing and too loud for him not to act on them. He started to hunt girls—not grown women. Girls that resemble the sister he lost. Taking them means he finally has some control over the story, over how life has shortchanged him. One victim at a time, he can overthrow the helplessness he felt as a boy, and exert a sense of power.

I'm deep in the swirl of all of this, utterly preoccupied, when I reach for the lights. They flutter on, dispelling shadows. And then my breath seizes. Caleb is here in the cabin, sitting in the middle of my couch.

Adrenaline kicks through me. I can taste it, cold and acidic, at the base of my tongue.

He's wearing all black, as if he means to disappear. His face above his dark collar seems to hover. "Don't try to run," he says with an eerie calm. His hand reaches out for the back of Cricket's neck. She's standing beside him just as calmly. They've already met, after all.

The unease I felt in town and on the drive home has turned instantly into violent, electric fear. It overwhelms me with such force I wonder for a moment if I can speak or move. On the coffee table in front of Caleb, there's a hunting knife with a serrated blade, seven or eight inches long. Somewhere in my mind, I've stored the knowledge that could help me now . . . how much damage a weapon like this could do, depending on where he plunged it into my body, with how much power, and how many times.

He's twice my size, easily. I'd need my gun to fight back, the one I've hidden under the mattress in my bedroom, on the other side of where Caleb is sitting. I'd have to get around him to make it. Impossible.

As if Caleb can sense my thoughts, he stands up, grabs the knife, and moves in front of the door to the bedroom. His expression is chilly and flat, as if he's thinking instead of feeling every move he makes. Floating above himself.

My diaphragm contracts with dread, my whole body stiffened to wire. I glance at Cricket. She's so smart and even more intuitive. I can see that she senses something's off in the way she keeps her eyes on me. Her position hasn't changed. She's still sitting by the coffee table, but her gaze is fixed and alert. She's telling me she's on duty. That I'm not alone.

"Why don't I light a fire?" I suggest, trying to buy time. "It's cold in here."

"Sure," he says stiffly, pointing to the woodstove with the tip of his knife. "Just don't try anything."

His warning makes me think he's read my body language correctly. I want to bolt, to scream, to attack him and take my chances.

Instead I kneel by the woodbox and take out the box of matches, narrow splints of kindling, newspaper. "What do you want?" I ask, aware that my voice sounds oddly hollow. "Why did you come?"

His mouth tightens almost microscopically. "I think I should be asking you the same, Anna."

I glance toward the blade he's holding lightly in his right hand, nearly grazing his thigh. He's not brandishing it, not behaving erratically. If anything, he's too calm, more than certain he has the upper hand here. Because he does. "What do you mean?"

"You're the one who came after me. I was leaving you alone. I was showing respect." The word rings out strangely, with heat and contour.

It means something. It's a key. My thinking is still slow and unreliable, perforated with fear. But I've been here before. Talked to dozens of murderers and psychopaths. Done complicated profiling, written oceans of case notes. I've also stood in Caleb's room, his laboratory. Somehow I have to use what I know to piece it all together. The origin story that's driving everything. Old and powerful. Propulsive. What he's done and still means to do. What's happening now, in this room.

"I respect you, Caleb," I say. "We've been friends a long time."

"That's right. We have." He leans against the doorjamb, his black sweater and black jeans like an unbroken slash against the white paint. "Except you're not the same, Anna. You used to understand me. I thought you did, anyway."

He's given me more information. Another small piece of the whole. I work to steady my breathing, to unclench the tension in my hands. "I want to, Caleb. Tell me why Cameron is so special. She is, isn't she? I love her, too."

Suddenly Caleb's face reddens. His throat above the collar of his shirt looks strangely corded, as if he's barely holding himself in check.

"You've been doing this a long time," I say, "but Cameron is different for you. You kept her for three weeks, but you didn't kill her. I don't think you felt good about hurting her at all."

Glancing over, I see his eyes narrow, as if I've hit a nerve, but he says nothing. I light the wooden match in my hand and a kick of sulfur burns my nose and eyes. Still, I'm grateful for the action and moments of camouflage. The last thing I want is for him to see me trembling. I can't be a victim in his mind. A deer in headlights. I'm his friend. He has to believe that I accept him. That I know he can't control himself.

"I'm just trying to put myself in your place, Caleb. Did you think you could keep Cameron because she reminded you the most of Jenny?"

"Don't talk about her," he snaps, bouncing forward a little on the balls of his feet. He's wearing large black sneakers and seems surprisingly light in them, considering his size. He has to weigh close to two hundred pounds, but moves like a smaller man, not with grace exactly but efficiency. Maybe the military had taught him that.

"I miss Jenny, Caleb. I'll bet you do, too."

Without moving, something seems to seize in him. "You didn't know her."

In front of me, the fire has taken hold, licking past the kindling onto the lengths of pine I've placed in a loose tripod shape. The smell of flame touching wood is one of the most familiar and soothing scents I know, deeply knitted into my memories of Hap and home. Of comfort. But all I can think now is how long Caleb will let me live. If these are the last few moments of my life.

However he's found me here, following me from town, tracking my movements for days, maybe, or even weeks, he obviously wants retribution now. I've stolen something from him. Something precious and irreplaceable.

I sit back on my heels to meet Caleb's gaze. "I wanted to know

Jenny better. I always thought there was something so sad about your sister. I wish now she would have talked to me more. I wanted to help."

I can't tell from Caleb's expression if what I'm saying irritates or interests him, but he moves away from the bedroom door and sits on the arm of the plaid sofa, facing me, perhaps ten feet away. The knife resting on his knee. "We used to have a secret language when we were kids."

"I've heard that about twins. I'm jealous that you had someone to love like that."

"It was very special." The muscle on his right forearm twitches, and the bowie blade jumps as if of its own volition. "You wouldn't understand."

"I'm sure it was special. But then someone took her. Hurt her."

He sits forward now as his pupils snap over me. He looks angry, as if I've flipped a switch. "Like I said, you wouldn't understand."

Cricket seems to sense a change in pressure in the room. She's been resting near the coffee table, not far from where Caleb is, but now her head pops up as she looks at me. I hold her eyes, silently willing her over. Not because she can stop him from hurting me if he decides to, but for the comfort of her body.

"Are you still mad at your mom, Caleb? Is that what some of this is about? Why you need to make women pay?"

"What do you know about it?"

"My mom left, too." I'm surprised to hear myself say the words, as if they've appeared in my mind unbidden. "She killed herself."

"I didn't know that."

"I never talk about it. You know how it is," I say, trying to align us carefully without setting him off. He's like a human bomb with dozens of trip wires. Some of them I can see, but most are deeply inside him. "Sometimes I wish she was still here so I could show her how much of my life she messed up. Do you ever wish that?"

His gaze narrows again, but he doesn't respond.

"How come your mom didn't come back after Jenny was murdered?" I'm goading him deliberately now. Testing wires. Hoping I'm not wrong. "Didn't she care at all?"

"She did care. She just couldn't come back. She wasn't a strong person."

Now it's my turn to react. It's like I'm looking into a mirror. Hearing lines from a script I wrote a long time ago. I have the strangest feeling that all of this has happened before. As if the path has already been laid. As if there's only one possible place to step. "Not everyone can be strong," I say. "I see that. I'll bet you had to do a lot for Jenny because your mom couldn't."

"I didn't mind," he says quickly. "I was good at it. Our dad was always so useless."

The word has an inflection that snags and rebounds. *Useless.* *Idiot.* Again I have the feeling that I'm looking into a mirror—a dark one. "You were the same age, but you were always the stronger one," I say. "She could get sad sometimes, but you made her feel better. You cooked for her. You tucked her in at night. I'll bet you read her stories, too."

Suddenly he frowns. Charged ripples of emotion cling to him as he stands up. "Stop trying to get into my head."

"I just want to understand, like you said. I feel like I've let you down, Caleb. I think a lot of people have."

He shifts forward and back, as if to test his balance. "Yeah," he mutters, almost to himself. "She shouldn't have tried to leave me."

The sentence lands with a jolt between my shoulder blades. He's not talking about his mother now. It's Jenny who let him down. Jenny who betrayed him. How could I have missed that before?

"Not everyone is strong, Caleb," I echo slowly, inching forward in my crouch. I've been kneeling this whole time in front of the fireplace, cutting off my circulation. My feet tingle as the blood reaches them. I risk a glance at the bedroom door, then at Cricket on the floor next to the couch, resting but aware, if I read her right, and finally back to Caleb. "She couldn't take it anymore, just like your mom."

"I would have gone with her." It's almost a moan. The boy in him is very much here with us, still hurting. That's where the rage lives. Right at the center of that wound. "But she didn't want to take me. She wouldn't listen."

"You had to stop her," I say. "That's how it happened." With him I'm calculated, trying not to set down a single wrong syllable, while internally I'm lunging through a pitch-black room for any familiar shape, as in a child's game. Blindman's bluff. "You argued. There was a struggle. You didn't know how strong you were."

His chin has tipped down, his eyes on some point in front of him, as if he's trying to blot all this out and focus on *that* instead, the bigger drama, the story of his life. They must have argued on her last day at home. She packed a bag, tried to go, but he stopped her and accidentally what? Broke her neck?

But no, Jenny had gone to work that day. Her coworkers had seen her leave to hitchhike back to the village. Which means he'd taken Jack's truck and waited for her, knowing she was going to be long gone otherwise. He'd pulled up while she had her thumb out. She'd climbed in thinking she could spend a few more minutes trying to explain why she had to go. And that's when he'd done it. Bluntly. He'd strangled her and then driven her to the river. All of it something he had to do. A horrible, soul-splitting thing. But part of him had liked it. Part of him had come alive for the first time.

"I don't think you're a monster, Caleb," I say. "You can trust me. Let me help you find a way out of this."

"No." It's barely visible, the way his muscles tense. Then a string breaks in him. He lunges with the knife toward the woodstove, toward me. Cricket snaps to her feet and rushes in front of him. It all happens faster than light moves. Slower than days whirl by, or years. Centuries.

Caleb loses his balance. Trips and stumbles over the dog's body, comes close to me, but Cricket has no doubt now that I'm in danger. The growl in her throat is low and terrifying as I run for the bedroom door, misjudging it.

My shoulder bashes against the jamb. A protracted bounce as I keep hurtling forward, chaotic sounds behind me, Cricket barking as I've never heard her bark, and then a high yelp as if she's been kicked or worse.

Now there are thundering steps along the hardwood floor. The fear in me is like something tectonic, but survival is even fiercer and more undeniable.

I reach the bed, plunge my hand beneath the mattress, feel the cool muzzle, the ridged grip like a message in braille to turn. Turn *now*.

But Caleb has lunged at me before I can lift my hand and pull the trigger. The force of him knocks the breath from my lungs. We crash hard to the floor together, his weight like a mountain on my chest.

I thrash beneath him, trying to get any kind of leverage, but gravity and strength are on his side. He pins me easily with his hip and elbow, his forearm like a club against my neck and larynx. The gun and my right hand crushed between us against my hip.

Dark spots swim through my vision as I fight for air. Fight to stay conscious.

He raises the knife, carves the air over my head. His face looms above me like some sort of warped and wretched planet as I search along the floor with my left hand, desperate for any kind of weapon. There's nothing but hardwood, worn smooth through the decades.

I reach over my head, keeping my eyes fixed on the knife, and *there*. My fingertips graze the iron bedpost. It's solid, or as solid as anything I'm going to find. I strain a bit farther, grip the post, and buck upward. Twisting from my hip and shoulder as hard as I can, harder, I get one foot under me. Then my left knee up. Blood rushes into my freed limbs.

Caleb's eyes bulge with rage as I struggle, the knife passing inches from my face, but maybe he can't bring himself to stab me. With one last thrust, I pitch him backward into the bed rail, his skull ramming solid iron. He cries out, a growl of pain and fury, as I stumble away from him with strength I don't really have.

This isn't just about saving my own life but for Cameron, so she'll never have to fear Caleb again, not for one more moment. I have to put an end to what she's suffered at his hands, and Shannan, too, and all the nameless wounded others, silenced now, stretching out and out in concentric rings.

I whirl to face him as he lurches to his feet, wrestling himself forward. His face is terrible. Twisted.

"Anna!" he shouts. But I've seen enough. Know enough now.

He'll never stop, not ever.

My right arm is half numb as I raise it in front of me. I steady the muzzle and fire into his chest, not fumbling this time. Not missing. The recoil slams through my clenched palm, three shots, but I only hear the first. The others thump-thump through my inner ear, no louder than my heartbeat, which seems to roll forward like a wave, shaking me out of my trance. Caleb's eyes are open but dull. Blanked out. His chest streaming blood.

I stagger into the other room, my nose stinging with gunpowder. Cricket is motionless in the center of the floor, a small river of blood and fluid near her mouth. For one excruciating moment, I'm sure he's killed her and can barely hold my hand still to check the pulse at her neck, but it's there. She's still alive.

I'm running on steam and shock, a distorted kind of euphoria. I bend over Cricket and pick her up. She doesn't struggle. She barely seems conscious against my chest as I carry her out of my cabin— *like a child,* I keep thinking—to my car, leaving the door open wide behind me, so they can come for him and process his body, and take him away, and scour the rooms, collecting evidence. It's a crime scene now. I never want to see it again.

Sixty-Eight

On November 4, I wake in the upstairs bedroom in Tally's farmhouse, the soft knitted blanket from her own alpacas resting lightly on my chest, Cricket at my feet like a warm stone. The side of her neck is still bandaged from where Caleb stabbed her. Initially the veterinary surgeon thought her trachea or esophagus might be damaged, but the injury had only reached soft tissue. The doctor had sedated her before cleaning the wound, draining the fluid and then closing her up with staples. She'd recovered in the Mendocino Animal Hospital for the first few days before coming to stay with me at Tally's. It was a temporary move, the first place I thought of in the aftermath of Caleb's death, since Will didn't have room for me.

As I push back the blankets, Cricket stirs and gives me a disgruntled look before yawning and going back to sleep. I throw on some warm clothes from my duffel in the corner and head downstairs smelling coffee and French toast.

It's Sam cooking, I notice. Tally is at the kitchen table reading the newspaper as I come up. She lays the paper down quickly. "How'd you sleep, Anna?"

"Not great, I'm afraid."

"Oh, dear. Did Cricket keep you up?"

"No, she's a perfect patient. I just had weird dreams. I have them a lot. It's nothing."

Sam wheels up behind me and puts a plate down that smells like heaven. Maple syrup and melting butter. Homemade bread.

"You know I'm never going to leave if you keep feeding me this way," I say gratefully.

"No problem," he answers with a wink. "I'll catch you two later. Heading into the studio now."

When he's gone, I turn to Tally. "So, what's in the paper you don't want me to see?"

"Oh," she sighs. "Now stop." She's in a dark green terry-cloth bathrobe and fusses with the sleeves. "It's just a story about Polly Klaas. I thought maybe you could rest longer before getting upset again."

"Why would I be upset?"

"Apparently the town is trying to pass a proposal to hire a missing-child expert, but the Petaluma police are set on rejecting it."

"That doesn't make sense."

"They say it would disrupt continuity or something." She pushes the paper my way, relenting. "That they're close to breaking the case."

I scan the page to see a quote from Sergeant Barresi about having plenty of resources and manpower without outsiders, then another from Marc Klaas about how frustrated he is that nothing significant in Polly's case has broken in more than a month.

"Maybe it's time for me to go to Petaluma," I say after a moment. "I'm not exactly sure how I can help, but I have nothing but time on my hands here. Cameron's home now. She's doing well."

Tally falls quiet, her blue eyes still. I watch her hands curl around the coffee cup in front of her and suddenly wish I had stayed in bed.

"What?" I make myself ask. "What is it? You've had another vision, haven't you?"

"I don't exactly know how to tell you this, Anna, but Polly's gone. They won't find her body for some time, but they will find it, and her killer, too. She'll be at peace finally. Not for a while, but she's going to get there."

I feel a stuttering wave of sadness. A weariness that's bone deep, endless. There are too many dead bodies behind me. And too much darkness ahead. "Her poor family. At least they'll have a body to bury. Maybe that will comfort them."

"I hope so," she replies gently. "Her murder won't be for nothing, though. Polly is going to be very, very important going forward. She will change things about how we look for the missing."

"You mean the Internet," I say.

"Other things, too. It will all unfold in time. She won't disappear. Decades from now, we'll still be saying her name."

I nod, wanting more than anything for Tally to be right.

"There's still work for you to do, Anna," she continues. "You really could stay here with us forever. I love having you around. But I believe you're supposed to go home now. Your family needs you."

I look away. The softest, most terrible wrecking ball smashes at my heart from the top of the sky. "I can't."

"Maybe you don't think so, but you're ready for this. Your son should have you there. He needs his mother."

Everything goes sideways then. I start to cry, but silently. I can't catch my breath long enough to make a sound.

"How old is he?"

"Almost seven months," I whisper. I haven't let myself think about how it would feel to tell this story, not to Tally or anyone. I've been hiding from it. The pain and the regret. The unbearable weight of my guilt. "He wasn't there the day Sarah died."

"What happened?" Tally's voice is gentle and compassionate. I know that I have to find a way to answer her. To tell the truth, no matter how impossible that feels. No matter how she'll look at me afterward. No matter what happens next.

"Brendan had the day off. He took Matthew over to his sister's house while Sarah was napping. I—" My voice breaks, but I make myself go on. "I'd been working on a big case for weeks and wanted to use the time to follow up on a few leads. When Sarah woke up, I realized we had no food in the house for dinner, so I put her in the car and strapped her in, but then the phone rang in the house. I'd been waiting for a call most of the day, about the case. The victim was an infant." I stop there as if that detail alone explains everything.

"She was in the car," Tally urges gently. "And you went inside to get the phone."

"I shouldn't have left her there," I explain raggedly. "But it was only for a second. I could see her through the front window in her car seat."

"The phone call rattled you, though," she guesses. Or maybe it's not a guess. Maybe she already knows all of this somehow in whatever way that knowing has come to her.

"It was my partner calling. The stepmother of the baby we'd found murdered had confessed. I'd interviewed her twice myself, but I hadn't seen it. I couldn't believe it. I just froze there, spinning on my mistake."

"And you took your eyes off of Sarah."

"Just for a minute. Not even *that*." The last word is a strangled croak. I take a deep breath so I can go on, pinching my eyes shut. "I'd left the car door open so I could see her better. She got out of her car seat somehow. I didn't even know she could do that. She was only two and a half."

"I'm so sorry, Anna. What a thing to live through."

Have I lived through it? Sometimes I've wondered. Is this living, reckoning with my guilt every day? Being without my family? My son?

I open my eyes. "The car was parked in our driveway at an angle. I only looked away for a second and then I heard an awful sound outside. Our neighbor Joyce had backed into the street from her own driveway and Sarah was there." Now that I've said everything, I feel almost numb. Vacant. There's nothing to hide, anymore. No secrets to keep.

"Oh, Anna." Tally's eyes are kind. "It was an accident. A terrible accident."

"For Joyce, maybe. She had no idea Sarah was there, but I was responsible for her. I'm her mother." The blank feeling inside me expands, as if I'm being swallowed alive, from the inside out. "She died instantly. She was so small."

"A thing like that could have happened to anyone."

"That's not true. I was too distracted. My work had taken over my whole life. I wasn't present. That's why Brendan told me to go. He knew the same thing could happen to Matthew. He said he can't trust me anymore."

"Grief is a powerful force," Tally says. "A lot of the families I've worked with over the years have come to similar places over a child's death. Maybe Brendan has had time to work out his feelings. Maybe he's ready to talk."

"Even if he could forgive me, I'm not sure I could do anything different now. I haven't changed."

"What do you mean? Why not?"

"I've never been able to have any distance from these victims. The kids I'm trying to help. My cases just swallow everything. That's how the accident happened." I lean against the table with my elbows. Everything inside me feels so heavy I wonder if I can go on. If I can ever again hold myself upright. "I miss Sarah so much."

Tally is silent as she moves her chair closer to mine. Her arms wrap around me, strong and tender, forgiving. Her body is like a harbor. Like a real place to land.

I stay there, anchored, until I start to feel stronger. Then I sit up and dry my eyes, and start to tell her about Jamie Rivera. It was late July when we found his tiny body in that icebox, covered in frost. I couldn't stop thinking about him, how his innocent life had just been stolen, for no reason at all. I wanted to find his killer more than anything. To make that person pay. Meanwhile my own family life demanded so much from me, and I didn't have it to give. I kept telling myself it was just this case. That once we'd solved it, I'd feel better and get back to what was really important. But in another way, I knew that would never happen. My work is a sickness—an addiction—and always has been.

Maybe I should have been more honest with Frank or asked for help, or gone back to therapy. I should have built that house in my mind and done everything I could to heal. Maybe then I would have been awake and watching—there. When Sarah climbed out of the car, I would have run out and stopped her. I would have picked her up in my arms, and carried her to safety.

"Nothing can bring your daughter back," Tally says when I've finished. Our coffee has grown cold. My breakfast pushed away long ago. "I can only imagine how much pain you've been carrying, but she doesn't blame you. Her spirit is as untroubled as any I've ever seen, Anna. She's like the sun."

I swallow hard. It's a beautiful image, and I want so much to believe it. That's what Sarah was like in life. Just like the sun. "Where is she now?"

"She's everywhere, like light. She watches over her brother and father and you, too. She's crazy about your dog. She says she always wanted one just like Cricket, and now she has one."

More tears then. Where do they all come from? Is the body made only of tears? "She's at peace? She doesn't feel any pain?"

"Only when she knows you're suffering. She wants you to forgive yourself, Anna. You have to find a way to come to terms with all this. There's so much more for you to do. That's how you can honor Sarah. You can live out your life's purpose."

Suddenly I think of Cameron. "I can't just abandon her," I try and explain to Tally.

"Cameron knows you care about her. Besides, she has a lot of people around who love her and will make sure she's safe." She tips her chin forward and gazes into my eyes with a clarity that startles me. "Are we really talking about something else, Anna? Or someone? What haven't you been able to let go of?"

I shake my head, wishing she'd look away or drop this. We've been sitting here forever already, discussing such terrible, unsurvivable things. And yet I know instantly what she means. Jason and Amy. Since that Christmas when I was eight, every story has been the same story. Cameron has come closer to my heart than most, but bringing her home hasn't freed the pressure at the center of my chest. Killing Caleb hasn't, either. "I don't think I can get better, Tally. I've been this way a long time."

"Anyone can change. We do it over and over, every time we do even one thing different. Don't sell yourself short. You've helped so many people, Anna. Help yourself. Help Matthew. Then see what happens."

"What if Brendan still blames me? I've hurt him so much."

Again, her eyes are soft and wise. "Maybe he does. Or maybe he forgave you a long time ago and is waiting for you to catch up."

A few hours later, Tally walks me to my car. I help Cricket into the back seat, and then throw my duffel onto the floorboard. None of this is easy. My emotions are still chaotic and my doubt is loud, but I know what I need to do now. Whether or not the strength will come to me, I have to try. Even if I have to show up on my knees, Tally is right. I have to go back and face everything. I have to be the mother I am. The sister I am, too. I have to find a way back to

Jason and Amy. Maybe they will slam a door in my face. Or maybe they forgave me a long time ago, too. There's only one way to find out.

Once I've settled behind the wheel of my Bronco, I say through the open window, "All the times we've talked, you've never mentioned Hap. Why is that? I just can't believe he wouldn't be watching all this from the other side. Watching me and helping me do what's right. Why would he leave me alone?"

"Do you feel him?"

That stops me. "Yes."

"Then how are you alone?"

"I never saw his body. I think that's why I can't let him go."

"Anna, I'm going to ask you something that might sound odd, but think about it for a minute. Where is Hap?"

Where? She's the psychic. Then it comes to me. He's inside me. I hear him all the time. All his lessons. His voice. "Here."

She looks down at her feet, still in slippers. Clutching the robe around her, she gazes at me with a level of directness that nearly takes my breath away. "The people we love never leave us, Anna. You know that already. That's what I mean by spirit. I mean love."

Sixty-Nine

I spend one more day in Mendocino. One long day—a map without edges. I walk out to the headlands in a cold wind to look at the wild sea, the Point Cabrillo light swinging toward me, then away. I go to Covelo Street and stand in front of Hap and Eden's house, wondering if it could ever be big enough to hold everyone and me, too, whole or not, missing or newly found. Our stars flickering on and on. Our souls and the shapes they make trying to find one another in the dark.

I go to Evergreen Cemetery with handfuls of ferns in a small ceramic vase. I go to Rotary Park to find Lenore and Clay packing to return to Denver, and clearly happy to see me. I give them my home number in San Francisco, then drive to the Curtises' to say goodbye to Emily and Cameron, hoping they'll agree to let me visit again soon.

Cameron is in her room with Gray, the two of them listening to music, sitting on Cameron's bed. Her right arm is in a sling bound to her chest, and her face still bears the evidence of her harrowing ordeal. And yet I can also see a light in her, newly kindled. There's a great deal of work ahead, but she's alive and in her body. How miraculous that is. They're both miraculous, hip to hip on Cameron's bed while Madonna sings "Like a Prayer."

I leave them there and find Emily in the kitchen. She's organizing her spice cabinet, and there are bottles strewn everywhere. It's a relief to see her surrounded by a mess somehow, even for a moment, even though she'll tidy it again.

"Will told me Cameron's starting to remember more about her early abuse," I say quietly. "Do you know yet? Has she been able to tell you?"

She nods heavily. "She's only getting pieces. The therapist is amazing. He's helping her a lot. I'm pretty sure it's my dad, though."

"I'm so sorry, Emily."

Her sigh sounds ancient. "Yeah. Me too. But I'm going to support her. Whatever it takes, however ugly it gets, the truth has to come out, Anna."

She's right. I think of the officer who will knock on her father's door one day soon. The long-overdue detonation of his secret self. The healing that might begin. "I'm proud of you," I say.

Her eyes film over. "At least Caleb is dead. I'm not sure she ever would have been able to go on with him still on the loose."

"Probably not." I have to agree, though the memory of our struggle in the cabin hasn't left me for a moment. Maybe it never will. "How's Troy?"

"Troy is . . . Troy wants to work it out. He's promising to stand by us."

"Well, you'll know what to do," I tell her. "It might take a while for you to feel what's right for you and Cameron. But you can do this. I've seen so much strength in you, Emily. I hope you can see it, too."

Then there is only Will to find. I hate telling him that I'm leaving, but this is the easiest of the things I have to say. The rest is too much to find words for, and yet I do, somehow. I tell him about Sarah, about Brendan asking me to leave. About the guilt and blame and raw grief I've been carrying. About Matthew. How afraid I've been to mother him. It's like moving a mountain off of my chest to say his name, even. To tell the whole story of how I got here.

"I should have trusted you more from the beginning," I finally say through tears, "but I didn't know how."

"I don't blame you. I can't even imagine what you've been dealing with. I'm so sorry. I wish I could have helped somehow."

"You've had too much to deal with too. The separation. Your family. The risk of losing your kids. That's a lot."

The muscles in his jaw clench as he wrestles with emotion. "It hasn't just been Jenny's case that's come between me and Beth," he says. "My drinking's been out of control for years. I want to get sober, but I don't know how."

"Me too. Maybe we can lean on each other. Anyone can change, Will," I say, trying on Tally's phrase. "Even if it's inch by inch."

He's silent for a moment, gazing down at his desk, the files and Post-it notes, the half-drained pens in a spill of light. Then he says, "I know it's crazy, but I still think we're going to work together to solve those murders from 1973, even if Jenny wasn't involved. It should be us. I just feel it."

I have to smile at that, just a little. "His famous feelings are back."

"Very funny."

"I do want to visit in a few weeks to check in on Cameron."

"Of course. Whatever you need. And let me know how you are, okay? You'll be on my mind."

"I love you, Will. You know that, right?"

"Yeah. Me too. Come back soon."

Seventy

Leaving town is harder than I imagined, even though I know I'll be back—for Will, for Wanda and Gray and Emily. For Cameron. I walk the length of Lansing Street, unable to get into my Bronco. Bristling with cold, underdressed for the bite of the wind, I look up at *Time and the Maiden,* starkly white against the blue fist of the sky, utterly cloudless and blameless, silent and everywhere. A single raven is perched squarely on the hourglass, looking not at me but away, its sharp head in profile, an arrow pointing at the sea. A symbol in a puzzle full of symbols, a mystery in plain sight.

For decades I've been drawn to the carving without knowing why. But just now, all I can see is the weeping maiden with her head bowed, and how like Jenny she is. Jenny on the beach, singing "Goodnight, California," her long hair blowing in front of her eyes. I see Shannan in the maiden, too, wearing her rabbit-fur jacket, her soul too heavy to carry. I see Cameron in the grove, and then Cameron as she is now, taking herself back, climbing off of the plinth and out of the puzzle. I see Amy with her white-blond hair in her mouth, sobbing the day she was taken out of our home, out of my arms. Finally, I see the girl I was on my first day in Mendocino, guarded and wounded, watching a simple sunset. The green flash of luck, Eden called it. But really it was the first moment I saw what love might still do to save me, if I had the courage to let it in.

For the longest time I stand on Lansing Street, thinking about beauty and terror. Evil. Grace. Suffering. Joy. How they're all here every day, everywhere. Teaching us how to keep stepping forward into our lives, our purpose.

Long ago Corolla told me that it's not what happens to us that matters most, but how we can learn to carry it. I'm starting to understand the difference, and how maybe the only way we can survive what's here, and what we are, is together.

I turn my back on the carving and begin to walk toward my Bronco, and as I do so, something flutters and knocks from behind me. The raven taking flight. Moving on. I smile a little, and then call for Cricket. She stands up in the back seat and tips her ears forward, eager to be on the road. Ready or not, it's time to go home.

Acknowledgments

In the three years I spent writing this novel I've leaned on far too many books, editors, colleagues, and friends to adequately thank, but the following deserve special acknowledgment.

My brilliant agent, Julie Barer, believed in this book and encouraged me to write it from the very first spark, over a long, wine-tinged lunch at Soho House in downtown Manhattan, as I remember. For her intelligence, unerring intuition, and huge, brave heart, I thank the universe for her now and always.

I'm ever grateful to my editor, Susanna Porter, for her excellence on the page, and complete investment in me and the worlds I'm trying to build; and to Kara Welsh and Kim Hovey for publishing my work with incredible integrity, thought, and care.

My dear friend and accomplice for twenty-two years and counting, Lori Keene, read dozens of drafts and also plunged with me through the real village of Mendocino, as we hiked many of the trails Anna and Hap do in the book and she listened to me find my way to these characters and their stories. For these and so many other reasons, I've dedicated the novel to her.

Retired detective Marianne Flynn Statz seemed to appear in my life randomly, but we know the universe doesn't do random! She read my manuscript with care, answered all of my questions with patience, wisdom, and a wickedly dark sense of humor, and gave me a richer and more granular template for understanding sensitive crimes. This book and Anna are deeper and truer because of her. Thank you, Marianne!

Chris Pavone, Kristin Hannah, and Christina Baker Kline all came through for me in a big way during the drafting process, pointing out things I didn't necessarily want to hear but absolutely needed to. This book is better by far because of their wise and responsive feedback. At the very least, I owe you guys more fancy cheese!

My amazing publishing team at Ballantine Books and Penguin Random House do their jobs brilliantly and have given me the best possible home these last ten years: Jennifer Hershey, Jennifer Garza, Allyson Lord, Quinne Rogers, Taylor Noel, Susan Corcoran, Kathryn Santora, Hayley Shear, and the incomparable Gina Centrello. Emily Hartley responded to a thousand emails cheerfully and efficiently. Dana Blanchette engineered the beautiful interior design elements and map. Thanks to Susan Bradanini Betz for her thorough and comprehensive copy editing of the manuscript, and to Steve Messina, who graciously and meticulously ushered these pages through a sometimes intense production process. I also need to thank senior VP and deputy general counsel Matthew Martin for his incredibly sensitive and responsive reading of this book.

Nicole Cunningham and the superb team at The Book Group have my back in every possible way and are the world's savviest and most delightful women. Elisabeth Weed in particular offered feedback on the manuscript at a critical time, for which I'm so grateful. I owe a debt of gratitude as well to Jenny Meyer and Heidi Gall, who help with every aspect of foreign rights and sales; to my consummately charming U.K. agent, Caspian Dennis of Abner Stein; and to my incredibly smart and wonderful film agent, Michelle

Weiner at CAA. Thanks to Kristin Cochrane, Amy Black, Lynn Henry, Valerie Gow, Sharon Klein, and their lovely colleagues at Penguin Random House Canada, and to Jenny Parrott at Point Blank/Oneworld in the U.K. for responding so enthusiastically to the potential in me and this story.

Diving into a new genre would no doubt have been a more staggering undertaking without the following books and resources as guideposts: *The Body Keeps the Score*, by Bessel van der Kolk; *Waking the Tiger*, by Peter A. Levine; *The Unsayable*, by Annie G. Rogers; *I'll Be Gone in the Dark*, by Michelle McNamara; *The Fact of a Body*, by Alexandria Marzano-Lesnevich; *No Visible Bruises*, by Rachel Louise Snyder; *In the Name of the Children*, by Jeffrey L. Rinek and Marilee Strong; *The Killer Across the Table*, by John Douglas and Mark Olshaker; *Criminal Minds*, by Jeff Mariotte; *Unsolved Child Murders*, by Emily G. Thompson; the Polly Klaas Foundation (pollyklaas.org); "Eddie Freyer: Polly Klaas Abuction and Murder", *FBI Retired Case Review* with Jeri Williams; the *Petaluma Argus-Courier* archives; "Polly's Face," by Noelle Oxenhandler, *The New Yorker*, November 22, 1993; *Who Killed Polly?* by Frank Spiering; *Polly Klaas*, by Barry Bortnick; the *Los Angeles Times* archives; *Images of America: Early Mendocino Coast*, by Katy M. Tahja; and *History of Mendocino and Lake Counties, California*, by Aurelius O. Carpenter; *The Light Between Us*, by Laura Lynn Jackson; *Gathering Moss*, by Robin Wall Kimmerer; and *The Songs of Trees*, by David George Haskell. I also very much need to thank the following authors whose work helped me understand what I wanted to accomplish in my own book: Tana French, Kate Atkinson, Louise Penny, Rene Denfeld, Peter Rock, and Gabriel Tallent. Thank you for your excellent mentorship, however unintended!

Brian Groh, Patti Callahan Henry, Beth Howard, Sarah McCoy, and Eleanor Brown are friends I've come to count on for solidarity and support when I most need it. You're incredible humans as well as phenomenal storytellers. Thank you! Kat Berko, my magnificent assistant, has been a godsend to me; I'm never letting her go. Other friends and family members continue to be indispensable in more ways than I can name: Sharon Day, Pam and Doug O'Hara, Beth Hellerstein and Dan Jaffe, Boo Geisse, Brad Bedortha, and the entire D'Alessio clan; Terry Dubow, Toni Thayer, Sarah Willis, Karen Sandstrom, Charlie Oberndorf and the Eastside Writers; Scott and Cherie Parsons; Heather Greene; the Kauai Gals, with a special shout-out to Cynthia Baker, Meg Wolitzer, Priya Parmar, Amanda Eyre Ward, and Michelle Tessler; and also David Kline and Jon Zeitler, who aren't gals at all, but who welcomed me so warmly, and made every moment of Kauai feel like home.

Thanks to Karen Curtis and to Cricket (the real Cricket!) for love and inspiration, and to the expansive Cleveland crew who have helped keep me sane, fed, dressed, coiffed, and on track during the writing of this book: Quincy D'Alessio, Sam D'Alessio, Alena Sorensen, Karen Rosenberg, Nan Cohen, Aaron Kamut, Kath Lepole, Brian Schrieffer, Leigh Sanford, Penny Conover, Krista Gorzelanczyk, Lindsey Campana, Erika Scotese, Karen Miner, Olga Chwa, Dave Vincent, and Ron Block.

I'm grateful to Rita Hinken and Letti Ann Christoffersen, my two mothers; to my nieces and nephews, Margaret Bailey, Jacob Bailey, and Sam and Mitchell Reller, for always encouraging my work and me; and to my sisters, Teresa Reed and Penny Pennington, who are my true north.

Finally, thanks to my children for being the most crucial element of my home team and the fabric of my life: Connor and Jamilya, Beckett and Finn. And Piper too, of course! I love and appreciate you more than words can say.

Author's Note

Ten years ago, when inspiration struck in the form of a real woman from history, Ernest Hemingway's first wife, Hadley, the idea seemed to come from nowhere. I had never considered writing a historical novel, let alone one that featured an actual person. And yet once I plunged into the research and writing process, it struck me powerfully that I wasn't just telling a story; I was honoring Hadley's life and spirit, and giving her a voice.

Something eerily similar happened in the writing of *When the Stars Go Dark*—the idea for which came just as unexpectedly and mysteriously, and with an electrical inner *yes* I've learned to pay attention to. I pictured a missing persons expert obsessed with trying to save a missing girl and also struggling to make peace with her past. Almost immediately I knew the story had to be set in Mendocino—a small coastal town in Northern California where I spent time in my twenties—and that the time frame of the narrative had to be pre-DNA, pre-cellphone, before the Internet had exploded and *CSI* had laypeople thinking they could solve a murder with their laptop.

Choosing 1993 was instinctual—random—and yet when I dug into the research, I was startled to learn that a rash of real-life ab-

ductions of young girls had occurred in the same geographical area
and time frame I was exploring, most notably the kidnapping of
twelve-year-old Polly Klaas. Polly was taken at knifepoint on the
night of October 1, 1993, from the bedroom of her home in Petaluma while her two friends watched. It was a horror story that triggered every parent's deepest fears, and set in motion the largest
manhunt in California's history. The town of Petaluma came together to aid in the search for Polly. Thousands of volunteers helped
search three thousand square miles, and kept her rescue center running twenty-four hours a day, until December 4, nine weeks after
her abduction, when her remains were discovered near an abandoned mill off Highway 101, near Cloverdale, California.

FBI agents were led to the body by suspect Richard Allen Davis,
age thirty-nine, a man who had an extensive criminal record, including two previous kidnappings, who had violated his parole numerous times, and who had evaded law enforcement officers twice
in the weeks following Polly's abduction, the first encounter being
only an hour after he took her, when two patrol officers helped him
get his battered Ford Pinto out of a muddy ditch, even though he
was notably inebriated and disoriented, with dirt on his clothes
and twigs in his hair. She may very well have still been alive, and
nearby.

I confess I didn't sleep well in the weeks and months I researched
Polly's case and others. The profound suffering of the victims and
their families crept into my dreams—and onto the page. It began
to feel imperative that I tell their stories as bluntly and factually as
possible, as a way to honor their lives and dignify their deaths and
disappearances. Saying their names became for me a sacred act. A
kind of prayer. And yet it feels crucial to note that writing about
real events and people requires the utmost sensitivity and care. For
this reason, and to respect their privacy and wish for anonymity,
I've changed the names of the friends who were with Polly the night
of her abduction.

Just a month after his daughter's kidnapping, Marc Klaas started the Polly Klaas Foundation, a grassroots nonprofit organization that has since worked with thousands of families, law enforcement officers, and volunteer workers to help find missing children. The foundation, as part of Polly's legacy, has also helped alter the California legal system, which now mandates life imprisonment for repeat violent offenders, and put Amber Alert laws in place across all fifty states.

Polly's parents have both repeatedly spoken of the way their community's search for their daughter showed the very best of humanity, a steady light in the midst of unbearable darkness. I realized I wanted to write about that. About how a town can come together when the worst happens. About how if we're ever going to truly heal, we need one another to get there.

Writing a novel is such an interesting mix of effort and surrender, of control and vulnerability. It wasn't until late in the stages of drafting that it fully dawned on me just *why* I was so drawn to tell this particular story and not any other. My troubled detective, Anna Hart, is obsessed with trauma and healing, with intimate violence and the complex hidden connection between victims and predators, because *I'm* obsessed with those things, and long have been. I've given her other parts of me too—a version of my childhood spent in foster care, and my abiding love of the natural world as deep medicine. What Anna knows and thinks about the hidden scars of sexual abuse, I know as a sexual abuse survivor.

It's a door we don't want to open, a conversation we don't want to have, and yet the facts remain: Every seventy-three seconds someone in America becomes the victim of a sexual assault. Every nine minutes one of those victims is a child. Eighty-two percent of victims under the age of eighteen are female. The effects of sexual violence can be long lasting and profound, triggering PTSD, thoughts of suicide, drug use and abuse, a sticky vortex of shame and powerlessness.

Sometimes I look up and down the street as I'm walking and wonder which of the girls and women walking the other way—masked and socially distant, now, in 2020—share my story. I believe that our sorrow connects us, yes, and that it can also be the source of our power as well as our empathy. Anna Hart's pain has led her to her path, her destiny, and mine has led me precisely here. To these characters, real and imaginary, to the fern forest, dripping with fog, to the bluffs above the roaring Pacific, to the cabin in the deep dark woods, and into the very heart of this book, which is as personal as anything I've ever written.

Cricket exists, as does the krummholz grove with its tortured and twisted cypress trees. I've sat at the bar at Patterson's, sipping whiskey just as Anna and Will do, and had coffee at the GoodLife. It's there, on Lansing Street, across from the Masonic Hall, where the carving of *Time and the Maiden* stands stark and white on a plinth above the village just as it has for over a hundred years. You could meet me there and we could walk together toward the bluff, talking as the wind carries our voices further and further on.

©Amber Ford

Paula McLain is the *New York Times* bestselling author of *Love and Ruin*, *Circling the Sun*, *The Paris Wife* and *A Ticket to Ride*, the memoir *Like Family: Growing Up in Other People's Houses*, and two collections of poetry. *Circling the Sun* and *The Paris Wife* were both picked for the Richard & Judy Bookclub. Her writing has appeared in *New York Times*, *Good Housekeeping*, *O: Oprah Magazine*, *Town & Country*, *Guardian* and *Huffington Post*. She lives in Ohio with her family.

paulamclain.com
Facebook.com/paulamclainauthor
Instagram: @paula_mclain